THE EMISSARY

KRISTAL SHAFF

Chapter One

After years of practice, Nolan still found lying difficult. It wasn't easy to hide a power that came as naturally as breathing. He had to continue, even if each flawless stroke of his quill exposed him for a fraud. As impossible as it seemed, he had to keep hiding to survive.

The candlelight danced across the half-finished parchment. A pile of identical rolled scrolls lay neatly stacked near his feet. It had been a long night, one that wasn't ending anytime soon. He covered a yawn and looked over his work.

His shoulders sagged. Crows! It wasn't supposed to be a masterpiece.

Dipping his quill into the jar of murky ink, he forced down his Shay of Accuracy. With a flick of his wrist, Nolan dislodged exactly two drops, splattering them across the parchment—not enough to destroy it, but enough to add the imperfection it so desperately needed.

Footsteps and voices echoed outside the door. He listened, making out Duke Ragnall's low rumble. If the duke bothered to visit this late, he'd have some "important" task he'd want Nolan to do. He stabbed his quill into the inkwell and wiped his hands on a stained rag. His long night just got longer.

He opened the door just as Ragnall poised his hand to knock. The duke's bushy brows rose briefly, then his pompous expression slid back into place.

"Nolan," he said. "There's an incident that requires your service." He glared at the grinning and puffed-up captain who stood off to his side.

"Of course, my lord." Nolan bowed and grabbed his workbag. "What's the situation?"

"Captain Finnis claims to have captured the Traitor of Faylinn."

Nolan blinked. He was tired. Probably didn't hear correctly. "Did you say the Traitor of Faylinn?"

"That I did," Captain Finnis said. "Having a drink at Aunt Bonty's, he was. The nerve of him, strolling into Alton like he hadn't a care or trouble in the world." He gave Nolan a yellow-toothed grin.

Wasn't the captain supposed to be on patrol instead of having drinks in a pub? From the duke's pursed lips and scowl, Nolan guessed the duke had noticed too.

Nolan had seen pretty much everything since coming to the manor two years ago, especially in the last year when taking over the duties of Master Irvin, the previous scribe. It was absurd how much needed to be recorded: every ridiculous party, every drawn-out tournament, and even the questioning of pickpockets and idiots who'd stirred trouble because they'd had one too many. Nolan suspected Captain Finnis had downed his fair share of drink by the looks of him—red bulging eyes, stupid grin—but more so, because of the absurd claim he made. How could a drunken slob have captured such a powerful and notorious traitor?

They proceeded through the gold corridor and entered the orange-painted halls. Continuing through the blue halls, then the red, they finally reached the section of the manor where bright colors became bare stone: the prison wing. The gray, colorless walls, signifying a wordless insult to those kept behind their doors.

As they neared the West Tower, raucous laughter boomed from the hall. They turned the corner to see guards, sporting the colors of all the districts in Alton, camped in front of the entrance.

Duke Ragnall stopped. "For the love of Brim, Captain. What in the Darkness is going on here?"

"The boys wanted to have a bit of fun. Didn't want to miss out on—"

"Unless they want to miss out on every free moment they have from now until they're ninety, they'd best get back to their posts."

The captain's smile vanished. He barked orders to his men, and the hall cleared—except for two standing at attention on either side of the door. Their chests were raised. Right arms hugged iron-tipped spears as they attempted to look important.

Skirting past the guards, they climbed the staircase and spiraled by cobwebs clinging to more gray walls. At the top, the captain unlocked the large oak door and shouldered it open. The smell of old filth and mold poured through. Captain Finnis thrust his lantern into the darkness, nodded, and led them inside.

Light flickered across a man standing at the far side of the cell. He wore brown breeches and worn leather boots, and a neatly trimmed beard covered his chin. He looked common enough, apart from the bloodstained rip in the shoulder of his tunic. He didn't acknowledge their entrance or glance in their direction; he just stared out the small window to the streets below. Calm. Not pleading. He was different than normal men who'd been thrown into Alton's tower.

Duke Ragnall cleared his throat. "You have been identified as Emery Cadogan, former general of the Shay Rol'dan army. What say you to this accusation?"

At first, Nolan thought the man hadn't heard as he continued to stare into the night. Finally, he turned. Dark purple bruises ringed his eyes, and dried blood coated his split and swollen lip. In spite of his injuries, he smiled.

"So *now* I'm asked for my name?" he said. "Is it common practice in Alton to beat a man before finding out who he is?"

Captain Finnis grabbed him, squeezing his arm. "Answer the question!"

"Do you think I'd be foolish enough to show myself if I were the Traitor of Faylinn?" he answered, his teeth clenched. "I'm just a traveler, for Brim's sake. Nothing else." He pointed to the other side of the room, as if he were reprimanding a disobedient dog. "So if you'd please, Captain, get your filthy hands off me, and go stand over there."

The savage expression on the captain's face faded. He blinked. And then, oddly enough, obeyed.

Duke Ragnall gawked, his face flushing. "Captain! What in the Darkness do you think you're doing?"

A faint purple light glimmered in the prisoner's eyes.

Nolan stared, then shook his head. It was late. He wasn't seeing properly.

"I'm sorry for this misunderstanding, my lord," the prisoner said. "It's a simple case of mistaken identity. I'm common enough. Could easily pass for someone else." He forced a laugh. "Though being mistaken for a traitor isn't something I'd like to repeat."

A glazed expression passed over the duke's face. "Yes, of course, my good man. I'm sure it's all a mistake."

My good man? Blood drained from Nolan's face. He inched toward the door; but as he slipped a hand around the opening, an overwhelming contentment washed over him.

As if moving through fog, Nolan turned to the prisoner. Nolan should be frightened, shouldn't he? No. Of course not. The man couldn't be the traitor. Captain Finnis was, after all, an idiot.

Nolan met the prisoner's light-filled gaze. Violet illuminated the man's head, casting a glow in the dim confines of the cell. How could he help him? They would need to sneak past the guards. Slowly, truth pushed through the haze. These thoughts weren't his own. They were *his.*

The prisoner's eyes narrowed and blazed brighter.

"No!" Nolan shoved the invading thoughts away, but the man's power shifted and probed deeper, as if turning the pages of Nolan's mind like an old book. The prisoner's power tore through him; shock and revelation flashed across the man's face.

Nolan staggered, his vision darkening. The workbag slid from his shoulder and thumped to the ground.

The captain shook his head. The prisoner's mental control had left him. He cursed before punching the traitor squarely between the eyes.

The prisoner's head jerked back, and he crumpled to his knees. Nolan stared, his mind reeling. The man had *seen* him. Somehow, he knew.

"Guards!" the duke bellowed. He grabbed Nolan's arm, yanking him from the room.

A rush of clanging swords and footsteps thundered up the stairs. A pair of guards raced past and into the cell. Violent commotion and pain-filled wails erupted from inside.

The duke shook his head. "I've never seen anything like it. He can bend one's will. Typically an Empathy Shay can only read a person's emotions."

Nolan's hands shook. The traitor could read far more than emotions.

"Nolan? Are you unwell?" he asked.

Nolan balled his hands into fists to control the trembling, at least a bit. "I'm fine, sir. Just a bit shaken."

Captain Finnis emerged, breathing heavily while wiping the corner of his mouth with a bloodstained knuckle. "He'll never use his nightforsaken Empathy power against us again, that's for certain."

Duke Ragnall looked nervously to the door. "For Brim's sake, you didn't kill him, did you?"

He hesitated. "Of course not, my lord."

Laughter and feeble moans echoed from inside.

Captain Finnis flinched. "But even if we did, he'd get what he deserves."

"He was the king's general!" Duke Ragnall said. "What would happen if King Alcandor arrived and discovered some commoner had killed him?"

"I'm no commoner, sir. I'm a captain of—"

"You're a commoner to the king. Unless you're planning to pull some dormant Shay power out of your backside, you'd best go in there and calm your men."

The captain paled and bowed. "Of course, my lord." He

returned to the cell, and the clamor hushed to an eerie silence. The rattling of chains followed.

The duke sighed. "Say nothing to anyone, Nolan. Though, with Finnis's mouth, I doubt this news will stay quiet for long. Question the soldiers and record how they discovered him. And of course, King Alcandor will need to be informed." He studied Nolan's face. "Can you remember all that transpired?"

Nolan nodded. How could he forget?

Two years of careful hiding. Two years of controlling himself, day after day. He'd given up his family, his career, any chance at a normal life. He'd pushed everyone away. Two years of loneliness...for nothing? This man could easily give his secret away! After a single, horrible moment, Nolan's fate now rested in the hands of a traitor.

Chapter Two

Nolan's hands still shook long after he'd returned to his room. He'd packed and unpacked his belongings three times before finally putting it all away—not that it took long. He had little to call his own: two changes of clothes, his inkbottle and favorite quill, and a few books he couldn't live without.

Finally, he sat on the edge of his bed taking deep, focused breaths. Control. He had to gain control. It would do no good to run away—it would only draw attention. He'd worked too hard to lose it now.

He distracted himself with the work he'd left earlier, doing little to hide perfection in his strokes. He was being careless, but half his attention was focused on the sounds outside his door. Would they come for him? Maybe they'd hurt the traitor too much for him to talk. Or maybe, just maybe, Nolan was wrong. Maybe the traitor *hadn't* sensed anything.

He concentrated on finishing the documents, but not even that work could calm his mind. Sleep didn't come. He dug into his towering bookshelf, removing book after dusty book, re-reading every account of the six Shay powers. They all mentioned how Empathy could judge the slightest change of mood before the person realized it. But apart from that, it didn't mention anything about it being able to sense others' powers.

Leaning back in the chair, he balanced it on two legs and ran a hand over his chin. He had no proof the prisoner knew his secret. Only the king had the ability to sense another Shay. Could the traitor be like the king? No. It was impossible. There was no one like the king.

Dropping the chair to the floor, he slammed the book closed. He crammed it back onto the bookshelf and picked up a small bit of parchment a servant had delivered earlier. The script was in the duke's nearly illegible scrawl.

Nolan,
Please join me in the dining hall for breakfast. There is much I need to discuss with you.
Duke Ragnall

He sighed. It was already almost time for breakfast, and he still had no answers. Then the most absurd thought came to him: What if he went to the prisoner and *asked* him what he knew? He quickly dismissed the idea. General Cadogan had nearly turned Nolan into his puppet just hours before.

"Right this way, General Cadogan. The door is just over here. Can I get you anything else while I'm at it, General Cadogan? Some food? Some wine? A sword to run me through?"

Even if Nolan wanted to speak to him, guards watched night and day. He had to find some other way. But not now. Duke Ragnall waited.

***

Everything in the duke's dining hall was gaudy. Portraits in gilded frames displayed over-dressed noblemen with arrogant expressions, and floral tapestries in every imaginable color hung from floor to ceiling on each wall. Every piece of furniture had some sort of lion or bear or other wild beast carved on its surface. The combination was nauseating.

A gigantic chandelier hung over a narrow dining table that stretched the length of the room. Today, the servants had set the table for three.

One place for Duke Ragnall.

One place for Nolan.

And the third...

Nolan groaned. Mikayla, the duke's young wife, glanced up, and her dark eyes locked on his. He had suspected for some time now that the duke needed spectacles more than he did. The way his wife stared at Nolan, like he was a roasted duck, made her strange obsession clear to everyone but the duke.

She was attractive and exotic. Her black hair shimmered with purple and blue hues. Her flawless, olive complexion outshone any woman's he'd ever seen. Not a single man, including Nolan, could resist turning his head when she walked by.

Her interest in him was baffling. He didn't see himself as remarkable, at least not by a woman's standards. He supposed that, compared to her old and overweight husband and the parade of idiot soldiers who came in, he won by default. Even though the attention flattered him, Nolan would never give in. He valued his life too much.

Duke Ragnall sat a ways from the table; his large stomach wouldn't allow him to fully pull his chair in. A servant stood next to him, cooling him with a fan of peacock feathers. The duke wiped his scalp and waved for the servant to speed up. Seeing Nolan, he dabbed his bushy mustache and waved him closer. Nolan adjusted the bag on his shoulder and approached them, wanting this meeting to be over already.

"Ah, Nolan! So good of you to come on such short notice." He motioned, giving him permission to sit.

Nolan placed his bundle within arm's reach and sat at the empty place setting next to the duke's wife. He put the napkin in his lap and attempted to appear comfortable, though Mikayla's gaze followed his every movement.

"Well," the duke said, "about last night's incident..."

Nolan tensed, unable to meet his eyes.

"I assume you have already recorded the information?" the duke said.

Nolan relaxed. "Of course, sir."

"Very good." Duke Ragnall took a large bite of sausage and chewed vigorously. "Do you have any new business?"

Nolan reached in his satchel and pulled out a piece of parchment, pretending to scan the list as he calmed the thrumming in his chest. He took a long breath. He'd probably spent all night worrying for no reason.

"Yesterday, we received a request from one of the merchants," Nolan said. "Mr. Bakker was interested in moving his clothing shop from Orange District to Blue District."

"The baker wants to move?" The duke snorted. "That's ridiculous." He picked up a roll and took a generous bite. "The bakery is just fine where it is."

Nolan resisted the urge to roll his eyes. The duke's wife snickered. Nolan caught her smiling gaze and quickly looked away. "No, my lord. Mr. Bakker is a tailor, not a baker."

Duke Ragnall paused mid-chew. "What are his reasons?"

"Well, my lord. He states his business has declined since his daughter came into the Shay of Accuracy last year, and the people of Orange District have been avoiding his shop and going elsewhere. He wants to go somewhere 'where he'll be appreciated.'"

Duke Ragnall turned his attention to his plate, shooing a meaty hand in Nolan's direction. "Of course, of course. If he has the means to move, then so be it. He has my permission."

"Very good, sir." Nolan rolled the parchment and slid it into his bag. After a brief inspection of the serving platters—which held far too much for only the three of them—Nolan selected a glazed pastry and placed it on his plate.

"I also wanted to speak to you about the upcoming Tournament of Awakening," Duke Ragnall said. "Our recent encounter with the prisoner will bring the king's army here sooner than expected. I've received word that General Trividar will be arriving this afternoon to question him."

Nolan stopped his fork midway to his mouth. *Kael was coming...today?* His stomach lurched.

Duke Ragnall continued, "Considering our current circumstances, I think it might be best to deliver the summons for the Tournament of Awakening as soon as possible. Perhaps you might make them available by tomorrow at the latest?"

"They're already done, sir." Nolan motioned to the bag, grateful he had stayed up to finish them. It would be one less thing for Kael to criticize.

"Why, Nolan, you never cease to amaze me." The duke turned to his wife. "My dear, isn't his performance outstanding?"

"Oh, yes," she said. "I'm sure it is."

Mikayla reached over and brushed her fingers across Nolan's hand.

Nolan coughed and rose quickly, jarring the table. "If Your Excellency would not object, I'd like to deliver the summons myself."

Duke Ragnall gawked, his mouth gaped, revealing his last bite of fruit. "*You* want to deliver them?"

He gritted his teeth, wishing he'd kept his big mouth shut. It wasn't like he wanted to run around in the horrid heat. And he could barely keep his eyes open. Nolan forced a smile. "The fresh air and exercise will do me good."

* * *

A puffy, gray blanket of clouds stretched the expanse of the sky like wads of dirty lamb's wool. It covered the town of Alton and the forest beyond, and even went to the distant mountains, obstructing the tops of the rocky fortresses from view. The sky appeared as it always did in the thriving city: dark, gloomy, and depressing.

Nolan walked the streets of the Yellow District, where every shop looked as if fading dandelions had sacrificed themselves on their walls.

A painter worked outside the herb shop, his clothes splattered in a prism of colors. The building's yellow hue peeled except where the man applied a new layer of pale, thick paint.

The man's rainbow-colored clothes sagged from his humped shoulders. His eyes met Nolan's, but he quickly averted his gaze, too ashamed to be seen by an employee of the manor.

Guilt gnawed at Nolan's gut. The only reason he had a privileged job was because he secretly used his Shay to succeed. He too could've become a painter—one of the lowliest jobs in the whole of Adamah. The poor man had no district color to claim as his own.

He turned at the corner. The buildings of the Orange District were always brighter than the others. Nolan passed the primary apothecary, where they made the paints each day. He shook his head. No wonder their district's colors always appeared the best.

He wasn't sure why they bothered. They said it honored the different Shay abilities; each color represented one of the six powers—like the Rol'dan cared or felt "honored" by them slapping paint on their walls. Maybe it was really because they were jealous of the Rol'dan; they claimed a color because they couldn't have one of their own. Or maybe it was just an excuse to not get along. The color districts always bickered, always presented long and detailed complaints. Lucky Nolan got to record every one.

He wound between rows of tightly constructed merchant shops, delivering summons for the Tournament of Awakening. Nolan *hated* this time of year. Parents dreamed their young one could become one of the "fortunate" few, one of the Shay Rol'dan. It was also when the city became more annoying than usual. With the tournament only two weeks away, people poured in from all the outlying towns. Law required every fifteen-year-old to participate, so families converged upon the city in noisy and excited droves, making the crowded city even more unbearable.

Morning stretched into afternoon before Nolan made it to his final destination in Red District. Turning at the candle shop, the clashing of swords rang nearby. On the front edge of the armory, a metal sign hung in the shape of a shield with *Deverell's Arms* etched on its surface.

He opened the door to a crowded room. The clang of

swords and the smell of soot filled the small space. People from all districts were there wearing clothes of every color. Nolan squeezed as politely as he could between the reeking bodies and past a large man entranced with the performance—of sorts—in front of him. Instead of a blacksmith or two tinkering around an anvil and coals, a rough-looking man with salt-and-pepper hair sparred with a boy only a couple years younger than Nolan.

The older one was Kardos Deverell, renowned arms maker; he had the large, developed forearms of a blacksmith. The boy resembled him, except instead of dark hair, tight, blond curls clung to his head. Although Nolan couldn't say for sure, he guessed he was the blacksmith's son, Alec Deverell. It was Alec Nolan came to see.

"Excuse me," Nolan asked the large man next to him. "What's happening here?"

The man only stared at the duel.

Nolan ground his teeth. He hated being ignored. He wiped a trail of sweat from his face before jabbing the stranger on the shoulder.

The man turned finally, annoyed. He stared...or more accurately, gawked at Nolan like he was an ignorant clod. "They're sparring, in case you can't figure that out."

"I can see that," Nolan said. "Why?"

The man shrugged, his large shoulder covered in a layer of grime and sweat. "Why not? Deverell and his boy do this all the time."

Kardos swung quickly around, blocking a blow; the crowd gasped in unison. Fringes of dark hair flared around the blacksmith's face, his eyes gleaming like a madman.

"They've done it for years," continued the man. "Every afternoon they're fighting. Only the past few years it's been worth watching. The boy didn't last long enough before."

Nolan flinched as the son dodged a swing at his shoulder and then swept his own sword around; Kardos blocked it easily and returned the attack. The crowd gasped again as the blow barely missed Alec.

"The boy's been putting up a good fight nowadays," the man said. "Matter of fact, he might win one eventually. Boy, I'd like to see ol' Kardos's face when that happens."

Both swordsmen glared at each other, nostrils flaring, veins protruding from their necks. If Nolan didn't know any better, he'd think they were trying to kill each other. Finally, with a wide sweep, Kardos tore Alec's blade from his grip, flinging it helplessly aside. The crowd erupted in applause.

Nolan strained to hear Kardos scold his son. Why was he angry? Alec had fought well.

After a few final curses—heard even above the noise of the people—Kardos turned and bowed with a flourish.

Alec withdrew to the back of the shop, his face turned downward as he tied a strip of cloth on his palm, as if dressing a wound. He peeled off his battered leather armor and drenched tunic and flung them to the ground.

Nolan stared. A large scar ran across Alec's chest. Another blazed his side. Numerous others crisscrossed his arms. Even his face had a long, straight scar below his cheekbone.

Nolan's own father hadn't been kind. At home, he'd yelled more than he talked. Nolan never did anything right while helping on the boat. Too much net. Not enough line. Too loud—he'd scare the fish. Too slow—they'll get away. But at least his father hadn't used him for sword practice. Nolan's father probably didn't even know how to hold a sword.

It took several minutes for the crowd to clear, leaving Nolan standing nearly alone in the center of the viewing area. Kardos caught Nolan's eye and smiled, displaying a row of straight, white teeth that contrasted with his soot-covered face. He extended a friendly hand.

"Enjoy the show, boy?" he asked.

He gawked. Kardos really didn't want him to answer, did he? Instead of saying something he shouldn't, Nolan crammed a scroll into the blacksmith's outstretched palm and recited his bland, rehearsed statement. "I am here to present an important document to Alec Deverell, from Duke Ragnall."

The merriment fell from the blacksmith's face. He stared

and then tore open the seal, unrolling the parchment. As he read, his brows furrowed deeper and deeper into a furious scowl. Alec approached and peered over his shoulder while Kardos muttered under his breath.

"No son of mine is going to be taken away from me. Those…I'll show them…They think they can tell us what to do." After Kardos finished reading it, for probably the fifth time, he crushed the document and chucked it to the ground. He opened his mouth to speak, his finger raised as if to jab Nolan's chest.

"I'll be there." Alec picked up the crumpled summons. "I'll be there as required."

"No, Alec," Kardos said. "I'll take care of this."

"Father, I'm going."

"Shut your mouth, boy. We don't have to put up with this."

"*We* don't." Alec's intense eyes locked on Nolan's with a resigned look. "*I* do."

Kardos grabbed Alec's arm and jerked him around. "Alec, I'm your father—"

"And this is the law. I'm fifteen now. I have to go."

"We can refuse."

"And what?" Alec said. "They arrest us? They close your shop? For Brim's sake, Father, I'll only be gone a month or so. I'm sure you can make do without me for that long." Alec turned. "If you'll excuse us, we have work to do."

Nolan didn't know how to respond. But before he had to, Alec walked to the forge. Kardos glared and then followed his son. The two began to work as if he weren't there.

Obviously, Kardos cared for Alec—when he wasn't slicing him to bits. He was willing to lose everything, his freedom and his shop, to keep his son from the Rol'dan. Nolan's own father sold him off to be a scribe for failing his Tournament of Awakening. Kardos fought to keep Alec away from the very same trials.

Suddenly, Kardos didn't look so bad, sword slashes and all.

Nolan left the shop and maneuvered through the crowded

streets toward the manor. The whole situation was strange. The Shay Rol'dan army had most, if not all, of their swords made at Deverell's shop, yet the man wanted nothing to do with the tournament. One would figure that, because of his business with the army, he'd be excited with the chance of Alec becoming one of them.

The glory and reputation of the Rol'dan blinded most people. They didn't see their true nature. Selfish. Bitter. Cruel. Maybe in his regular dealings with the Rol'dan, Kardos Deverell saw what most didn't. The truth.

As soon as Nolan came within sight of the manor, he stopped. His palms were slick, and he wiped them on his breeches, trying to steady himself.

A crowd gathered at the main gate. A father held a small boy on his shoulders; the smiling youth waved a yellow flag. Several maidens huddled together in a ridiculous, giggling mass. Nolan, however, could only cringe. Only one person, besides the king himself, could cause this much excitement. General Kael Trividar had arrived.

Chapter Three

Nolan stood in the gold-adorned hallway near the entrance as voices echoed from inside the Great Hall. A year had passed since Nolan had seen him last—a peaceful year that flew by much too quickly. Last year, Master Irving had dealt with Kael while Nolan simply ducked away.

Now, Nolan held the position and responsibilities of master scribe. This year he'd have to face his self-absorbed brother, whether he liked it or not. He stepped closer, stretching so he could better hear.

"Where is he now?" Kael asked.

"Safely locked in the tower, General," Duke Ragnall answered. "You may question him at any time."

Kael chuckled. "I'm surprised your men had the capabilities to apprehend him. But I suppose he's *only* an Empathy user. I'd be amused to see your pitiful lot try to capture someone with Speed."

Nolan huffed. Kael always thought his Speed Shay was better than the rest of the powers. Typical Rol'dan.

"Of course, General. We were quite fortunate." The duke cleared his throat. "You should be pleased to know that the last of the summons for the Tournament of Awakening are being delivered as we speak. Everything is ahead of schedule."

Nolan peeked around the corner. Daylight filtered through the glass in the high, domed ceiling. Kael strutted under the dim light, adorned in his golden tunic and waist-length cape. A leather jerkin stretched snugly across his broad chest. Duke

Ragnall waddled behind him, acting more like a servant than the Lord of Alton.

The way everyone loved the Rol'dan, doted on them, gave them free goods from their shops, frustrated Nolan to no end. Even the duke fed Kael's massive ego. Nolan was so tense, he almost didn't hear the delicate padding of feet coming down the corridor. He turned, and his heart stopped. Mikayla stared at him, her slender hand on her hip. He snapped his jaw shut and dropped his eyes, taking in the rest of her.

Twisting gold bands encircled her upper arms, and a blue-jeweled pendent hung low on her chest, drawing attention to her revealing neckline. He forced his gaze from her chest to her gown; it cascaded down long, olive legs in numerous strips of sheer blue fabric. Several gold rings adorned the toes of her bare feet—a hint of her Talasian culture. She balanced a tray on one hand, gracefully moving closer with cat-like steps.

Nolan stepped back as she came toward him, but the wall stopped any chance of escape. When he opened his mouth to speak, she placed a finger against his lips. The intoxicating scent of sweet-and-spicy oils permeated her skin.

They said nothing for several long seconds, only studying each other in the lantern-lit hall while warmth flooded Nolan's cheeks. She smiled as her hand slid down Nolan's neck. He needed to stop her, but he couldn't move. With a quick yank, she undid the tie on his tunic.

He jolted to reality and grabbed her wrist, but not before her fingertips sent a fire-like jab into his chest. He inhaled sharply and glared at her, shaking his head.

She paused, reluctantly stepped back, and wrenched her wrist free. With a playful pout, she turned and disappeared into the Great Hall, making her way toward her husband. Nolan remained against the wall, his heart pounding against his ribs.

"Ah, Mikayla! Thank you, my dear."

A moment later, Mikayla reappeared, empty handed.

Nolan flinched, bracing himself, but she did nothing but glance over her shoulder, teasing him with her eyes as she disappeared down the corridor. He watched her swaying hips as she glided out of sight.

The voices drifted from the Great Hall, pulling Nolan back to his eavesdropping.

"How many will be attending this year?" Kael asked.

"I believe there are around eighty from our region," the duke said. "Nolan could tell you for certain. He has them all recorded in the city's census reports."

"So my *brother* is still in your service?" He stressed the word brother like he'd just tasted something disgusting.

"Yes. Of course! He recently assumed the position as my personal scribe. I've never seen one with such a natural talent for the job. He surpassed my previous scribe in just a few short years."

Nolan scowled; he really needed to make more mistakes.

"That young man has been such an asset to me here in the manor," the duke said. "I am most certain his work cannot be matched even by the king's personal scribe."

"Your sentiments are…touching. As if scribbling on bits of paper is an asset." Kael paused, taking a gulp of ale.

"It's more than scribbling," the duke said, completely missing Kael's insult. "I've never seen someone with such a perfect hand. Each stroke is…well, it is magnificent."

Nolan groaned. His nightforsaken Accuracy always got in the way. One of these days he'd slip up and find himself locked up in a cell.

The duke began describing some of Nolan's finer attributes. Nolan shook his head. At least the conversation dislodged the image of Mikayla's legs from his mind. Sometimes he wondered how long he could keep it all up—hiding his power, avoiding Mikayla. Someday she would catch him off guard. Crows, what would happen then? He'd have to take everything one cautious step at a time.

He sighed, knowing he needed to get this over with. Nolan pushed off the wall, cleared his throat, and entered.

Kael's smirk widened when he saw him. "Nolan! The duke was just telling me how hard you work here at the manor." He drained his mug in one gulp, set it on a nearby table, and slowly scrutinized the full length of him. "These are new." He jabbed at Nolan's spectacles, knocking them out of place.

"Yes." He straightened the frames. "Duke Ragnall was generous enough to have them made for me. With all the writing I do, it puts quite a strain on my eyes."

Kael laughed. "Now even your eyes are weak. How appropriate. One might say it makes you look smarter. I suppose you need all the help you can get."

Nolan strained a smile.

Kael slapped his hands together and rubbed them as if trying to stay warm. "I suppose you'll need to record the questioning of the prisoner, as the law requires. And since you're here, well, there really is no need to wait, is there? Nolan, why don't you be a good boy and go get the record book? We're going to have a chat with our friend up in the tower." He paused and held up a finger. "On second thought, let me grab it. By the time you return, he might die of old age."

Kael's eyes glowed golden-yellow before he sprinted out of the Great Hall in a blur of golden cape and tunic. He reappeared a few seconds later, holding the Book of Records, a quill, and a jar of ink from Nolan's personal quarters located on the other side of the manor. Kael shoved the quill and ink into Nolan's hands and opened the book.

"Hm..." Kael's finger traveled down the page. "So Cadogan was just sitting in a pub? Well, it serves the idiot right." His eyebrows rose, and the corners of his mouth twitched. "And he used his Shay power."

"Ah, yes," the duke said, wringing his hands. "We won't have that problem anymore. We've blindfolded him. And I doubt he would want to try again; my men made him regret that action."

Kael rolled his eyes. He slammed the book closed and shoved it into Nolan's chest. "Come on. Let's take care of this annoyance as quickly as possible."

***

On either side of the door to the West Tower sat two of Alton's guards. Their swords lay tucked under their chairs, and their chins rested on their chests in peaceful slumber. One of them let out a soft snore. Nolan cringed.

Kael cleared his throat.

The snoring stopped. One guard stretched before opening his eyes. He looked around casually, at least until his gaze locked on Kael.

Eyes popping open, he slugged the other guard in the arm. Both jumped to their feet. "General Trividar," he said. "I had no idea you'd arrived in Alton already."

Kael grunted and examined them as if doing a routine inspection. "Is sleeping your usual manner of watching prisoners?"

"Of course not, sir."

"So I can expect to never find you in this position again?"

The man shifted uncomfortably. "Of course not, sir."

"For your sake, I should hope not. If I ever find you sleeping on duty again, the consequences will be...grave." Golden-yellow light glowed in his eyes. He leaned toward the man. "Now let us in."

The two men fell over each other trying to open the door first. After a monumental struggle, one soldier came out victorious. He opened the door with a pathetic flourish, allowing Kael and Nolan to pass through.

The door closed with a reverberating *thud*. Finally, unable to control himself, Kael erupted into boisterous laughter that echoed off the gray walls of the empty stairwell.

"Was that necessary?"

"Oh, Nolan." He wiped tears from his eyes. "You never had a sense of humor."

"They were afraid of you *before* you showed your light," he said. "You're such a twit."

Kael's grin vanished, and his eyes glowed again. He pressed his face close to Nolan's, his teeth clenched. "Those men out there, though they wear the crest of the king, are just as pathetic as you." He jabbed a finger into Nolan's chest. "They need to be reminded that the soldiers of the Shay Rol'dan are the only ones with real power and control." His Shay light faded. He turned and climbed the stairs as if the quarrel had never happened.

Flaunting powers was control? More like stupid. Arrogant. Nolan had hid his Shay the last two years. Now *that* was control. He'd like to see Kael pull that one off.

Nolan inhaled, calming the frustration grating his already frazzled nerves. Then he remembered the task. He would come face to face, once again, with the Traitor of Faylinn. Would the traitor say anything in front of Kael? Nolan's stomach knotted and his mouth turned to wool. *What in Brim's name am I doing?*

"Nolan!" Kael called. "You're not *that* slow, are you?"

He could do this. He really had no other choice. At least they'd blindfolded the prisoner.

"Nolan!" Kael growled.

Nolan forced his feet up the stairs and joined his brother.

Kael pulled at the handle, muttering a curse under his breath. Kael awakened his Speed, shot away, and reappeared with a key. After unlocking the door, he said, "Take this." In a toss obviously meant to plummet down the stairs, Kael threw the key.

Without thinking, Nolan seized it from the air.

Kael eyed him suspiciously for a long time.

Nolan forced a smile and held up the key. "Got it."

Kael grunted. "Well, don't lose it." He turned his attention back to the door.

Nolan swallowed hard. It was a good catch. *Too* good. This tension between them had distracted him. Nolan glared at the offending key. Not knowing what else to do with it, he crammed it into his leather pouch.

The door groaned open, and Nolan squeezed the Book of Records in his hands. Four chains connected the prisoner to the wall, securing his limbs like a savage animal. The links piled in a heap by the traitor's hands, enough for him to stand and walk around the cell; however, the man didn't look as if he could move much at all. He sat with his battered head resting against the wall at an awkward angle. It surprised Nolan how many more injuries the man had acquired since just last night. Most of his face was cut, bruised, or swollen. And judging by his stuttered breathing, not all of his injuries were visible.

The traitor, Emery Cadogan, shifted his head. Nolan took a step back, a shudder traveling down his spine; the traitor's blindfold was gone.

As if he had heard Nolan's thoughts, Emery searched the ground, his chains clattering. Finally, he picked up a dirty rag that had been his blindfold.

"I hope we can speak without pretenses," Emery said. He eyed Kael while fingering the cloth. "It's been a long time, Lieutenant. Six years, I believe. Oh, but wait...You're the general now, aren't you? I suppose your heroics the night I escaped helped in your early promotion."

"Shut your mouth, Cadogan." Kael drove a heel into Emery's knee. "The only time you will speak is to answer my questions."

Emery pressed his lips together, stifling a cry. He peered up at Kael, clenching his teeth in an expression that resembled a grin.

Kael turned to Nolan, scowling. "Let's pretend like you aren't an idiot. Do I need to open the book for you?"

Nolan resisted the urge to chuck the book at Kael's head; instead, he placed the Book of Records on the dirty floor and sat. The cold stones seeped through his breeches, sending a shiver through him. He arranged the jar of ink, removed the cork stopper, and readied his quill. After all was in order, he found Emery's brown eyes fixed on him. Nolan choked a breath and looked away.

"What were you doing at the pub?" Kael began.

"Usually, people go to pubs for drinks," Emery answered. "I figured Aunt Bonty's was as good a place as any to get one."

Nolan flinched as Emery's head wrenched to the side. Kael's eyes blazed golden-yellow, and fresh blood painted his knuckles.

"Maybe I didn't make myself clear," Kael said. "Why are you here in Alton?"

Amusement hinted in the corners of Emery's bleeding lips. "I already told you," he said. "I wanted a drink."

The telltale sign of fury flickered on Kael's face. Nolan recognized it all too well.

Without warning, Emery slammed to the ground.

Kael appeared on top of him, straddling his chest, his hands wrapped tightly around Emery's throat.

Nolan jumped to his feet. He thought Kael would stop, but the fury that lined his face only increased. Emery struggled, gasped for breath, and then made no sound at all.

Nolan's eyes widened. Kael was arrogant, yes. But he'd never seen him quite like this. He'd lost it. And now, he was going to kill this man, right in front of him. Conflicting thoughts flashed through his mind. If Kael killed him, then Nolan wouldn't have to worry. His secret would be safe.

The prisoner's face started to turn purple. As much as Nolan wanted the threat taken away, he'd have to live with this image the rest of his life. He couldn't do it. It'd make him as bad as Kael.

Nolan grabbed Kael's arm and yanked. "Kael, stop!"

Something hit Nolan hard, and he flew backward. Pain shot through his head as it collided with the wall.

Kael stood, nostrils flaring, as his Shay light blazed. "Keep your mouth shut, Nolan! I'm the king's general. You *will* respect me. Just write down what's said like the stupid little scribe you are."

Kael picked up the Book of Records and tossed it in Nolan's direction. Then he turned to Emery and kicked him solidly in his side. Emery curled into a ball and moaned.

"You may think you can get away with your little games, Cadogan," Kael said, "but if you hide your answers from King Alcandor, you'll wish I had killed you instead."

Emery coughed and wiped his lips, leaving a streak of blood and saliva across the back of his hand. "You wouldn't kill me," he wheezed. "That would take the pleasure away from the king doing it himself. And you wouldn't want to disappoint the king, now would you?"

"Why did you come to Alton?"

Emery smiled. "Aunt Bonty's is near the center of town. You really should try one of her ales."

"You lie!"

Emery answered, almost too quiet to hear, "If you had Empathy, you'd know for certain, eh?"

Nolan's jaw dropped, and he quickly closed it so Kael wouldn't see. Though Kael beat him, wore the Rol'dan colors, and led the entire army of the king, this Emery fellow was the one in charge.

"If you were hoping I'd kill you," Kael said, "then you'll have to be disappointed. But don't worry, Cadogan, once you see the king, you'll get your turn."

Kael kicked the quill and ink. The bottle fell over, oozing thick, dark ink onto the floor. "Nolan, in your records state that the traitor was uncooperative and needed to be reprimanded. And inform the duke that the traitor must be kept here until I return from the Tournament of Awakening. At that point, I will escort him to Faylinn. The soldiers of Alton can continue their watch. And, I can see by his current condition, they'll give him everything he deserves."

Nolan stooped and turned the inkbottle up, staining his fingers in the process.

"I hope you can remember all of that, without having to jot it down," Kael said.

"I'll do my best, Kael." Nolan laced his words with as much sarcasm as he could.

Kael sneered. "That's General Trividar to you."

Nolan didn't respond; instead, he studied the inkbottle to see how much remained. He'd had enough of Kael to last until next year.

Kael's Shay light brightened. "I'll return in two weeks for the tournament. Try not to screw this up, Nolan." And without another word, Kael sped away.

Nolan's head pounded, his leg still throbbed, and half his

ink coated the stones. But despite that, he felt much better now that Kael had left. He started to relax, but his blood froze when he realized Kael had left him alone with the prisoner.

Nolan fixed his gaze on the ink-stained stones. Several minutes crept by. Nolan knew he should leave, but he couldn't. Not yet. He *had* to find out what the man knew. As time continued, his fear passed along with it, ebbing away until curiosity took hold.

Nolan raised his eyes slowly, expecting to find two purple orbs glowing. Instead, Emery sat on the ground, his head hung low as he took slow, labored breaths. He coughed, and his body went rigid while his face contorted.

Nolan took a step toward him. Emery's bruised face raised, but instead of a violet light, kind brown eyes studied him.

Emery smiled, his swollen lips stretching across white teeth. "Are you always impressed when someone gets beaten?"

Nolan started. "What did you say?"

"You were impressed when the general beat me."

He'd been horrified and frightened. But impressed? He didn't remember feeling that way at all.

"No, you're right," he said, as if answering Nolan's thoughts. "It wasn't when he beat me. I felt your emotions afterward."

His question finally took form in Nolan's mind. He *was* impressed, but it wasn't because Kael beat him.

At that moment, Nolan realized this traitor was no different than he was. He'd evaded the army. Nolan could easily be him, trapped in some tower, waiting for death. And it could still happen, if his secret got out. However, the difference between Emery and him was that Emery fought, while he hid.

Emery stared, as if waiting for an answer.

Nolan finally said, "You impressed me, because you stood up to him."

"Ah! So *that's* why." He chuckled. "Yes, I suppose I did. It's partially habit, I'm afraid. I was his superior at one time. And then there's just the enjoyment of antagonizing him. He's always been easy to annoy." Emery flinched while taking a slow breath. "So why would that impress you? You stood up to him as well. You even called him by name."

"Brothers at odds still call each other by name."

"Brothers, eh?" He nodded. "Yes, I can see the similarities, especially in the eyes."

As he examined Nolan, his Empathy light glowed, and his power pushed into Nolan's mind. Nolan recoiled, and the Empathy abruptly left.

"Forgive me, Nolan," Emery said. "I didn't mean to frighten you."

Sweat trailed down Nolan's face, his instincts nudging him to run.

"I *am* sorry," Emery said, his eyes pleading. "I promise. I won't search you again." He studied Nolan again before speaking. "How old are you?"

Nolan tensed. *Why does he want to know?* Nolan considered making up a random number, but then he changed his mind. The man was an Empathy user, for Brim's sake. He'd know if Nolan lied. And honestly, what difference did it make? It wasn't as if he were hiding his age. "Seventeen," he finally answered.

Emery's brows raised in surprise. "Seventeen? How very interesting."

"Interesting?"

"Well," he said. "You are seventeen and not in the ranks of the Rol'dan."

The blood drained from Nolan's face. By Brim, he knew. He'd expected as much, but to hear him say it aloud...

Nolan didn't notice Emery's hand supporting his elbow at first. When his head finally cleared, Nolan gasped and yanked his arm away.

"Are you all right?" Emery's muscles trembled as he examined Nolan.

Nolan's fears ebbed away. The man could barely stand, let alone attack him.

Emery staggered to the window, chains dragging, and grabbed the sill for support. "I felt your power last night," he said weakly. "I must admit, it surprised me to discover you. I had no idea I could find one so powerful, right here in the manor. And your age makes it that much more intriguing."

"Powerful?" Nolan asked, still dazed.

"Why, yes, Nolan. You see, when I use my power on someone, their Shay talks back to me. The stronger their power, the stronger it answers." He smiled slowly. "Let's just say your Shay has a very loud voice. And I am most curious to know which Shay it is."

His comment slapped Nolan from his numbness. He stared. Emery didn't know?

Emery pulled up his sleeve and examined a nasty gash. "You don't have to tell me, but I'd hoped, very much, that it might be Healing." He eyed Nolan expectantly. "You don't have Healing, do you?"

Nolan didn't answer him, but his silence apparently satisfied Emery.

"Hm," Emery said, "what a shame."

Nolan licked his dry lips. "I thought you'd tell."

"Tell them of your power? Of course not, boy. Remember why I'm here: I'm a traitor because I *left* the army. I'm in the business of saving people from the Rol'dan, not throwing them into their arms. Your secret is safe with me."

Relief flooded through him, and then a question smacked his mind. He was in the business of *saving* people from the Rol'dan?

"I find those with powers before they take part in the trials," Emery answered Nolan's silent question. "Then I give them the chance at a different life."

A different life? Nolan's mind lingered so much on the idea, it took him a moment to realize Emery had asked him a question. "Did you say something?"

Emery's expression softened. "I said, I have a favor to ask of you."

"I can't free you," Nolan answered. "There are guards—"

"Of course not. This is far more dangerous than helping me escape."

Nolan gawked. *What could be more dangerous than that?*

"Since you are the scribe for Alton Manor," he said, "I assume you're the record keeper for your sector of the Tournament of Awakening?"

Nolan nodded.

"I'd like you to watch the new recruits, the ones who come into their powers. Find who might want a different path than the Rol'dan."

"And how am I supposed to do that? I can't read minds."

Emery smiled slightly. "So Empathy isn't your gift then?"

Nolan grimaced. "How am I supposed to know such a thing?" he asked, hoping to redirect the discussion away from his Shay.

"I believe you're a good judge of character."

Even if he could figure out who might be interested in a different life—whatever that meant—how could Nolan keep them from the Rol'dan? Once someone came into a Shay, they were automatically placed into their ranks. Deserting the army marked them as a traitor. Emery was a perfect example of those who avoided the king's calling. Offering someone an alternative life sounded like a guaranteed way to reveal himself and get killed. Most people *wanted* to be Rol'dan.

"Some of my friends will be arriving in Alton soon," Emery said. "I came to Alton to search for Shay users who had not yet come into powers. My friends are meeting me here for the results of my search. But of course, I have found none… apart from you.

"I've struggled this time, finding those with powers," Emery said. "Something is happening that I can't explain. I believe my own power is weakening somehow, as well as those of my friends. It takes all of my concentration to find new Shay users. I had thought perhaps I was just missing them, that it was just me. But we've noticed that the numbers of Rol'dan recruits have dwindled as well. If what we suspect is true, I believe that soon there will be no more Shay users in all of Adamah."

Ridiculous! Powers don't weaken. But the more he thought

about it, the more it made sense. Just a year before, Nolan could barely keep his power under control. He'd figured that he'd just gotten better at hiding. Or maybe it was both.

"Though I can't prove it," Emery continued, "I believe King Alcandor is responsible. His powers and abilities are like none other. I suspect he is harnessing our Shays, using them to increase his own."

Emery squeezed the window ledge so hard his blood-smeared knuckles whitened. "It's essential that we save these children before they are lost to the king's army. Increasing our numbers also gives us a better chance of finding a solution to our fading powers. Do you understand our plight? Nolan, can you help us?"

He couldn't answer. Emery was asking him to alter everything. His life was safe as a scribe. He should tell Emery to shove off; but something made him pause. Nolan was as much a prisoner in the manor as Emery.

"I can understand your hesitation," Emery said. "It's a serious crime I'm asking you to commit. Even if you refuse, I'd like for you to go with my friends. Our life isn't safe, but neither is the one you're attempting now. With my friends, at least you'll no longer have to pretend."

His jaw dropped. *Such a place exists?*

The echo of footsteps approached. Nolan's supplies lay strewn on the floor near Emery's feet. Nolan scrambled to retrieve the book and quill. As he rose, Emery grabbed his arm and whispered, "What is your gift, friend?"

A guard entered and Emery quickly dropped his hold.

"General Trividar, sir?" The guard looked around. "Where's the general?"

"He just left," Nolan lied. "Didn't you see him pass?"

"I uh...Yes. Of course." He cleared his throat. "Are you done then?"

"Just a moment." Nolan bent to retrieve the bottle of ink off the ground and locked eyes with Emery. In that brief moment, he made a decision.

He relaxed, letting a pulse of his Shay leak through his

control. The blue light of Accuracy flickered in Nolan's eyes, just long enough for Emery to see, and then he hid it away again. For the first time in his life, he'd shared his secret.

The guard led Nolan from the room and pulled the heavy door closed. He casually reached into a small pouch around his waist, digging into it with a confused expression. "Strange. Must've left it downstairs."

"Left what?" Nolan asked.

"My key." The guard grunted. "It's not like the traitor can go anywhere with those chains, but still…"

"I'm sure it'll turn up." Nolan reinforced his words with his best reassuring smile and readjusted the pouch…which held the key.

Chapter Four

Nolan brushed his hand over the battered red cover. Inside, the book listed the results of the Tournament of Awakening for the last hundred years. He opened it and thumbed back two years prior, the year of his own tournament, the year his life drastically changed. Nolan's name was under the large list of people who'd failed. The list of those obtaining a power contained twenty names.

Nolan pulled his eyes from the book to the activities of the pub. It was mid-morning—well past breakfast and well before lunch. Every table was filled, and people hovered at the outskirts of the room, all waiting their turn to grab a chair.

A robust woman appeared at Nolan's table. Her rosy cheeks crinkled in a pleasant smile, and a mane of salt-and-pepper hair framed her round face. "What can I do for ya?"

"Ale please."

"Of course, love." She wound her way through the crowd to the bar, chatting and laughing with several patrons on the way.

Nolan assumed she was Aunt Bonty, but he wasn't sure. He'd never set foot in the woman's famous pub before. When he arrived, the crowd nearly made him turn back around. However, the smell of freshly baked bread wafting from the open door—and the fact he still had an hour to kill before the tournament—finally lured him in. Aunt Bonty's pub was one of the few places in Alton where everyone was welcomed. Clothing of all shades filled the room—segregated into their own sections, of course. Luckily for Nolan, working at the manor allowed him to sit wherever he wanted.

Nolan repositioned the book and flipped back to Kael's tournament year. He was one of thirty-two discovered that year. The number of Rol'dan recruits increased the further back he looked. Thirty-eight. Then forty. Then sixty-five. The most recent tournament listed just nine names.

He stared at the page.

Why hadn't he noticed? The numbers had radically dropped. How much longer until the Shay powers would disappear completely?

"You all right there, love?" Bonty stood at Nolan's elbow, waiting patiently for a place to put the ale.

"Sorry." He closed the book and stuffed it into his pack.

"Ah, not to worry." She placed the mug on the table. "You meetin' someone?"

"Um, no. Why?" He picked up the mug and took a drink. It tasted much better than he'd imagined.

Bonty smiled. "Just wondering. I thought she might be looking for you." She pointed toward a young woman seated at the bar, patted his arm in a motherly fashion, and continued to the next table to drop off a bowl of savory smelling stew.

A girl, maybe a few years older than Nolan, sat straight on a stool. Her dark brown hair hung down her back, tied loosely with a strip of gray cloth. She was pretty. Not exotic like Mikayla, but still quite lovely. Wearing simple clothes—a light blue dress and no jewelry—she could easily fit in with the girls back home.

He took a prolonged drink and murmured a laugh. *Don't be an idiot, Nolan.* He shouldn't think of home—or admire pretty girls, for that matter. The manor was his life. Today, he'd leave to record the proceedings at the tournament, just like last year and every year to come. And when he returned, he'd hide in his gloomy room and die of old age as scribe of Alton Manor. No trip home. No girls. No life. Just him, his ink, and his quill.

A boisterous laugh rebounded off the walls. A large, hairy man perched on a stool too small for him with his back to the pub's far wall. His eyes sparkled. His beard hung long and matted. Everything about him was huge. If Nolan guessed, he would assume the man to be a Higherlander, the people from the other side of the mountain range. But that would be ridiculous; they didn't usually leave their lands.

An energetic group of children, dressed in every shade of the districts, sat on the floor surrounding him, hanging on his every word.

"Nay!" the man said in answer to a child's question. "I've never seen them. No living man has. But I have seen a man after the fact, after the dark beasts took his soul." He leaned forward for effect. "Aye, you best listen to your mums about the night. Everything she's said is true."

The children leaned their heads together, whispering.

The Higherlander was quite a storyteller. The activities of the pub died as others started hanging on his words. Nolan reclined in his chair and stretched his legs to get comfortable.

"And the Demon Wars?" a girl asked.

"That, my lass, I do not know. I've heard a man who can tell those tales, so he says."

"And the magic stones!" a boy asked. "Do you have the magic stones?"

The man stroked his long beard, smiling. "And what do you know about those?"

The boy looked around shyly. "My friend, Tommy, showed them to me. He said you gave him magic stones that keep the night beasts away. He said he got them from you yesterday."

The man laughed so deeply it rumbled in his chest. "So that is why I have so many here to listen to my tales! Aye, laddie, I still have some."

The children rose, pressing in closer. Nolan stretched to catch a peek.

"Now, remember, these here aren't real," the man said. "There are legends of real stones, hundreds of years ago. They say the light inside them can scare any darkness away. So don't be wanderin' out in the dark and getting yourselves killed. These here are only rocks, not true magic stones."

The children didn't seem to care if they were pretend. They chattered excitedly as he handed out small bundles. The brood scampered away with their new treasures, some running out the door and others joining adults at nearby tables. Conversations started up again. A boy at the table next to Nolan's held out his bundle, showing it to his father. The man scowled, yanking it away.

"Don't be ridiculous!" He tossed it on the floor and led the crying boy away.

Nolan scowled. *Oh, for Brim's sake; let the kid have some fun.*

The storyteller rose and threaded his way through the pub, talking with those he passed. He headed to the bar where the pretty girl waited for him. She tapped her fingers impatiently, speaking to the man in low tones. Nolan straightened, his stomach dropping in disappointment and shock. The girl was with…him?

How in the name of Brim did a hairy oaf end up with a girl like her? She only came to his shoulders. And for crow's sake, he was way too old for her. A smattering of gray went through his dirty-blond beard.

Nolan studied the girl's profile. And while staring at her might've been rude, he found the view much better than the smelly tradesmen crammed around the tables surrounding him. After several moments, she placed a few coins on the counter and swept the room with her eyes. Nolan panicked and jerked his head down.

The table wasn't very interesting, but there was no way he was going to look anywhere else. Nolan traced a finger on a jagged knife gouge, and when he couldn't stand it any longer, he raised his head.

The brown-haired girl and the mountain man had gone.

Nolan pushed back disappointment and downed the last of his drink. He reached to retrieve his overstuffed pack and noticed a small wad of cloth lying on the floor—the one the father had tossed away. Nolan glanced around, seeing if anyone else had noticed. Conversations continued. He plucked it from the ground and set it in front of him.

It consisted of some sort of animal fur—deer, maybe—tied closed with a thin bit of leather. Nolan pulled the strap and it came undone. Inside lay six small stones, each painted a different color. Nolan smiled. Magic stones. He palmed the small rocks, rolling them, inspecting them. He then placed them back in the pelt and tucked the bundle into his pack.

As he rose to leave, Kardos Deverell, the blacksmith, burst through the door like an angry badger. Nolan sat again and pulled out his book, pretending to read. Things were too interesting to leave now.

"What can I get for you, Kardos?" Bonty asked.

"The same as usual."

"Aren't you and your boy swingin' swords about this time of day?"

"It's a bit hard to fight yourself now, isn't it?" He downed the mug in a long gulp and slammed it on the bar. "Alec is leaving for that nightforsaken tournament, and he won't bother listening to reason."

"It's not like he had a choice."

Kardos grunted. "I swear…If they lay one hand on my boy, those Rol'dan dogs will be on the other side of a Deverell blade."

The room quieted into whispers as eyes darted toward Kardos. Either Kardos didn't notice or he didn't care.

"Here, love." Bonty refilled his mug and pushed it toward him. "Set your mouth to this instead."

"Forget it." Kardos shoved the mug away, sloshing its contents onto the bar. He threw a couple of coins on the counter. "I need to get to work. The Rol'dan might not be able to murder anyone else without a good weapon. Good day, Bonty."

"Take care, Kardos," Bonty said, and then shifted her attention to cleaning the mess.

The conversations swelled back to loud drones. If Alec was anything like his father, the tournament would be interesting, indeed.

Nolan stood, grateful to leave the overcrowded pub, but dreading the start of his day. The streets outside were even worse than the pub. The merchant shops in Alton were typically swarmed with shoppers and travelers. Today, the entire city—and probably the surrounding ones—had all come to wish the competitors a good journey. Nolan couldn't take two steps without some passerby jostling him.

He finally reached the river where three long boats rested peacefully along the docks, waiting for departure. In the center of each boat, a canopy sheltered reclining Rol'dan soldiers from the scorching sun. Kael sat in the lead boat with his feet propped on a chair. He drank from a large mug, seemingly bored.

Nolan slid his bag off his shoulder and rotated his arm. A table had already been set on the pier. He situated his inkbottle and the tournament book in front of him. Nolan opened the book and ran his finger down the page. He was ready, he supposed, to begin his first duty of the tournament: the tedious process of calling off the names.

Nolan scanned the hopeful faces pressing toward the docks. A few of Alton's guards held off the expectant throng, waiting for Nolan to give his cue to begin. Emery's plea for help prodded the back of Nolan's brain. Nolan *couldn't* help him. Not now. Not ever. He was only a scribe, for crow's sake.

Forcing back his guilt, Nolan focused on his task at hand. He had a job to do. Some of these people were about to confront their greatest desires and darkest futures. In just a few moments, their life-altering journey to the Tournament of Awakening would begin.

Chapter Five

After seven days rowing down the Curlew River, and another seven on foot through the Forest of Vidar, Nolan and the traveling party broke through the trees into a breathtaking view.

On the farthest edge of a grass-covered field, a lake sat at the base of a towering cliff. Branches and twisting vines draped over the rock face, giving shelter to a small waterfall that cascaded and churned over a medley of red and brown stones at its base. Small shafts of light broke through the cloud cover—unlike the low, endless clouds over Alton—making the water sparkle in spots. The grouping of nearly one hundred travelers gawked, muttering a few "oohs" and "ahhs." Many had probably never seen the sunlight at all.

The other thing that amazed Nolan was the colors. The grass was green—not the artificial green smeared over the district buildings in Alton, but green unlike anywhere else. The flowers smattered on the grass and clinging to vines all shouted natural colors, making the brightest paint in Adamah seem just another shade of gray. Nolan loved this place, even if it reminded him of the tournament. He shook his head, pushing aside memories of swords and arrows and blood. He scanned the mass of excited faces as they collapsed, one by one, in the grass. Poor fools. They didn't even know what was coming to them.

Nolan wiped his forehead. For a brief moment, he considered running to the small lake and jumping in fully clothed. From the murmuring, it seemed similar thoughts crossed the others' minds as well.

A short distance away, a sea of tents burst with competitors from other cities and towns. In all, over five hundred were supposed to come for the trials. Since Alton was the largest of the cities, and Nolan being the scribe of that city, he had the "honor" to keep track of everyone. His shoulders sagged thinking about it.

Nolan's eyes drifted to the others, and he thought about Emery Cadogan's request. A girl with red hair flipped it over her shoulder. A heavy-set boy chatted with a tan-skinned friend. How in the Darkness did Emery expect Nolan to do anything? Everyone looked the same before coming into their powers. How could he "keep an eye out" for anyone? Excitement buzzed. They couldn't wait for their trials to begin.

He'd watch them, of course. That was his job: to watch and to record. But there was no way he'd ever try to coax them from the Rol'dan. Knowing his luck, whoever he talked to would report him. Then Nolan's secret would be laid bare. And if that happened, he couldn't help anyone, including himself. He'd be marked as a traitor and hanged. Guilt stabbed Nolan. Emery was on his own.

A hearty laugh sounded from the group of Rol'dan where Kael chatted. Unlike the rest of the travelers, they had ridden on horseback.

"Why do they get to ride anyway?" a boy whispered.

"It's because they're the Rol'dan," a girl answered. "They deserve to ride."

Several nodded in agreement.

"They probably forgot how to walk," another voice said.

All heads turned to Alec Deverell, who, instead of resting, yanked a tall blade of grass out of the ground and flicked it. "Or they're just too fat and lazy to walk on their own."

The group giggled and gasped. The Rol'dan soldiers quieted, and a Perception officer's eyes glowed orange as he listened with his Shay. Nolan held his breath; this would not bode well.

"Let *them* walk behind piles of horse dung for a change," Alec continued. "Or maybe it was their own droppings, otherwise they'd have to actually get off their fat backsides to relieve themselves."

Those who'd thought him funny before went silent, their eyes wide.

Nolan stared. *Is he really that stupid? Or does he want to die young?*

The Perception officer leaned over to Kael, and a few words passed between them. He pointed in Alec's direction, and the whole lot made their way over, causing everyone to quickly rise to their feet.

Kael stopped directly in front of Alec and studied him. "What's your name?"

"Alec Deverell...sir," he replied, though the "sir" sneered with nothing close to respect.

"Deverell...Deverell..." He snapped his fingers. "Ah! You're the bladesmith's son."

Alec didn't answer.

"Yes, I see the resemblance. Dreadful man that Kardos. At least he turns out a good blade." Kael slid his sword from its sheath and laid the shining blade against his open palm. "I carry one of your father's swords."

Alec only glanced at it. "Yes, I know that blade."

Kael stabbed his sword into its sheath and flicked a finger across the scar on Alec's cheek. "It appears you know your father's blades quite well."

The soldiers laughed, but Alec's expression darkened.

"And unless you show the Rol'dan more respect," Kael said, "you will be reunited with your father's sword."

"General Trividar," Nolan said, cringing inwardly. "Under the law of Adamah, all competitors are protected during the Tournament of Awakening." He paused, inhaling a slow breath. "Wouldn't be a good idea to hurt one of them."

"Nolan, might I have a word with you?" Kael's voice was tight.

Nolan flinched. Crows, it wasn't like he hadn't seen this

coming. His stomach twisted as if he'd just swallowed a snake. As he bent to get his pack, he caught Alec's eyes. Alec's scowl melted into a strange, questioning stare. Nolan forced a smile, but it only made the confusion in Alec's face deepen.

Nolan followed Kael and the other Rol'dan to the main portion of camp. They made their way past the Rol'dan lodge—a large, two-story building permanently made for the tournament. The six flags of the Shay fluttered lightly in the wind. Three were posted on either side of the entrance, each displaying the symbol and color of the Shay Rol'dan's six sects.

"I will be with you in a moment," Kael said to the rest of his men. The soldiers cast knowing smirks from one to another, then nodded and turned toward the lodge.

Soon the duo approached Nolan's quarters: a larger tent away from the bulk of the crowd. Kael grabbed Nolan's arm, yanking him toward the tent's entrance.

"Now, Kael," he reasoned, "you need to calm—"

Kael flung him inside. He stumbled and fell, tripping over the leg of a chair. His spectacles flew from his face.

The blurred image of Kael rushed him. Nolan crawled away like a crab on a beach. Kael hauled him to his feet, and sudden, blinding pain erupted through Nolan's cheek. A fist in the gut doubled Nolan over; Kael yanked him straight, twisting his arm upward.

Nolan coughed, and his eyes watered, blinding what little vision he had left. "Kael, can't we just talk—"

"It's General Trividar to you!"

Nolan's vision burst with a flash of light, and he hit the ground. Kael pushed him, his boot shoving Nolan's face into the dirt.

"You will remember your position, Scribe!" Kael pushed harder. "And I'll personally run anyone through who attempts to heal you."

Kael released him and leaned in, close enough for Nolan to see regret flick across his brother's face. Nolan paused, staring. *He was...sorry?*

"I expect you at the lodge," Kael said, his scowl back in place. "You have a lot of work to do." Kael turned and left Nolan alone.

Nolan closed his eyes, his body trembling. Kael had always been hard on him, even when he was a kid. But since he'd joined the Rol'dan, he'd gotten worse. Much, much worse. These last two years, Nolan didn't know his brother anymore.

Then he remembered Kael's brief look of regret. Had Kael been sorry? After weighing the possible hope against his fresh agony, Nolan decided he must've imagined Kael's sympathy after all.

After the ache lessened a bit, he tried to stand. He swept the ground with his hand, searching for his spectacles. He flinched when someone grabbed his arm. Alec stood next to him, glowering.

"What are you doing here?"

Alec hesitated. "I, um…followed you."

Nolan groped once more for his spectacles until Alec shoved them into his hand. Sliding them on his face, he saw with perfect clarity the chaos of his room. Upturned desk. Emptied bag. Papers and quills strewn.

"You shouldn't have gotten involved," Alec said. He studied Nolan, and his expression flickered with guilt. "Maybe you can find a Healer. They're swarming all over. Like roaches."

"Great idea," Nolan said. "Except I've been ordered to suffer."

"Ordered to suffer? Who ordered—" Realization fell over his expression. "The crow-loving piece of filth."

Nolan smiled, even though it hurt. He wasn't going to argue with truth.

"You should've stayed out of it," Alec said again, looking a bit too much like his father. "It was my problem, not yours. Why'd you get involved, anyway?"

Because you were being stupid, Nolan thought. Truthfully, he wasn't sure why he had jumped in. Probably because Kael wouldn't kill *him*. Nolan bent to pick up a disheveled stack of books; a stab of pain shot through his side. He moaned.

"I could've handled it," Alec said.

Nolan stopped and stared. "Handled it?"

"Aye. I could've handled it, much better than you."

Nolan opened his mouth then stopped, seeing Alec's muscled arms. He was probably right. Alec spent his days fighting or pounding metal. Nolan, on the other hand, sat in a dark cave of a room with a quill. Maybe Alec *could've* taken a beating better. He cleared his throat. "It's done now. Besides, I'm not the one in the tournament tomorrow. You're going to need to be in one piece."

Alec snorted. "Ah, yes. The tournament."

Nolan limped toward his pack, righted his things, and went to the tent opening. He motioned for Alec to follow. "Come on. The sooner we get this over with, the sooner we can get home."

***

A long, impatient-looking line of people waited near the Rol'dan lodge where Nolan would perform the monumental task of assigning five hundred fifteen-year-olds to groups.

He set his things on a large oak desk. It would be a long night, especially since it hurt to breathe. To make matters stranger, Alec hovered over his shoulder. Nolan wasn't sure why, though he assumed guilt played a role. Instead of joining the other competitors, Alec stood watch, his arms crossed over his chest like Nolan's personal guard. *Am I so pathetic that I need a guard?*

Alec caught Nolan's eye and nodded, as if his position were completely natural, like it was commonplace for scribes to have escorts protect them from the abuse of passing Rol'dan generals.

Nolan forced back a smile. He'd ignore the odd behavior, for now.

"All right now. Who's first?" Nolan said.

A redheaded boy came forward.

"Name?" Nolan took the scroll from his outstretched hand.

"Alden Sullivan."

"Where are you from, Alden?"

"Tydros."

Nolan dipped the quill and copied his name into one of the four color groups that would begin to take form.

"You join the red group. Your camp is to the far right." He handed him a red strip of cloth and pointed toward a grouping of tents where a flag flew.

The boy stared. "Red?"

"Aye, red." Nolan sighed. It had started already. The color segregation made this task much harder than it had to be.

"No," the boy said, "I can't be in red. Father told me specifically to be in blue. My grandfather's brother was an Accuracy archer in his day." He puffed his chest. "So our family needs to stay in blue."

Nolan met his eyes, hardening his stare. "Well today, you'll be red."

He started to protest, but Nolan ignored him. "Next!"

The boy had no choice but to trudge away. After a solid hour of constant arguing, and the occasional cheer when Nolan got a color "right," a girl came forward, her hair bouncing around her shoulders in golden curls.

"Name?"

"Taryn Trividar."

Nolan lowered his quill. "I'm sorry, could you repeat that?"

She smiled. "Taryn Trividar."

Nolan gawked. No. It couldn't be. Had she changed that much in two years?

She cocked her head quizzically. "Is something wrong, sir?"

"Sir?" Nolan snickered "By Brim, you look just like your mother now."

"You know my mother, sir?"

"Of course. Uncle Camden wouldn't let us forget how pretty she was. He went on and on about it every single day. And it's hard to forget Aunt Alana's cooking." Nolan sighed and leaned back in his chair, savoring the memories.

"Nolan? Crows!" She scanned his face, then frowned. "What happened to you? I didn't even recognize you."

Nolan coughed into his hand. "Just an accident. I'll be fine."

Alec snorted behind him.

"How's Uncle Camden?" Nolan said, hoping to distract her. "Have you missed me?"

Her concern transformed into a wide grin. "It's been so calm since you left. I think Papa actually misses the trouble."

"Cousins?" Alec said, gawking.

Taryn's lips quirked.

"This is Alec Deverell," Nolan said. "He's attending the tournament as well."

"Pleasure to meet you, Alec." She extended her hand.

Alec grabbed it and shook it like a sailor. He must have realized his mistake, because he quickly dropped his grip and gave a small, awkward bow.

It was so good to see her. Nolan wanted to talk, to ask how everyone back home was doing. Curiosity even made him wonder how his father had been. Nolan was about to say something, but noticed the huge line winding around the lodge. The boy behind Taryn shifted his feet impatiently.

Nolan cleared his throat. "I suppose I should get to work." He motioned toward the line. "Maybe we can talk again later tonight or between challenges?"

"Oh, yes," Taryn said. "I'd like that very much."

Nolan handed her a blue strip of cloth. "Take care of yourself, Taryn."

She scowled as her eyes examined the bruises on his face. "Take care too, Nolan."

Alec watched her leave, his mouth hanging open. Taryn turned to wave, and Alec quickly averted his gaze.

"Here, Alec," Nolan said, tossing him a blue cloth. "You can be in the blue group too."

Alec stared, horrified at the simple strip of fabric. "I uh... It really doesn't make any difference."

"Then blue it is." Nolan then called the next person in line.

***

The torches surrounding the camp had been lit, as well as a large bonfire where most of the competitors gathered. A medley of drums and flutes played, and a bit of jovial dancing began. It was good for them to have some fun. He remembered having a splendid time that first night at his trial; he'd been just as clueless as them. Most of them had gotten over the shock of the color sorting and relaxed into their groups. However, their cheerful mood wouldn't last long, especially after the tournament started.

Nolan closed the book and stood, aches stabbing his ribcage and stealing his breath. Alec, who had never left him, grabbed Nolan's arm to help.

"Thanks, but I'm fine."

Alec ignored him, nabbed Nolan's pack, and slung it over his shoulder. Nolan thought about telling him to stop treating him like a war casualty. Although, he felt a bit like one, and probably looked the part too. He limped pathetically forward, trying to ignore his throbbing leg.

"So this Taryn…is your cousin?" Alec asked after a few steps.

Ah. So that's why he's still here. "Father and Uncle Camden have a fishing business in Galva. Taryn, Kael, and I spent more time on the sea than on dry ground."

"Kael?"

"Kael is…was my brother."

"Was? Is your brother…"—he hesitated—"…dead?"

Nolan snorted a laugh and watched Alec's face for his next reaction. "He's alive, unfortunately." He motioned toward the Rol'dan lodge. Kael stood on the porch, laughing with some of the other soldiers.

Alec stopped, his eyes widened. "One of them?"

"The general," Nolan added, smiling. "You had the pleasure of meeting him today."

"You're General Trividar's brother?" Alec shook his head,

his eyes wide. "How's that possible?"

"If your father hasn't explained those sorts of things to you by now…"

Alec was confused for a second, and then his brows knit in annoyance. "You know what I mean. He's such an idiot, and you're…well, you're not."

"I'm not?" Nolan's mouth, the side not swollen at least, turned up.

Alec's scowl softened and he met his eyes. "Not yet."

Nolan laughed. "Kael and I aren't so different. At least, we didn't use to be." A memory flashed into his mind. Nolan and Kael were supposed to be bringing in the fishing nets, and they ended up tangling each other instead. They laughed until their sides hurt. After their dad found out, their backsides hurt much more. Kael won their games, of course. He was eight years older than Nolan, so he'd always get the upper hand. Nolan touched a knot on his head and frowned. Some things never did change.

Nolan and Alec reached the tent, and Alec handed him his bag.

"Thanks for your help," Nolan said. "You should get back. You have a big day tomorrow."

Alec didn't move. He shifted his feet. Nolan waited, expecting him to speak. But when a few other competitors walked by, Alec stiffened his posture and then briskly walked away.

The protective torches surrounding the camp cast a flickering light on Alec's retreating form. He made his way to the blue camp, away from the festivities of the others.

Alec was odd, for sure. It was his father's fault, probably. Why did he push Alec so hard? For some reason, Alec and his father both hated the Rol'dan, and that hatred had reared its ugly head that afternoon. Had a Rol'dan hurt them? Wronged them? Obviously, something had happened. Every time Alec looked at a Rol'dan, his eyes burned.

Today, Alec had started something with Kael that wouldn't be easily resolved. And from this day forward, Alec would be balancing on the blade of a completely different kind of sword. Nolan only hoped Alec didn't try to push that blade in deeper.

Chapter Six

Alec Deverell stared at the crowd, his mood growing grumpier. He adjusted the blue armband, the one Nolan had forced on him the night before.

Taking a deep breath, he tried to calm his anger and his nerves. He wasn't sure why the dumb tournament made him anxious; it wasn't as if he'd gain a Shay power. Not him. Not a Deverell. He'd just have to get through the thing so he could get home.

He really didn't know much about what happened at the tournament. However, from his father's grumbling and extra practice sessions, he guessed it wouldn't be good. He dragged Alec to the armory every single day and had even increased his training the two weeks before leaving for the trials. Alec touched his side, low on his ribs, where a bandage hid a fresh gash under his shirt. He would take ten more injuries just like it to be away from here.

The trees rustled, casting shadows across an absurd outdoor banquet. Four long tables stretched across the forest's edge in the gathering area, waiting for the opening feast of the Tournament of Awakening to begin.

A savory aroma wafted over, making Alec's stomach rumble. *Crows, it smells good.* The last few weeks, all he'd eaten on the trail was dried meats and stale bread, and breakfast had been slim. He headed to the tables. At least he'd make the best of the situation and eat well.

Cloth runners stretched the length of each table, each a

different color: red, blue, green, and yellow. A group with colored bands matching his own sat at the long table adorned in blue.

Alec scanned the bench, trying to decide which spot would be the least annoying—there were far too many idiots around him. It would be hard to choose.

"Over here," a voice called. "Alec!"

He glanced over a mop of red hair and saw Taryn, Nolan's cousin, waving him over. He looked over his shoulder to see if she was calling to another boy named Alec. There was no one. Realization fell on him like a sword strike. *Crows. She's talking to me?* Warmth rushed to his cheeks. *I can't sit next to her!*

"Alec!" she yelled again. She broke into a wide grin when their eyes met.

Too late. He couldn't pretend he didn't hear.

He took a deep breath and shifted his shoulders—much like he did before a sparring match with his father. If he could get sliced on a daily basis, he could find the nerve to sit next to Taryn. She pointed to a space across from her, a blue cloth dangling from her wrist.

"Did you sleep well?" Taryn asked. "I could barely sleep at all. I'm so nervous."

Alec swung his legs in, wedging in a space. "Yeah, I suppose."

Her violet eyes sparked. He leaned forward. Yes. She had violet eyes. Why hadn't he noticed last night?

"I'm glad I found you," she said.

"Why?" He cringed as soon as the word left his mouth.

Taryn giggled and shook her head as if he'd told a joke. "Nolan seems pretty busy. I'm not sure when I'm going to be able to talk with him."

Nolan leaned against a tree ten paces from a grouping of Rol'dan. The bruising on his face had gotten a lot worse. His right eye was swollen nearly shut and had turned purple.

"He looks even worse today!" Taryn said. "What happened to him? Must've been quite an accident."

She waved enthusiastically. But for all the energy she exerted, Nolan only forced a smile, barely waving in return.

She lowered her arm and bit her lip. "Wonder what's wrong?"

Alec opened his mouth to answer, then changed his mind. It would probably be best if she didn't know.

After an awkward silence, they were thankfully interrupted by a group of servants carrying in food. Platter after platter was set in front of them: berries and grapes and some type of large, green fruit and fresh baked rolls and sausages and ham. It all made Alec's mouth water. He thought about stacking his plate as high as possible until he noticed Taryn watching. Alec stopped with only a few things. He didn't want her to think he was a greedy slob.

"So where are you from?" Taryn finally asked.

He'd just shoved a bite of ham in his mouth. He chewed quickly and then swallowed. "Alton."

"Oh! Is that where you met Nolan? Father told me he worked there."

Alec nodded and took another bite. He'd met Nolan briefly in Alton, but hadn't much cared for him then.

"I've never been to Alton," Taryn said. "I've heard it's quite big."

"It keeps Father and me busy."

The loud drone of the group lessened as people ate.

"So your father's a tradesman?" she asked. "Or does he work in the manor with Nolan?"

"He's an arms maker," Alec answered, feeling pretty good about the conversation so far.

Taryn put down her fork, and a strange expression passed over her face. "By Brim! Your father isn't *the* Deverell, is he?"

How do I answer? It could mean anything, especially when his Father was involved. She stared at Alec, studying every detail of his face, waiting for an answer. Then thankfully, her eyes darted to someone standing behind Alec. She grinned.

"Nolan!" she said.

Alec took a bite from a roll and chewed vigorously. A

twitch jolted his stomach.

"How's your meal?" Nolan asked.

"Great," Taryn said, "though I'm so nervous, I'm not sure I can eat much of anything."

Nolan attempted a smile. "You shouldn't force yourself to eat."

"Why don't you join us? You can have as much as you want of mine."

"No, thanks," Nolan said.

Nolan's eyes held a strange expression, as if struggling with telling them something. "Like I said, no sense stuffing one's self. That is, if you aren't feeling well."

"Nolan!" General Trividar's voice blared.

Nolan's cheek twitched. "Excuse me." He returned to the idiot Rol'dan.

General Trividar yanked Nolan off to the side, his face red as he jammed his finger into Nolan's chest.

"What's that about?" Taryn said. "Who's that?"

"General Trividar."

"Kael?" Taryn sat straighter, watching with more interest. "So he's my famous general cousin. I barely remember him from when he left for the Rol'dan. Hm...he doesn't seem as impressive as my Uncle Belen made him out to be."

Alec stabbed another serving of meat onto his plate. "No. He's not impressive at all."

Taryn gave Alec a puzzled expression and turned to her cousins. General Trividar's eyes roved over the tables, and a predatory grin spread across his lips.

"Well, at least they've stopped fighting," Taryn said.

From what Alec had seen so far, it was never over between them. It wasn't as if Nolan had committed a crime by coming over and saying hello.

Alec's stomach twitched again, not much, but enough to get his attention. What had Nolan said? Not to force himself to eat if he wasn't feeling well? How would Nolan know how he felt? Did he look sick? Unless Nolan knew something the rest didn't.

Alec pulled his eyes from his plate to the others gorging themselves. He couldn't help but notice the smirks on the faces of the Rol'dan. They laughed, as if about to pull some sick practical joke. He put a hand to his gut and pushed the plate away. He didn't feel so well.

As the last platter was emptied, General Trividar sauntered to the head of the tables. "Greetings!" he said. "Welcome to the first day of the Tournament of Awakening."

The group erupted in cheers, and a cluster of Rol'dan handed out tightly wrapped scrolls.

"Did you all enjoy your feast?"

The crowd cheered louder.

General Trividar's grin widened. "My men are handing out a document for your first trial. Once they have been distributed, we will go over them together."

Those who had already received their scrolls opened them and confused conversations spread. Alec unrolled the parchment and found a very strange list.

1 Root of Tardock
1 Mitimum Beetle
5 Violet Taum Berries
10 Perridrake Seeds
1 Bonnie Bird Feather

A middle-aged woman with her hair pulled tightly in a bun stepped forward. Her eyes darted back and forth, radiating the orange light of Perception. "My name is Captain Rossen. I will explain each of the items on this list. If you haven't yet opened your scroll, please do so now. We will start at the top.

"The first item: one root of tardock," she began. "Its outer foliage is very small with yellow tips on its leaves. It can be found in large patches of weeds as it prefers shade." She held a small green plant. "The best way to recognize the tardock plant is by its distinct smell. We will pass it so you may sample the fragrance."

Several soldiers walked around holding bundles of similar

green plants. Alec couldn't smell anything, except the stench of horse and day-old sweat from the Rol'dans' hands.

"Very good," Captain Rossen said. "And when you dig up the roots..." She held a small, brown root branching in furry tentacles. Once again the soldiers walked around with the roots so all could see them properly.

"Seems like quite a bit of traveling to learn about plants," Alec whispered.

Taryn snickered.

Captain Rossen continued, "The mitimum beetle has a shiny, iridescent shell." She opened a small wooden box and removed a beetle, no bigger than the nail on her little finger. She placed it on her palm and angled her wrist, like they were supposed to be seeing something more than a bug.

"The next item," the captain continued, "is the violet taum berry. It can be mistaken for a sickle berry, which is quite plentiful in this region. The difference between the two is the taum berry has a bitter taste when consumed.

"However, you don't want to eat them, for the inner meat of the sickle berry, although quite tasty, has been known to turn one's skin purple for several weeks. You can obtain enough of the taste by rubbing them gently on your tongue, like so..." Captain Rossen held two small berries and brushed them on her tongue.

Servants circled the tables with two bowls filled with dark purple berries. Alec took one from each bowl and examined them. They were exactly alike.

Around them, a multitude of tongues dangled out of mouths as frantic hands rubbed berries against them. Alec considered tossing them in the grass until one of the Rol'dan soldiers cast him a suspicious glare. Alec turned his back to him, reluctantly stuck out the tip of his tongue, and gave both berries a quick swipe.

Nothing.

He stuck his tongue out farther and rubbed a bit harder.

Still nothing. This was so stupid.

He stuck it out the rest of the way and rubbed vigorously,

determined he'd taste the nightforsaken things. Everything would've been fine if he hadn't looked at Taryn mirroring the same action. Their eyes met and she smiled. And as hard as they tried to keep going, they had to stop. It was very hard to stick out your tongue and smile at the same time.

Laughter rang from the yellow table where a boy sat, his skin now a strange shade of violet. The others around him rolled off the bench, tears running down their faces. The boy, on the other hand, was miserable.

"Now, now," Captain Rossen said. "You see what can happen if you don't follow directions precisely."

A few whispered comments of "blue boy" circulated.

"Let us continue." Captain Rossen cleared her throat. "The perridrake plant can be identified by the texture. It has a plush, fur-like coating on the underside of the leaf. Once you find the plant, break open the pods near the base and obtain the seeds."

A soldier passed by with two leaves. One supposedly a perridrake and another some other common weed. Alec rubbed them, not feeling any difference. He scraped a hand through his hair. This little treasure hunt was going to be harder than he'd first thought.

"The last item is the feather of a Bonnie Bird."

A man approached with a cage holding a very small, very nervous brown bird. It opened its beak with a soft chirp.

"Its call is the best method of finding where it nests. It prefers to build in low bushes. So once you find it, you should have no problem obtaining a loose feather."

General Trividar stepped forward. "Now that you have a description of all the items on your list, your first test will be to go into the Forest of Vidar and find them all."

"How are we supposed to do that?" a boy in the green group said.

"To bring forth a Shay, one must focus intense emotions into the center where the Shay lies dormant. However, bringing a Shay forward is a much more complicated task than just searching blindly in the forest for leaves or feathers. We must find an incentive—such as fear—to bring forth the power."

General Trividar crossed his hands over his chest, one side of his mouth curved up. "To aid you in discovering your power, if you so have one, your incentive will be to search this list of ingredients for the antidote of the poison you just consumed."

Silence followed. After the initial shock, a wave of angry voices rose.

"The first sensation will be an illness in your stomach," General Trividar said. "More than likely, many of you are feeling it now. The second symptom will be fever and dry mouth. No amount of water will aid you. Then your stomach will sour, feeling like it's been turned inside out. Vomiting, weakness, and dizziness are all the later symptoms. By then, you will wish you were dead.

"But before you dig your graves," General Trividar continued, "the poison is not fatal. The quicker you find the antidote, the fewer symptoms you will suffer. So urgency is a priority in your quest."

A girl jumped up, as if to run to the forest. A few others did the same.

General Trividar held out his hand to stop them. "I need to tell you two other items of information. The first: All the objects we used in this demonstration are unavailable to you. They will be placed under lock and key and under careful guard. The second: Once you find your ingredients, you will need to bring them here. Captain Rossen will combine them properly. Oh, and one last thing. It *is* possible to find the items without Perception, but it would be difficult to do so before the poison starts taking effect.

"Good luck to you all. May the king's grace shine upon you, if you are so fortunate."

Chaos erupted. Panic-stricken participants jumped from their seats and dove into the forest, yelling and squabbling as they went.

A wide-eyed girl next to Taryn jolted from her seat and grabbed Taryn's arm. "Come on!"

Taryn rose and staggered a few steps before stopping. "Are you coming, Alec?"

"No," he replied. Alec couldn't say anything else. His blood boiled so hot he could melt the knife in his hand if he sliced open a vein.

Taryn gave Alec a nervous smile, but allowed the girl to drag her away.

The whole gathering area cleared in moments. Only Alec, the Rol'dan soldiers, and Nolan remained.

Alec locked eyes on General Trividar. The Rol'dan were devious and manipulative, but to be as deceptive in such a thing as a meal—something sustaining life and strength. No. He wouldn't be a puppet, especially not to *him*. He refused to dash around the woods like some hunted deer. General Trividar would have to find his sport another way.

Instead of heading off to the edge of the woods, Alec stomped straight toward camp, passing directly between the Rol'dan.

General Trividar stepped into his path. "I didn't think you were stupid enough not to know the location of the forest. Over there, Mr. Deverell."

"I know where the forest grows." He took a step around the general, but was blocked again.

"One of my Strength Rol'dan would be more than happy to throw you in," the general suggested. "However, the landing would probably be more painful than walking yourself."

"Get out of my way."

General Trividar snarled, striding toward Alec.

Nolan stepped between them. "I'm sorry, Alec, but all competitors are required to participate."

Alec gawked at Nolan. What was he doing? How could he take their side?

"It's the law." Nolan gave Alec a look that said, *I'm sorry.* "You have to enter the forest to complete the trial."

"I must enter the forest?"

Nolan nodded. "Otherwise you'll be considered a traitor."

Alec clenched his teeth. He couldn't let them win. But there was no way around this. If he didn't do this, they'd arrest him. It would serve no purpose at all, except to hurt Father more. If Alec let the general arrest him, he would win. Alec tried to calm his rage. Then an idea came to him. Maybe there was one more option…

"How long must I remain in the forest?" Alec asked.

Though it was subtle, Nolan smiled. "The laws note nothing of time."

Alec turned toward the woods, stepped into the edge of the trees, and trailed it toward camp. General Trividar matched his pace, stalking him with each step. When Alec reached the outcropping of tents where the blue camp stood, he stepped from the woods.

General Trividar glared. As Alec passed him, he purposely bumped the general's shoulder with his own. "Shame," Alec said. "Looks like I've failed."

He continued on, ignoring the vein protruding from the general's neck and the golden-yellow light of his Speed Shay blazing from his eyes. Alec even ignored him when the general gripped the hilt of his sword. Alec had succeeded in making him furious, and that fact alone made him smile. And his smile remained the next several hours, at least until the poison took hold.

***

When Alec woke the next morning—or closer to afternoon—he wasn't alone in the grass under the blue flag. Sprawled all throughout the camp were what looked like dead bodies after a gruesome battle. But the groaning and retching reminded Alec that they were all alive.

He closed his eyes and tried to ignore another wave of nausea. He couldn't even imagine how he would've felt if he had gorged himself like he'd wanted.

A steady tapping jarred his head. He opened his eyes, stood, and staggered around several people on the ground. The camp waved and lurched before his eyes, the smell of vomit everywhere. He grabbed a tent pole, focused, and kept going until he reached a familiar figure nailing a document to a post.

Nolan grimaced as he pounded the curling paper. Messy brown hair hung in his eyes. Behind the purple bruises mottling his face, Nolan was as pale as if he'd eaten the poison too. He finished hammering and gripped an arm across his chest. He was strange. For some reason, he kept protecting Alec. It wasn't like Nolan knew him at all. Alec wanted nothing more than to enrage that general. But his wiser half knew he was being stupid. And Nolan kept risking himself so Alec would stay in one piece.

"You okay?" Alec asked.

Nolan released a stuttering breath. "Strange you should ask. You look dreadful."

"I feel dreadful," Alec said. "But at least not as bad as them."

Nolan's blue eyes passed over the others. "Hm, yes. It's not much better anywhere else. I'm glad to see you're up and about."

"Thanks to you."

Nolan smiled faintly. "I didn't do much."

He grabbed another nail and pounded the paper in place. After he'd finished, he buckled over, resting his hands on his knees.

"I think my rib is broken." Nolan straightened, though it took him a lot of effort. "It's a good thing I only have to lift quill and parchment." He glanced at the hammer in his hand. "Well, at least for the most part."

Alec pointed at the document Nolan had just posted. "What's this?"

"The schedule for the rest of the week: Tomorrow, blue group will do the Challenge of Accuracy; the following day will be Strength; then the next day Speed; and the last day will be Empathy. The other colored groups alternate days. Everyone will get a turn at each trial."

"Only four more days?"

Nolan nodded.

Alec did a quick calculation. "What about Healing?"

"You'll get lots of chances to test that power."

"Doesn't sound very promising."

"No, I'm afraid not."

"And the Perception trial yesterday?" Alec asked. "Did anything come from it?"

"One came into their power. A girl."

Panic washed over Alec. He scanned the pathetic people across the grass, draped over rocks, propped against tress, and those who just fell where they were on their faces. She wasn't here. Matter of fact, Alec hadn't seen her at all.

"A girl from yellow group," Nolan said. "I believe her name is Sussan. Taryn is waiting this off inside her tent. I checked on her a few minutes ago." He slipped the hammer into a leather pouch on his side. "Well, only three more signs to go."

"Want some help?" Alec asked, and then a wave of dizziness clouded his vision. When it cleared, Nolan had a hand on Alec's shoulder.

"Thanks for the offer, but I don't think you're in any shape to do anything." Nolan studied his face. "And, Alec, quit making my brother angry. He'll make you regret it."

"I can take care of myself."

"I hope so." Nolan released Alec's shoulder and gave him a sympathetic smile as he turned and walked away.

Whatever pity Alec felt for him was replaced with annoyance. What did Nolan expect him to do? Ignore the general when he taunted him? Alec wouldn't let General Trividar, or his arrogant friends, get away with it. All he needed was a sword, and he'd show them a thing or two.

A shiver went through his body, and his stomach flipped with such force he couldn't hold it. He retched while leaning a quivering hand on the post. Alec pulled back up and wiped his mouth across his sleeve.

Yes, he'd show them…just not today.

Chapter Seven

Alec watched as Captain Faal's eyes glowed a deep sapphire blue. With a simple motion of the captain's hand, he cued a group of blue-caped Accuracy archers forward. They positioned themselves next to quivers embedded in the ground and nocked blue-feathered arrows in their bows.

"The Shay of Accuracy complements the art of archery perfectly," Captain Faal began. "With our special ability, we can hit anything within our range of vision."

The bows creaked as the Rol'dan pulled back and aimed toward numerous colorful targets at the far end of the field.

"Ready?" Captain Faal said. "FIRE!"

A volley of arrows sang through the air and *thudded* into the targets, each finding their mark perfectly in the center blue circle.

"Red."

A swish of arrows all landed in the red rings.

"Yellow."

The arrows impaled the yellow rings.

Captain Faal called off numerous colors in quick succession before calling "blue." With a crack of wood, the arrows found the center targets, splitting the previous arrows in two.

The trial bearers erupted in cheers.

"Fantastic," a nearby girl said.

Taryn nodded with wide eyes as she clapped in approval.

Alec wasn't impressed.

Nolan leaned toward Alec. "Your father probably doesn't

make many bows or arrows in his armory, does he?"

"No," Alec whispered. "Not enough steel to suit him."

"For those of you who are untrained in archery," Captain Faal said, "we'll give you an opportunity to learn before your Challenge of Accuracy begins."

Captain Faal separated them into groups, giving a quick lesson on the proper way to hold the long bow, where to position the arm, and how to sight the arrow. When it was Alec's turn, he found that—much like swordplay—he had natural talent. Unlike many of the others, Alec could hit the target.

"Hold your fire," Captain Faal called.

General Trividar came over the hill with a group dressed in black robes. Green sashes strung across their chests, marking them as the sect of the Healing Rol'dan.

Alec had been feeling pretty good about his archery skills. But seeing those Healers…Well, that couldn't mean anything good.

Captain Faal gave a quick bow to the general before speaking. "Sir, we are about to begin."

"Very good, Captain. Proceed."

Captain Faal motioned to two of his Accuracy Rol'dan, and they took a place on the opposite side of the field, a good twenty paces on either side of the centermost target.

"As you know," Captain Faal said, "the Shay of Accuracy gives one perfect aim. Your task for this trial will be to hit with perfect aim as well. You will have only three chances. If you miss, the result could prove quite painful."

A boy raised his hand.

Captain Faal pointed at him. "Yes? Questions?"

"What do you mean by painful?"

The captain smiled. "As mentioned before, to bring forth a Shay, one must focus intense emotions into the center where the Shay lies dormant. But shooting targets alone will not bring forth a Shay. Which is why if you miss the target, our archers will return fire."

The boy's mouth dropped open. "They'll shoot us?"

The crowd murmured, anxious energy spreading.

"They may shoot you. Or they may not. As long as you hold still, our Accuracy Rol'dan will avoid a fatal blow. The result of dodging may be an arrow between your eyes"—he motioned to the black robed Healers—"and our Healers will not raise the dead. So far in our history, we've never had a death with this portion of the trial."

Alec snorted. So far...How reassuring.

General Trividar stepped forward, false concern plastered on his conceited face. "I'm sure you can all agree that the temporary discomfort is necessary. How else can you discover if you can be an honored Rol'dan?"

Alec's stomach lurched with disgust. *Honored Rol'dan?*

The participants calmed slightly, though fear still trickled through them.

"Perhaps a demonstration is in order?" General Trividar suggested. His eyes roved over the group, stopping on Nolan. "I believe our scribe would be more than happy to show us."

Nolan's face paled.

Captain Faal frowned. "It isn't really necessary—"

"I must insist." The general held out his arm, as if giving Nolan a warm invitation.

Alec thought Nolan might refuse, but he squared his shoulders and stepped forward, grimacing as he bent to get an arrow. He was in no condition for archery. He nocked it and closed his eyes for several long moments.

"I didn't call you to sleep," General Trividar said.

Several of the Rol'dan chuckled.

Nolan opened his eyes, pulled the bowstring, and his lips contorted. He released it, and it landed with a quiet thump into the soil in front of the target.

"Perfect example. Thank you, Nolan," the general said.

Nolan inhaled deeply and straightened his posture, awaiting the return fire. The arrow whistled through the air and *thudded* solidly into Nolan's shoulder. He jolted back a step and stifled a cry, but made no movement to remove it. Instead, he leaned over, trembling, his eyes closed.

Alec clenched his fists, and Taryn clung to his arm. General

Trividar hadn't used Nolan just for example. He wanted to make a fool of him.

General Trividar strode in front of their shocked and silent group. He made an annoyed gesture to the Healers before he spoke. "As you can see, a missed shot resulted in a shot returned. And as you can also see, he is very much alive."

Captain Faal stepped forward. "I should also note that hitting the target does not signify a successful shot. A center shot is the only one accepted. Only a truly accurate shot will pass the trial."

"That's impossible," Taryn whispered. "None of us can do it."

"That's the idea," Alec whispered back. "We aren't meant to pass unless we have Accuracy."

Captain Faal began arranging the group, leading them to the other side of the hill away from the range.

"I can't even hit the target." Taryn's eyes widened. "What are we going to do?"

"Nothing," Alec said, frowning. "We have no choice. Besides, it'll be a few hours before it's our turn. We should check on Nolan and see if he's okay."

She nodded, though still pale. She glanced at their linked arms, gasped, and quickly dropped her hands to her sides. He stared at where she'd held him, disappointed; the spot felt suddenly cold.

They pushed through the crowd toward Nolan, and a Healing Rol'dan stepped into their path.

"Just a moment," the Rol'dan said. He turned to Nolan and yanked the arrow free.

Nolan grunted out what sounded like a curse.

The Healer ripped open Nolan's bloodied tunic, placed his palms on Nolan's pale chest, and closed his eyes. When he opened them, an emerald light glowed.

The Rol'dan shuddered; spots of moisture seeped through his robe on his shoulder, exactly where the arrow had been. But the most amazing sight was when purple bruises swelled on the Rol'dan's face, and after a moment, faded to normal again.

When he'd finished, the Healer dusted himself off and walked away as if nothing had happened.

Alec stared. He'd never seen anything like it.

"Crows, Nolan," Taryn said. "Are you okay?"

Nolan smiled. "I'm feeling quite well, actually." He ran his hand across his face where the bruising had been.

Alec couldn't get over it. He knew he shouldn't be impressed—especially of a Rol'dan—but he couldn't help it.

"Was this your first time?" Nolan asked.

"What?" Alec shook his head. "Sorry?"

"Was this the first time you've seen a Healing Shay at work?"

"Y-yes. Your face..."

"And my rib." Nolan grinned.

"How much can they heal?" Taryn asked.

"Well, they can't grow a limb," Nolan said, "or your head. So keep that attached at the trials. They absorb the injury before healing." Nolan frowned while examining the bloody hole in his tunic. "That's why they won't bring back the dead. They can do it, but they sacrifice themselves in the process."

"Mr. Deverell," General Trividar called as he approached. "You will not fake your way out of your challenge this time." His smirk vanished when he spied Nolan. A vein protruded from his temple and his lips twitched. If the idiot hadn't remembered Nolan's injuries before, he did now. "You're still a terrible shot, Nolan," he said. "Isn't there something you should be doing?"

Nolan grinned with his eyes and bowed. "Of course, General. I must observe the different trials and record the results, just as I was doing before you gave me an extra assignment."

General Trividar's face reddened, but it faded quickly when he spied Taryn.

"This is Camden's daughter," Nolan said.

"Uncle Camden?" General Trividar's mouth dropped open, just a little, and then he closed it again. "By Brim, you look just like your mother."

"I hear that a lot."

He bowed and lifted her hand, bringing it to his lips.

Taryn sucked in a small breath.

When he lifted his head, subtle sadness lingered in his eyes. "I take it back. I believe you are even more beautiful than your mother."

Her eyes widened and her cheeks flushed.

Alec stared, open-mouthed. He didn't dare move lest he punch the general in the face.

The general let go of her hand and straightened to his regular, overconfident stance. "The challenge starts in a moment. Go join the others." His eyes flashed golden with his Shay of Speed, and then he was gone.

***

"One moment," Captain Faal said.

Alec relaxed the bow, but kept his arm tense. It was bad enough he had to wait the entire morning for his turn, let alone having to stop before he even began.

General Trividar sauntered down the field and halted in front of the Rol'dan soldier in charge of impaling Alec. Both men spoke with their faces lowered, like they had a secret. The conversation ended, and the general stepped off the field.

"All right," Captain Faal said. "You may continue."

Alec pulled on the bow and sighted the target. He still preferred his sword, but this bow thing wasn't half bad. The arrow zipped through the air and landed in the middle of a yellow ring. It wasn't the center, but still not an awful shot. Alec lowered the bow and stiffened to prepare for the return fire.

More swords had cut him than he could count, but an arrow would be a whole new kind of injury. A small part of him, the one not scared, was morbidly curious. The Rol'dan aimed and released. The arrow whizzed between his legs, ripping his breeches and exposing the uppermost portion of his inner thigh. If it had been a half an inch higher…Alec's face heated. That shot was no accident. He grabbed another arrow, raised it and took aim, this time at the archer's groin.

The soldier grabbed the arrow out of the air, glared with eyes glowing, and sent the same arrow back.

Fire shot through Alec's foot as an arrow pinned it to the ground. Alec yanked it out, his foot erupting with white hot pain. He ground his teeth and sent the blood-coated arrow back at the crow-loving Rol'dan.

As soon as the arrow left his bow, Alec reached for another, not caring what happened. Out of the corner of his eye he could see Captain Faal step forward. Alec had shot three arrows. His trial was officially done. But before the captain could say anything, Alec shot again.

"That is enough," Captain Faal said.

He ignored him and let loose another failed shot. His leg erupted in fire with the returned arrow. It hurt badly, but Alec's anger flared to the point where he didn't care.

"I said enough. Stand down."

The creak of a bowstring drew Alec's attention. Captain Faal stood, an arrow drawn and pointed at Alec's throat.

"Are you done, boy?" he asked. "If not, I can make you be done."

Alec held the bow and arrow, shaking with anger, fatigue, and pain. He glared at the archer on the other side of the field and drew the bow.

"Reconsider, boy," the captain warned.

Alec eyed the archer, and then the captain, his gaze falling to the point of the arrow aimed at him. He cursed and threw the bow. Once the battle lust left, the agony of his injuries came in a rush.

He collapsed, his leg failing. Blood soaked through his breeches where the shaft embedded in his thigh. It dripped down his leg, mingling with the blood from his foot.

General Trividar squatted over him and wrenched the arrow from Alec's leg. Flesh tore as it pulled free. Alec growled and ripped a wad of grass from earth. Crows! It hurt more coming out than going in!

With the arrow in his hand, the general examined Alec with pleased interest. He fiddled with it before tossing it to the side. "You must enjoy discomfort, Mr. Deverell."

Alec's rage returned. He tried to stand, but couldn't as tremors of pain stabbed his leg.

Four Healers rushed over. Alec resisted, his vision clouding at the edges.

"Sit still," one of the Rol'dan Healers scolded.

Alec very much wanted to grab one of those arrows, and cram it up his—

His body jerked. Strange warmth started in his chest where the Rol'dan's hands touched him. It spread like a hot broth on a winter's day. Then all the pain oozed away, his body relaxing. He exhaled slowly, the sensation...intoxicating. He pushed down the lingering pleasure as bile rose in his throat. How could he *enjoy* it? Memories flooded his mind: his mother... the armory. *Rol'dan don't heal. They only destroy.*

It ended as abruptly as it started. The Healers stood, giving Alec resentful looks as they walked away. Alec staggered to his feet, regaining his balance. Even though the injuries were gone, weakness lingered.

Nolan grabbed his arm to steady him, his face set in a serious scowl. "What did you think you were doing?" he whispered

Alec yanked away from Nolan's grasp and headed to camp. He didn't want to talk about it. Still, Nolan followed.

"Alec!"

Alec stopped. "What business is it to you? I completed the trial, just like I was ordered to."

"Yet you couldn't do it like everyone else. You had to cause as much trouble as possible."

"I was trying to teach that Rol'dan—"

"Teach him? Teach him what? That you make a good target? The only reason you aren't dead is they aren't allowed to kill you."

"I was teaching him that he couldn't get away with insulting me. Did you see what he did?" He motioned to the crotch of his torn pants.

"Yes. He was trying to make you mad. And it worked."

"What was I supposed to do?"

"Nothing."

"Do nothing? You mean, like you?"

"Yes, like me."

Alec snorted. "I can't just sit there and let them walk all over me. I'm no coward."

Nolan's jaw tensed. "A coward...like me?"

Alec didn't answer.

He couldn't.

That was exactly what he'd implied, and they both knew it.

Finally, Nolan released a long sigh. "It's not about being a coward. It's about controlling yourself. I know you want to win, Alec. I get that. However, my brother is more stubborn than you. And more powerful." He met his eyes. "The more you keep fighting Kael and trying to make him angry, the more you'll end up just like him. And that is exactly what he wants: to push you over the edge. He wants a *reason* to kill you." Nolan smiled weakly. "Be careful, all right?" Then he turned and walked away.

Nolan's words slapped Alec across the face, sealing any arguments. He stared at Nolan's retreating back, his blood heating even more, if it were possible. *The more I try to make him angry, the more I become like him? Ridiculous! How dare Nolan compare me to a murdering Rol'dan!*

An iridescent flash caught Alec's eye. He bent over and watched a mitimum beetle make its way through the grass. Just two days ago, at the trial of Perception, people desperately searched for them. Now, this one marched along as if taunting him. With a sudden burst of rage and frustration, Alec ground the beetle into the earth.

Chapter Eight

Alec sat on a large rock and rummaged through his pack for a waterskin. Tipping it back, he took a long swig, letting the lukewarm water drain down his throat. It was cooler today, but the lack of wind and the brisk hike made him sweat. He wiped his forehead and glanced over in time to catch a group of girls staring and looking away. Unfortunately, gossip spread fast.

For some reason, everyone knew exactly what had happened at the Trial of Accuracy. Alec could tell by the way they whispered any time he walked by. He wondered if they thought him brave or insane. Alec hadn't decided yet himself.

He thrust the waterskin into his bag and did another scan over the group, searching for Taryn. They hadn't spoken since yesterday, and he had a terrible feeling she was avoiding him. He couldn't blame her, really. He'd probably do the same.

A short, athletic soldier dressed in the red tunic and cape of the Strength Rol'dan strolled in front of the group, his hands casually behind his back. A thick, braided beard hung mid-way down his chest.

"I am Captain Ekon," the Rol'dan said. "Before we begin, I want to share with you about the Shay of Strength, the focus of your next challenge.

"Some people believe the Shay of Strength only makes you stronger. Our Shay gives us strength. Yes, that is true. We can lift objects the common man would envy. However, it also transforms our bodies. Our bones harden like iron rods, and our skin strengthens like the toughest of leather. A foe might discover, too late, that it is most difficult to stab, slash, hit, bruise, or crush one such as us. We are the most powerful of all the Shay Rol'dan."

Captain Ekon smiled arrogantly, as if expecting them to keel over from awe and admiration at his mere presence.

"I am sure you are all anxious to find out if you have this powerful Shay. Perhaps among you, we might find a new champion."

Another Rol'dan soldier appeared at the top of a steep path littered with small stones. He waved, giving a silent signal.

"Ah! I see it's time to begin." Captain Ekon scrutinized the group until his eyes rested on a tall fellow with blond hair. He motioned him forward and pointed the boy up the hill.

For several long minutes, the others waited for something to happen. Birds chirped. Feet shuffled. Just when the atmosphere began to relax, and conversations started again, a terrible yell rang out.

The group went completely silent, staring in horror at the path above. The yell choked into silence, followed by a chorus of laughter.

Alec repositioned himself on the rock and breathed, trying to tell himself he wasn't at all nervous. Then he remembered the arrows. What terrible things lay just over the hill?

The process continued throughout the morning: a terrified scream, then silence, then laughter. Alec took to people-watching to distract himself. A few boys wrestled, more than likely trying to show off to the girls. Several others sat alone, shaking their legs with nervous tension. A skinny fellow toyed with a sling, knocking off small stones stacked on a larger one. Someone else stood with him, apparently getting a lesson.

Alec leaned forward and squinted. It wasn't hard to recognize Nolan. His crumpled clothing, spectacles, and mop of messy brown hair could belong to no one else. Alec slid from where he'd been sitting and walked over.

"Try it like this," the skinny boy said. He held an empty sling in his hand then flicked it over his head to release an imaginary stone. He handed the sling to Nolan.

Nolan stood in a silly squatting sort of stance. Alec snorted, trying not to laugh. Nolan glanced from the corner of his eyes, swung the sling once, and released his imaginary stone.

"Hey! Not bad," the boy said. "Let's try it for real this time."

Nolan put a small rock in the sling, gave it a fling, and released. It struck the base of the large rock, missing the smaller ones entirely.

"At least it's going in the right direction," the boy said.

Nolan laughed. "Perhaps we should clear the area before I try again."

"No, no…very good for a first try." He bent to pick up another stone. "You should have seen my first go. I was standing in the field with my father. He said that I…" His voice trailed off as the Strength captain approached and motioned for him. The smile on his face disappeared. "Well then. I guess I'll tell you the rest later. It's a good story."

"I'm sure it is, Rylan. I'll be looking forward to it," Nolan said, holding the sling out to him.

"You keep it. It's a spare." He smiled weakly. "Besides, you need the practice."

Nolan laughed. "That I do."

Nolan placed a stone in the sling, rocked it back and forth a few times, and whipped it toward the rock. This time the small stone whizzed overtop and barely missed the leg of another boy. He shot Nolan an annoyed glare. Nolan held up his hands in apology.

"I didn't realize you had to fend off wild animals in Alton Manor," Alec said.

Nolan ignored him and slung another stone. This time, it skidded across the ground, hitting the trunk of a nearby tree.

"Maybe you should take up something else," Alec said. "Range weapons don't seem to be your talent."

Nolan stopped mid-swing and glared at Alec. The rock, instead of shooting forward, flew straight up. Nolan took a step back and winced as he caught it in his palm on the way down. "So you came over here to insult me again? First I am a coward. Now I am clumsy?"

"Crows, I didn't mean to…" Alec kicked the ground, picked up a stone, and whipped it at the large rock as hard as he could. It hit the smaller rocks with an echoing crack. He'd had all night to think over things. He'd over-reacted and taken his frustrations out on Nolan. He'd lost his temper. Again. Though he didn't agree with him about doing nothing when the Rol'dan tormented him, he also knew Nolan was only trying to help. Alec sighed. "No, I didn't come to insult you. I guess rudeness just comes naturally."

"As well as other things." Nolan motioned toward the rock pile. "I'd offer to let you try the sling, but you don't need it."

It *was* a pretty good throw. Good thing, too. He'd chucked it hard enough it would've left a mark on someone. He turned and found Nolan watching him, brown hair hanging over sun-reddened cheeks. His wire-rimmed spectacles sat askew, probably from the beating he had received from his brother. Alec cleared his throat. "I'm…I'm sorry about yesterday."

Nolan's mouth quirked up. "I know."

A gut-wrenching scream turned everyone's heads. This time, it was not a scream of fear, but of agonizing pain, like a pig slaughtered on a hunt.

Alec forced saliva down his dry throat. "What was that?"

Nolan sighed. "Well, Rylan won't need his sling."

He tore his eyes from the hill. "What do you mean?"

"Strength users typically are trained with large, blunt weapons. A sling will do him little good."

A Strength Rol'dan? That skinny kid? No. He couldn't be.

The Strength captain stepped toward him, breaking Alec's shock. A crooked-tooth sneer poked through the bush of his beard. "Deverell. You're next."

Alec couldn't move. What waited for him over the hill?

"You'll do fine," Nolan said. "Just don't be yourself."

He whipped his head toward Nolan, ready to explode, until he saw Nolan's concerned face.

Alec relaxed. "I'll *try*."

Nolan smiled grimly. "Good."

"Deverell," the Rol'dan said again. "Any time now."

Alec nodded and numbly followed the Rol'dan, wondering what trouble he'd get himself into this time.

***

The clouds seemed closer and thicker on the hill. Alec looked from the gray, puffy mass and met the faces of a group of grinning Rol'dan. A short distance away, a stone-slab bridge stretched over a deep chasm. A second group of Rol'dan—including several black-robed Healers—watched from the other side. Alec felt as if he'd become part of some demented entertainment, much like wild animals fighting to the death. He wiped his hands on his breeches, gripping his hands into fists. Crows take them. Why did the Rol'dan have to make them feel so helpless and small? They stripped them of any defense and surrounded them, watching with morbid fascination. He filled his lungs and released it in a rush. *Just get it over with, Alec. And don't do anything stupid.*

A groan grabbed his attention. The skinny fellow clutched his legs and writhed in a tight ball on the ground.

"Coming into the Shay of Strength can be excruciating," a woman said as she strolled toward Alec, wearing a gown cut far too low to be respectable. He forced his eyes away from her neckline to her smiling face. Her hair was almost black and tied loosely behind her head. She didn't seem much older than Alec, perhaps just a few years, but she was definitely old enough to be completely woman.

"I'm Kella. I'll be implementing your trial."

"You?" Alec asked, hardly believing his luck.

She stepped in very close and studied Alec's face. Then she gave a quick passing glance over the rest of him. Alec swallowed hard.

"This one's adorable," she said.

The Rol'dan snickered.

Adorable? Puppies were adorable, not men.

The girl reached around him and, for a moment, Alec thought she would kiss him. But then he realized she had tied a thick rope around his waist.

"There you go...nice and comfy." She smiled close to his face, her soft breath brushing Alec's cheek. And then she walked away.

Alec watched her retreating form with great interest. Her hips swayed nicely from side to side. As she crossed the bridge, she glanced over her shoulder and smiled, *almost* making Alec forget the rope.

Alec followed the path of the rope along the ground to the chasm where it stretched to the other side. Kella, now across, picked up the opposite end of the rope, and her eyes flared with red light. Alec groaned. So *that's* what the screams were about—she was going to pull him over the edge.

The rope went taut. Alec dug in, pulling in the opposite direction. On the ground ahead, foot-sized trenches plowed the earth and disappeared into the chasm below, the evidence of the people who had gone before.

Across the distance, Kella smiled, eyes red as fire. She was taking her sweet time. As she hauled Alec toward the edge, the tops of the trees loomed in the chasm below. She gave a final yank. Alec jumped as his feet lost purchase. His heart leapt into his throat.

Time stood still. Alec propelled forward and slammed hard against the side of the slab bridge, his chest aching as breath left him.

He wheezed, attempting to fill his lungs. Grappling, his sweat-coated hands slipped over the moss covering the bridge's side. He reached, stretched, and at long last, his frantic fingers found hold. But his victory was short lived.

Alec's body jerked away, and he soared toward the dark, cloudy sky. He choked back a scream. By Brim, he was going to die! As the rope stretched taut, Kella yanked Alec down to the opposite side of the chasm. The ground came all too quickly, the scenery blurring by him. He braced his legs, attempting to catch his fall. As he slammed onto the ground,

Alec heard the bones in his legs crack, followed by searing pain. The cheers of the Rol'dan rang faintly over the pumping blood in his head. Alec could hold it no longer; he screamed.

He opened his eyes, expecting to see sky, but instead Kella squatted over him. She ran her fingers through his hair.

"You *are* a brave one." She smiled. "However, it would've been better if you had taken the fall. I would've caught you, silly boy."

She stood, and two other Rol'dan came in her place and healed him.

Chapter Nine

Alec dressed early, hoping to find Taryn before their next challenge. There were only two days before they'd be going their separate ways: She would be heading south to Galva, and Alec would return to Alton.

So why did he care if he never saw her again?

He barely knew her. And the chances he'd go to Galva anytime soon were thin. But there was something about her that made him go all numb and stupid, and as dumb as it sounded, Alec didn't want to lose that feeling.

He stepped out of the tent and did a quick scan. Usually, only a few hung around this early, but today, a stream of people headed for the lodge. The Challenge of Speed was today, nothing else as far as he could remember. Why then all the interest with the lodge?

A pair of girls walked back. Alec almost asked them what they knew, but their conversation quickly changed his mind.

"King Alcandor? I can't believe he's here."

"Did you see him?"

"No. I've heard he's wonderfully handsome."

The girls giggled.

"Sean said he arrived in the middle of the night."

"How would he know?"

"I don't know. I'm just telling you what he said."

"He can't be right. No one ever travels with the Dor'Jan wandering at night."

The first girl laughed. "King Alcandor doesn't fear the

Dor'Jan. He's much too powerful for them. I've even heard he travels alone."

The two girls continued to jabber as they darted away.

Alec stood frozen, hardly believing what he'd just heard. *The king? Here?* He glanced at the lodge. He couldn't believe it...*wouldn't* believe it. He wasn't about to trust gossip from ridiculous girls. But there *was* one person who could tell Alec the truth.

Alec went the opposite direction of the others, catching more snippets of information on the way. He arrived at Nolan's tent feeling both angry and annoyed that so many people would be excited about a rumor.

Nolan was awake, standing outside, and staring at the lodge. Alec put a hand on Nolan's shoulder, making the scribe gasp and whirl around.

Nolan relaxed. "Alec."

"Sorry. Didn't mean to scare you. Thought you saw me coming."

"I'm fine." Nolan glanced at the lodge again.

"So, uh..." Alec said. "I've heard the king arrived last night?"

Nolan frowned as he continued to stare at the lodge.

"It's true?"

Nolan shrugged. "I've never known him to come to the tournament before, but it's possible, I guess."

"So you don't know?"

"No," Nolan said.

As they stepped off, Alec matched Nolan's stride. Unfortunately, Nolan didn't know any more than himself. As they walked toward the morning gathering, Nolan kept glancing back to the crowd. He was usually so calm, but today he acted like a bear might jump out and maul him.

"How are you doing, anyway?" Nolan asked. "I heard you had quite a fall at the Strength challenge yesterday."

Alec grimaced. "Um, I'd rather not talk about it."

"At least you didn't get into any arguments."

Alec snorted. "I suppose."

They continued in silence before Nolan finally said, "Are you ready for your next challenge?"

"Well, I'm ready for the nightforsaken thing to be over with, that's for certain," Alec said. "Then I can go home to normal life."

"Your life is anything but normal, Alec."

"It's normal enough for me. Besides, I miss the sword. I feel as if I'm going soft."

Nolan laughed. "Soft? Try being a scribe."

As they continued on toward a grassy hill, a mischievous smile crept on Nolan's face. "As soft and girl-like as you've become, you might have to shake the dust off of your sword arm today."

Alec stopped. "Swords?"

Nolan answered with a grin.

"We're being tested with swords?" Alec asked again. He felt like he'd just inherited a fortune.

Nolan shrugged in response, but the mischievous grin on his face answered his question. "Don't forget that this is to test for the Shay of Speed. Even on a good day, you can't best them."

"I'm used to losing," Alec said. "Father beat me all the time. But at least I won't be helpless. These nightforsaken trials make you feel like you can't do *anything*." Alec quickened his steps. He'd lose, but he'd make a good show doing it. For once, he couldn't get to the trials soon enough.

***

When they arrived, most had already assembled in a large circle around a grassy hill. Taryn wasn't hard to spot with her golden curls.

"Hey," Alec said, "Taryn's over there."

Nolan didn't seem to hear, he was so distracted. Alec waited, then he nudged him to get his attention.

Nolan gasped and whirled toward him.

"It's me," Alec said, hands up defensively. "Crows, Nolan.

Are you okay?"

"I'm fine. Just worry about your challenge."

Even though he hadn't known Nolan very long, Alec knew a lie when he heard one.

Taryn brightened when they approached.

"Hi, Taryn," Alec said. "How have your tournaments been?"

Her violet eyes met Alec's. "Better than most. I seem to be getting away without a scratch. Even in the Accuracy trial, the arrows missed me completely."

"That's quite an accomplishment," Nolan said.

"I know! If I didn't know any better, I'd think someone was protecting me." A strange expression passed over her face, and she darted a quick glance toward the Rol'dan. General Trividar spoke a few words to his soldiers and then disappeared with his Speed.

"I'm sure it's all luck, though," Taryn said. "I can't imagine coming away from this sword trial without a scratch. You would know, wouldn't you, Alec?"

At first Alec didn't know if she was criticizing or complimenting him. But from the admiration on her face, he guessed it was the latter. Alec cleared his throat, excitement churning in his stomach. He wiped his sweaty palms on his legs. Even though he could barely put two words together when around her, Alec couldn't wait to show her how well he could swing a blade.

A woman dressed in the male Rol'dan tunic and breeches stepped forward. Her hair hung down her back in a thick braid. She was in her middle years and much plainer than the girl who'd broken Alec's legs.

"I am Captain Rohonin," the Rol'dan said. "Today, we will be searching for the Shay of Speed."

Just as she began explaining the marvelous attributes of the Shay of Speed, and how it was superior to any other dumb power sect, another group of Rol'dan approached.

General Trividar crossed the field, but all heads turned to the man beside him. King Alcandor, the supreme ruler of

Adamah, had visited them after all.

Alec's jaw dropped.

King Alcandor wore a uniform not too unlike the Rol'dan soldiers—leather breeches and a tunic—except instead of a leather jerkin, he sported an expensive-looking vest. His ground-length cloak billowed behind him, reflecting light in the golden fabric. A crown, of sorts, rested against black hair. It was more of a circlet—three intertwining gold bands with an unusual stone set in the center of his pale forehead. The stone changed colors with every movement he made. His ice-blue eyes scanned the group, pausing intermittently on a person from time to time.

Nolan mumbled something Alec didn't understand, and then he darted around the outside of the circle and ducked behind a group of nearby Rol'dan.

"What's that about?" Taryn asked.

"I have no idea. He's been acting funny all morning."

Taryn didn't seem too worried, for her eyes drifted back to the king. Alec pressed his lips together. He guessed the king could be handsome. Several of the other girls whispered to each other, giggling. Alec should hate him—that's what his father would want. But he couldn't help the curiosity pulsing through him. His father told him King Alcandor never aged—he looked exactly the same as when Father was a boy. There were also tales that claimed he was centuries old. Crows! How did a man live that long and still look so young?

"Have you seen the king before?" Alec asked.

"No," Taryn answered. "He's not what I expected."

Alec grunted. "Me either."

"You may continue, Captain," King Alcandor said as he took a place next to the other Rol'dan.

Captain Rohonin blushed, then regained her composure. Even she acted like an idiot.

"You will be first," she said to a dark-haired boy across the circle.

He sauntered forward, looking to his friends. Alec folded his arms across his chest and grinned. This would be good. As soon as the boy turned, Captain Rohonin thrust a sword into his hands. He had barely enough time to move when her sword crashed against his.

The boy backed away, flinging his sword in pathetic swipes as he tried to block the captain's blows. Occasionally, her sword would meet flesh and the boy would yelp.

Golden light shimmered in the captain's eyes. Her Speed increased until her blade was nothing but a blur. When she stopped, the dark-haired boy lay curled on the ground, his arms and legs covered with numerous cuts. A trio of Healing Rol'dan surrounded him and got to work.

Unlike a normal duel where the crowd cheered their favorite to victory, this group fell uncommonly silent. As the trial continued, Alec shook his head at each pathetic attempt. He hadn't realized how intense his training had been. Every mistake was obvious and every failed block absurd. And as each person lost, Alec got more excited for his turn.

The captain scanned the group. Her eyes locked on Alec's. She opened her mouth to speak, but the voice of the king spoke instead.

"One moment, Captain."

Captain Rohonin turned from Alec, gave a tense bow of her head, and stepped aside.

King Alcandor stepped forward and strolled through the inner circle of the competitors, occasionally stopping to examine someone, then continuing on. Then the king walked straight to Taryn and smiled.

"What is your name, my dear?" he asked.

"Taryn Trividar, Your Majesty." Her voice shook a little.

"My cousin, Lord Alcandor," General Trividar said.

"Your cousin? She is very beautiful, General." The king smiled warmly. "So tell me, child, how have your trials fared so far?"

"Um, as good as can be expected, Your Majesty."

"Very good, Miss Trividar. And I suspect you have avoided any unnecessary injury?"

"W-why, yes, sir."

The king nodded. "Captain, this young lady will not need to participate in this challenge today."

A murmur spread.

Alec stared, first at the king, then at Taryn. Not that he minded the king excluding Taryn, but he just couldn't fathom why.

King Alcandor placed his hands on Tayrn's shoulders, traveled down her arms, and grasped her hands. He took a step, pulling Taryn along with him. Heat flared to Alec's cheeks. Why was he touching her? His sword hand twitched; his attempt at self-control was fading quickly.

He searched for Nolan. Nolan was level-headed. He'd have proper perspective on this whole thing. He finally found him, hiding behind a grouping of Rol'dan archers who'd come out to watch. Nolan's pale face gawked at Taryn with an expression of horror. Alec's stomach dropped. What was King Alcandor going to do?

Alec followed their progress across the practice field, pushing people aside so he could better see. The king stopped in front of the other Rol'dan and examined Taryn. The violet light of Empathy shone from his eyes.

"Have I done something wrong, Your Majesty?" Taryn stammered.

"Of course not, my dear. Nothing at all."

The king's expression darkened. He reached behind her and yanked her close. She tried to object, but stopped, a strange haze clouding her eyes.

Alec's chest heaved. He pushed two people out of his way. When the king reached down and pulled a dagger from a holder at his thigh, Alec reacted without thinking. He lunged forward, not caring if he was the king or not. But a Strength Rol'dan grabbed Alec in his iron hold.

"Leave her alone!" Alec yelled.

"Everything will be just fine, my child." The king positioned the knife under her ribs.

The cloud lifted from her eyes, and she moved her hand up to stop him, but the king grabbed her arm and pulled it behind her back.

"No!" Her voice trembled. "P-p-please, Your Majesty…"

In helpless shock, Alec watched King Alcandor push the blade in.

Taryn screamed.

"Shh…hush, hush now," the king cooed in Taryn's ear. He smiled and yanked the dagger free.

Her body shook, and her breath came in deep, ragged gasps. King Alcandor held her close until her head lolled, her eyes fluttered opened, and a faint green light began to glow from her eyes.

Alec stopped struggling and gawked, his heart dropping to his knees. He took a step, realizing the soldier had released his hold. No. This couldn't happen. Not her.

As the light of Healing faded in Taryn's eyes, the king gently pulled her away.

"Captain Tiohan," the king said.

An old Healer bowed. "Yes, my king."

"Take our new Rol'dan to the lodge. She needs rest and has much to learn."

Tiohan took Taryn's hand. She staggered as he led her away.

Alec stared. He couldn't wrap his head around the fact she'd become a Rol'dan Healer. Numbness came over him so thick he didn't even notice the king approach.

"Who is this?" King Alcandor said.

"His name is Alec Deverell," the general said. "He's been difficult at the tournament this year."

"That doesn't surprise me, considering his display a moment ago." A purple light glowed from the king's eyes, and he circled around Alec, examining him.

"Did you say Deverell?" King Alcandor asked.

"Yes, Your Majesty," the general answered. "He's the blade maker's son."

The king gave a curt nod. "This young man shall be tested next. General, you will conduct his trial."

Alec's head jerked toward the king, coming out of his

stupor. He wished he hadn't. When their eyes met, a strange sensation went through him, and he couldn't pull away.

"Would you like to fight the general, Alec?" the king asked, smiling.

A surge of anger and hatred swelled. *Yes, I would.* There was nothing Alec wanted more.

"I see this pleases you," King Alcandor said. "I will enjoy watching you use your skills, young Deverell."

The general smirked, untied his cape, and flung it off to the side. Then he yanked a sword out of the ground and tossed it to Alec.

Alec caught it easily and swung it back and forth in an arc to get a feel for the blade. It wasn't one of his father's swords. The weight was off, and it was too bulky. Still, it felt good to hold steel.

The general unsheathed his sword and lunged in a single, fluid movement. Alec's trained instincts met his blow. For several minutes, they circled each other, only swinging on occasion to test the reaction of the other. Alec's nerves twitched at the meaningless duel.

Finally, General Trividar stopped and grinned. "Shall we fight, Mr. Deverell?" And then in a burst of jabs and slashes, the true battle began.

Fighting him was amazing. Alec had never met someone with such natural talent. Father's swordsman skills were of the highest repute, but this man goaded Alec like none before. Alec fought with every fiber of strength and will and determination he could muster.

As the battle stretched on, it would seem neither could gain on the other. That is, until the yellow fire in the cheater's eyes began to glow. Slowly and steadily, the general's Speed increased.

Alec matched him as well as he could. Sweat poured down his face, obstructing his view. Finally, the general struck Alec and his sword arm went limp. Alec cursed and grabbed the sword with his other hand to block another blow.

"You are multi-talented, Mr. Deverell," General Trividar said.

"Only for you, General," Alec said between clenched teeth.

Alec barely heard the crowd cheering as the general's Speed increased even more. Several more gashes appeared on Alec's body, so fast he didn't see them come: one on each leg, one across his chest, and finally, one that loosed his sword.

He fell to his knees, trembling with pent up fury. Although Alec couldn't defend himself, he glared at the general as battle pounded in his blood. General Trividar wiped his sword on the grass, crammed the blade into its sheath, and turned away.

Several Healing Rol'dan ripped open Alec's shirt, and the all-too-familiar pulse of healing coursed through him. After they finished, Alec fell on his hands, his chest heaving with exhaustion.

"Splendid, young Deverell," King Alcandor said. "I knew you would not disappoint me." The king's eyes glowed purple with Empathy, and that odd sensation shot through Alec again.

"Once more, General," the king said.

Alec looked up. *Another fight? This is too good to be true.*

"Your Majesty?" the general said.

"Fight him a second time, General."

"My pleasure, Lord Alcandor."

Before the general could make a move, Alec pushed to his feet, grabbed his sword, and sprinted toward General Trividar, swinging with all his strength. The general's sword seemed to appear from nowhere, blocking Alec's blow with a resounding clang.

"Now, now, Mr. Deverell," the general said calmly.

Alec couldn't remember a time when he'd been angrier. His blood felt as if on fire. Alec couldn't stop thinking of what they'd done to Taryn. Somehow, they'd taken her innocence and turned it into something putrid; she was too good to be transformed on her own.

Alec fought for Taryn and for his dead mother and for the memory of others wronged by the Rol'dan. He would give them a voice, even if for a short time. He turned and jabbed and blocked and dodged and swung. At least until the general's eyes glowed.

It took every bit of his skill not to be completely overcome. Just when Alec thought it would be over, General Trividar slowed. If he meant to toy with him, Alec would gladly accept it and use it to his advantage.

Alec's stomach lurched. He ignored it and raised his sword for a perfect strike. His sword arm began to shake, so he gripped the sword tightly with both hands. Tremors traveled up his arm.

The general sliced Alec's side. He ignored the rush of pain and lunged, his sword finally connecting.

The general roared and only paused for a second before striking again.

Alec dodged the strike, and a wave of nausea nearly knocked him down. He pulled himself upright and gashed the general again.

He was elated. He got not one, but two strikes in. But why had the general allowed it? He should've overpowered Alec by now.

Alec pierced him a third time, and the realization struck him harder than any hammer blow. The general's face no longer mocked. His expression showed concentration and hatred as the golden light of Speed flamed from his eyes.

Alec's muscles jerked uncontrollably as an unknown energy coursed through him. Another wave of nausea finally took over. He choked it back but could no longer hold his sword; it fell helplessly to the ground.

Alec paused, as if in a dream, just as General Trividar lunged. His world stopped as if he'd plummeted off a cliff and finally hit bottom. Only then did Alec realize how fast he'd been moving. Faces had blurred, unrecognizable; trees had become a vague mass of green. He looked down—slower than he thought possible—to his father's own creation impaled through his chest.

It was oddly painless. Then a dull throb took hold.

As another wave of convulsions wracked through Alec's muscles, the edge of the blade cut new. Agony spread over his chest, more intense than he'd thought possible. This was not just another cut given on the floor of the armory.

He heard a gasp, then a scream. A rush of pain jerked through him as the general's arm yanked, pulling the sword free. Pressing trembling fingers to his tunic, he brought them away warm with his own blood. His legs lost their strength, and slowly, he crumpled to the ground.

Chapter Ten

A rainbow of colors spilled before Alec when he opened his eyes. Six banners, each representing one of the sects of the Shay Rol'dan, hung around the perimeter of a large common room. He stretched, finding himself resting in the most comfortable bed he'd ever slept in. Alec had been dreaming terrible things: Taryn coming into power, his fight with the general, the general stabbing him. He grasped his chest, his fingertips finding a new, faint scar.

He gasped. He hadn't been dreaming after all.

Another memory surfaced: He'd come into a Shay power.

"Alec?"

Taryn sat on a chair next to him. He sat up quickly—much too quickly—as the foreign Shay power pulsed through him. Taryn squealed in surprise and jerked away. Alec collapsed, cursed, and hugged a plump pillow to his face.

"This can't be happening," he muttered beneath the pillow.

"I know," Taryn said. "I can hardly believe it myself."

Slowly, he pulled the pillow away and met Taryn's concerned eyes. She was dressed in the black robes of the Healing Rol'dan. A green sash crossed her chest. Even in black she looked beautiful.

"How long have I been here?" he asked.

"Just a day," she said. "At least we didn't have to participate in the last trial. From what I heard, Empathy must play some sort of guessing game with boxes. And you know how fun their games are." She forced a nervous laugh, and then her smile dimmed. "What happened to you, Alec? Did they do this to you?"

She brushed her fingertip across an old scar on Alec's arm. A jolt of healing energy pulsed into him.

She gasped. "I'm sorry. I didn't mean—"

"It's okay."

"No, really. I'm sorry. I can't control this. Every time I touch someone..."

Alec sat up, this time pushing back the infernal Speed Shay and doing so at normal speed. "Most of these scars I've had for years. You know, we spar at the shop and all." He touched the newest addition. It was amazing, really. He should've been dead! Taryn shook her head as her eyes roved over him, making Alec's face warm.

"I've heard of your duels," she said, "but I never imagined...I was frightened when they first brought you in. You were completely covered in blood. And when they took off your clothes..." She shut her mouth quickly. "I mean, they had a terrible time trying to clean you..." A pink glow tinted her cheeks.

Alec lifted the edge of the blanket. He wore nothing. He scanned the lodge, noticing soldiers milling about. "I suppose they did it here in the open?"

She smiled slightly, but couldn't meet his eyes.

"And you were here too?"

Her blush deepened.

Crows! He didn't even want to think about how much she had seen. By the way she was acting, he guessed quite a bit. He cleared his throat, pushing down the warmth spreading up his face. "I suppose that's one way to keep me from running away."

She finally met his eyes. "Keep you from running away?"

"By taking my clothes. Running through the woods wouldn't feel so good, especially with all the pointy branches and such."

She snickered. "Yes, I suppose so."

The doors to the lodge burst open, and King Alcandor

entered, followed by a group of Shay Rol'dan with General Trividar in the lead. The soldiers in the lodge rose to their feet and bowed. King Alcandor ignored them and made his way directly to Alec and Taryn.

"I see we are feeling better," King Alcandor said.

The king's blue eyes glowed purple with Empathy, and a warming sensation came over Alec. Alec grabbed the blanket and pulled it up, suddenly self-conscious.

King Alcandor made a motion, and a soldier placed a folded garment on Alec's bed: black breeches, a gold tunic and cape, and a leather jerkin. It was the uniform of the Speed Rol'dan.

Alec's stomach turned.

"I am sorry this displeases you, young Deverell," King Alcandor said. "Despite your disgust, your new uniform suits you well." He picked up the garments and held them expectantly.

"Remember your Shay," the king said softly. "You will move so quickly, no one will be able to see you. Well, except maybe those who share your skill of Speed." He grinned. "But I am certain they won't watch."

The other Rol'dan chuckled. Alec couldn't believe it. The king wanted him to get dressed in the open, in front of everyone…including Taryn. A familiar energy awakened deep within, and Alec knew, unfortunately, the king was right. He'd move faster than they could see.

Grabbing hold of what he guessed to be his Shay, Alec threw aside the covers and put on the uniform. Not that he wanted it, but he'd feel better with some clothes on. Alec knew, somehow, he'd done it in a sightless moment.

Taryn gawked, open-mouthed.

"Well done," King Alcandor said. The man's eyes traveled down Alec's body in a way that made his skin crawl. "I will see you at dinner tonight. I am looking forward to getting to know you better."

King Alcandor turned toward Taryn, and she inhaled. He took her hand. "And you, Miss Trividar." His lips lingered on her open palm while she flushed a deep scarlet. "I will enjoy getting to know you much, much better, as well."

The king turned away, his cloak billowing in a sea of golden silk behind him. He strode through a pair of massive wooden doors. Among the Rol'dan, only General Trividar followed.

"Dinner?" Alec asked.

Taryn smiled nervously. "It's for us. Typically, new initiates dine with the king when they return to Faylinn, but since he's here…"

Alec's muscles felt strangely foreign; tremors of energy vibrated through them. He dropped his gaze to his new clothes, starting at his too-bright golden tunic and traveling down fine leather breeches to bare feet. Knee-length boots, adorned with brass buttons, sat next to a neatly folded golden cape waiting to complete the ensemble. His stomach ached, not from hunger or nervousness, but disgust. How could he face Father now that he'd become one of *them*—just like the one who had murdered his mother?

***

It was difficult getting to the dining hall. Not because it was hard to find, but because his legs had a mind of their own. He'd be walking normally, then Speed off, running into more walls and doorways than he wanted to remember. Taryn caught up to him each time, trying to cover the laughter splattered across her face. At least one of them found his nightforsaken power amusing.

When they finally reached the dining room, Rylan—the skinny fellow who had been slinging with Nolan—pulled his chair and accidentally threw it across the room. It shattered into splinters with the force of his newly acquired Shay of Strength. At least Alec wasn't the only one struggling with their new power.

"This is horrible," a redheaded girl said. She wrinkled her freckled nose as she lifted a goblet.

A boy next to her tapped her arm in a brotherly way. "You'll get used to it, Sussan."

"Get used to it!" she screeched. "It tastes like metal!"

"Oh no," the boy said. "This is good. At least it's fresh water here. Might be some iron ore nearby in the earth, that's probably what you're tasting. Wait till we get back to Faylinn. They boil the seawater, but it still tastes like salt. The better you get at your Perception Shay, the more you can block it out."

"Faylinn?" Alec asked.

"He came into his power a few months ago," Taryn explained. "He's already moved to Faylinn."

"I still say it's horrible," Sussan said, frowning at the glass.

"It's just water." A boy smirked from across the room, his eyes turning blue with Accuracy. He launched a small nut and, with a perfect *plink,* it landed in her glass. "It *was* just water."

"Owen!" She slammed her glass on the table, water sloshing, and glared at the boy as her eyes flared with the orange light of Perception.

"So, you are Alec Deverell?" The brown-haired boy next to Sussan pulled a lopsided grin. "Sorry, we haven't met yet. My name's Daren Kinsley. I must say, the soldiers have been talking about you a lot this week."

Alec grunted. *I bet they have.*

"They were all surprised at your transformation. I can't speak for the rest, but I'm quite glad," Daren continued. "I'm from Tremain, originally. I've helped my father mine ore in the mountains for years. We were able to see your performances from time to time when we brought ore to Alton. Sold a lot to your father. He always gave us a fair price, too."

Daren waited for a response before continuing. "Well, at least they train the Shay of Speed for sword skills. I've watched them practice. Compared to most of the Rol'dan, you're an expert already."

"Yeah. An expert. That's why I got run through."

"Well, you *were* fighting the general. He's the best swordsman in the entire Rol'dan army, if not the entire land. You put up a real good fight; *I* was impressed."

Alec wasn't—the general was still alive.

"So...Alec, is it?" A boy with black hair glared, his eyes glowing purple with Empathy. Alec felt as if someone poked around his brain. "Why do you dislike the Rol'dan?"

Alec started. *Night's shadows! Did he just read me?* "I...I didn't say that."

"You didn't need to."

"Maybe it's because annoying Empathy users barge into people's minds." Daren winked at Alec. "This here is Fanior, our newest intermeddler."

"Empathy Rol'dan," Fanior corrected, puffing his chest.

"Same thing," Daren said.

The sound of breaking glass drew everyone's eyes to Rylan. The remains of a goblet fell from his fist. Opening his palm, he examined a tiny cut. Taryn sighed, reached over to touch his hand, and her eyes glowed emerald green with Healing. She flinched and opened her palm as a similar cut faded away.

"Hey, thanks," Rylan said.

"I have to start sometime, I guess." Her hand lingered on top of Rylan's before she shyly took it away.

Alec watched the brief exchange, and heat spiked his vision. As Alec reached for his glass, his hand bolted, flinging the glass, and its contents, over everyone.

Taryn smiled as she grabbed her napkin to dry herself.

"Sorry," Alec said.

"That will get better, too," Daren said. "It took a few weeks before I could eat much of anything, or block out noise to sleep. With Perception, every sensation is amplified, so much it's hard to function. Your body adjusts to the power eventually." He forced down a piece of bread, like he was trying to eat mud.

"So how'd you get your power a few months ago, before the trials?" Alec asked.

Daren pushed bread around on his plate. "A trial isn't the only way one can come into their power. There was a mining accident back home. I came into my power then."

The doors to the small dining room opened, and a throng

of servants paraded in, placing platter after platter of food on the table, a mixture of aromas filling the air.

Sussan clasped her hand over her nose. "I'm going to be sick."

Daren put an arm around her shoulder, though he looked as green as she did. "It gets easier...with time."

The door opened again and two soldiers wearing the floor-length purple cloaks and deep purple vests of the Empathy Rol'dan came in and stood on either side of the room. They crossed their arms over their chests and glared at the group. A glimmer of purple light flickered in their eyes.

The door swung open a third time. With a flourish, King Alcandor made his entrance, pulled out a chair next to Alec, and sat. Alec tensed and lowered his eyes, his muscles twitching with pent up Shay energy. Crows. Why did he have to sit next to him?

Silver forks and knives scraped across plates in silence. The king didn't eat; instead, he stared with nearly translucent blue eyes, his posture motionless except for a single, long finger running circles across the rim of his goblet. When his gaze reached one of them, they tensed, squirming in their seats. After several long minutes of his scrutiny, all eating stopped entirely; nervous tension filled the room.

As the servants removed uneaten dinners and served dessert, Fanior, the annoying Empathy user, spoke.

"So, Your Majesty," he said. "Will you be accompanying us to Faylinn?"

King Alcandor's goblet lingered before his mouth. He glared at Fanior, his stern eyes glowing with Empathy. Fanior turned pale and jerked his head down.

"Miss Trividar," the king said, ignoring Fanior.

Taryn dropped her fork with a clatter.

"I believe your father is a fisherman in Galva?"

Taryn swallowed. "Uh, yes, sir."

"And Alec..."

Alec cringed.

"You are from Alton?"

He didn't answer. His tongue felt as thick as a rope.

"Kardos Deverell is your father?"

He nodded.

"He does excellent work. I have known only one other who has managed to surpass your father's skills."

Alec slowly lifted his eyes.

"Ah! You are wondering who?"

Reaching into the folds of his cloak, the king pulled out a jeweled dagger. Alec clenched his fists under the table. The last time Alec had seen that blade, it had dripped with Taryn's blood.

King Alcandor turned the blade, offering Alec the handle. As much as Alec wanted to tell the king to shove it up his backside, his curiosity made him look. He took the dagger and studied it in his open palm.

Discolored with age and use, ivy carvings accented the dagger's ivory handle, as well as numerous multicolor jewels—more a work of art than a weapon. Alec studied the blade and changed his mind; it wasn't only art. He'd never seen a weapon like it. It was absolutely amazing.

"Who made this?"

King Alcandor's eyes fixed on Alec. "A man named Zareh. But the secrets of his craft died with him over two hundred years ago." He took the dagger. "He was a strange little man, but definitely had a way with metal, much like your father."

King Alcandor continued to question everyone, but his gaze rested on Alec the most. He placed his hand on Alec's forearm. Alec's first impulse was to yank it away, but he couldn't bring himself to do it. A tug of contentment pulsed through him, pushing whatever revulsion he had away.

"Well," the king said as he rose from the table, "all of you should rest this evening. Tomorrow you will begin your journey to Faylinn. I hope you will transition to your new lives in the Shay Rol'dan well. Though I have enjoyed our evening, I will be departing immediately. I look forward to greeting you once again when we are reunited." With a toss of his cape over his shoulder, he walked toward the door. "And, Alec, I wish to have a word with you...alone." Then the king left the room.

Alec sat stunned. Daren cleared his throat and made a frantic motion for him to move. Alec followed. What in Brim's name did the king want with him?

In Alec's mind, he'd only meant to do a quick jog. But with his first step he was already in the next room, his body arriving far before he realized. When Alec stopped, he found himself only an arm's reach from the king.

Alcandor smiled. "You will learn to control it in time. Eventually, it will be as common to you as breathing." He reached over, slid his arm through Alec's, and winked. "So you don't go darting off on me."

Alec nodded, but doubt flicked through his emotions. Just as quickly, it was gone.

A pair of soldiers opened the doors, and the duo emerged on the lodge's landing. The king led Alec stiffly, arm in arm, down the steps. Sunlight shone low over the treetops, and a hint of orange reflected in the layer of dark clouds, framing the edges of the trees and the lower mountains like a painting.

"Look at them," the king said, motioning to a large fire where the others celebrated the end of their trials. "They know little of what true pleasure is. They believe one can experience life to its fullness with a silly celebration. A warm fire. Simple music. Dancing. Those ignorant children have no idea of what fullness is." The king stared at Alec, his icy gaze penetrating. "You don't even realize it yet. Right now, you can only taste the first sip of your Shay power. Those commoners will never fully experience life the way you will. They are nothing compared to you."

He led Alec along the outskirts of the camp and then stopped and placed a hand on each of Alec's shoulders. Where he touched, peace filled Alec. He should be disgusted, shouldn't he? Why couldn't he pull away?

Alcandor leaned closer, staring fully into Alec's eyes. "I wanted to speak to you privately, away from the other Shay Rol'dan. I see great potential in you. The talents you wield are beyond your years, and your soul burns with Rol'dan fire. Yes, you are special, and this is your destiny."

All his life, Alec's father told him he wasn't good enough, that he didn't try hard enough. But now the king—the very man whom Father taught him to hate—told Alec he was something more. Alec didn't know how to feel.

"I must leave now, Alec, but I anxiously await your arrival to Faylinn. Once your training begins, every Rol'dan will see your talents. You will be glorious among them."

Backing a few steps away, King Alcandor's eyes glowed golden-yellow with Speed. He gave a curt nod in farewell, and then he ran into the woods.

The pleasure abruptly left Alec and loathing washed over him. He shook his head, coming back to himself. *What just happened?*

Alec stared at the empty space left by the king. On one side of Alec, people celebrated. On the other, the lodge of the Rol'dan towered with arrogant splendor.

He belonged to neither world.

All Alec wanted to do was disappear, to run away.

He paused. *Why couldn't I?*

He headed in the direction of the celebration, to the tent where he'd stayed before he'd changed. Without speaking to anyone, ignoring the awe-inspired stares of his former tent-mates, he grabbed the bag he'd brought with him. It wasn't much, but it was all he had—the remnants of a life now gone.

He turned from the competitors—the music and laughter had stopped—and stared into the line of trees on the outskirts of camp. The Forest of Vidar stretched before him. And before Alec could talk himself out of it, he awakened his Speed and ran into its depths.

Chapter Eleven

Alec stopped abruptly, and the leaves whirled around his legs before settling to the ground. He leaned against a tree, shoulders heaving, lungs burning. The vast green expanse of the Forest of Vidar surrounded him. Trees stretched as far as he could see. He turned. Every direction looked exactly the same. *Crows!* In the midst of all the running, he'd gotten lost.

Sliding off his bag, Alec cursed and tossed it to the ground. He'd have to retrace his steps, though it was getting hard to see.

His stomach dropped.

Images of the Dor'Jan flashed in his mind, the nightmares and stories from childhood surfacing. Night Beasts. Soul Stealers. They had lots of names. If they were real or imaginary, he didn't know. He'd always figured they were tall tales meant to keep children in at night. It had worked, too. He didn't want to find out if the stories were right or wrong.

Alec raked his hand through his hair. There was little choice but to make the best of his stupidity. He gathered a pile of sticks and branches, stacking them as he'd done many times before. After work, Alec's father would often make a similar fire. Alec always thought it ridiculous to sweat over the forge all day and then "relax" near another fire at night. However, right then, he was thankful his father had taught him how.

He grabbed a piece of bark along with some old leaves and brown pine needles and prepared the kindling like his father had taught him. From the pile of wood he pulled a long, straight stick and looked to the darkening sky. He spun the stick, forward and backward, applying pressure to the bark. At first he started slowly, and then his Shay took hold.

The energy traveled from his chest, up his shoulders, and into his hands. Along with the speed, the friction increased; blisters formed on his palms. Alec gritted his teeth, and when he could hardly continue, a thin trail of smoke drifted upward, and an orange ember glowed.

He spun the stick quicker still, forcing the throbbing from his mind. A small flame sparked to life. He gingerly picked up the bark, cupping his bleeding palms around the tiny flame. He placed it in the campfire, and then built a second fire.

Positioning himself between the two protective flames, the sun sank completely, surrounding him with darkness unlike any he'd ever seen. Exhausted, both physically and emotionally, Alec wilted to the ground. And as the night came to life, he drifted into a fitful sleep.

***

Alec jerked awake. The low flames crackled, but the dark forest was otherwise silent. He stoked the fire with a few more logs, and a spray of sparks swirled upward into the night sky. Something had woken him. An owl? Some other night creature? He wasn't sure, but he had the strange feeling something watched him from the shelter of the trees.

He leaned toward the darkness, and a symphony of crickets answered. The flames flickered and cast shadows, giving the trees the appearance of life. The nearby branches reached for him, resembling dried and withered hands.

A shudder rolled through Alec, but he pushed back his terrible imagination. Nothing there. Just branches. Nothing at all. Even after calming himself, his eyes fixated on the branch-like hands. Then, one of the branches moved.

He blinked and stared at the spot. Must be the wind. Or an animal? All sorts of creatures came out at night. But even so, fear rushed back, his heart thundering. He stood slowly, placing a hand to his belt. He realized, with a groan, he had no sword.

What in the Darkness was I thinking? Running off in the forest without a weapon? Crows, I've lost my mind!

He wasn't allowed to bring one with him to the trials, but he was a Rol'dan now, for Brim's sake. He could've stuck around long enough to get a sword. Or nabbed a knife from dinner, at least. Coming into his Shay had affected more than his body; he'd become stupid as well.

Slowly, he knelt and grabbed a stick—like it would do much good against a wild animal. If something were to jump out, at least the thing would have to work a bit before getting its meal. Gripping it tightly, Alec ignored the pain of coarse bark against his injured palm.

The branch moved away from the tree and circled outside the light of the fire, moving like a man.

He relaxed. Not an animal. He mentally prepared himself to bash the nightforsaken thief over the head. But what glided into the fire's illumination was no living man.

A robed creature emerged, its skin ashen gray. The skin stretched, dried and sunken, over its skeletal frame. Whatever hair it had once possessed now wisped in gray fringes, partially hidden under a dark hood. Colorless. Soulless. A Dor'Jan. Alec's blood ran cold.

The stick in Alec's grip quaked. The dark beast drew closer—then another, and another joined the first. All different heights. Some resembled men, others women. All with gray skin stretched over bone; all with sunken cheeks. They stared with hungry, darkened eyes, drained of any natural color.

Alec's Shay tugged, like it wanted to reach out to the Dor'Jan. He gasped and grabbed his chest. The creatures lingered at the edge of darkness; only the flames kept them away.

Alec's eyes darted to the fire. It was dying and needed more wood. He moved to grab a log, but froze, his muscles like marble. His Shay wrenched. He inhaled sharply. Crows!

What in Darkness was going on?

Collapsing to his knees, Alec crawled to the fire as if dragging through sticky mud. His Shay pulled, fighting against every advance. He reached for a log, but his rebellious arm froze, unable to grasp, unable to move at all.

Alec forced down the panic, focusing only on the log just out of reach. His arm trembled, refusing to do the simple task.

"Dear Brim, I can't do this," he prayed. Not that Brim would answer. Not that the god-legend was even real. Sweat streamed from his face and dripped on the blanket of decomposing leaves. "Someone, please help me."

But no help would come.

Alec would die. Alone. Maybe it was better this way. He wouldn't have to disappoint Father.

The firelight dimmed, and the creatures stepped closer. If Alec gave in, he wouldn't have to worry about being a Rol'dan. He'd be...dead.

With his last bit of resolve, Alec reached, this time not for the log, but directly into the embers. Alec screamed. The fire seared his flesh, but the pain freed him from Dor'Jan control. Hope surged. At least he'd die fighting like a Deverell! He drew a flaming stick and thrust it toward the nearest Dor'Jan.

The creature hissed and lurched back. Alec whipped around, his heart hammering, as another Dor'Jan closed in on him. The creature cowered from the flame. As Alec's Speed flared to life, his body froze.

His eyes widened as his limbs resisted. *Crows, what's happening?* He pushed with all his strength, but his muscles became like stone. What had changed? Why couldn't he move? It happened as soon as his Shay—

Realization smacked him. His Shay power. The Dor'Jan. They were connected somehow. As if pushing back bile, he withdrew his Shay. The heavy weight lifted, and his body regained control. He swung the flaming torch just as a Dor'Jan closed in. It backed away.

Alec couldn't rely on his new power, couldn't use it at all without the monsters taking hold of him. He rolled his shoulders. Pain shot through his arm as his injured hand tightly gripped his stick. He'd have to fight on his own.

Alec steadied his shaking, burned hand and focused on the battle in front of him, as well as the internal war of resisting his emerging Shay. Sweat trailed down his face, stinging his eyes. The Dor'Jan had doubled, then tripled. He wasn't even sure how many there were anymore; they surrounded him.

He turned, gritting his teeth, as he waved the flames at the closing Dor'Jan. A creature dodged and grabbed Alec's face. Alec screamed and dropped the stick; the flame sputtered and choked out, enveloping him in darkness.

Pain, sharper than the fire, filled his lungs, as if he'd swallowed hot coals. His Shay pulled from deep within, trying to rip from Alec's soul.

Alec gasped as the creature let go. Another Dor'Jan grappled it away. Alec crawled across the ground on elbows, away from the skirmish, his pulse racing. But after a few pitiful paces, another Dor'Jan slammed against his back.

Long, ragged nails stabbed his face. Alec's breath left again, his Shay struggling to stay within. The Dor'Jan released him as another creature yanked it away. The dark shadows fought each other, struggling to reach their prize. Alec dragged himself across the ground, away from the tangled, wrestling throng.

But it wasn't far enough.

Another Dor'Jan grabbed him, pushing him to the ground. And its hand was cold...so very cold. The meager air trickling through Alec's nostrils smelled of rotting flesh. He tried to push the beast's bony wrist away, but it was too strong. Alec's mind drifted. Nobody—not even his father—would find what was left of his dead body.

A flash of light burned through the darkness, bright as the sun. The Dor'Jan released Alec, and a high-pitched scream filled the air. More animalistic squeals joined the first. Horrible howls lingered in the darkness, some of them choking off short.

As Alec's eyes adjusted to the light, he saw a man—or something like a man—standing over him, dressed in golden armor. Light shone from him and around him as he slashed and stabbed with a sword shining brighter than the flames of a forge. The Dor'Jan burst into flames as the warrior pierced them. The creatures fell to the ground, shrieking, and then went silent and still. The warrior gazed down at Alec, studying him, as if making a decision. Through the haze muddling Alec's brain, he saw two bright lights shining where the warrior's eyes should be.

"Get up," the warrior ordered.

Disoriented, Alec stared.

"Get up, I say!" The warrior hacked into another Dor'Jan, grabbed Alec from the ground, and threw him over his shoulder like a rag doll.

The trees whirred by with the power of Speed, except the light of the warrior surrounded them, protecting them like day. Alec's head bounced as the warrior's powerful muscles shifted as he ran. The shrieking diminished, and Alec's last conscious memory was the steady drum of the warrior's feet upon the ground.

Chapter Twelve

Nolan sat on the edge of his bed, candlelight flickering on the six stones in his ink-stained palm. Candle wax dripped down the sides and pooled on the table. Nolan had maybe an hour or so before the light ran out completely. It didn't matter so much. Morning was almost there.

He swatted a mosquito and rolled the rocks in his palm. He wasn't sure why he liked the silly things so much. He'd played with them daily since he'd gotten them in Aunt Bonty's pub. They served no purpose—except for being a child's toy. They were even too small to use on his new sling. Seeing the colors mix and mingle, not separated, filled him with longing. He wished for their land to change. He wished that it didn't matter how you painted your house or what color shirt you wore.

He put the stones into the pouch, refastened it, and sighed. Both Taryn and Alec were part of the Rol'dan now. It was too late. And he'd stood back and watched it happen, hiding behind a group of Accuracy archers. Crows! Maybe Alec was right: He was a coward after all.

But what could he have done? The king sensed power. Nolan had hid behind the archers so he wouldn't be detected. If he had run out to help Alec and Taryn, he'd have been arrested and probably hanged by now. He couldn't have done anything.

A distant, nagging voice drilled in Nolan's head, reminding him of one more option, one given to him in Alton's prison tower.

Lying down, he pulled the blanket under his chin, forcing

the guilt away. The hum of the insects' serenade sang in his ears. Not to mention the raucous laughter of the late-night celebrations from the end of the trials. Tent walls were too thin. Nolan blew out what was left of his candle and sunk farther into bed, trying to tune out the noise and the busy drone of his own thoughts.

Outside his tent, someone groaned. More than likely, some idiot had taken his celebrations a bit too far. Nolan tried to ignore it, but the pathetic moans grew louder.

Nolan threw off his covers, put on his spectacles, and emerged into the humid night air. The sorry sap was easy to find, lying under the light of a torch. Nolan shook his head and smiled, but his amusement faded when he noticed the gold fabric reflecting in the firelight.

A Speed Rol'dan? What in the Darkness was he doing here?

He cautiously approached, rocks digging into his bare feet. As he got closer, he stared in astonishment. The soldier was Alec Deverell.

If it weren't for the groaning, Nolan would've thought him dead. His sickly, pale skin resembled a corpse's. He turned Alec's limp body over, put an ear to his chest, and heard a steady heartbeat and even breathing. He sighed. The last time he'd seen him, Alec had a sword stuck through his chest.

Nolan shook Alec's shoulders. "Alec?"

He didn't respond. Nolan lightly slapped his face.

Alec's eyes popped open. He gasped, flailing.

Nolan dodged a fist. "Whoa! It's me!"

Alec blinked, staring at Nolan with unfocused eyes. "Nolan? Where am I?"

"Outside. At camp."

Alec looked around, his breath in short pants. He brought a hand to his chest, rubbing it, cringing as if in pain.

Nolan scanned him and relaxed. No blood. No wounds. Maybe he'd been celebrating? Or maybe he'd been drinking to forget the whole Rol'dan situation? Yes, that was it. He'd seen Kardos do the same.

"How'd I get here?" Alec asked.

Nolan smiled. "I didn't take you as one for drinking so hard."

"Drinking?" Alec shook his head, and his forehead wrinkled. "No...no...This isn't right."

"Come on." Nolan put a hand under Alec's arm. "Let's get you to the lodge."

Alec yanked his arm away, the light of Speed flaring in his eyes. "The warrior. Where is he?"

"The warrior? Alec, you should get back to the lodge and lie—"

"I don't want to go to the lodge," Alec said through clenched teeth.

"Maybe I should get one of the Strength Rol'dan to help."

"Crows, Nolan. Didn't you hear what I said? I don't want to go to the lodge or go with the Rol'dan." He tried to stand, but fell back, his shoulders sagging. "Maybe I should go find the Dor'Jan," he said. "I'd be better off with them."

"Dor'Jan? There's no Dor'Jan here. You just had some sort of bad dream."

"Not here." Alec pointed to the forest. "Out there." He held out a trembling hand, turning it, inspecting it. "The warrior must've healed me."

Nolan studied him.

He scowled. "Don't look at me like that."

"Like what?"

"Like I'm drunk or insane."

Nolan laughed.

"I'm *not*," Alec said, as if trying to convince himself. "Those monsters attacked me in the forest. I would've died if that warrior hadn't saved me. It was some kind of light warrior or something..." His voice trailed off. He glared at Nolan. "You're doing it again."

Nolan shook off his expression. "Sorry, but it does seem a little strange."

A group of competitors passed. Their talking faded into silence when they saw Alec. Leaves and grass stuck out of

Alec's curly hair, and lines of soot smeared across his pale face. His uniform was a mess. Unbuttoned. Disheveled. Covered in grime and dirt. The group quickened their pace and, after they had gotten a good distance away, began to whisper.

Nolan leaned in. "If you don't want to go to the lodge, at least get inside."

The scowl on Alec's face softened. He pursed his lips and gave a curt nod.

It took all of Nolan's strength to support Alec's limp weight as they proceeded slowly to Nolan's tent, gaining more stares on the way. Once inside, Alec crumpled on the bed. For several minutes, they sat silently as new morning light filtered into the tent.

Nolan sat next to him, the bed creaking. "Tell me again. What happened?"

"The Dor'Jan—"

"Not there," Nolan said. "Tell me what happened before. You said you were in the forest?"

A strange expression passed over Alec's face.

"How did you get in the forest?" Nolan prodded.

Alec hesitated. "Last night, the new Rol'dan had dinner with the king."

"In the forest?" Nolan had never heard of such a ridiculous thing.

"No," Alec spat. "We had dinner in the lodge."

"So something happened at this dinner?"

Alec looked away. "I guess the dinner was okay. Taryn was with me, and a few others seemed pretty nice. The food tasted good too..."

"But the king?"

He nodded slowly. "He kept singling me out, talking to me. After we finished eating, he pulled me aside. Told me how wonderful I was and—" He cleared his throat. "It's like he manipulated my head. I wanted to leave him, but I just couldn't."

"Ah," Nolan said. *He used Empathy.* Memories of Emery Cadogan controlling Nolan flashed in his mind. He shuddered.

The king was more powerful than Emery.

"After he left," Alec continued, "I was so disgusted I ran into the forest. A stupid idea now that I think about it. The sun was setting, and I was completely lost by the time night came. That's when the Dor'Jan came for me."

Nolan sat straighter. "You saw the Dor'Jan?"

"Aye," Alec said. "And they're even worse than the stories. If it wasn't for the warrior…"

Alec's hands shook. He'd obviously been through something terrible, whatever it was. Nolan wasn't sure if he could believe Alec. No one had ever seen the Night Beasts and lived. If it was truly the Dor'Jan that had attacked Alec, he was lucky to be alive.

"You know," Nolan said, "if you needed somewhere to go, you could've come here."

Alec snorted. "Here? Why? So you can tell me to do nothing, like at the trials?"

Nolan started as if he'd been slapped. "No. You could've come to talk—"

"Talking won't change anything. Talking won't take away this nightforsaken power. Talking won't make my father hate me less."

"Hate you?" Nolan said. "Oh, come now. He doesn't hate you."

"Once he finds out I'm a Rol'dan, he will." Alec sighed. "The only good Rol'dan to him is a dead one."

"I'm sure he won't—"

"You don't know my father. There's nothing in the world he hates more than the Rol'dan. When he finds out, I'll no longer be his son."

Nolan laughed.

"You find this funny?" Alec glared.

"I'm sorry. It's just…well, your father might disown you for becoming a Shay Rol'dan, while my father disowned me for *not* becoming one. He shipped me off as apprentice scribe as soon as I came home."

"Your father was ridiculous."

"Why?"

"It's not like you could help..." Alec's voice trailed off and he winced. "Even if it isn't my fault, Father will still hate me."

"Give him a chance," Nolan prodded.

"Nolan." He stared at his hands resting limply in his lap. "One of them killed my mother."

Nolan ran a hand over his chin, drawing in a slow breath. That explained a lot. Kardos had his reasons for hating the Rol'dan, but Nolan would've never guessed this.

"It happened when I was eight," Alec said. "Two Rol'dan soldiers came to collect an order. I heard my mother crying. When I looked through the door..." He sniffed. "She hadn't a chance. A Strength Rol'dan had his way with her. And after he was done, he killed her. All I did was stand there."

"What could you do?" Nolan said. "You were only a boy. Even a grown man can't fight a Strength Rol'dan."

Alec shook his head. "I don't know. But I should've done something."

A few voices passed outside, and a sliver of sunlight broke through a crack in the tent.

"It destroyed my father." Alec pushed himself up and staggered to the desk. "Afterward, the soldier said she attacked him. My father denied it, of course. He could've been locked away for the things he said to them. Instead, the king ordered him to continue with his work, forcing him to create weapons for them.

"That's why he's pushed me," Alec said. "He's taught me how to defend myself against the Rol'dan. And now I've become the very thing he taught me to kill." His shoulders slumped and his arms hung limply. "It makes no difference anyway. It's not like I can go home. The Rol'dan will force me to train, and I'll become like them."

"Just because you have a Shay, doesn't mean you'll become like them," Nolan said. "*You* decide how to use your power."

Alec snorted. "Name one Rol'dan—man or woman—who hasn't embraced the king's service. Name one kind thing a Rol'dan has done that didn't benefit them first." Alec leaned forward in challenge.

His words pierced Nolan. Alec was right, of course. Even Nolan's choices had been selfish ones. He'd avoided the Rol'dan to save himself. Even now, Nolan had the knowledge to save Alec, yet he hesitated. A coward. He was more interested in his own safety than Alec's.

Nolan knew, right then, what he should do. There was no other way to make Alec understand.

He looked into Alec's tortured face and let his Shay power emerge. His body warmed and relaxed as the blue light of Accuracy shone from his eyes.

The anger on Alec's face melted away and his eyes widened. Staggering, he swept his arm across the desktop, scattering its contents, and landed—rather ungracefully—on his backside. Eyes bulging, he stared at Nolan as if he'd seen a Dor'Jan.

Nolan took a step, and Alec held up his hand, palm open, to stop him.

"It's impossible," he whispered. "You can't be a...a..."

"A Shay user?" Nolan answered.

"B-but how?"

"I received my power like anyone else."

"Why didn't you tell me?" Alec snapped.

Nolan picked up some papers from the ground. "Your opinion of the Rol'dan hasn't encouraged me to share." He eyed Alec. "Besides, it's my deepest secret. I don't tell anyone."

"But you show me now?"

"I...I didn't know any other way to help you understand."

"Understand?" Alec glared. "You want me to understand you're a liar! That I can't trust you any more than I can your brother?"

"No," he objected. "It's not like that. I wanted you to understand that you don't have to be like them."

Alec scowled. Then he rose slowly, examining Nolan's eyes.

"You're Accuracy?" he finally asked.

"Yes."

"But you were terrible on the archery range."

"I hit exactly where I'd aimed."

"But you missed every shot." Realization washed over Alec's face. "You missed on purpose? Crows, Nolan. You knew what would happen."

Nolan cringed. "Yes. I knew."

Alec stared again. "But you aren't even a Rol'dan? You did the tournament, didn't you? You said your father disowned you for failing."

Nolan set a book on his desk and straightened a few crumpled pages. "I failed my trial on purpose."

"On purpose?" Alec said, eyes wide. "I didn't even recognize my power until it came on me. Didn't your Shay come at your trial?"

"It did."

"How could you hide it? It'd be impossible."

Nolan sighed. "Not impossible. But it was the hardest thing I've ever done."

Alec stared at the ground, his face knotted into a troubled frown.

"When I failed my trial," Nolan said. "I thought I was the only one who didn't want to be a Rol'dan. Kael used to be good. A cocky, arrogant fool at times, but he was a good person. He was my friend as well as my brother. After he left for the Rol'dan, it all changed. He changed.

"I hid because I saw what the Rol'dan did to him. It was the only way I knew to avoid becoming one. And until now, I thought this life was my only choice."

"It must be nice to have a choice," Alec grumbled. "I have none."

"Maybe. Maybe not," Nolan said.

A puzzled expression crossed Alec's face.

Nolan hesitated. His next words would change everything. "What do you know about the prisoner held in Alton?"

"The Traitor of Faylinn?" he asked. "Not much. He was the general, wasn't he?"

Nolan nodded. "His name is Emery Cadogan. Six years ago, he deserted the Rol'dan."

"And now he's rotting in Alton's prison."

"He's got friends," Nolan added. "Others who have powers like us. They have this place where we can go."

"Where'd you hear such stupid rumors?"

"Emery told me. If we can free him somehow, we could join him and—"

"You talked to the traitor?" Alec stared, open-mouthed. He lowered his voice to a whisper. "Do you realize what you're suggesting? If we get caught—"

"Yes, if we're caught, we'll die. But at least you won't be Rol'dan."

Alec nodded. "But what about you? You're already free. Why would you become a traitor? Why risk your life for me?"

"I'd gain a chance to be myself for the first time in two years. And besides…" He inhaled and released a breath slowly. "I need to stop hiding and doing nothing."

Alec met his eyes, and a flicker of Speed light flared in their depths. His lips parted into a wide grin. "Aye. And it's about time, too."

The tent flap opened, and a young Rol'dan soldier poked his head inside. "Alec, we need to get back to the lodge. They're giving us our last-minute orders before we prepare for the journey home."

Alec punched Nolan's arm. "Talk to you later." He ducked around the young soldier and went outside.

Nolan rubbed his stinging arm and opened the tent flap; his stomach dropped. The young soldier bore the orange cape of the Perception Rol'dan. *By Brim! What did he hear?*

Alec and the soldier passed the torch post where Nolan had found Alec earlier. They stopped. Alec picked up a bag, flung it over his shoulder, and then continued on.

Nolan closed the flap, his heart racing. Their plans could be ruined before they even started.

With shaking hands, Nolan gathered scrolls for the families of those who would not return. He couldn't even imagine how Uncle Camden would feel when instead of a daughter, a scroll returned in her place. Camden was not the type of man who took pleasure in glory or fame. Unlike Nolan's father, Camden would feel the loss deeply.

Nolan wrote a proclamation for Alec's father as well, though Alec would arrive in Alton to tell his father personally; Alton was one of the many stops between here and Faylinn. It would be an unpleasant reunion between Alec and his father. Unlike Nolan's uncle, the news would bring a whole different type of grief upon Kardos Deverell.

He packed the rest of his meager belongings and scanned the tent one last time. This would be his last trip to the Tournament of Awakening. An odd mixture of sadness, fear, and excitement stirred inside him. Either they'd free Emery, or they'd be discovered, labeled as traitors, and put to death.

Nolan wasn't sure which option scared him more.

Alec and Taryn flashed in his mind, as well as Emery Cadogan, sitting in the West Tower of Alton alone. There was no turning back. Three people now depended on him. A new, open page of Nolan's life had begun.

Chapter Thirteen

Nolan leaned against the side of the boat. The warm breeze brushed his face, and the sun filtered through his closed eyelids. He inhaled and released it slowly, doing his best to enjoy the beautiful weather while he still could. The water's gentle churning was peaceful, as well as the soft melodies of the frogs and birds as they drifted along. But nothing Nolan did, nor any forest sounds, could calm his nerves as they neared Alton.

The task before them was immense. Some might say impossible. Guards were stationed around the clock, and the Rol'dan would be among those who watched. There would be only a short amount of time to rescue Emery before Kael took him to King Alcandor. Poor Emery's only chance lay in the hands of a scribe and a hotheaded youth. But even so, they weren't without hope.

Nolan could come and go in the manor without suspicion. He also now had a sling—the first weapon he'd owned—and though most might think it a worthless weapon, it was easy to hide, quiet, and went well with his Accuracy Shay. But Nolan's most important tool had nothing to do with him. That weapon lay in the superb sword skills and Speed of Alec Deverell.

A shadow blocked the sun from his closed eyes. Nolan opened them to Alec standing above.

Nolan smiled. "I was thinking of you."

"Good things, I hope."

"Are you allowed to come amongst the inferior, common

folk?" Nolan asked.

"I don't think they noticed." Alec motioned toward a group of Rol'dan. They reclined under a canopy, sipping frothy mugs and laughing obnoxiously.

"Besides," Alec said, "it's getting far too crowded over there with their swollen heads."

Nolan laughed. "Well then, welcome to where the smaller heads reside."

Alec exhaled a deep sigh. "Thanks. I can't take it anymore." He plopped next to Nolan and placed his leather bag in his lap. Side by side, they sat in silence.

After some time, Nolan yawned and noticed Alec gazing at the riverbank as it slowly drifted by. Nolan's eyes dropped to Alec's lap where his hands rested casually on his leather bag. It was simple, as far as bags went. Worn spots marred the edges. He started at it, unable to pull his eyes away.

"Nolan?"

Nolan shook his head.

"You awake?" Alec asked.

"Yes, of course."

"Well, I asked you how you've been getting along, but you never answered."

"I'm sorry. Tired, I suppose." Nolan ran a hand over his face. "Have you gotten a chance to talk to Taryn?"

"No," Alec said, his expression becoming more serious. "She's on the first boat. General Trividar hasn't let her out of his sight. I think he separated us on purpose."

It sounded like Kael, considering all the attention he'd lavished on her.

"What's with him, anyway?" Alec asked. "They're cousins, for Brim's sake. And he's too old for her."

"I don't think it has anything to do with Taryn."

Alec grunted. "Oh? Did you see the way he looks at her?"

"It has more to do with her mother."

"Her mother? How so?"

Nolan sighed, trying to decide the best way to explain the complicated relationship. "When my mother died, Alana,

Taryn's mother, sort of stepped in and helped our family. She was a neighborhood girl. I was only a baby, and she became the mom I never knew. Kael, on the other hand, was old enough to notice her differently."

"I see." Alec sat up and moved his hands to his lap, fidgeting with the strap on his bag, drawing Nolan's attention to it again. "So he loved her?"

"More like an obsession," Nolan answered. "She was eight years older than he was, old enough that she never saw him the same way he saw her. Eventually, she fell in love with my uncle, Camden. They married soon after. Kael has never gotten over her."

Their conversation faded into silence. Nolan's memories of his family muddled with escape plans, but his eyes kept darting to the bag in Alec's lap. *Why in the name of Brim am I so focused on the cursed thing?*

Finally, Nolan couldn't take it any longer. "What are you carrying?"

Alec looked puzzled, and then followed Nolan's gaze. "In here?"

"Yes. In there."

"Why?"

Nolan shrugged, trying to appear indifferent. "Was curious."

Alec opened it and removed a crumpled, bloodstained tunic. "Some clothes, mostly. At least what's left of them. Most of what I brought was destroyed in the tournament."

Nolan craned his neck, trying to peer in. Alec stuffed the contents back in and placed it on his other side.

"I'm sure your bag is more interesting than mine," Alec said.

Nolan forced a laugh. "I'm not sure how exciting ink and quills would be." He looked to the barge in front of them. A Rol'dan soldier leaned on the railing, staring. Nolan's heart choked in his throat; it was the Perception Rol'dan who had reclaimed Alec from the tent the other night, the same one who might've heard their conversation.

Nolan nudged Alec. "Who's that?"

The soldier quickly looked away.

Alec's arm tensed. "His name is Daren Kinsley. He's pretty new. Came into Perception a few months before the trials. Some type of mining accident or something. Never did find out all the details. But I guess it was bad enough it forced his Shay power."

Nolan and Alec's eyes met in silent understanding. Their conversation wasn't safe anymore.

***

The boats rounded the bend in the river, and the city of Alton came into view. Behind the docks, large stone walls surrounded the city. Guards stood at their posts atop the wall, leaning forward as they watched the approach. A horde of people gathered on the docks, cheering loudly as they caught sight of the boats.

The people pushed each other while madly waving flags of the Rol'dan.

Though Alec hadn't mentioned home since starting their journey, Nolan could see the fear of confronting his father lining Alec's scarred face.

They bumped against the dock and jumped from the boats, wedging behind a wall of guards pushing against the crowd.

Alec yelled over the commotion, "What's with these people? Don't they have anything better to do?"

"It's our welcome home," Nolan said. "Don't tell me you've never seen this. You've lived in Alton all your life."

"I could always hear the noise from the shop, but I never imagined…" Alec shook his head. "My father always kept me at home. Said he wouldn't watch the Rol'dan parade their new dogs…" He flinched and said no more.

"Over here!" Nolan motioned toward a heavily decorated wagon. Rol'dan banners draped the edges, and gaudy, rainbow-plumed horses shifted nervously on their reins.

Alec gawked at Nolan with a sour expression, one that

obviously said, *You can't be serious.*

"You don't have a choice." Nolan prodded. "Besides, do you really think it's a good time to bring attention to yourself?"

The jailbreak would happen soon. Conflict pinched his face, the war between stubborn resolve and wise judgment. After his brief internal battle, he cast Nolan a glare quite similar to Kardos Deverell and climbed into the wagon.

The remaining passengers boarded and, with a crack of a whip, the wagon began the slow procession through the streets of Alton. The excited mob gave a robust cheer and followed along, all trying to get a glimpse of the fortunate few. The only people who remained with Nolan were the families of those who returned from failing the trials; they hugged their children as they led them back to lives of mediocrity.

Nolan smiled at the happy reunions, that is, until he spotted a man standing alone. Unlike the others, his solemn face paled.

Kardos Deverell stared at the retreating procession as if it were a death march. Nolan took a step toward him, not knowing what he'd say. But he needn't worry, for a body blocked Nolan's path.

Nolan looked around the annoying person only to see Kardos stomping off. Nolan had a feeling the man was making straight for the pub to drown his sorrows.

"I'm sorry to bother you," a voice said, "but are you Nolan?"

For the first time, Nolan focused on the woman in front of him. He inhaled sharply. Several weeks earlier, he'd admired this girl when he'd sat in Aunt Bonty's pub.

"W-what did you say?" Nolan stammered. *What is she doing here?*

"Are you Nolan?" She bit her bottom lip, waiting.

In the pub, her hair had looked plain brown. Daylight brought out reddish tints in the thick, brown locks. She wore it down today, and it made her prettier than before, if that were possible. His eyes fixed on her mouth, and he wondered what it would be like to kiss her.

"I'm sorry," she said. "I made a mistake." She turned to leave.

"Wait!"

She faced Nolan again.

"Yes, I'm Nolan. We haven't met before, have we?"

"No. We have a mutual friend."

Perhaps Aunt Bonty had decided to play matchmaker? But it made little sense since she already had her mountain man, didn't she?

She leaned toward Nolan. He could smell violets or some other flower on her skin. His pulse increased. She put her face near his ear, and her breath sent a shiver down his spine.

"Emery told us you would return," she whispered.

Nolan jerked back. "Emery?"

She shushed. "We have little time."

"Did you say Emery?"

She wrinkled her nose, annoyed. "Please, can you come with me?"

"The duke will be expecting me," Nolan said. "But I can meet you outside the manor once I'm finished."

"Good. I'll be waiting." She peered around, as if someone were watching, and headed toward the nearest street, blending back into the meandering crowd.

Who was she? Was she one of Emery's friends? Even if she was, how in Brim's light had she spoken with Emery? Nolan was, of course, telling the truth when he'd said the duke would expect him. But his pitiful excuse had been more to give him time to think. The duke had enough to keep him busy with the manor bursting full of Shay Rol'dan. That, along with the preparations for the feast tonight, would mean Duke Ragnall would hardly miss Nolan.

If Nolan wanted to find out more, he'd have to meet with her. He only hoped he wasn't stepping into a trap.

Chapter Fourteen

Nolan left the manor. The sun was veiled behind the clouds and cast eerie shadows on the stone-lined streets. He'd gotten so used to the light at the tournament, he'd nearly forgotten the dreariness of Alton. Hopefully, if the escape went well, he wouldn't have to put up with Alton's gloomy skies for long.

He'd reported to the duke earlier, then spent the next several hours hiding in his room having a heated argument with himself about why he shouldn't meet this mystery girl. He'd lost, although he knew it probably wasn't the smartest decision.

Scanning the thinning crowd, he searched the faces, almost hoping she wasn't there. He was about to change his mind when he saw her. She leaned against a broom shop painted gold. Taking a deep breath, he stepped toward her.

"Thanks for coming." She pushed an amber lock behind her ear.

He nodded, his voice now missing.

She motioned and led Nolan into the marketplace and down several busy streets. With each step, doubt prodded him. They'd planned an escape, and here he was, risking everything for a pretty face? She looked over her shoulder and smiled, but it didn't reach her eyes. She appeared worried, somehow.

They wound through at least three district colors before coming upon Aunt Bonty's pub. The pub was crowded—much like the last time Nolan had come. Several card games were in progress, and each chair was filled. Aunt Bonty's had a reputation for good food and service. The smell of roasted meat and freshly baked bread permeated the room, and suddenly, Nolan remembered he hadn't eaten since arriving in Alton. He'd been too nervous. He glanced at the bar longingly, but thoughts of food quickly fled. Kardos Deverell sat slumped at the bar, surrounded by empty mugs.

The girl gently touched Nolan's arm, her fingers icy cold. "This way."

Nolan nodded, took a final glance at Kardos, and followed her up a flight of stairs, leaving the lively pub activities below.

The hallway to the inn portion of the pub was clean and well maintained, though it filtered little of the noise. Gradually, the pub's bawdy laughter joined with music. Somewhere close by, a stringed instrument played a sad, dissonant song. The music grew louder as they continued down the hall, and then it stopped. A door opened, and a monster of a man with a long matted beard blocked their view. Nolan blinked. It was the mountain man from the pub. He was a lot taller close up than from across the room.

The man's eyes flared orange. Nolan tensed, not quite believing what he'd just seen. *He has Perception?*

"You all right, lass?" the man asked.

She nodded and went inside.

Nolan lingered in the hall, all of his fears coming back in a rush. *This mountain man has a Shay?*

Another man with dark red hair stood by the open window. He set a lute against the wall and turned toward him, his eyes flaring violet. Then an Empathy Shay searched Nolan. His heart thundered; his breath quickened.

The redheaded man's Shay extinguished. "Don't be afraid." He motioned with his hand. "Please, come inside."

Standing before Nolan were not one, but two non-Rol'dan with the power of the Shay. Or were they? Maybe they were part of the Rol'dan after all. He eyed the girl, wondering what power she could wield. Had that Daren fellow ratted out Nolan and Alec's plan? Were they testing him now? Nolan met the girl's eyes. He wanted to trust them. Emery told him he had friends; they could be them.

Taking a deep breath, Nolan entered. He'd come this far already. The mountain man shut the door and motioned to a worn table set with four mismatched chairs. "Have a seat, lad."

Nolan took a deep breath, eyeing the large man. He had smile wrinkles around his eyes—a friendly face. Resigned, Nolan sat. The man with red hair, whose expression was more serious than the other man's, took another seat directly across from him. His green eyes bored into him before he finally spoke.

"What's your name?" the man asked.

"I thought you already knew my name."

He ground his teeth. "Your *full* name. We need to make sure we have the right person. We're risking a lot bringing you here."

"Nolan," he answered. "Nolan Trividar."

"And your profession?"

"Personal scribe for Duke Ragnall."

The man flared his Empathy, prodding Nolan's mind, probably searching for truth. Nolan let him, though he hated how it felt. Invasive. Rude. Finally, the Empathy withdrew.

"You know why we brought you here?" the man asked.

Nolan hesitated. If they were Rol'dan spies, his words would condemn him. "You brought me here because a mutual friend has found himself in a difficult situation."

The man grunted. "I was able to talk with Emery briefly."

How? Nolan thought.

"I made an Empathy connection with him from his prison window. As you might know, those with Empathy can link minds, as long as they can see each other," he said and shifted on the chair. "He told us about you. And, for some reason, he trusts you. However, I need to confirm you're this Nolan he speaks of. If you're him, then you're hiding something of importance—something that defines you more than most know."

Nolan swallowed. *My Shay power.*

"My gift isn't as powerful as Emery's," the man continued, "so I can't verify it like Emery can. But I can still sense your intentions in meeting us here, and they seem to be honorable, I suppose. So if you want to help us free our friend, I need you to show us your power."

Nolan would rather strip naked than show his Shay to three strangers. It was bad enough he'd already shown Emery and Alec. He glanced at the girl. She smiled.

He swallowed. Maybe not naked, but still...Revealing his power was something very personal. Unfortunately, it was the only way to gain their trust.

Taking a deep breath, Nolan released his Shay. As if taking off a constrictive tunic, he let it expand. He looked each one in the eyes, blue light shining fully, and then he hid his Shay and looked away.

"I'm sorry," the man said. "Emery told us of your special situation. I can sense your discomfort and also your understanding. You know why this was necessary."

He nodded, still unable to meet their gaze.

The man sighed. "My name is Flann McCree. This is Hakan, and my sister, Megan. We're a few members of the same clan, so to speak. As you can see, we have no ethnic boundaries—"

The large man, Hakan, snorted a laugh.

Flann glared at Hakan and then continued, "Our group consists of those with gifts, and their friends and families. If anyone resists the responsibilities of the Rol'dan, their families are at risk as well.

"We asked you here because we've spoken to Emery. He has a plan for escape. He insisted you would be a part of this as well. Tonight we'll free him and escape in the dark."

"Tonight?" Nolan straightened. "At night?"

Flann's expression flattened. "He believes it's the only way to put enough distance between us and the Rol'dan."

True. No sane—or insane—Rol'dan would follow us. But how are we supposed walk around in a dark forest full of Dor'Jan?

"Hakan will guide us in the darkness with his Perception," Flann answered.

Nolan's eyes drifted to Megan, who twirled a strand of hair.

Is she a Shay user or a family member? Nolan wondered. *Flann said Megan was his sister, and she's not shown any power. She's quite pretty.* Nolan ran his hand over his chin, realizing he was probably getting as shaggy as Hakan. *Maybe I should've cleaned up a bit...*

Flann's expression changed. Before, it had been stern, but now, a fierce glare stabbed, one only a protective brother could give. Nolan held his breath. If he was going to be hanging around Empathy users, he'd really have to start paying attention to his thoughts.

"Well, tonight doesn't give us much time," Nolan said, forcing Megan from his mind.

"No, it doesn't," Flann said, still scowling.

"There are two others," Nolan added.

"Rol'dan initiates?" Flann asked.

Nolan nodded.

"Emery hoped you would find others."

"What gifts do they have?" Megan asked.

"Alec has Speed and Taryn has Healing."

"Speed could be useful," Flann said. "Can he fight?"

Nolan's mouth quirked. "He can hold his own."

"If things get difficult," Flann said, "I'm afraid we might depend on his Speed. Even so, it will still be a challenge to get to Emery."

A memory twanged. Nolan slid his leather pouch off his shoulder and shuffled inside it. He'd nearly forgotten. Finally, his hand closed around something cold and hard. He pulled out a key. "Would this help?"

"What is it?" Flann asked.

"The key to Emery's prison tower."

Hakan gave a guttural laugh. "Crows! Where'd you get that?"

"Let's just say it was a gift from my brother."

Flann almost smiled. "Yes, I believe we can make this work. We've heard of a banquet tonight, in honor of the new Rol'dan?"

"Yes," Nolan said. "That's right."

"It'd be a perfect distraction. All we need is a way inside without alerting the guards."

Nolan noticed the lute leaning against the wall, and an idea formed. "You're musicians?"

Flann raised a questioning eyebrow. "Yes. Megan and I are."

"Then I'll get you inside easily."

Chapter Fifteen

Nolan straightened his blue jacket, probably for the tenth time. For the sake of blending in, he'd dressed for dinner. With the nobles in their fancy clothes and the Rol'dan strutting in spotless uniforms, this ridiculous jacket was the only way to disappear.

A large part of him still wanted to change his mind. He could give the key to Flann, and nobody would know better. But he'd already started the wheel turning. He'd written the summons that would bring Megan and Flann inside the manor. His treachery would return to him, one way or another. No. Nolan couldn't turn back now.

A quiet knock sounded at the door.

"Come in."

The door opened. Flann and Megan entered quickly and shut the door behind them.

"You got my summons?" Nolan flinched. Of course they'd gotten it. Nolan had written it at the inn and handed it to Flann himself.

Flann did his best to hold back a grin. "Yes. It worked perfectly."

"No problems?"

Flann's grin left abruptly. "There was one guard who I'd like to throttle. I read his filthy thoughts when he was—"

"No problems," Megan said.

"It went as smoothly as could be expected," Flann said reluctantly.

Grabbing a parchment off the desk, Nolan handed it to Flann. Flann took it and unrolled it to reveal a map of the manor.

"Wait until the banquet begins and the corridors have emptied," Nolan said. "We'll meet here." He pointed to a small "X" on the map.

Megan peered over Flann's shoulder. Her eyebrows rose. "You drew this?"

Nolan opened his mouth to answer, but paused. *She doesn't like the map?* Their gazes met, and she gawked with wide-eyed awe. *No. She likes it.*

"I'm supposed to attend the banquet," Nolan said, his voice cracking. "I'll return as fast as I can." He smiled at them nervously. Then, after a stiff bow, he walked from the room and shut the door behind him.

As he made his way through the colorful corridors on his way to the Great Hall, he couldn't get Megan out of his mind. *Do I look okay? She was staring at me.* He straightened his jacket. *Does she think I'm an idiot? Probably. I couldn't even talk without sounding like a dying crow.* He exhaled sharply. He *was* an idiot. Obsessing over this girl wouldn't help their escape. *Refocus, Nolan. Don't get everyone killed.*

Inside the Great Hall, evening light filtered through the high-domed ceiling, accenting the room's splendor. Polished metal lanterns hung from every pillar and pole, and six long tables were spaced evenly in places of honor. To complete the pageantry, each table was draped in different shimmering, colored fabrics to represent the power sects of the Shay Rol'dan.

Alec—who sat amongst the Speed Rol'dan—looked as comfortable as Duke Ragnall would be in one of his wife's gowns. Alec had scooted as far away as he could from a drunken Speed captain, doing his best to avoid conversation.

A bellow of laughter erupted from the group. The laughing Rol'dan leered at Alec, as if he were the butt of the joke—which might be likely. Nolan stepped toward them, not certain what he'd do when he got there.

An Empathy Shay passed over Nolan on the way. It was faint, nothing like Emery's. He was grateful most Empathy users could only read emotions, not sense powers. Still, he'd have to be careful. His tension might be noticed. More than likely, it was only a casual glance.

As Nolan approached the table, Kael swung his hands, elaborately telling one of his absurd stories. His fellow soldiers leaned in, hanging on his words.

"My last time in Renfrew," Kael said, "there was this bar wench—a pretty little thing. She was in the Talon's Pub, if you're ever there. Now she was one who was more than willing to please."

Stian, the thick-necked—and thick-headed—captain next to Alec, bellowed in laughter so loudly that several people at the next table turned.

A blond serving girl flitted throughout the room, pouring spiced wine. She leaned between the captain and Alec, looking at Alec like no proper girl should.

"I know the one," Stian said. "Bright red hair and full lips." Stian held his hands in front of his chest, pretending he had breasts—quite large ones, too. "She has a generous amount of 'quality,' that one."

Kael downed another mug and pointed at the servant to refill. "What was her name, anyway?"

"Does it matter?" Stian said, his words slurring.

Kael laughed and motioned toward Alec. "True, but if our new friend here wants to pay her a visit, it might help him to know her name. That is, if he knows what to do with a woman."

Stian exploded into laughter.

"Well, Mr. Deverell?" the general asked, leaning forward.

Alec glared and looked away.

"Ah, I see," Kael said. "The young stallion has not yet saddled a mare."

Nolan cleared his throat, and the entire table turned to face him. Nolan bowed for affect. "If you'd excuse me, General, sir. I need to borrow Alec Deverell for a moment."

"Why in the Darkness do you need him?" Kael said.

"I need his signature in the Book of Records," Nolan improvised. "A new policy."

Kael snorted and grinned. "I need to relieve myself shortly. When you are done, you can record me wiping my backside. Or are you already booked with Duke Ragnall?"

The table erupted in laughter once again, enough that Captain Stian almost slid backward off the bench. The banquet hadn't even officially started, and the idiots were already drunk. Nolan smiled; it would help in their escape if something went wrong.

Using his Speed, Alec appeared next to Nolan, apparently quite eager to be away from his fellow Rol'dan. They strode to the far side of the room where the Book of Records sat on a table.

"You have no idea how much I owe you," Alec whispered.

"Shh," Nolan said. "Don't thank me too much. You'll have to go back, for a little while at least."

Alec groaned. "Do I have to?"

"Yes," Nolan hissed. "And please, watch your thoughts. There are far too many Empathy Rol'dan here."

Nolan wrote the title, Rol'dan Initiates, on a blank page and pointed to a place for Alec to sign. He leaned over and whispered as Alec dipped the quill, "When the second course starts, meet me in the west wing under the portrait of the previous Duke of Alton."

Alec's eyes jerked up. "Tonight?"

Nolan nodded once.

Alec grinned. "About time."

The buzz of the room faded as the duke took the platform with Mikayla on his arm.

"Can you let Taryn know?" Nolan asked.

Alec nodded. "I talked to her already; but I didn't know it would happen so soon. Why the change?"

"It's...complicated." Nolan swallowed, his throat dry. *Crows, I hope this works.* Not that their original plan had much merit—run in, grab Emery, and run back out. At least this plan had stealth.

Alec cocked his brow but didn't ask.

Nolan then noticed the eyes of Kael and his men on them. He nudged Alec's arm. "You need to get back."

"Until the second course," Alec said, pointing at Nolan matter-of-factly. He forced a nervous smile and returned to his seat as Duke Ragnall raised his hands to make his annual announcement.

"My lords and ladies," Duke Ragnall said. "Welcome! It gives me great pleasure to introduce to you this evening the newest members of the Shay Rol'dan."

The applause from the nobles, along with the pounding of the goblets from the Rol'dan soldiers, made quite a spectacle. Whether they wanted to or not, all seven initiates rose to their feet to acknowledge the praise, and only after they were seated again did the banquet officially begin.

Chapter Sixteen

Nolan crept down the red hall as it transitioned into gray stone. It was strange having so many lives in his hands. He glanced over his shoulder, meeting five pairs of eyes. Megan, Flann, Alec, Taryn…and Rylan, the boy who had given him the sling, all waited for his direction.

Nolan still wasn't sure who'd been more surprised when Rylan first showed up—Alec or himself. Taryn had been the one to invite him. Nolan was happy, of course. He'd liked Rylan. Alec, however, didn't seem quite as glad.

After making it across the manor undetected, they positioned themselves near the West Tower. Nolan peered around the corner, and thankfully, only a pair of guards dozed in their chairs against the wall.

Nolan held up two fingers. Alec nodded and silently unsheathed his sword. But before he had removed it entirely, Flann put a hand on Alec's arm, whispered in his ear, and handed Alec a coiled rope. Alec nodded, and the golden-yellow light of Speed flared in his eyes.

He vanished, and the sound of scrambling and thrashing bumped in the hall. After the commotion subsided, Alec stood triumphantly over two wide-eyed guards bound and gagged on the floor.

"Well done," Flann said. He turned to Nolan. "Where's the key?"

Nolan leafed through his leather pouch—pushing rocks, Hakan's colored stones, quills, and inkbottles aside. He withdrew the key. Flann took it and stepped over the struggling guards. Motioning for Megan, the pair disappeared up the stairs.

Waiting for Flann and Megan was agonizing. Every breath the bound soldiers took, or any scuff of their feet upon the stone floor, sounded louder than normal. After a few more minutes of struggling, the guards stilled and watched them with frightened eyes. Nolan averted his gaze. He doubted the guards would escape punishment from the Rol'dan.

"What's taking him so long?" Taryn asked, breaking the silence.

"There are quite a few stairs," Nolan assured her.

She looked at the door, wringing her hands and biting her lower lip. But her fidgeting ceased when a faint, steady beat sounded nearby.

"What's that?" she whispered.

The noise turned into echoing foot strikes. Someone was approaching at a run.

Alec grabbed his sword as a lone figure rushed around the corner. Daren was dressed in his Perception uniform, red-faced and heaving for breath as if he'd sprinted all the way from the Great Hall.

"You all have to leave now," Daren said between pants. "They're coming."

Before they could react, Kael appeared with his Speed, his cape swinging as he slowed. Shrugging off the golden cape, it fell in a shimmering heap onto the floor. His eyes still flared with golden-yellow light, hiding the red-tinged edges from his drinking. He glared murderously and opened and closed his fist.

"Starting a new life of crime, Nolan?" Kael said. "I know your job is quite dull, but aren't you taking this a bit too far?"

"Get back!" Alec pointed his sword at Kael.

Kael raised one eyebrow. "Mr. Deverell? I'm not surprised you're involved, though I believe King Alcandor will be quite disappointed."

The door to the prison tower swung open. Flann and Megan

emerged with Emery. Emery looked surprisingly better than when Nolan had seen him last, as if the injuries were nothing but a memory.

Kael grinned and drew his sword. "You have children and simpletons helping you to escape, Mr. Cadogan."

"Not that you would know, Mr. Trividar, but friendship does inspire bravery at times," Emery said.

Kael's lip curled. "You're mistaking bravery for stupidity."

"I don't think so." Alec pushed Kael's sword away with his own.

Kael threw his head back and laughed. "So now that you're a powerful Shay Rol'dan, you believe you can beat me?"

Both Kael's and Alec's eyes flared with Speed. They would fight. This time, one would die.

Nolan yanked out his sling, reached into his bag, and grabbed the first thing his shaking hand closed over. "Kael!"

Kael froze. The sneer on his face fell, and his mouth dropped open as Nolan's Shay light shone.

Using the brief moment of shock, Nolan sent a jar of ink flying, smashing it against Kael's forehead. Kael staggered backward, hitting the floor with a hard crack of his head. Both blood and black ooze striped his face, mingling in his hair and dripping onto the floor around his motionless body.

Nolan's heart thundered. He had used his light of Accuracy to surprise him, to distract him and Alec from killing each other. But it had come at a price. Kael now knew Nolan's secret—that is, if Kael lived to remember.

"Well done!" Alec sheathed his sword and knelt next to Kael.

Kael wasn't moving, and crows, there was so much blood. Nolan's stomach tightened. *Oh, Kael.*

Alec grunted. "You didn't hit him hard enough. He's still alive."

Nolan released a breath. *He's alive!*

Alec touched the black ooze and rubbed it between his fingers. "What'd you use anyway? Ink?"

"I...uh..." Nolan hadn't thought much about it. He'd

reacted instead. Blood oozed where glass protruded from Kael's face.

Emery stepped forward, staring at Kael's body. Ink dotted his somber face where it had splashed from the impact of the throw. Emery shifted his eyes to Daren, who still watched from the wall, his eyes wide with terror.

"You," Emery said. "Why have you come?"

Daren tore his eyes from the general's still form.

"Yes, you boy," Emery said.

"I...I don't know," Daren stammered. He found Alec. "I heard what you were planning. Was curious, that's all. Been listening in. That's when I heard the general. Somehow, he knew too." He held up his hands. "I didn't say anything. None of my business. But I just couldn't sit there when they were coming to kill you."

"So you came to warn us?"

Daren said nothing, his face pale.

"Considering you're now a traitor," Emery said with a smile, "you might want to come with us."

***

With the addition of Daren and his Perception Shay, they maneuvered through the manor, avoiding the sight of any Rol'dan, and crept out a rarely used servants' exit. Flann led them across the street, where they met Hakan behind a building. They continued weaving between the shops as the light of the sun dimmed. After several blocks, they turned a corner on to Red District. Deverell Arms came into view.

Alec stopped so abruptly, Taryn ran into him.

"Ow—" Taryn rubbed her arm.

"Shh," Flann said.

"Why are we going there?" Alec whispered.

"Quiet," Flann scolded again.

"We bought some travel torches from the smith," Megan said. "We need them for our journey."

Alec still wouldn't move.

Taryn gave Alec a shove. "Come on!"

"Both of you shut your mouths," Flann said, "unless you want to tell the Rol'dan where we are."

Emery had also stopped mid-stride and stared at the shop, his face turning ashen.

"Are you all right?" Megan touched Emery's arm.

Color returned to Emery's cheeks; he forced a smile. "I'm fine. I've just had enough of this city to last me quite a while."

After some Strength-forced assistance on Rylan's part, they convinced Alec to move. They opened the door to the armory and saw Kardos Deverell leaning over his anvil. Aunt Bonty's well-rounded form rested against a nearby wall, watching him work. Both their faces lifted and fell in shock.

"You forgot a few of your things at the inn," Bonty said to Megan, her voice quivering slightly. "So I brought them out. By Brim! What have you folks gotten yourselves into?"

"I'm sorry, Bonty," Megan said. "You shouldn't be here."

"Well I *am* here, so you can tell me what's going on." Bonty crossed her arms. The serious scowl on her face disappeared as soon as she saw Alec. "My! Don't you look handsome."

"What are *you* doing here?" Kardos growled.

"Father, I'm sorry—"

"You should be sorry, thinking you could step foot in this shop."

"Believe me," Alec said, crossing his arms, "not *my* choice."

"I'm sorry to break this up," Hakan said, "but we're about to get company."

A Speed Rol'dan burst into the shop, and a blur of swordplay erupted.

"Get back," Emery said, motioning for them to get some distance.

Nolan gawked, unable to discern any part of the battle. The swords rang so fast, sounding like a metallic hum. They didn't need to wait long; the fighting abruptly stopped. The Rol'dan soldier crumpled, his chest bleeding dark crimson.

Alec stood erect, red-coated sword in hand. He deflated

and staggered back, staring at his victim. He wiped a sleeve across his mouth as his face paled. Another Speed Rol'dan appeared, and Alec recovered and attacked again.

"Isn't there something we can do?" Taryn asked.

"No," Emery said. "We'll just have to hope the boy can fend them off."

While the others gathered supplies, Nolan yanked out his sling and palmed a handful of coal from a nearby sack.

"Nolan, come on," Taryn prompted.

He ignored her, fixing his eyes on the door. Alec needed help. Nolan squeezed the leather straps of the sling so tightly his fingers numbed. When a soldier burst through, Nolan loosed a large piece of coal with more reflex than thought. It found its mark with a dull thud, and the soldier dropped.

Alec yanked his sword from another Rol'dan's chest and met Nolan's eyes. What had they gotten themselves into?

Captain Stian appeared, his arrogant face sneering as he raised his sword. Alec's Shay light swelled, but Stian was hurled backward before their swords could meet. The far wall splintered as the captain crashed through it.

Nolan inched closer and peered through the gaping hole. Stian was pinned to the ground, an anvil on his chest. His body jerked with his final death throes, and then he lay still.

Rylan ran up behind, his eyes wide and still flaming red with his Strength. "I didn't mean—"

"It's all right," Nolan said. "You did what you had to do."

"What the Darkness!" Kardos's face flushed with rage. "My anvil! My wall!"

"Your belongings are the least of your problems, Mr. Deverell," Emery said. "From now on, you'll be considered a traitor by association. You must come with us."

Kardos scowled and glared from one to the other with disgust, stopping at Alec and quickly looking away. "Why would I come with a bunch of filthy Rol'dan?"

"Because if you don't, you'll die," Emery said. "And your presence could serve us well. We need a craftsman like you to help us make weapons."

Kardos's expression softened briefly before it hardened again. "To kill the Rol'dan?"

"To defend ourselves, and yes, some Rol'dan may die because of it."

"There're more coming," Hakan warned.

"All right," Kardos growled. "I'll come."

Kardos yanked a bag from a hook and shoved tools into it.

Bonty hovered nearby, wringing her hands. "You take care of yourself, Kardos Deverell—"

"I'm afraid they probably already know of your involvement as well," Emery said. "It'd be best if you come with us."

"B-but my shop…" Bonty stammered.

"They're getting closer," Hakan said. "Is there some other way out of here?"

Kardos nodded and led them out the back of the building.

"We need to get far away from the main gates," Emery said. "As close to the river as we can."

The panic on Bonty's face smoothed, and she inhaled deeply. "I know the perfect spot. Follow me."

Bonty led them in a most confusing manner, weaving down several streets, until they reached the northeastern wall of the city. They stopped near an unmarked building, next to a garden edged with decorative stones. It was one of the few places in Alton not filled with shops, where some of the merchants lived.

Alton's city wall stretched above them, at least five men tall. A tower along the wall's edge held a platoon of useless Alton guards.

Nolan squatted next to a cucumber plant and grabbed a handful of stones. He was fresh out of inkbottles; he'd need something to throw.

"The river is on the other side," Bonty whispered and pointed at the wall.

"There are too many guards," Hakan said. He listened, his eyes flaring orange with Perception. "There's the group up there, another at the gates, and a whole swarm of them searching the city. For now, they don't know where we are."

"Ideas?" Flann asked.

Taryn pointed to some steps leading to the tower. "We can climb there, take out the guards, and jump down the other side?"

"Jump down the other side?" Daren said. "Ouch."

"Should I..." Rylan said hesitantly, "Should I break through the wall?"

"I've considered that," Emery said. "However, the wall is too thick, even for you. It'd take several attempts, and even then, the stones might come down on you."

Nolan leaned against a gnarled oak and looked up. The tree was taller than the wall, but too far away. If the branches were only longer, they could climb. Of course, the drop on the other side would hurt.

Emery followed Nolan's gaze. "Excellent idea!"

Excellent idea? "But it's too far." Nolan said.

Emery turned to Rylan. "You can make us a ladder."

Realization washed over Rylan's face as he gawked at the tree. "With that?" His voice raised a pitch.

Emery smiled. "You'll do fine."

"Um...okay." Shaking out his hands, Rylan approached the tree. His eyes glowed red with Strength, subtly at first and then bright as flames. He braced his palms against the trunk and took a prolonged sigh. Then, with teeth bared, he pushed.

Veins protruded on his thin neck, and a yell broke from his clenched teeth. The earth moved beneath their feet as roots popped free from their soil bed.

"By Brim..." Kardos said.

A horn sounded, and Alton guards stormed from the tower to the ledge on the wall, spears in hand.

Things were about to get ugly.

Nolan placed a rock and slung it. A soldier yelped and tumbled backward off the wall, hitting the other side with a pathetic moan. Nolan threw another, then another, picking the soldiers off until he'd cleared the wall.

Rylan pushed harder until the tree hit the wall with a cracking thud.

"Quickly!" Emery said.

Kardos grabbed Bonty's hand and helped her up; together they made the climb. Kardos reached the top first, his heavy tool bag clanging. He slid down the draping branches, using them like a dangling rope. Both he and Bonty disappeared from Nolan's vision as they descended to the opposite side of the wall.

Nolan palmed more stones as he waited for the others to start their climb. Swords rang out on the opposite side of the wall. Apparently, the poor guards Nolan had dislodged would have to face the blade of Kardos Deverell.

Nolan and Alec stood by the tree's base. Shouts and cries sounded from somewhere inside the city, breaking through the quiet air. He couldn't see them yet, but their voices drew closer with every barked command.

Alec nudged him. "Get going. I got this."

Nolan was about to object until he saw Alec, blood-coated sword clenched in his fist, snarling expression on his scarred face, and golden light blazing from his eyes.

Nolan nodded and scrambled up the tree.

Hand over hand Nolan climbed, heart thundering, palms sweating. Branches and bark scratched his arms. He reached the top and looked down, vertigo clamping his mind. He grabbed a branch, steadying himself.

Most of their group had reached the bottom where a circle of injured guards surrounded Kardos. Hakan still descended, the thin branches bowing under the mountain man's weight. A dozen blue lights caught Nolan's attention farther down the parapet to the west. His heart stopped. Rol'dan archers.

Nolan's eyes jerked back to Alec. He was fighting more guards, his back to the wall. One Accuracy shot, and he'd be dead before he hit the ground.

"Alec!" Nolan yelled.

Alec spun, scowling. "I'm busy!"

"Alec! Get your arse up here. Now!"

Alec turned again, his face tight in irritation until he caught sight of the Rol'dan. He cursed and—after a few sword slashes for good measure—sprinted up the tree.

One thing Nolan could say about Alec: He was an excellent warrior. Another thing he noted: Alec didn't know a rat's backside about climbing.

Nolan gasped and gripped a branch every time Alec slipped. By the time he'd reached the top, Nolan's heart beat out of his chest.

"Wow," Nolan said. "That was...not so good."

Alec's jaw clenched and his nostrils flared. He opened his mouth to speak just as the sound of bowstrings filled the air.

Nolan yanked down hard on Alec, pulling him behind the trunk. The first volley of arrows *thudded* into the wood.

"We have to get down," Nolan said. He only hoped the others hugged the wall or were smart enough to get out of range. Dark was closing in, at least. It would make it hard for the archers to see.

The archers repositioned for better aim. Behind them on the wall, Strength Rol'dan closed in, eyes shining red, massive war hammers outlined in the dying light. He and Alec could hide from the arrows, but once the Strength Rol'dan reached them—

"Heads up!" Alec yelled.

An arrow whistled through a gap in the branches and slammed into Nolan's shoulder. He reached, grasping for a branch as it slipped through his fingers. And, as if in slow motion, he fell.

Branches cracked and twigs scratched his arms and face as he plummeted through the limbs. A resounding snap rang in his ears when he hit the ground. Darkness that had nothing to do with the night hovered before his eyes. He gasped for breath.

"Nolan!"

Nolan shook his throbbing head and saw Alec's bag lying next to him on the muddy earth. He must've dropped it. His shoulder and arm throbbed, the pain buzzing in his head. The pain drifted in the background of his consciousness as the longing for the bag pulled at him. He reached, but recoiled when his broken arm protested.

"Nolan, get up!" Emery stood over him.

Nolan staggered to his feet, his legs nearly buckling. He groaned as pain stabbed through his shoulder and arm. Nolan looked up, expecting to be impaled, but the branches blocked the archers for the time being. It wouldn't last long, though. They were already climbing around the tree to get better aim.

The Strength Rol'dan hovered on the wall, not daring to descend now that night approached. Nolan jerked his eyes to the line of trees. Night. With the darkness came the Dor'Jan. Crows! They'd left one fire and thrown themselves into another. Maybe the Rol'dan were the *wise* ones, after all.

Alec slid ungracefully down a branch and landed. "Nolan? You okay?"

"I think so." His head swam and his arm throbbed. The arrow shaft had broken off in his shoulder, the stub of bloody wood protruding. Nolan pulled his gaze from the wound and his gaze fell on Alec's bag.

"Forget it," Alec said. "I don't need it."

The bag drew Nolan, compelling him. It was close enough to nearly touch, but it was out in the open, away from the safety of the tree.

"Seriously, Nolan," Alec said. "There's nothing there. I don't need it. Can you walk? Do you need help?"

"I'm fine," Nolan said. At least his legs were good enough to run.

Alec jogged off, looking over his shoulder, waiting for Nolan to follow.

Nolan should go. He knew that. It was only seconds before the Rol'dan would be back in range.

"Nolan!" Alec said in a raised whisper from his place at the river's edge. The others were already crossing, wading in water to their waists, disappearing outside the torchlight into the darkness, but Nolan's feet couldn't move.

Without rational thought, Nolan sprinted toward where the bag lay.

As soon as he looped the bag over his head, a chorus of bowstrings twanged. Pain erupted as half a dozen arrows punched into his chest. He fell and gasped, but no air would come, only the warm flow of bitter blood. Blackness edged into his vision, making the world muddy and dark.

A figure appeared over him, Alec perhaps, tossing arrows with his Speed.

Then someone lifted Nolan.

He heard more yelling and splashing water.

And then, finally, Nolan heard nothing at all.

Chapter Seventeen

Nolan's back arched, and then collapsed, splashing into the cold currents. The agony was gone, but in its place, a weakness enveloped him, as if he'd forced aside the heavy cloak of death.

The moon glowed through the cloud cover, casting pale light on the figure of a girl standing shin-deep in the caressing river. Wet strands of hair hung over her downcast face, and her sagging shoulders heaved in labored breaths. Nolan had been healed, but at what price? Poor Taryn had gone above and beyond the call.

She lifted her face, and the moonlight reflected on her hair. The blond strands Nolan expected weren't there. The locks were brown, and tears still lingered on her cheeks. It wasn't Taryn at all. Megan wiped her eyes and gave Nolan a weary smile. Large spots of blood soaked through the front of her dress.

Nolan opened his mouth, but no words would come. He could hardly believe it. Megan was a Healer? The memory of the arrows returned in full clarity. Not only had she healed him, she'd saved his life.

"I told you to stop!" Flann grabbed Megan's arm and yanked her to her feet. She staggered, sloshing in the water as she clutched her brother's arm for support.

"Stop?" she said. "You'd rather I'd watched him die?"

"*You* could've died!"

"The risk was my choice to make, not yours—"

"Our whole mission is a risk. Each of us must make choices. What Megan did was dangerous, but it was also right," Emery said.

Emery waded toward Nolan. His wet hair clung to the side of his bearded face. He knelt, examining Nolan as the faint purple in his eyes glowed brilliantly in the darkness.

"Where are we?" Nolan asked

"Downstream from Faylinn. The Rol'dan won't follow us, but we need to move quickly. Can you walk?"

Barely able to feel his arms from the cold water, Nolan placed his palms against the gravel-and-slime-covered riverbed. As soon as he pushed up, both hands slipped, and he collapsed into the water. "I…I don't think so."

Emery nodded. "You've lost a lot of blood. I'm afraid you'll have to travel by other means." He made a motion toward Rylan.

"I can do this." Nolan braced his hands. They trembled, and he fell into the water again.

"I'm sorry, Nolan," Emery said. "We can't wait, at least not for you to walk on your own."

Emery was right. Nolan was as useful as a sack of rocks. He resisted the impulse to sink below the water and disappear.

Rylan stepped toward him, his shirt covered in bloody gore. Stripes of red streaked down one shoulder to his back, as if he'd carried a deer carcass across his shoulder after a hunt. Nolan swallowed. So much blood. He must've carried Nolan away after he'd been shot.

Rylan smiled sheepishly, lifted Nolan, and pitched him over his narrow shoulders like a sick lamb from the field.

"Now that we're out of danger…for the moment," Emery said, "we'll travel the river a bit farther and then through the Forest of Vidar. We mustn't light a torch, nor utter a sound of any kind. If we do, we could bring the Dor'Jan upon us."

"So this is how we're supposed to evade death?" Kardos said. "By Brim, you're mad."

"So it would seem." Emery's mouth quirked. "Hakan, you'll take the lead from this point on. You can recognize the creatures by sight or sound?"

Hakan frowned. "Aye, and smell as well. I can't forget that stench."

"Is there anything I can do?" Daren asked. "I have Perception as well."

Emery patted Daren's shoulder. "I'm afraid your gift is not developed enough to withstand the efforts." At the confusion that flitted over Daren's face, Emery explained, "Our powers weaken as the sun sets. Perhaps you might help by keeping watch over our group, making sure we all stay together. It'd be death for anyone who falls behind."

Kardos stepped forward, his fists clenched into fists. "What makes you think the creatures haven't heard us already, especially with all the loud-mouth yelling?"

Bonty swatted bugs around her head. "Calm down, Kardos. It won't help losing your temper either."

"The Dor'Jan will search the roads first, where most people travel," Emery said. "No one strays far from the roads. We can use this to our advantage. However, if we alert them to our presence, then we'd be helpless to stop them. From this point forward, we must say absolutely nothing and walk like one of the creatures of the forest."

"So a bear would be fine then, eh?" Hakan said with a nervous grin.

Emery shook his head. "Keep us safe, friend. I'm afraid it will take the perseverance of a bear to keep us alive."

Hakan nodded, scowling with all seriousness, as Perception glowed from his eyes. He squared his large shoulders, took a deep breath, and with a steady sloshing of feet, their silent night journey began.

***

Although Megan had healed Nolan's injuries, the awkward position on Rylan's shoulder inflicted a whole different type of pain. When Nolan's limbs weren't asleep, he'd find himself drifting in and out, awakening to darkness. What little moonlight shone from behind the clouds was blotted out by the foliage. The only thing visible was the faint orange glow coming from Hakan's eyes.

The silence and monotony were taxing. They didn't even have conversation to pass time. After awakening again—much like the many other times—Nolan noticed the darkness seemed a little less. And after a short time more, he could see the outline of his fingers when he wiggled them in front of his face.

Sunlight filtered through the trees, and with it, a collective sigh sounded from the group. Rylan gently placed Nolan in a bed of leaves.

"This will have to do, Nolan." Rylan smirked, looking more like a boy because of the freckles scattered across the bridge of his nose. Several lines of sweat dripped down his face. He wiped them away with a shaking hand.

"I'm so sorry, Rylan." Nolan's voice croaked from lack of use.

"There's nothing to be sorry about," Rylan said. "If it weren't for you, I'd be heading off to Faylinn instead." He grinned. "It's the least I can do. But a little break would be great."

Rylan retreated toward the others, swinging his arm in a circle as if trying to gain sensation. Ahead, Hakan fell to his knees, covering his face with quivering hands. Emery went to him, exchanged a few words, and returned.

"Hakan is exhausted," Emery said. "We'll make camp here." He gave them all a weary smile, dark circles under his eyes. "Well done...all of you. We should get some sleep, though we won't want to stay long. We must distance ourselves from Alton. Tonight, when the night falls, we should be able to camp and sleep normally again. Today we must keep watch closely. The Rol'dan will be searching for us."

As discussions progressed to who would be at watch and who would sleep, Nolan relaxed, barely noticing the sticks and rocks jabbing into his back. Alec stood a good distance away, his arms crossed over his chest, glaring at Nolan with his golden Shay light blazing. He was angry. As much as Nolan wished he could ask him why, he couldn't keep his eyes open.

***

The smell of roasting meat roused him. Nolan opened his eyes, realizing he'd slept far longer than anyone else; they were already preparing to depart. He attempted to stand.

"Not yet," Taryn said. She sat next to Nolan, her face smudged with mud, and her blond hair matted and wild.

She handed Nolan a wooden plate with meat cut into bites small enough for an infant. Nolan forced himself up against a tree trunk, took the plate, and placed the first bite gingerly in his mouth.

After several minutes of silent eating, he put down the empty plate and ran a hand over his chin. It was a strange sensation. Though he felt well, Nolan struggled to even lift his arm. "I suppose Rylan will have to carry me the whole way."

Taryn smiled. "It's okay. It's daytime now, so it will be a lot easier for him."

Rylan moved a large stone from one side of camp to the other, as if testing his Strength. He laughed, set down the heavy boulder, and brushed the dirt off his hands.

"See? Like I said, he'll be just fine." A strange expression passed over Taryn's face. "Um, Nolan...About last night. I'm really sorry. I didn't do anything."

"Do anything?"

"When you were dying, I panicked. I didn't know what to do. If Megan wasn't here..."

"There was a good chance you couldn't have done anything."

Her brows furrowed. "What do you mean?"

"Emery said the powers aren't as strong at night. Also, you heard what he said to Daren, that he hasn't used his Perception long enough to help much. You just got your Healing. How much have you actually used it?"

She scraped a bit of mud off her fingernail. "I healed a cut on Rylan's hand once."

"Did it hurt?"

Her eyes came up. "Maybe a little."

"And what else?"

She shrugged. "Nothing else, so far."

Nolan snorted. "And you are feeling guilty for not healing an arrow in my chest?"

"Six arrows, actually."

Nolan started. "Six arrows?" He pulled down the front of his blue jacket—which now resembled dirty rags. Six new scars joined his previous arrow marks, concentrated on the center of his pale chest. How in the Darkness had he lived?

Taryn shook her head, eyes wide. "I thought you were dead. Then Megan pushed everyone aside and healed you anyway."

"Crows, Taryn. Anyone would've panicked."

"I suppose." She sniffed and looked away. "I could've at least tried."

Nolan put his hand on hers and squeezed. "Where's Alec?"

She bit her lip. "He went for a run, I think. He's pretty upset with you. About the bag and all."

"About me going to get it?"

She nodded.

"They didn't leave it behind, did they?"

"Alec's bag? Why I...I don't—"

"It's right here," Alec said, speeding out of the woods.

His voice caught everyone's attention, and the rest of the camp went quiet. He stood, frowning with dried blood smeared across his tunic and face, blood that was more than likely Nolan's.

"It's just a bag," Alec said. "Why in Darkness would you risk the whole plan? There was an entire wall full of Accuracy archers for Brim's sake."

Nolan started to speak, but couldn't. Alec was right.

"I told you to leave it, but you wouldn't listen," Alec continued his rant. "Instead you nearly got yourself killed. Crows, Nolan. What about Megan? She risked her life to bring you back—all for a nightforsaken bag."

"Now, Alec," Emery said as he came closer, "there was no permanent harm done."

"And what the Darkness do you know?" Alec spat. "Apart from what you steal from other people's minds? The only reason I helped you in the first place is because Nolan trusted you, and considering his bad choices, I'm not so sure anymore. Why should I trust a Rol'dan anyway?"

"I'm as much a Rol'dan as you," Emery said.

Alec glared at Emery, and then at his own Rol'dan uniform, now dirty and torn. "Well, I can make sure this doesn't happen again." Alec removed his bag from his shoulder, walked toward the edge of the forest line, and drew his hand back as if to toss it into the woods.

Nolan staggered to his feet. "N-no, Alec. Please…"

Alec gawked. "After all that, and you still want it? No. It's for your own good."

"Alec, may I see it?" Emery asked.

Alec stopped the forward momentum of his throw, frowned, and chucked the bag toward Emery instead. Emery opened it and handed items to Taryn: a clean Rol'dan uniform wadded into a ball; a small dagger; bread wrapped in cloth, suspiciously looking like linens from Alton Manor, and a flask that sloshed with water. As he dug deeper, the contents deteriorated: a ratty, bloodied tunic, a leather belt, some cloth bandages—some slightly used, and a half-eaten apple turning brown.

"Disgusting. Don't you ever clean out that thing?" Taryn said quietly.

Alec cast her an annoyed glance, but ignored her. "I told you. Nothing important."

"Wait a moment." Emery reached to the bottom and pulled out a palm-sized bundle wrapped in a frayed white cloth. The color and age of the fabric didn't just look old, it looked ancient.

Alec's eyebrows went up. "What the—"

"Is this yours?" Emery asked.

"I've never seen it before."

Nolan leaned forward, the bundle in Emery's hand pulling him. Nolan swallowed. He'd never felt like this before. He held his breath as Emery unfolded the layers of cloth. Inside, a smooth, translucent stone filled the entirety of his palm. *It's just a rock?*

Kardos scowled. "Where'd you get that, boy?"

Alec stared in wonderment. "I don't know."

"What do you mean, you don't know?" Kardos said. "How can something appear in your bag without you knowing it?"

"I told you, I don't know."

"Didn't you at least feel the thing knocking around?" Kardos asked.

"It's light," Emery said. "Much lighter than it should be."

"Where'd you leave your bag? Someone must've put it in there," Kardos continued.

"I didn't leave it anywhere!"

"You must have," Kardos said, "otherwise that rock wouldn't have ended up in there, now would it?"

Alec jerked his bag from Emery's hand. "I already told you!"

"What about the lodge?" Taryn said.

Both Kardos's and Alec's heads jerked toward her.

She swallowed, like she regretted speaking at all. "After the Speed challenge, when you were unconscious at the lodge."

A muscle twitched in Alec's face, making the scar on his cheek lighten.

"Unconscious?" Kardos said.

"It's nothing."

"How is unconscious nothing?"

"I don't want to talk about it." Alec stuffed his things in his bag.

"Do you think there might've been a chance for someone to put it in?" Emery asked.

"No. I mean...I don't know. I suppose it could have been then. Why should it matter? It's a rock, for Brim's sake."

"What were you doing unconscious?" Kardos asked.

"Father, just drop it!"

"I taught you well enough. You shouldn't be knocked out by anything. Why weren't you keeping your guard?"

The bickering continued as Nolan staggered toward them. He felt as if his limbs had gained five times their weight. Concentrating on putting one foot in front of the other, he trudged to where they argued. With a tap on Emery's shoulder, the yelling ceased.

"Nolan? You shouldn't be up. What are you do—?"

"May I see it?" he asked, holding out a shaking hand.

They all stared at him, blank faced.

"Please," Nolan begged.

Emery didn't hand it over immediately, but examined it first. "Nolan, we don't know what this stone is or where it came from."

Nolan's skin crawled with anticipation. "For Brim's sake, Emery. Please…"

Emery pursed his lips. Finally, he sighed and shook his head. "All right, Nolan, though I don't approve of it in the least."

As soon as Nolan's fingertips brushed across its smooth surface, an overwhelming peace came over him. His tense muscles relaxed. His fatigue melted away. He cupped it between his palms and sighed. And strangely enough, his strength returned.

Chapter Eighteen

A white flame danced across the logs, licked upward, and then sank into the orange glow from where it came. Nolan stared at the hypnotic fire and listened to the quiet drone of conversations. It'd been a long day. With one hand in his bag at his side, he fingered the stone. He didn't know what it was, or how it had helped him, but now he couldn't put it down.

Behind their small camp, Emery arranged the travel torches to protect them from any threats. Nolan felt safer with the fire. Though they saw no sign of the Dor'Jan, Nolan swore he could feel them watching just outside the circle of trees.

With both the campfire and the torches, the stifling heat made Nolan drowsy. He inhaled a cool breeze and glanced to Megan. She sat with her foot propped on a rock, her elbow on her knee, and her chin resting on her fist. The firelight flickered across her thoughtful expression...her full lips...her slightly upturned nose...her green eyes. Those eyes came up, and Nolan strangled a breath and jerked his attention back to the fire.

Crows. She made him feel like he was ten years old! And to top it off, guilt kept prodding him. She'd risked her life because he'd been an idiot, yet Nolan didn't have the decency, or courage, to thank her.

"Thank you" was easy enough to say, wasn't it? Nolan grabbed a twig and dug it into the earth. No. It was harder than dodging a grip of arrows. But at some point, he'd have to say *something.*

"So, Nolan," Hakan said. "What does a scribe do? You know, besides jotting bits of this and that." His eyes sparkled and crinkled the corners of his eyelids while the fire's light flickered off his weatherworn face.

Nolan smiled, thankful for the change of thought. "I wrote documents and summons and recorded day-to-day events in the manor."

He grunted. "So you just wrote all day?"

It did sound a bit boring when he said it like that. "Yes, I guess. We did have other things from time to time."

"Such as notorious traitors being dragged in?" Emery stepped into the circle and sat next to Nolan. Smiling, he rested his arms on his propped up knees. Bonty handed him a steaming plate and patted his arm.

Nolan chuckled. "One or two, maybe. Though you topped them all."

"You flatter me." Emery shoved a bite of roasted rabbit—Hakan's latest kill—into his mouth.

"And what about your spare time?" Hakan asked. "What'd you do for fun?"

"The fine art of crafting words isn't fun?"

Hakan laughed. "I suppose someone might think so. That is, if they were quite dull."

Nolan flinched. "Well, I did read."

Megan leaned forward. "Oh, really? I suppose there were quite a few books in the manor."

A bead of sweat dripped down Nolan's face; he promptly brushed it away with the back of his hand. "No. I mean, yes. But not the type of books you're probably thinking of. My room had two huge cases, stocked with historical documents, some of the oldest known books I've ever seen. All filled with Adamah history."

"And you enjoyed this sort of reading?" she asked.

Nolan thought about lying, but he did enjoy studying history. "Well, yes. I did, actually. I learned a lot."

Hakan snorted. "What about sport? Did you get out much?

Do some hunting?"

Nolan laughed. "I've never hunted."

"What a waste!" Hakan said. "You'd be quite a hunter with that Accuracy of yours. Just think! I could track the biggest buck in the forest, and you could bring it down with a single shot." His eyes glinted.

"He's always trying to find a hunting partner," Emery noted.

"And what's wrong with that?" Hakan asked.

"I'll tell you what," Nolan said. "When we get to this camp of yours, I'll go hunt with you. Promise."

Hakan beamed. "Aye! And I won't forget your promise, either."

"You have no idea what you've gotten into," Megan said.

"Gotten into?" Hakan said. "Why, I've done him a favor, I have. The only thing he's done is look at dusty old books."

"I'm sure he's done more," Megan said. "Do they have lots of parties at the manor?"

"A few," Nolan answered. He didn't mention how he'd hidden during those parties. He hated crowds.

Afterward, conversation thankfully drifted from Nolan. He rose from the fire, went to the edge of camp, and stood next to one of the travel torches embedded in the ground. The darkness of the forest sang its usual sounds as night followed its routine. Sometimes, Nolan wondered if his escape was pointless. It wasn't as if he could fight like Alec. All he could do was read books and write well. Really well. But a good map wasn't going to help them in a fight. He supposed he could sling a little. That did come in handy when they were trying to get away.

Taryn laughed with Alec, Daren, and Rylan. Nolan relaxed his tense shoulders. Yes. The escape wasn't totally pointless. He saved Alec and the others, too. Now they'd have a chance at a real life…whatever that was as a traitor.

"Nolan?"

He whipped around to find Megan standing close. He'd been so lost in his thoughts he hadn't heard her.

She bit her lip. "Mind if I join you?"

He gawked before answering. "Sure." He shifted, making room next to him. He touched the metal sconce holding the torch by mistake and yanked away, welts forming on his fingertips.

Megan sighed, and before Nolan could object, she touched him. A pulse of healing energy surged into him.

"Um...thanks."

She dismissed it with a wave of her hand. "Don't worry. It's what I do."

He wiggled his fingers. She was good. "Speaking of... thanks for the other day too."

She shrugged. "You don't need to thank me."

"Don't need to thank you? You nearly died."

"Not true," she said, green eyes twinkling. "*You* almost died. I merely saved you."

She had a point. An embarrassing one. He'd been quite an idiot to grab that bag, but at least now he knew the stone made him do it. It wasn't his fault.

"Besides," she said. "You've already thanked me. With your eyes."

He snorted. His eyes had been grateful...and guilty...and a lot more. He'd struggled to keep back all the strange feelings inside him, especially with her brother, Flann, watching. Nolan had never met anyone quite like Megan. And though he barely knew her, he was starting to really like her.

She stared beyond the light of the torches to the forest. The remnants of a smile faded on her lips and her brows furrowed.

"What's wrong?" Nolan asked.

"There was one other thing I wanted ask you." She pursed her lips before continuing. "The stone. The one you got from Alec? Can I see it?"

He stared at her. Why would she want it? He reached into his bag, and his hand instinctively closed around it. Once again, an overwhelming peace came over him. As he placed the stone into Megan's outstretched hand, a tremor of apprehension came over him. It took all of his willpower to let go.

Megan studied it, running her fingertips across its smooth surface. "It might be a healing stone."

"How so?"

"Well, it restored your strength." She tilted her head. "As a Healer, I can mend wounds, but restoring strength is beyond me."

Nolan shrugged. "It didn't restore me."

"Yes, it did."

"No. It did more than that. I feel lighter. More alive. I haven't felt that way for...Well, I've never felt this way before."

She turned the stone over in her hand. "And it doesn't go away? You're still rested and strong?"

"I'm still rested, yes." Nolan smiled. "Hard to gain back strength you didn't have to begin with."

She nudged him and laughed. "You know what I mean."

"I can walk around and not be a limp rag, yes." A tremor of impatience went through him as he stared at the stone. "Can I have it back now?"

She placed the stone into his palm, but her hand lingered. He met her eyes, and a tremble of excitement went up his arms.

A pulse of Empathy touched Nolan's emotions, probably Flann checking up on him. Nolan yanked his hand away.

"Well now, everyone." Emery stood and stretched. "We'd better rest as much as we can. Hakan, how much farther do we have?"

"A good four days, I think."

Emery sighed. "Well then. We best get a good night's sleep. We'll leave at first light."

The wind shifted and Daren gagged. "For Brim's sake! I think something died."

"No, lad," Hakan said. "It's much worse."

Daren's face paled. "You mean..."

Hakan nodded.

Both Megan and Nolan took a step back behind the protective torches. Nolan stared into the darkness. It took on a whole new sinister feel.

"They aren't coming any closer," Hakan said. "Been hovering for an hour or so."

"And you didn't say anything?" Kardos said. It was the first time he'd spoken since his argument with Alec that morning.

"I just said something, didn't I?" Hakan raised a bushy eyebrow. "Besides, what good did it do? Made you all worried for nothing."

"For nothing?" Alec said, his face turning red. "Those creatures are hovering at our backs, and you call it nothing?"

"They're not coming to get us," Hakan said. "So why should I make everyone in a huff? We might as well enjoy our evening instead of burning holes in our guts with worry."

"Have you ever seen a Dor'Jan?" Alec asked. "Have you ever seen what they can do?"

Hakan nodded. "Aye, I have. I knew a fellow in our clan who stayed out late hunting. We searched for him the next day. Found him—or what was left of him—fifty steps or so from camp. Isn't something I'll forget."

"No. I mean, have you *seen* what they can do?"

"See them take a man? Crows, lad! Of course not."

"I've seen them," Alec said.

Everyone stared at Alec.

Flann snorted. "That's impossible. No living man has seen a Dor'Jan."

Alec tossed a log into the fire. Sprays of sparks flew up, swirling into the night sky. "I have."

"You need to discern reality from your dreams," Flann said.

"Enough!" Emery said. "Right now our main concern is rest so we can get home safely. Hakan. Daren. Take turns keeping watch for the Dor'Jan."

Hakan nodded, and Daren turned a bit pale.

"The rest of you get to sleep," Emery said. "There'll be no more arguing. If we're in any real danger, they'll alert us." He glared at Alec and Flann, his eyes flaring purple to reinforce his words.

Flann jerked his pack from the ground and went as far as

he could go in the small confines of camp. Alec did the same, except he went to the opposite side.

Alec sat on a rock, his back to the group as he stared into the forest. He had spoken to Nolan about the Dor'Jan before they left the trials. Alec was adamant then, too. Nolan closed the short distance and sat next to him on some moist weeds. He waited for Alec to speak first.

Alec sighed, as if irritated. "What?"

Nolan shrugged. "You want to talk?"

"I have nothing to say." Alec stabbed the ground with his sword, his face set in a scowl. "No one believes me. Even Flann and Emery think I'm lying. I thought maybe, just maybe, someone with Empathy could see I'm telling the truth."

"I doubt they think you're lying."

Alec's sword hand paused. "So they think I'm crazy?"

"Maybe."

Alec's head jerked toward Nolan. At least he was looking at him now.

"Even if they did, it's what you believe that matters," Nolan said.

"Do you think I'm crazy? The last time we talked about the Dor'Jan, you thought I was drunk."

Nolan didn't answer. Alec was right, of course.

"Drunk or insane, what's the difference?" Alec said. "You don't believe me either."

"Well, I didn't before." Nolan pulled out the stone and held it toward Alec. "But that was before this."

The others stopped talking. With such a small campsite, conversations weren't very private.

"Maybe you already had the stone when you were attacked by the Dor'Jan?" Nolan suggested. "Maybe it saved you?"

Hakan stood, his bushy face animated; obviously, he'd been eavesdropping. "Blimy! Maybe it's a magic stone!"

"A what?" Alec said.

"A magic stone!" He rubbed his large hands together, as if about to eat a meal. "From the legends. They say the light inside the stones can scare the dark creatures away. Aye, it makes sense. If you had a stone, you could've survived the Dor'Jan."

Flann stalked from his side of camp. "Ridiculous! There are no magic stones."

"But the legends—"

"Legends from your mountains. Not here. Not now," Flann said. "They are stories people tell children."

Hakan's jovial face fell. "And what's to say the stories aren't real?"

Alec stood, glaring. "A warrior saved me, not some worthless stone."

Silence followed. All stared.

"You say a warrior saved you?" Emery asked.

"It was the stone!" Hakan said.

Emery shushed Hakan and turned back to Alec. "Tell me about this warrior, Alec."

"Why? So you can tell me I'm wrong?"

"Of course not. I'm not trying to discredit you."

Alec laughed sarcastically. "Like Flann a few minutes ago?"

"That was Flann, not me. I've also seen the Dor'Jan, though maybe not in the same circumstances as you."

Megan gasped and silence followed once more. This time all attention fell on Emery.

"You've seen them?" Flann asked.

"I have." Emery sighed, his mood darkening. "And no, I won't share with you when and how." He turned to Alec. "Tell me about your warrior, Alec."

"He isn't *my* warrior."

"Still, tell me what you saw."

He looked from Emery to Nolan, a nervous expression on his face. "I saw a warrior, larger than any man I have ever seen."

Emery motioned toward Hakan. "How tall in comparison to our friend?"

"Taller," Alec said. "Much taller. And he glowed like the sun."

Emery's eyebrows shot up.

"See!" Alec said. "I knew you wouldn't believe me."

"Who said I don't believe you?" Emery pulled at his beard in thought. "It sounds a lot like the tales my steward, Jared, likes to share. I believe him, so why shouldn't I believe you?" His eyes glowed violet. "And besides, there's truth in your words."

Alec stared at him skeptically. "The warrior came from nowhere. He fought with a gigantic sword that glowed as if it was still stuck in the coals of the forge. When he sliced the Dor'Jan, the creatures burst into flames. Then the warrior threw me over his shoulder and ran away."

"He was unconscious when I found him," Nolan added. "And he was pale and weak when he woke up. But he did regain his strength quickly."

"Like you did?" Emery asked.

Nolan nodded. "Yes, like me. But he didn't have the stone at that time."

"How can you be so certain?" Emery asked.

"His bag wasn't with him."

"I had my bag," Alec said. "Wait! No, I didn't." His brows wrinkled. "That's odd."

"What?" Emery asked.

"I'd left it in the forest where the Dor'Jan attacked me. But after I talked with Nolan, I found it lying under the torch on the way to the lodge."

A memory came to Nolan. It was when Daren and Alec had left his tent. Alec had picked up the bag outside. The very next time Nolan saw him on the boat, his obsession started.

"So you left it unattended?" Emery asked.

Alec opened his mouth and then closed it. "Yes, I suppose I did."

"This warrior of light could have given you the stone."

"But, what is he?" Alec asked. "I was burned, and he healed the blisters on my hands. He also ran as swift as my Speed. And by the way he carried me, I'd say he has Strength too. No one wields more than one Shay power."

Emery's brows furrowed. "There *is* one. Only one."

Chapter Nineteen

T he next several days, they followed Hakan deep into the woods. Nolan couldn't fathom how he knew which way to go; all the trees looked the same.

Nolan had done some traveling in the forest before—from his hometown of Galva to Alton, and from Alton to the tournament and back. Even then, he'd only been on the organized paths. Permanent camps lined the well-worn roads through the land, adorned with unlit torch lamps that people could use to keep themselves safe at night.

Instead, they paved their own way, tramping over soil that had possibly never been touched by human steps. Fuzzy green moss coated the gnarled roots protruding from the ground. Vines climbed thick trunks, stretching to sunbeams splashing through the leafy canopy. Wild creatures, ones Nolan had never even read about in his books, skittered from the brush and ignored the interlopers. And the flowers. Beautiful wildflowers grew in multicolored clumps, with sweet fragrances that made Nolan's nose clamp and sneeze.

Conversations flowed easily from the group until Hakan's humor faded into silence. His relaxed posture became rigid, muscles protruding on his thick neck. His brows met to become one, intimidating scowl.

Emery kept glancing over at the mountain man, concern plastered on his face.

"Does he have a fever?" Megan whispered to Emery, finally breaking the silence.

"I've got no nightforsaken fever," Hakan said, overhearing her from quite a good distance away.

"Well, considering we're lost," Emery said. "I believe you aren't well at all."

Hakan stopped abruptly. "I know exactly where we are!"

"Do you?"

A strange expression pinched Hakan's face. "I'll get us there. Don't you worry."

"What if we *are* lost?" Alec asked.

Hakan whirled on his heels. "I'll find our way! I can see a clearing just ahead. I'll figure it out when we get there."

And just as he'd said, a clearing broke through the wilderness. Beyond the branches, the remnants of a stone wall appeared, broken apart by the encroaching forest. Piles of rubble and half-destroyed walls stretched out to the distant trees. Somehow, Hakan had led them to the ruins of a vast city. He staggered a few steps and sat hard on a large pile of stones.

"What is this place?" Alec asked.

Emery rested his hands on his hips and heaved a deep sigh. "I have no idea."

Megan approached some rubble that might have been a house or shop at one time. Small yellow flowers bordered its edge. She picked a cluster of the blooms and inhaled their fragrance. "What happened here?"

"A battle?" Nolan fingered a small section of broken wall. "Catapults, maybe?"

"Cata-what?" Rylan asked.

"Catapults," Nolan said. "Machines used to throw large rocks."

"Like a big sling?"

Nolan chuckled. "Not quite. They are big wooden structures made to hold and fling boulders. Don't think you can make a sling quite that big."

Rylan's grin widened. Nolan could tell this wouldn't be the last of their conversation.

"How'd a war get here in the middle of nowhere?" Alec asked.

Nolan shrugged.

"Did you study something that might resemble this, Nolan?" Emery asked. "In your history books?"

Nolan ran a hand over his chin, scanning the wreckage. It was probably bigger than Alton. "I don't remember any large cities falling. Not sure why this one wasn't mentioned."

They spread apart, picking through the rubble. Trees overgrew the wreckage, obstructing a large portion of the city from view. Much like the land at the tournament, the sunlight was stronger. Warm rays smattered here and there across the wreckage.

Emery picked up a chipped plate and looked at the sun's position. "We'd best keep moving." He flung the artifact to the side. It smashed to bits on the ground. "How close are we to home, Hakan?"

Hakan hadn't moved since arriving. He sat on a pile of rubble, his large hands pressed to either side of his temples. "I hear some life an hour or two to the east. Pretty sure it's the village. Right direction. Must've gotten turned around a bit and ended up here."

"That close?" Emery said. "How could've we not known about this place?"

"Don't know." Hakan groaned as he bounced his knee.

"Surely when you've gone hunting—"

"I don't know!" Hakan growled, rose to his feet, and stalked several paces away.

Kardos pulled an enormous sword from some thistles. Unlike the other bits of weapons they'd found, this one was undamaged and shone like new.

Alec inhaled audibly, and his face went white.

"By Brim, I've never seen anything like it," Kardos said.

Alec swallowed. "I have."

"Don't be daft, boy," Kardos said. "I've never made anything this big."

He shook his head slowly. "It belongs to him."

"Speak clearly, boy. Make some sense."

Alec's eyes flickered golden-yellow as his temper flared.

"It belongs to the light warrior!"

Everyone stared at Alec. Nolan hadn't seen him this pale since the day he'd found him unconscious on the ground at the trials.

Kardos snorted. "You're going on about that warrior again?"

"Don't believe me if you want, Father, but there's proof right there."

"Doesn't prove a thing. Except someone has way too much time on his hands. Look at it! It's not practical." He made an attempt to swing it. "What'd you suppose it's made of?"

"If you don't know," Alec said, a bitter edge to his voice, "I'm sure none of us do."

"It doesn't belong here, not in this rubble." Kardos ran his finger over the edge of the blade. "Magnificent work. Recently forged, I'd guess. Not a scratch on it."

Everyone stared at the sword, unable to speak. If the sword was hidden in the rubble, what did it mean? Not that Nolan knew a lot about weapons, but the thing was *huge.* He shuddered. He'd hate to see a man—or worse yet, something not human— big enough to actually swing it.

Emery rubbed the back of his neck. "Well, if what you say is true, Alec, someone—or something—has passed here of late. And whatever it was, it's come too close to our village."

"Then we'd best leave straight away," Hakan said. Without waiting for anyone else, he trudged into the forest.

"I agree," Emery said. "Though, I'd like to return and examine it more closely. An entire city doesn't get lost without reason." He motioned to where Hakan disappeared. "We'd better move."

Kardos heaved the large sword over a shoulder.

"You're taking that?" Alec asked.

Kardos snorted in reply, stepping around Alec; Alec dodged a near miss with the shining blade.

"Come, boy," Kardos growled. "Standing here won't get us anywhere."

Nolan lingered, not quite ready to leave. He scanned the

fallen city one last time. *So much to learn. What happened? How did it fall?* Then, reluctantly, he followed, questions flashing through his mind.

***

They continued through the forest, and thankfully, Hakan's mood lightened. Nolan also noticed Daren wiping his forehead with his sleeve and scowling as he stomped along.

"What's wrong with him?" Nolan asked Taryn.

"He's been like that for a while, since before we found the city. He's been ignoring Rylan and me like he's mad at us." She pressed her mouth tightly in annoyance. "Maybe he caught whatever Hakan has."

"For Brim's sake, Taryn," Daren said. "I can hear you." He cast a foul glare her way and jogged ahead to walk next to Hakan.

"I see what you mean," Alec noted. "Maybe that stone is messing with their minds." He eyed the bag at Nolan's waist.

"It's *not* the stone." Nolan yanked on the strap of his bag, adjusting it from Alec's reach.

"He has a point, Nolan," Taryn said. "It made you lose your senses in Alton."

"It's different. I wasn't like either of them."

"Of course," Alec said. "You only ran into a wall of arrows."

Nolan winced. Like he needed a reminder.

Away from the ruined city, the forest took on a more civilized feel and paths cut through the dense foliage. The flattened soil underfoot was wonderful after days of cutting their way across the vast woods. After a very long hour, a man stepped soundlessly out of the forest.

A sword seemed to appear in Alec's hand.

"It's okay," Emery said. "He's a friend."

The man wore only a pair of leather breeches: no shirt, shoes, or weapon of any kind. His torso—bronzed darker than Nolan had ever seen—was well developed. He crossed his arms over his chest, not returning Emery's warm greeting.

"It's about time." The man's dark eyes scanned the group as he pushed a strand of black hair from his face. "You have new initiates, I see."

"Indeed, Maska. We've added four."

"Not as many as your last excursion," Maska said. "Are you all well?"

"Some more than others." Emery gestured toward Hakan.

Hakan growled. "Enough of this. You all think you know everything? Well then, find your way without me." He clomped ahead of them on the path, like a small child throwing a tantrum.

Maska studied his retreating form. "It would appear Hakan has come upon the same ailment as many in the village. The mood has grown exceptionally foul today."

Emery and Maska led the way, discussing the strange atmosphere passing over their home. Nolan noticed Maska's fluid movements. Every sweep of his arm, every step he took, resembled a synchronized dance. And his accent, though faint, reminded him of someone...something...

Nolan snapped his fingers. "Ha! You're Talasian."

They all stopped. Maska turned with a curious expression, the first hint of emotion Nolan had seen since they'd met.

"Duke Ragnall's wife is from Talasi," Nolan said. "You remind me of her."

"Duke Ragnall?" Maska asked.

"He's the duke of Alton," Emery answered.

Maska nodded. "I doubt one of my people would marry a duke, especially one from this land. Our people tend not to stay long. We are rarely welcomed, let alone married to leaders. This woman you speak of, I doubt she is Talasian. You must be mistaken." He turned and continued the conversation with Emery as if the Nolan hadn't spoken.

Megan gave Nolan a sly smile. "Don't worry too much about Maska. He's not rude, really. He just isn't allowed to show emotions. It's part of the culture of Talasi. Emotions are a sign of weakness."

"I don't think he needs to worry about weakness." Nolan noted the muscles chiseled onto Maska's bronzed back.

"He was disowned by his people," Megan said. "That's why he's here in Adamah."

"Disowned? What he'd do?"

"He won't say," she answered. "He's a man without a country. He doesn't feel comfortable in Adamah, yet he isn't allowed into his own land."

She casually linked her arm in Nolan's. He'd seen her do it enough times with Emery and Flann; he tried not to make anything more of it. But even so, he took a deep breath to calm his pulse.

"We think his power has something to do with it," she said. "As far as we know, he's the only Talasian with a Shay."

Nolan didn't know much about Talasi. None of the plethora of books he owned talked much about them. His only experience was with Mikayla.

"What's his Shay?" Nolan asked.

"Strength."

Strength fit him. "And how did he end up here?"

"Emery found him," Megan said. "He saved some idiots who were going to attack Maska." She shook her head. "Little did those men know what they were up against. Luckily, Emery prevented it before it happened. He could read their intentions. And, of course, he also saw Maska's gift. Emery has a knack for finding people."

Her gaze rested on Nolan; she wasn't just speaking of Maska.

"I suppose he's found quite a few," Nolan added. "Probably you as well?"

She laughed. "No. He found Flann. I came along because I'm family. My power didn't emerge until two years after I arrived at the village. I fell, broke my arm, and ended up healing myself."

"That was convenient," Nolan said.

"Very." She smiled. "Though, with all the healers in the village, I would've been just fine."

"So how old are you, anyway. Sixteen? Seventeen?"

She giggled. "No. I'm twenty."

Twenty? His heart sank. *Crows, what must she think of my dumb ogling.*

They walked in awkward silence while Emery and Maska continued to speak of what had happened since Emery left for Alton. It was strange to see such a lack of expression in someone when speaking of such horrible events. Even when Emery spoke of his capture, Maska only nodded, as if he were mildly interested at best.

"Why would a whole race of people choose to hide emotions?" Nolan whispered.

"Perhaps they have no choice," Megan answered.

"No. The duke's wife has no problems expressing emotions."

"Maybe Maska's right. Are you sure she's Talasian?"

"I'm positive." Nolan saw Mikayla's emotions a lot more than he wanted to, especially the *"I want you"* kind.

"How'd the duke get a Talasian wife, anyway?" she asked.

"She was a gift."

"A gift? From whom?"

Nolan frowned. "King Alcandor."

"We're almost there," Emery said. "It's right through—"

A group of people clustered in a clearing, yelling. An older man's voice, in particular, rose above the rest.

"If you'd excuse me," Emery said and went toward the group. They stopped fighting and presented their case to Emery without even a hello.

"Oh my," Megan whispered. She pointed to the older man. He was tall and thin with wavy brown hair. "That's Garrick. He's one of the founders of our village, one of the original Rol'dan who escaped with Emery. He's also one of the calmest, most steady men you'll ever meet."

Garrick jabbed his finger into Emery's chest as he screamed curses.

"He doesn't seem very calm."

"Exactly," she said. "And those others are his students.

He helps train those who come into Accuracy. While in the Rol'dan, he was the highest ranking archer..."

Her voice trailed off. "I don't understand. Garrick's usually so calm."

A violet light took hold in Emery's eyes. The curses in the group faltered and then stilled. Emery spoke to the group briefly, then they trudged off the field. It was then Nolan saw a grouping of structures in the center of the huge clearing. Small houses. People coming and going. Carrying baskets. Hanging clothes.

Emery approached with the tall man; light brown hair hung in the man's face. "I wanted you all to meet a good friend of mine, Garrick Grayson," Emery said, frowning.

Garrick offered his hand and shook Alec's first, a hard smile plastered on his face. "It's good to meet you. Welcome to our family."

He shook hands with everyone, shifting from one leg to another like he'd rather be anywhere else. When he got to Nolan, his countenance changed slightly. "What did you say your name was?"

"Nolan Trividar." He held out his hand; however, the man only stared at him with a strange, hungry expression. Nolan pulled back and stepped away.

Emery placed an arm on Garrick's shoulder. "Flann, can you show the others around and find them a place to stay?" He pointed toward the buildings. "The smithy shop is still empty. Alec and Kardos can go there."

Emery met their gazes, apology lingering in his brown eyes. "We'll get to the bottom of this, I promise. Please, make yourselves at home."

Emery led Garrick away. Nolan tried to forget Garrick's strange look, and the way it made his skin crawl. Instead, he focused on the new sights around him.

They stood in a pleasant field, a grouping of practice targets an easy shot away. The town—or village, they'd said—was centered in the clearing. To the east of the village rested a calm and welcoming lake. Several trees lined its edge strategically.

Nolan wondered if some Strength user had transplanted them. To the west of the structures a grouping of people sparred with swords. Surrounding the entire clearing were poles with lanterns.

"This way," Flann said with a smile.

As they drew closer, details of the structures came into view. Warm smiles greeted them as they walked a dirt road between rows of small cottages. The buildings stood close together, but it didn't seem crowded. Instead, Nolan thought the whole place was cozy. The cottages were plain wood and stone, natural grays and browns instead of Alton's gaudy colors. Nolan had never seen anything so wonderful.

Without saying a word, a woman handed Nolan a warm basket and smiled; a flash of Empathy flared in her eyes. He blinked back confusion before the smell of fresh bread met his senses.

"That's Mary," Megan added. "She likes to bake."

They'd suddenly become the center of attention as people came outside.

"Welcome," said a man with a full moustache. He patted Nolan's shoulder as they walked on.

A little girl ran up to Taryn, giggling, and handed her a handful of dandelions. Taryn knelt next to her and they whispered together as if they'd known each other for years. Somewhere close by a dog barked, and children played. For some reason Nolan had imagined a group of hard-faced traitors, sulking over a fire as they discussed their imminent capture. He'd never imagined such a place.

Nolan began to realize how void his life had been the last two years. He had no friends in the manor. Only his books. His brother—the rare moments he'd see him—went out of his way to make his miserable life even more miserable. Even before then, when he'd lived at home, his father criticized him like he wasn't even his son. And now, strangers welcomed him? Without question and with open arms?

"Nolan?" Megan broke into his thoughts. "You okay?"

Nolan smiled. His nose was running. He wiped his face

and...Crows! He was crying? *What must she think of me?*

"It's amazing, isn't it?" she said, as if she didn't notice his humiliating display.

Nolan didn't dare answer. Even when he was home with his family, he never felt like he totally belonged...like he did now.

Chapter Twenty

Nolan pushed his spectacles to the top of his head and stared at the stone with his naked eye. He'd seen pretty much everything, as far as stones went. Growing up near the sea had given him plenty of opportunities. He'd collected rocks and shells as a child, but none of those gave him strange sensations like this one.

He turned it over. No matter how many different angles or in how many sources of light he held it, it still looked like... well, like a rock. A nice rock—smooth, milky white, and translucent—but still only a rock. He tossed it onto the bed next to Hakan's "magic stones." The palm-sized stone and the painted pebbles looked nothing alike. He couldn't shake Hakan's comment about them being the same. Was this, in fact, one of those legendary magic stones?

Nolan shoved his hands behind his head and lay down. He sighed, sinking into the feather pillow. He now called a one-room cottage home. It was bigger than his room at Alton manor—but not by much. The walls held no towering bookshelves, nor were there stacks of parchment piled in the corners. The desk remained empty, not covered in quills, ink, or miscellaneous projects half finished. New morning light drifted in through the windows. His Alton room had no windows of any kind. Nolan had depended on candles, even in the day. It was odd to wake to sunlight, and he wrapped his mind around the idea of freedom. No projects loomed over him. No responsibilities...yet. He wasn't sure what to do.

Nolan jumped when a rap sounded at the door. He put on his spectacles, picked up the stone, and swung his legs over the side of the bed.

Someone knocked again, this time more impatiently.

It was probably Alec. He'd talked of getting together this morning. The knocking turned to pounding.

"Hold on a second!" Nolan called.

In a few strides, he closed the distance and lifted the latch; but to his surprise, it wasn't Alec. It was Garrick. *What in the Darkness is he doing here?*

The tall, thin man stared at him, wringing his hands. Finally, he cleared his throat. "Emery asked me to fetch you. We're meeting to discuss the ruins you saw yesterday, as well as the..." His voice trailed off, and his eyes dropped to Nolan's hand. "He wanted you to bring a stone of some kind. Crows, is that it?"

Nolan clenched the stone. If Emery thought he'd just hand over the stone, he was mistaken.

"He won't take it from you."

Nolan's eyes shot up. Garrick had Accuracy, not Empathy.

"He told me you'd react like this." Garrick leaned against the doorframe.

"Are you okay?"

The older man forced a smile. "Not really. Emery sent me so I'd have something to do. Get my mind off of this...anxiety." Garrick's eyes were pinched. The expression reminded Nolan of his own when Emery found the stone in Alec's bag. Blood left his face. Crows, no. He didn't want to consider it, but had to. Was Emery right? How could he be right?

Garrick didn't notice Nolan's turmoil; he was too caught in his own. Nolan squeezed the stone in his palm. If he shared it with Garrick, he'd no longer have it to himself. But this man was important to the village, Emery's friend. He couldn't keep it from him...could he?

Nolan groaned inwardly and took a deep breath. Before he could change his mind, he grabbed Garrick's hand and placed the stone in his palm.

Garrick gasped, and all the tension slid from his shoulders and disappeared into the ground. After a lengthy pause, he looked at Nolan, wonderment on his face, and then his eyes dropped to the stone.

"Just don't walk too far away from me." Tension ticked through Nolan's arm.

"What is it?"

"I'm not sure."

"Where did you find it?" Garrick's gaze remained fastened to the stone.

"It found us, actually. I think Emery suspects the king gave it to us."

"Alcandor?" Garrick huffed. "I couldn't imagine that to be true."

"Neither could I. But I also didn't think it could make people feel so terrible." Nolan frowned.

"Not everyone is feeling bad. So how could it be the stone?" Garrick said. "Maybe the stone is a cure, not a cause."

"A cure for what?"

"I...don't know."

Nolan held out his trembling hand. "I'd like it back, if you don't mind."

Garrick cleared his throat. "Of course." He moved slowly, hovering the stone over Nolan's outstretched hand. Finally, he placed the stone in Nolan's palm.

Nolan relaxed, feeling the peace of the stone wash over him.

Garrick's hand lingered, the stone resting between their two palms. Finally, he let go and rubbed his empty hand with his other. He followed Nolan's movements as he slipped the stone into his pouch.

"I know we've just met," Garrick said, "but I'm afraid you're stuck with me now."

"I know." Nolan exhaled slowly. "We've become best friends."

Garrick laughed. "Ah! Emery said you were a good fellow. I can see why he likes you."

They stepped outside, and Nolan closed the door. "What else did Emery say?"

Garrick displayed a friendly, crooked-toothed grin. "He mentioned I might have competition with my Accuracy gift. Considering we'll be spending a lot of time with each other, we can test his theory soon."

They continued down the small road, and Garrick waved at an old woman sweeping her front entrance. He smiled at another child as she darted by.

"Morning, Garrick," a young man said.

He was quite different than the cursing madman from the night before. Garrick was actually a nice guy.

They turned toward the center of town. It didn't take long, for the village was quite small. A larger building loomed above the rest of the cottages. It had the same plain wooden walls, no adornments of any kind. Functional, not decorative. When they reached it, they walked up three steps and Garrick opened the doors, letting Nolan go in first.

He flanked Nolan, standing not even a hand's width from his arm.

The building consisted of two rooms. One was large enough to hold quite a few people, probably most of the village. It was comfortable, though it resembled a stable compared to the Great Hall in Alton. An improvement, in his opinion. No ugly tapestries, no glass-domed ceiling. Small windows lined the walls with shutters propped open with twigs, letting in a cool breeze. Nolan paused and inhaled, taking it all in.

Conversation drifted from the second, smaller room. Hakan's angry voice carried over the rest.

Garrick opened the door, and every head turned.

Seated around a thick-legged table were Hakan, Emery, Flann, and Maska.

"You know most everyone," Garrick said. He motioned toward an old man standing off to the side with slumped shoulders and a small circle of gray hair ringing his nearly bald head. "This is Jared."

The old man nodded.

Emery stared at Garrick, and his eyes flared with Empathy. "By Brim, man. What happened?"

Garrick smiled. "You'll have to ask Nolan."

Nolan recounted what happened and then reluctantly handed the stone to Hakan. The mountain man held it in his large, dirt-stained palm for a long time, staring at it as if waiting for it to move. Finally, he huffed an exaggerated sigh and said, "What in the Darkness am I supposed to do with this anyway?"

"If you were silent and waited a bit longer," Maska said, "perhaps you would know."

"And maybe if you'd shut your trap and not add your opinions—"

"Enough," Emery said. "Arguing won't give us answers."

"I am not arguing." Maska crossed his dark arms over each other. "I am merely stating fact."

Hakan rose from his seat, his massive form towering over the table.

"Sit, friend," Emery said.

Hakan sat slowly. "I don't know why people are so worried. There's nothing wrong with me. I mean, besides what a couple good nights' sleep might fix. Perhaps yesterday there might have been a bit of a problem, but I'm much better today."

"Your condition is better?" Emery asked.

"Aye. Much better. Matter of fact, I'm pretty much back to myself."

Flann cast a doubtful look at Emery. Even Nolan, who didn't know Hakan very well, knew the man wasn't his normal self. For some reason, the stone didn't work on him. So much for the stone being a cure.

"Well," Emery said, "the only commonality between Nolan and Garrick is their Accuracy. Otherwise, we have no explanation why it doesn't calm you as well."

"It's because there's nothing wrong with me," Hakan growled.

A clatter sounded behind Emery's chair. The old man crouched on the ground, picking up a tray of mugs.

Emery rose and started helping him. "Jared, you're supposed to be a part of this meeting, not a servant to it."

The old man smiled. "I was getting a few drinks, that's all."

"Leave them," Emery said. "Come, sit with us, please."

The man avoided everyone's glance as he awkwardly chose a chair on the farthest end of the long table.

"Perhaps this stone affects those with Accuracy," Flann added. "Are there others with Accuracy who are feeling unwell?"

Garrick grunted. "Most of them."

"We could test the theory," Maska suggested, "by asking for volunteers."

"I'm sure there would be at least ten or more willing to try," Garrick said.

Nolan imagined a cluster of people clinging to the stone. How could he manage that? What if someone took it away? He shifted in his seat, his heartbeat accelerating. "What about the city?" he desperately suggested. "Maybe we should go there first."

Emery's Empathy passed over Nolan.

"A good idea. Perhaps we *should* go there first," Emery said.

Nolan heaved a sigh of relief and gave Emery a grateful smile.

Emery turned to the old man. "Jared, the reason I wanted you here was because of your knowledge."

Jared's bald head wrinkled. "My knowledge? I'm not sure how much I can help."

Emery's smile widened. "It's time we put all of those stories your great-grandfather told you to some use."

***

They set off for the ruins immediately. Once they arrived, it didn't take long to find the center of the city. Looming above the rest of the chaos stood a partially intact castle. Time and weather had crumbled many of the towers into rubble. The portions standing were made of mismatched stones—some round, some square, some in no specific shape at all. They were plastered together strategically to form, apparently, indestructible walls.

Maska used his Strength and tossed gigantic stones to clear a path to the opening of the castle. Garrick stood next to him, offering suggestions to where the boulders should go. Jared, Emery, and Nolan did nothing but watch. Nolan had seen his fair share of Strength Rol'dan over the years. But Maska, with all of his grace and natural skill, made the other Strength Rol'dan clumsy in comparison.

A movement caught his eye. Hakan paced, his broad shoulders slumped and his face set in a permanent scowl.

Another boulder crashed aside.

"He's gotten worse," Emery said, concern lacing his voice.

"Should I go talk to him?" Nolan wasn't sure what he'd say, but he felt useless at the moment.

Hakan stopped pacing and frowned. "Best leave me alone, lad." And then without another word, he stepped over a pile of rubble and out of sight.

Emery sighed. "So, Jared...now that you've been here a few hours, do you have any ideas of what this place might be?"

Jared pressed his thin lips together.

"It's okay, Jared," Emery said. "You can tell us anything."

Jared nodded and stood as straight as his slumped shoulders would allow. "I believe this is where the final battle took place."

Flann snorted. "Emery, do we really have time for these tall tales?"

"We have time." Emery flicked a warning glance at Flann before smiling at the old man. "Go on, Jared. Tell me about this battle."

Jared shuffled his feet. "Legends say Adamah's capital was not always in Faylinn. Before Alcandor, there was a grander city. Some believe the king began his rule at a different city five-hundred years ago. It was there where he saved Adamah from the demons who tried to kill all who lived. This could be that place."

"Most everyone knows of the dark times," Flann said.

"Yes, Master Flann," Jared said. "That is when Alcandor took the throne. However, my great-grandfather told me a far different tale." Jared leaned in, as if telling a secret. "It wasn't demons who tormented us. Those demons were actually Guardians who protected us."

"Oh, come now, Emery," Flann said, rolling his eyes.

Jared continued. "This battle—The Demon War—was not the start of our salvation, like the traditional legends tell, but it was really the downfall of man."

"So in your opinion," Emery said, "would this be the location of that battle?"

"Aye, sir. This is where the Guardians fell."

"What are these Guardians?" Emery asked.

Jared wrung his hands. "Protectors, sir. Light-filled warriors."

Nolan froze. Light-filled warriors? Could these be the same as what Alec saw? Maybe the warrior wasn't Alcandor after all.

Emery caught Nolan's eyes. "Light-filled warriors? And where are these Guardians now?"

Jared's face fell. "Extinct, as far as I know."

"Demons...Guardians...whatever they were," Flann said. "What difference does it make? Legends don't apply to us now. Our primary concern should be our people. Have you forgotten?" He motioned to where Hakan disappeared. "Hakan—as well as a third of our village—is suffering. Shouldn't we try and figure out why?"

"And also why this stone helped some of us, but not others?" Nolan added.

"And what of the weakening powers?" Flann said.

Emery ran a hand through his dark hair. "Yes, there is that problem, as well. Perhaps this new illness and the diminishing powers are connected. Even so, let's focus on what we know. We've come because we found the sword here. Alec seems to think it belongs to the warrior he saw, which is when we suspect he received the stone."

Jared leaned in. "Master Emery, what sword? What are you speaking of?"

Just then, Hakan appeared on top of a boulder. The crazed expression had left his face, replaced by a small grin poking through his bushy beard. He held out his hand, and a smooth, translucent stone lay in his open palm.

Instinctively, Nolan's hand flew inside his bag. He relaxed when it closed around the stone.

Emery stepped toward Hakan. "Nolan? Is that—"

"Not mine."

"Where did you find that?" Emery asked.

"It sort of found me, I suppose," Hakan answered. "Called to me, it did. Buried under a bunch of rocks. Strange, eh?"

"Two stones? Strange, indeed." Emery held out his hands. "May I see them?"

Hakan jumped down, anxiety on his face. Nolan handed Emery his stone, already feeling its loss.

Emery held one stone in each palm, moving them up and down like he was weighing them with scales. "They're identical as far as I can tell."

He handed them back, but the moment the stone touched Nolan's palm, it felt wrong. Hakan held a similar scowl. Without needing to speak a word, they swapped stones. Contentment returned immediately.

"But as you can see, they're not identical at all," Emery said.

"So what are they?" Nolan asked. He was now more confused than ever.

Hakan grinned. "Magic stones."

Flann sighed. "Do we really need to consider it?"

"We'll consider anything we can," Emery said. "Jared, do you have any ideas?"

Jared's face was neither puzzled nor thoughtful. If Nolan were to pick an emotion, he would have said the old man looked...frightened.

Jared shook his head. "No, sir."

"And what of you, Hakan?" Emery asked. "Tell us about these magic stones of yours. Are they the same ones you've been making for the children?"

"Aye!" Hakan reached into his side pouch, leafing through it. He scowled. "I'm all out, I'm afraid."

"Here." Nolan plucked the small pouch from his bag and tossed it to Hakan.

Hakan caught it. A wide grin spread across his face. "Now where did you get these?"

Nolan cleared his throat, and heat rose to his cheeks. "Found them in the pub in Alton. Stuck them in my bag for safe keeping."

A flicker of a smile touched Emery's lips, yet he didn't comment. He took the bundle, opened it, and fiddled with the stones. "Why six of them?"

Hakan shrugged. "Dunno. Always been that way."

"And the colors?"

"Don't know that, either," Hakan said. "My father gave some to me as a lad, as well as his father before him. There have always been six and were always painted those colors. It's just a child's toy. Something all proper kids should have."

"In *your* culture," Flann said.

Hakan smirked. "Aye, in a proper culture."

Flann was about to retort, but Emery glared at him, a flare of Empathy light in his eyes. Flann closed his mouth, scowling.

"Have you noticed the six colors are the same as the Rol'dan's?" Emery asked.

"Aye," Hakan said. "But colors are common enough. Adamah is obsessed with them. Their houses. Their clothes. Why wouldn't the stones be colorful too?"

Emery motioned toward the rock in Hakan's hand. "And, isn't it strange that this one responds to Nolan and Garrick, both of whom have Accuracy? And the other responds to only you."

Nolan gawked at the stone. No. It couldn't be, could it? Like Hakan said, the magic stones were only toys.

Garrick and Maska approached.

Maska bounded across the sharp rocks on his bare feet without flinching. A layer of sweat gleamed on his bare torso. His gaze flickered to Nolan and then to Hakan. His dark eyes dropped to the stones in their hands. "I have the way cleared. The inside has been relatively untouched."

"Very well," Emery said. "Let's see what you've found."

They followed Maska to the structure and entered a demolished corridor. The walls still stood, but the ceiling was nonexistent, allowing full view of the dark clouds above.

Nolan felt strange as they walked, as if he'd already been down the corridor a hundred times before. They turned at another hall, and the eerie familiarity sent a shudder down Nolan's spine. He'd never been here. Why did it feel so familiar?

They turned once more and walked through an archway. It opened into a magnificent hall with intricate ivy carvings chiseled into trim along its walls. Nolan froze as recognition hit him. It was true. He'd never been here, but he'd practically lived in a room like it.

"It's an exact replica to the Great Hall in Alton." Nolan ran a hand over his chin.

Emery raised a brow. "Is it now?"

The domed ceiling in Alton's hall held fine glass; this particular one had no glass remaining. Instead, birds roosted. Nolan scanned the floor and, just like Alton, darker stones were embedded in circular patterns across the floor, evenly spaced from the center of the room. As crumbling and broken as the rest of the city was, this room appeared to be untouched.

"Over here," Hakan said.

On the wall, where a gaudy tapestry hung in the Great Hall, an ornate grouping of words was carved into its surface. Nolan blinked. *The ancient text of Adamah? Here?*

"What's that?" Hakan asked.

"A language of sorts," Maska answered.

Hakan shook his head. "It's old, for sure. That there are Brim's words."

"Brim?" Maska asked, his dark brows rising ever so slightly.

"Aye, Brim. The god of light."

"Ah." Maska's brows resumed their unemotional position. "The old Adamah religion."

"Just because your kind doesn't believe in Brim," Hakan said, "doesn't mean he isn't real. Some say it's the sun where Brim lives. Some say it's in the night sky or in the flames. But most believe Brim is the source of our Shay powers."

"Or perhaps it is a tale for brutish clansmen."

"Brutish clansmen?" Hakan snorted. "You're the brutish clansman."

Hakan and Maska continued to argue while Nolan read the text. He was beginning to think they *liked* arguing. Nolan pressed fingers to his temples. *Crows, they make it hard to think.* Nolan knew this text, but it had been too long. *Think, Nolan, think.*

"Everyone knows who Brim is," Emery interrupted them, "not only Higherlanders. Though few actually believe in him anymore."

"Maybe this is where the people worshiped Brim," Hakan said, his eyes bright with excitement. "What a find!"

"Perhaps." Emery stepped closer, squinting up at the wall. "Jared, do you know anything about this ancient text?"

Jared frowned. "I'm sorry, sir. I can't read."

Nolan adjusted his spectacles. Time had worn the symbols. "I think it says, 'All come to the light, and the living power of Brim will shine through you.'"

All turned toward Nolan, several with their mouths slightly ajar.

"You can read it?" Emery asked.

He cleared his throat, blood rushing to his face. "I did study the ancient text."

"You taught yourself the ancient text?" Hakan said. "Blimey. Now that there is dry reading, for sure."

Emery smiled. "How old are you again?"

Nolan was about to answer, until he realized Emery was

joking. "I told you I like to read."

Emery chuckled then focused back at the wall. "So Hakan might be right. This seems to be a temple to Brim."

"Then perhaps the Great Hall in Alton was one as well," Nolan suggested.

"And come to mention it," Garrick added, "the throne room in Faylinn resembled this, too."

Emery wheeled and looked at Garrick. "You're right, Garrick."

Flann stepped forward. "And once again it has nothing to do with our problem. It's a ruin. Nothing more."

Nolan's mind drifted as the conversation continued. *Who would've believed reading those dusty old books would come in handy?* He stared at the words again. How did people worship Brim anyway?

The dark clouds shifted, casting a flicker of sunlight across the dirty stone floor. Like the tournament location, the sky was a bit clearer in the forest. More blue. Nolan lifted his hand and let a ray of sunlight spray across his palm. "Come to the light," the words said. Did both the Great Hall and this temple have ceilings to let in the sun? Both displayed the same symmetrical patterns on their domed ceilings: a small ring in the center, surrounded by six more iron rings spread in equal distance.

A bird landed on one of the rings, holding a worm in its beak. In the Great Hall, those places held expensive gems. But here, the spots were empty.

Nolan scanned the floor. Surely, stones like those would've been stolen long ago. His hand wandered to his bag, turning the translucent stone round and round in his palm—a habit now.

He thought more about the text:...*the living power of Brim will shine through you.* Why did it say *through* and not *on*? It was a strange way to state it. Maybe he misread it. It wasn't as if he was an expert on the language. He'd studied it out of boredom. Sunlight could never shine through a person. It only shone through things like the gems, or glass, or...

He stilled the stone. It wasn't as clear as glass, but it most definitely could allow light to shine through.

The voices stopped, and a pair of Empathy Shays passed over him. Both Flann and Emery must've noticed his tense silence.

"What is it, Nolan?" Emery asked.

"Maybe nothing." Nolan moved the stone toward the light. He nearly dropped it when the sunlight brightened. The clouds scurried away from the sun, like a roach from a flame. A blue symbol shone underneath the stone onto the floor: three Vs, one inside the other, with a solid circle nestled in the smallest of the Vs. It was the symbol of the Accuracy Rol'dan.

Nolan could scarcely breathe. Hakan joined Nolan, placing his stone in the light next to his. A second ray of sunlight burst through the clouds, and another symbol appeared on the ground. This time, it was an orange light consisting of three intersecting lines. It was the symbol of Perception.

"Blimey, Nolan! How'd you figure that out?" Hakan asked.

"I...I don't know," he stammered. "Just came to me."

"It explains quite a bit. Why your stone didn't work on me." Hakan barked a laugh. "It wasn't my Shay!"

"Two stones?" Garrick motioned to Hakan. "Where'd you get that?"

"Found it in the ruins."

Emery slapped Hakan on the shoulder. "They are different. Just like your magic stones."

Hakan grinned. "Aye! Like my magic stones!"

"Remarkable," Emery said. He knelt and touched the symbol of Accuracy. Blue light reflected on his hand.

Garrick knelt next to Emery, repeating the same action. Except as soon as the light touched him, he gasped and yanked his hand away.

"Garrick?" Emery asked.

Garrick studied his fingers. "I'm not sure. It felt...strange. Not painful, really. Just strange."

Nolan examined the ceiling and the intersecting bars. An idea came to him, one so obvious now. "I could be wrong," he said, "but I believe they go up there."

Emery followed Nolan's eyes. "Well then. Let's find out."

They went outside and searched the temple. It didn't take long to find the crumbling remains of a ladder, carved out of the stone, climbing the outside of the temple and disappearing over the top.

Maska took both stones and made the perilous climb. He swung and leaped so smoothly; Nolan marveled as he watched. Above, the clouds parted once again, and two beams of sunlight shot down. The stones were in place. A moment later, Maska descended at a speed that would've caused Nolan to plummet to his death. Maska dropped lightly to the ground.

Nolan didn't know quite what to expect when re-entering the temple. He assumed the circles of light would be bigger. What he didn't expect was how they fit with the darker stone circles embedded into the floor. Six dark circles circled the perimeter of the room; two were now filled with lighted Shay symbols.

He glanced up, looking at the two spots cradling each stone. They were fashioned, somehow, so they leaned ever so slightly to direct them to their prospective spots on the floor. There were four more Shay powers. Nolan ran his hand over his chin. But there were five spots left on the framework above. What significance was the centermost spot, where all the others branched from?

"Now what?" Hakan asked.

"Well, the text said to come to the light," Nolan said.

"I would call this coming," Hakan said.

"Not exactly." Garrick looked at his hand, as if remembering touching the light.

"Are you sure?" Emery said, answering Garrick's thoughts. "We have no idea what will happen."

Garrick displayed his crooked smile. "Well, there's one way to find out."

Everyone held their breaths when Garrick stepped into the light.

"I don't feel—" Garrick said. "Wait. There *is* something."

A cluster of lights twinkled into existence. What looked

to be white fireflies started at the ground and gently moved upward, winding in a shimmering cylinder around him.

"Garrick, you okay?" Hakan said anxiously.

Garrick didn't answer. The lights increased, and in a few breaths of time, they enveloped him like a translucent blanket. Garrick gasped, his head jerked back, and his feet lifted from the ground as a band of blue light encased him. Nolan covered his eyes from the blinding radiance. It dimmed, and Garrick drifted slowly down, his feet touching the ground lightly. The pinpricks of light ended their dance as Garrick's head rolled forward, the blue of his Shay fading from his eyes. He staggered, and Emery caught him.

"Are you okay?" Emery asked.

Garrick smiled wide. "Oh, yes."

Chapter Twenty-One

After Garrick stepped from the light, both Hakan and Nolan took a turn. It was unlike anything Nolan had ever felt. More intense than coming into his Shay power.

Standing in the light focused his Shay, making it more powerful. He also didn't feel trapped by the stone's pull; the anxiousness was completely gone.

When they returned to the village that day, they realized finding the first two stones caused a series of problems. The illness spread to others in the village, those with different Shays from the ones they'd found. Somehow, finding Perception and Accuracy had awakened a longing they didn't know they had, until now.

Over the next days, Nolan watched the progress of those taking the light. He found it interesting, and he jotted down differences, trying to note how each person acted when it was their turn. Alec had given him some parchment and ink. By the sly expression on his friend's face, Nolan wasn't about to ask Alec where he'd found it. The supplies *did* look suspiciously like the ones he'd left back in Alton.

Emery meandered through the temple silently. He would step into the different Shay lights, his hands outstretched as if sunning himself. At first, Nolan thought he simply liked the sunshine. Nolan had never seen it so bright; the dark clouds seemed to give way. But as hours passed, Emery's mood got worse. Much worse.

Nolan left his work to fetch Garrick in the village. When they returned, several villagers lingered in the temple, taking turns as they stood in the light. Emery sat on the floor, leaning against the far wall. His hair hung in strings as he rested his face on his knees.

"How long has he been like this?" Garrick asked.

"Hours," Nolan said.

"Emery?" Garrick squatted next to him.

Emery slowly raised his face, revealing dark circles under his brown eyes. "Ah, Garrick. Nice of you to drop in."

"Why don't you come home and get some rest?"

"I will. But not yet."

Emery's head dropped; apparently he was done talking. Nolan tapped Garrick on the shoulder and motioned him away.

"Maybe it's the Empathy stone," Nolan whispered.

"Of course it is," Garrick said. "The Accuracy stone did a number on both of us. It was terrible for Hakan as well."

"Yes, that's true," Nolan said. "But Hakan practically stood on top of the stone at his worst. You saw Flann this morning, didn't you?"

"He's feeling the stone's call as well."

"But not like this."

"Maybe it's because Emery's power is stronger than Flann's," Garrick suggested. "I was much more foul-tempered than most of the other Accuracy users in the village."

"But once again, that's when I brought the stone into camp. Emery has been here the whole time. And unless someone is bringing that stone here—"

"No one is bringing the stone." Emery stood in the light again, this time in Accuracy. Blue lines striped the pain-filled scowl on his face.

"What in Darkness is he doing?" Garrick said.

"He's been at it all morning," Nolan said. "Not sure why, though."

"The more I stand in the light," Emery said, "the more the Empathy stone calls to me."

Nolan gawked. Why would he do such a thing? Feeling the

call of the stone was horrible. It was one of the worst things Nolan had ever experienced.

"The fool," Garrick muttered under his breath.

Emery smiled weakly.

"Why?" Garrick asked.

Emery stepped from the light, his shoulders slumped. "I have a reason."

"Which is?"

"We must find the remaining stones."

"Of course we must," Garrick said. "It doesn't mean you need to torture yourself."

Emery's eyes searched theirs. He looked older, more tired. "It's helping me focus on its location. I'm leaving tonight."

"Oh no, you're not!" Garrick said. "Every time you leave, you get into trouble."

Emery put a hand on Garrick's shoulder. "It shouldn't take too long. A few weeks. Maybe a month."

"Very well," Garrick said, "I'll get my things together and—"

"No," Emery said. "I'm going alone."

"Over my rotting corpse, you are," Garrick said. "You aren't in any shape to be traveling anywhere, especially alone."

"I'll be fine. You need to watch the village."

"The village will survive without me," Garrick said. "We'll take Maska, Hakan, and Flann with us." He snapped his fingers. "And Megan as well."

Emery's head whipped up. "Not Megan."

"We'll need a Healer." Garrick glared at him in challenge.

Emery sighed. "Megan will be fine."

"It's settled then," Garrick said. "And Vikas can come for Speed."

"Who's Vikas?" Nolan asked.

Garrick smiled. "A friend."

A whoosh of air hit Nolan, parting his hair and sending a shiver down his spine. He didn't need to turn around to know who arrived.

"Hey, Alec." Nolan turned and Alec grinned.

Alec's eyes darted to Emery. "What's wrong with him?"

"It's the stone."

"Ah," he said. "A lot of that going around."

"How are you taking it?"

"Pretty good," Alec said, still grinning far too much. "I can feel a little something...maybe. But it's hard to tell if it's just me getting used to this power, or if it's the call from the Speed stone." His smiled faded. "Now, Rylan...He's grumpy."

"Rylan?"

Alec nodded. "But at least he's found a way to get it out of his system."

"Such as?"

"Come. See for yourself."

Nolan glanced at Garrick and Emery, who were deep in conversation planning for their trip. He waved a brief farewell and left the temple, walking through the ruins. A group had gathered near a pile of rubble—where the city walls must've stood. They faced a tree-covered slope overlooking the distant mountain range.

As they approached, Rylan loaded a stone, bigger than his head, onto a thick, braided sling. He slipped his wrist through a loop and grabbed the other end of the strap. The onlookers backed away. He whipped twice and released, sending the stone rushing over the treetops. The sound of snapping and popping branches faded as the stone disappeared into the distant forest below.

Daren bounced on the balls of his feet. His good humor had intensified since he had stepped into the Perception stone's light. And by the looks of it, he enjoyed testing the extent of his refortified powers.

"Fantastic!" Daren said, his eyes glowing orange. "You almost got it in the pond."

Alec craned his neck. "There's a pond down there?"

Rylan loaded his sling with an even bigger chunk of the ruined wall. "So, what do you think, Nolan? Would this be an example of a catapult?"

Nolan laughed. "Not bad. Although, it might be closer to a trebuchet."

Rylan's head whipped toward him, his eyes blazing red. "Trebuchet?"

"A catapult has more of a basket, where a trebuchet uses…" Nolan's voice drifted away; Rylan wasn't listening anymore.

Rylan growled as he launched another rock into the forest. He *was* crabby.

"Ha!" Daren cheered. "Bull's-eye. In the water."

Nolan listened, unable to hear the splash. He shivered. A whole battalion of sling-yielding Strength users would be a dangerous thing.

Nolan pulled his own sling out and stood next to Rylan. He aimed for tree trunks and then specific knots on the trees. After a while, Alec added to the game by tossing stones into the air. With a loud crack, Nolan hit those too.

Rylan smiled for first time. "Crows, Nolan. Did you miss any?"

"Of course not." Nolan rubbed his throbbing arm, trying to make his muscle stop twitching. "I'm done."

Rylan tossed another boulder. "So soon?"

"My muscles aren't made of iron, like yours," Nolan said. "Besides, I've embarrassed you long enough. You can't hit the side of a tree."

Rylan forced a laugh. He was *trying* to be in a good mood. He flung another rock, this time following its progress with a glare. At least he was taking it out on the rock.

"It's getting late," Nolan said. "We should get to the village before it gets too dark. Takes a good two hours to get there."

Alec grinned. "What? It only takes a few seconds."

Rylan punched him on the arm, and Alec grabbed it, grimacing. "Easy man, you're going to break something."

"And would that be so bad?" Daren said. "You could go visit Taryn for some healing."

Alec's face flushed. He glanced around, as if checking to see who'd heard. He glared at Daren, a sly smile spreading across his face as his eyes flared golden-yellow. "Now…where is that pond?"

In mid-laugh, Daren disappeared, his scream marking his

progress down the hill.

Rylan jumped down the rocky ledge to follow. He paused and looked back to Nolan. "You coming?"

"Nah," Nolan answered. "Best to get away while I can. Besides, I need to go talk to Emery."

"All right," he said. "See you at the village!"

Nolan waved and headed back to the temple. The other villagers had cleared, probably wanting to get home in good time. The sun lowered enough so the Shay lights disappeared from the floor. A few torches flickered in the dimming light, illuminating two people in the room. Emery lay covered with a blanket, his eyes closed as if sleeping. Megan stroked his dark hair.

Nolan stopped mid-stride, jealousy spiking. *But why be jealous? Emery is way older than her. Like a father, isn't he?*

Megan stood and stretched as Nolan walked closer to the pair. "He's refused to go back," she whispered, her voice echoing in the empty room. "He wants to sleep here."

"Here? Is it dangerous?"

She motioned toward the torches. "Not any more than when we camped."

"Are you staying?"

"I suppose so," she said, her eyelids drooping.

"You should get some sleep. Aren't you traveling with Garrick and Emery tomorrow morning?"

"I am," she said. "Crows, I feel like I just got home."

"I can stay with him," Nolan offered. He had nothing better to do.

Her face lightened. "Really, Nolan? That would be great. I still have to pack."

"Are you going to be okay...tomorrow, that is?"

"I'll be safe." She glanced at Emery. "I have no idea how long we'll be gone. I don't mind helping, but I had hoped..." She stole a quick glance at Nolan. "It would've been nice to spend more time here."

Megan met Nolan's eyes and held them. "You'll see us off in the morning?"

He shifted, suddenly feeling awkward. "Of course."

"Thanks again, Nolan." She hesitated, as if she wanted to say more, before turning and stepping out the doorway.

After she left, Nolan stared at the entrance where she'd disappeared. He wished he could read her emotions. His experience with girls was pathetic, to say the very least. Most of his interactions had been with his aunt and his cousin, and all his free time had been on the fishing boat at sea. The only time he had the opportunity with any girl was when Duke Ragnall's wife threw herself at him. And as pretty as Mikayla was, Nolan wasn't stupid.

An Empathy Shay touched Nolan. He whirled, finding Emery's glowing eyes resting on him.

Nolan flushed. "She was tired. I told her to go home."

Emery propped up on his elbow and ran a hand through his dirty hair. "Very thoughtful of you."

Nolan joined him, and they sat in silence.

"I must admit," Emery said, breaking the stillness, "I'm surprised someone has finally won her over."

Won her over? Nolan straightened.

"She is a beautiful and wonderful girl." Emery released a long sigh. "One of the most caring minds I've ever seen—and I've sensed a lot of minds."

Emery kept rambling about Megan. About when they met. About how pretty her hair was—which Nolan agreed. After a while, a revelation came to Nolan. *Crows! Does Emery like Megan?*

"Emery, if I'm getting in the way—"

"With what?" Emery's brows rose. "Megan and I? You do realize I'm old enough to be her father."

"Yeah, I know, but—"

He laughed. "Don't worry. Any chance between us is nonexistent. I wouldn't inflict my burdens on her." His eyes dropped to the floor. "Or any other woman, for that matter."

What in Brim's light was he talking about? Certainly he had a lot of responsibilities, but not enough to keep him from having a wife.

Emery studied Nolan. "I can feel your confusion, friend. I should explain. It's just…well, everyone has different ways to deal with hardships. Some turn to depression. Others withdraw, as I have. And some turn to violence, such as your brother."

"Kael?" Nolan's stomach tightened. "What does Kael have to do with this?"

He met Nolan's eyes. "I've wanted to speak to you on this subject for some time now."

Nolan stared at Emery, confused.

"If you give me a moment to explain." Emery inhaled and released it slowly. "I'm sure you know of the king's ability to control emotions."

Nolan paused before answering. "Like how you controlled me in the tower?"

"Oh, no," Emery said. "I can only push feelings that are already there. King Alcandor is much more powerful. He can alter someone's wishes completely, such as change your desire from Megan to Hakan."

Nolan laughed, but he stopped when he saw Emery's serious expression.

"Very early in my service, I was chosen. My power of Empathy is strong, and Alcandor could sense it immediately. Alcandor favors those with Empathy above all other Shay users. He claims they are the most…" He scowled. "They are the most talented of lovers."

Blood left Nolan's face.

Emery looked Nolan in the eye. "King Alcandor would call me regularly to his bed chamber."

"You mean…" Nolan paused. "He would…force you to his bed?"

"He never forced me," Emery said. "As I said, he has the talent to bend one's will. Unfortunately, he favored me more than any of the others. Day after day, he summoned me, and I would pleasure him, as he commanded me to.

"Only after I'd left his presence did my true will return." He lowered his face and drew undefined shapes in the dirt on the floor.

Nolan turned, unable to look at him as mental pictures flooded his mind. He took deep breaths, trying to calm the knot twisting his insides.

"You have no idea what it's like to be so out of control," Emery continued. "And then, when the forced emotions fade, memories remain. You recall everything, but can change nothing. To this day, I can't dislodge those images from my mind. So you see, I'm damaged. I will never subject a woman to my past. I will never marry."

Nolan's throat went dry. Emery had served in the Rol'dan for how long? He did a quick calculation, and his stomach turned. Emery had been under Alcandor for nearly seventeen years—as long as Nolan had been alive! The king held special powers, but he hadn't expected this. Did the king do this to all his Rol'dan?

Nolan sucked in a breath and his body tensed. *Kael.*

"Your brother was well into the king's ways when I left Faylinn," Emery said. "The king chose him early, like me. His Shay is very strong. Those with the most powerful Shays attract Alcandor the most. After I left the Rol'dan, the king probably focused more attention on him. He'd been made general, after all."

Nolan swallowed hard, remembering how violently Kael had beaten Emery. Did Kael blame Emery for his current situation? How much of his brother's anger was fueled by the king's abuse? The insults. The violence. It explained more than Nolan wished it did, especially how much Kael had changed. He'd been so angry at Kael for all his arrogance and self-righteous indignation. But now, he realized Kael was just another victim of the king. His frustration and disgust for his brother washed away in a rush. *Poor Kael.*

"Does the king only desire men?" Nolan asked, his voice shaking.

"No. It's the power to control. Whether man or woman, it makes little difference to him. Alec would be a prime target as well," Emery continued. "Bringing the boy along saved him from a far worse fate than becoming a Rol'dan. And from the strength of your power, determination, and leadership, you chose the right path to hide your Shay. The king would've favored you...very much."

Me? Favored me? His stomach lurched. Then the rest of what Emery had said came to focus. *Strength? Determination? Leadership?* He snorted. Emery didn't know what he was talking about.

Emery studied Nolan, sorrow embedded in his brown eyes. "There are qualities in you. Not many have been able to resist my influence. And you convinced not just one, but three people to leave the Rol'dan."

"I only spoke with Alec. I had nothing to do with the others."

"Yet when Alec mentioned you, they followed," Emery said.

Nolan shook his head. "I didn't do anything."

Emery put a hand on Nolan's shoulder. "Many times, the most humble people make the greatest leaders of all."

They remained in silence as the sunlight faded completely. Emery reclined on the floor and pulled the blanket to his chin. After several minutes, Emery's chest rose and fell with his steady breathing. Nolan, however, couldn't sleep.

He drifted off, and horrific images of Kael forced into submission clouded his dreams. Then, without warning, Kael would transform into Emery. Then Alec. Then Megan. Then himself.

Nolan gasped and sat up. Morning. A jolt shot through his shoulder, probably from slinging and sleeping on the hard floor.

The new sun peered through the top of the temple, casting colorful Shay lights on the floor. The circle, which held the blue Accuracy light, flickered softly with each passing cloud.

Emery had already woken and stood under the orange light of Perception. His shoulders were slumped, his eyes closed, and his face contorted into an expression of agony.

"Emery?"

His eyes fluttered open. "Ah, you're awake. I'd ask how

you slept, but your restless night already told me; I felt torment coming from your dreams." He furrowed his brows. "I'm sorry."

"It's okay," Nolan said. "I'm glad you told me. Though I don't know what to think of the Rol'dan anymore."

"It does change one's opinion of them, even if slightly. And it makes it much more difficult to consider destroying them," Emery said. "That's why we need to defeat the king before others fall into the same trap. The Rol'dan make you forget who you are. Being one of them inflames everything depraved about yourself you didn't know existed."

"And the stones might help, somehow?"

Emery sighed. "I don't know. However, the happiness of our village is as stake without them. And if we can restore our full abilities, we might have a better chance to defeat him... somehow."

*Defeat the king and...*A spark of hope flared in Nolan. *Perhaps we can save Kael after all.*

Emery stretched and walked toward the entrance with slow, dragging steps. "I need to return. Garrick is probably fuming." He hesitated. "Are you coming? Or perhaps you might like a few minutes alone?"

"A moment would be great."

"If you don't make it back in time for us to leave—"

"I will," Nolan interrupted, feeling a little embarrassed. "I promised Megan—"

"Ah, yes," Emery said, smiling. "Then I'll see you shortly."

After Emery left, Nolan paced, his thoughts lingering on Kael and Emery's dark past. Then he remembered Megan, and the fact Emery said she liked him.

Nolan's daydreaming ended abruptly when he considered the stones. What if they were calling—not only to the village— but to the Rol'dan as well? The stones could be their salvation and ruin at the same time. *What if they lead the Rol'dan here?* His chest tightened. No wonder Emery was pushing himself in the light. They needed to find the stones first!

Nolan stepped into the light of Accuracy, letting the blue

lines flicker across his skin. He didn't *need* the light anymore—
not since he first stepped into it—but he liked it anyway. His
Shay swelled, and he savored the pulsing power.

Reluctantly, Nolan left the light. He needed to return
before Emery and Megan departed. He flung his pack over his
shoulder, walked past the light of Perception, and paused.

Curious, he held his hand in the light; the orange symbol
illuminated his palm. Wiggling his fingers, his Shay spoke to
this foreign beam. It felt different than Accuracy. Not bad, just
different. A comfortable, warm feeling. Like an old friend.

The ancient text had said each light was a part of Brim.
Were they bound to each other? Yes, of course. Why else
would Emery's stone call louder when he stepped into the light
of these?

Nolan glanced around. Finding himself alone, he stepped
into the orange light. It tugged inside him. He waited, letting
the unfamiliar glow of Perception pulse deep within. Just
when he was about to step out of the glow, the tips of his
fingers twitched, and his heartbeat quickened. Tingling spread
through his palms.

Nolan clenched his fists, tremors overtaking his arms. He
threw back his head and screamed as the light of Perception
exploded inside him. Lights and sensations drifted into
nothingness, and the temple dimmed before his eyes.

Chapter Twenty-Two

Nolan stepped into a sea of white mist. It curled around his legs, filled his vision. Mind racing, he pushed aside one thick cloud only to have another take its place. It covered reality in a formless shroud.

He walked faster, unable to see his feet, as he searched the infernal fog. With each step, his heart jolted: Would the next step be off a cliff? Would another step equal death? Yet he pressed on, searching. The fog closed in.

Finally, in the distance, he saw a shape. With breathless excitement, Nolan ran toward it and stopped abruptly. A man towered out of the whiteness, as tall as a living monument, standing like Brim himself.

Nolan closed his eyes and pressed the heels of his hands into his sockets. When he opened them, the man was still there.

Nearly twice Nolan's size, the man's muscled arms crossed over a massive, plate-covered chest. His armor glistened pure gold and shimmered with hidden light. The bracers strapped to his thick arms, and the intricately decorated greaves on his legs, appeared to be gold as well. He looked down at Nolan. Tight, brown curls hung down his face, framing his square jaw. But the most unnerving feature of the man was his eyes: Where normal eye sockets should've been, white light shone.

Nolan swallowed. "Are you…?"

"Brim?" His voice rumbled. "No."

"What are you?" Nolan asked in a breathless whisper.

He blinked slowly, studying Nolan with his light-filled

eyes. "I would ask the same of you."

Nolan jerked back. "Me? I'm only a human."

"Are you?" One side of the warrior's mouth turned up.

Despair filled Nolan. "Crows! Did I...die?"

The warrior chuckled. "You are not dead."

Both relief and confusion flooded him. If he hadn't died, what happened? And if this wasn't Brim, then who—or what—was he?

Nolan gasped as realization hit him. Alec had described him: a warrior glowing with light. And Jared had given him a name. "You're a Guardian!"

The smile left the warrior's face. "No. Not anymore."

The mist circled, surrounding them in a white tunnel. Steadily, it increased in speed, so much so it appeared solid and whole.

"What's happening?" Nolan asked.

"Our time is up."

"Time? What time?"

"You must return."

The tunnel increased its speed like a tornado as it darkened from white to gray.

"Please. Who are you? Do you have a name?"

The warrior took a step back into the swirling tunnel. "I am Greer."

He disappeared, and with him his light, leaving Nolan in darkness. Then faint voices pierced through it. They were familiar somehow, and grew louder and clearer.

"Any change?"

"No."

"You can't do anything?"

"I've tried," a woman's voice said. "There's nothing physically wrong with him."

Nolan gasped, filling his lungs with air. The overpowering smell of bacon surrounded him. His eyes flew open, but everything was unfocused. He closed them quickly as the blurry images swam.

A soft, warm bed hugged him. Opening his eyes again,

several people stood over him, but he couldn't see clearly enough to recognize them.

"He's awake!"

"Thank Brim."

Nolan opened his mouth to speak, but it was dry as wool.

"Relax, Nolan," Alec's familiar voice said. "Here, have a drink."

Alec placed an arm under Nolan's shoulders and pulled him up, pouring a small amount of water down his dry throat. Nolan gagged. It tasted like dirt.

"What happened?" Nolan finally croaked.

"Don't know," Alec said. "Daren heard your scream from the temple nearly three days ago. At first we thought you were dead. Your heart was still beating, but you only took a breath every minute or two."

Three days? No. That's impossible.

"We've been trying to figure out what happened," Alec continued.

Nolan closed his eyes, trying to remember. The last thing he recalled was white mist and the Guardian. He exhaled, pushing back the rising panic. No. It was a dream. The Guardian had obviously been a dream.

"We should send someone out to tell Emery and the others you're all right," Alec said. "They left the day after we found you, although it took a lot of convincing to get Megan to move."

"I need my spectacles," Nolan said.

"Your spectacles?" Alec said, a strange tone to his voice.

"I can't see a—" Nolan touched his nose, but the frames were already resting there. His heart raced so strongly, he could hear it hammering in his ears.

"Nolan, what's wrong?"

"I...I can't see. Where am I?" He flung the covers aside and tried to stand.

"Sit," Alec said. "You're at my place. Taryn, can you look at his eyes?"

"I've already looked at him at least twenty times," she

said. "Like I said before, there's nothing wrong with him."

Nolan slumped. His eyes were poor before, but now he was practically blind! "I need to go."

"You're not going anywhere," Alec said. "At least, not until we know you're all right. Crows, man. We thought you died."

Nolan shook his head. It felt funny. "I just want to go."

"Bonty's been cooking," Taryn said. "At least eat."

A door opened as if on cue, and the large silhouette of Bonty entered, followed by the smell of bacon and eggs.

Nolan's stomach lurched. "No. Not now."

"All right, love." Bonty patted Nolan on the arm and slid the tray onto the nearby table. "I'll leave it here in case you change your mind."

A wave of nausea swept over him. He jumped to his feet, pushing past Alec toward the door. "I need air."

"I really don't think that's a good idea," Alec called.

The sunlight hit Nolan's face like a torch; he slammed his eyes shut.

"He shouldn't be by himself," Taryn said.

"I'll give him a few minutes, then follow him," Alec replied.

Nolan cracked his eyes, looking for Alec and Taryn. He started. He was alone.

"What a shame," Bonty said. "He didn't eat a thing."

"He said he wasn't feeling well."

"He might just need some time."

"I'll bring him something later today," Bonty said. "Poor dear."

A baby cried...somewhere. Then birds chirped, as if they sat on Nolan's shoulder. *Too loud!* He clamped his hands over his ears, but it made little difference. So many noises jumbled together. It was hard to sort out. *What in Darkness is happening to me?*

Blurred trees swayed before his vision. He ripped off the useless spectacles and gasped. In breathtaking, sudden clarity, everything came into perfect focus. He could make out fine lines on the bark of a nearby tree. A parade of ants marched along the branch. And in the practice field, a group of people pulled back their bows. He could even hear the twang of their bowstrings.

Then Nolan felt his Shay power emerging; however, it wasn't the Shay he knew.

Chapter Twenty-Three

Nolan lost track of time. He couldn't sleep—sounds were too loud. He couldn't eat—food tasted worse than dung, not that he had the motivation to eat anyway. Sunlight finally didn't blind him, not that he wanted to emerge from his hole. He'd finally found a place he could show his Accuracy after two years of being a hermit. And now...He took a long, shallow breath. And now he had to hide again.

Nolan held the mirror, watching orange light flare in his eyes. He focused and listened to a nest of birds twittering outside. Pulling back, the orange light faded under the surface of his normal blue. He could hear the birds, though not as clearly as before. He ran a shaking hand over his chin. Learning control was exhausting.

He switched to Accuracy, feeling its familiar presence take hold. The orange light changed to sapphire blue. Summoning Perception again and leaving Accuracy in place, his eyes turned from blue to a strange gray with hints of blue and orange flaring around the pupils. Two powers at the same time? Crows. What was he going to do?

When he'd hidden Accuracy, his naturally blue eyes covered his mistakes. The orange light wouldn't cooperate that way.

He focused on Perception again and, instead of the birds, he listened to the world outside his self-imprisonment. People carried out day-to-day activities, oblivious to Nolan's struggles. Then he heard footsteps, closer than the others. He put down the mirror, focusing on hushed conversation approaching.

"Do you think he'll talk to us?" Taryn's voice said.

"He'd better," Alec's voice replied. "He's locked himself in there for a week now. I'll get him out of that house if I have to drag him out."

Nolan hid both Shays and took a slow, calming breath. He waited for the knock before opening the door.

"Hey there, Nolan," Alec said a bit too casually. "Mind if we come in?"

Nolan forced a smile and motioned for them to enter. The combined smell of metal and lavender followed them.

"We haven't seen you for a while," Taryn said.

A scraping sound drew Nolan's attention. She rubbed a trim of fabric on her dress.

"How are your eyes doing?" Alec asked.

"Better," Nolan said, leaving out the fact his vision was now perfect.

Taryn studied Nolan. "You don't look so good. Have you eaten anything?"

"A little," he admitted. "I'll try and do better."

A satisfied smile played across her face.

"Bonty can bring you something." Alec said. "I'm spoiled with her staying so close. She cooks for us every day."

"No, thanks. Unless it's some fruit or something."

Nolan waited for them to speak, to see how Alec would "drag him out of here."

Alec shifted his weight to his other leg. "I've been thinking…"

"Yes?"

"What do you think about learning to fight? You know, just some sparring or something. Nothing too intense."

"Spar?"

"You know. With swords."

Nolan laughed. "So as soon as I'm feeling better, you want to kill me?"

"Oh, come now." Alec smirked. "I'll go easy on you."

Nolan was sick of wallowing behind closed doors, sick

of staring at his pathetic reflection while practicing his lying again. He'd have to come out eventually, otherwise people would start thinking he was crazy. He'd also gotten a decent grasp on hiding his new Perception, shoving it away in the same internal box with his Accuracy Shay. He straightened and inhaled deeply. "Sure. Why not," he answered. He needed a distraction. Getting thumped by Alec would more than accomplish that goal.

***

Alec lied; he hadn't gone easy on Nolan at all.

It was his own fault, though. Nolan had taken to sword fighting quite well.

Defense movements had structure and order. An opponent moved, and a set of responses followed. Nolan quickly memorized the series of blocks and strokes Alec taught him, then, of course, he let his Accuracy execute them with perfection.

"Well done," Alec said as they finished another round with wooden practice swords. "I haven't seen anyone catch on to basic defensive moves so quickly. But, I suppose, cheating does make things easier." Alec mopped his face with a cloth.

"Cheating?" Nolan put a hand to his chest.

"Of course." Alec grinned. "*I'm* not the one using my Shay power, am I?"

He pushed back a smile. "I can't shut it off if I tried. In the manor, I'd use it for writing, hours at a time. I'm sure your Speed flairs now and then. Maybe when you're working at the forge, or sparring with your father or me?"

Alec laughed. "Don't tell me that! I thought I'd finally bested my father because of my skills alone." He snatched two swords from the grass and tossed one at Nolan.

Nolan caught it and shot Alec a skeptical glance.

"It's time we used steel."

Taryn, who had been sitting in the grass watching, groaned. Up until now, she'd only healed a few bruises from the wooden swords, or soothed the sore muscles from Nolan's shoulders after he could hardly move.

"Now don't worry. I'll keep it safe," Alec said.

"I'll believe it when I see it," Taryn said.

Alec lunged.

Nolan blocked, and the clang of swords rang out.

"Nice one!" Alec said. He lunged again.

Nolan pushed back panic, concentrating on the fight. This was real swordplay, not the banging of two sticks against each other. It was metal upon metal, singing a song of real combat.

It was exciting and a bit scary.

His panic died as he concentrated on the moves. Alec tried to trick him, and Nolan compensated.

After a while, Nolan noticed others gathering. Daren. Rylan. And quite of few others he didn't know by name. Nolan's body dripped with sticky sweat, and he gasped so hard he struggled to breathe.

"Giving up yet?" Alec taunted. A huge grin spread across his face. He was much more used to this sort of thing than Nolan.

"Not a chance," Nolan said between gasps. Alec wouldn't take him that easily.

Several observers drifted away. Nolan figured they'd gotten bored. But when he saw a larger crowd headed toward the central hall, he flared a bit of Perception, just enough to hear what was going on. Nolan dodged another strike then stopped mid-fight at hearing the name of Emery mentioned. Sudden, fiery pain shot through his arm.

"Crows, Nolan," Alec said, throwing down his sword.

A deep gash cut between his wrist and elbow, and bright crimson blood gushed from the wound. Nolan pressed his arm against his chest trying to stop the flow, covering his shirt in red.

"Why didn't you block?" Alec said. "Taryn!"

Taryn's eyes opened wide. "You said you'd be safe."

"He was safe," Nolan said. "I was distracted; it's my fault."

"By Brim," Alec said. "It's a bad one."

Nolan's head swam as the red on his shirt spread. Taryn

laid her trembling hands on Nolan—one on either side of the angry wound. Her head flew back, and she choked on a scream.

Healing coursed through Nolan's body, and he watched helplessly as her wound opened and his closed. Her arms shook as she took in the gash. When her wound healed completely, she fell to her knees in the blood-soaked grass.

"I'm so sorry." Nolan's chest tightened and guilt washed over him. *So stupid! How could I be so careless?*

With a dazed expression, she nodded. "It's what I'm supposed to do, right?"

Alec grabbed Nolan's wrist and wiped the blood with his hand. "Crows, you're amazing, Taryn. You can barely see it. I wish you'd been around when I fought my father all those years. Maybe my body wouldn't be so wrecked."

"Your body is fine," Taryn said, still trembling. She froze as color rushed to her cheeks.

Alec stared as if he hadn't quite heard her correctly.

Nolan's hearing tuned to the distant conversation again. He wanted to flare Perception to hear better, but he wasn't so sure he could do it without giving it away. He looked at Taryn and Alec. The pink tint to both of their faces was enough excuse to go.

"Well, I should clean myself up. I'm a mess." He put a hand on Taryn's shoulder, guilt prodding his gut. "Um...thanks."

She nodded, though her eyes remained fixed on the ground.

Alec tore his eyes from Taryn. "You okay?"

"Don't worry. It's my fault. I'll pay attention next time." He took a few steps. "Tomorrow?"

Alec relaxed. "Sounds good."

Nolan made his way toward the conversation, making sure no one watched before increasing his Perception.

"Where are they?" an older voice said. It sounded like it could be Jared.

"They're going west for the Strength stone. Maska feels its pull greatly, so we've decided to continue and collect them both before coming back," said another voice Nolan didn't recognize.

"Where's the Empathy stone now?"

"They kept it with them. It gives Emery and Flann comfort, at least enough to continue on."

Nolan rounded a corner and saw the conversation. Jared stood next to a middle-aged man, slight of build and short of stature. His dark-blond hair grayed at his temples. His posture was erect. They both quieted as Nolan approach. The stranger seemed not to notice Nolan's gory appearance. His piercing hazel eyes met Nolan's.

"Nolan?" Jared said. "What happened to you? Are you hurt?"

"I'm fine," Nolan said. "Just sparring with Alec."

The stranger chuckled. "You need more practice." He offered his hand. "Nolan, it's good to meet you. We were introduced briefly, but you were unresponsive at the time."

Nolan shook his hand, cringing when he'd bloodied the man's palm. It didn't seem to bother him.

"I'm Vikas," he said. "I was just telling Jared we found the Empathy stone past Numa, half buried in a field of grass. If it weren't for Emery and Flann, I would've thought it was only another stone lying there."

Nolan shifted uncomfortably. "How is…everyone?"

"Fine," Vikas said. "We were glad to hear you'd recovered."

Nolan's head swam, his vision fuzzy. He needed to lie down. "Give them all my greetings."

Vikas nodded. "That, I will." He turned back to his conversation with Jared.

Nolan headed home, still listening in as he stumbled along. It would be another month before Emery's group returned.

Nolan crossed the village, catching the horrified stares of several people. Finally, he opened the door of his house, and a wave of exhaustion fell over him. He crumpled onto his bed, falling asleep almost instantly.

His dreams were littered with Megan, then of a light-filled warrior standing over a pile of stones. Nolan dropped to his knees, tossing stones to the side. Searching. The rocks thudded against the wall, over and over again. And even when he held one in his hand, the noise continued. The stone glowed, this time with a light so white it blinded him. He covered his face as the light swelled. When it completely enveloped him, Nolan awoke. His clothes were soaked in perspiration and caked with dried blood.

The pounding continued.

"Nolan!" Alec called from the door.

Nolan rose, staggering. Morning sunlight hung low in the eastern sky, framing Alec in the open doorway.

"I was wondering where you were," Alec stammered. "We were supposed to meet for practice. Crows, you look terrible."

Nolan examined himself. He *did* look terrible. "I guess I fell asleep."

The scar on Alec's cheek puckered as he frowned. "You all right?"

"I'm fine," Nolan lied. He was a little weak, and he hadn't felt right since coming into Perception. He motioned Alec inside. Nolan stripped off his clothes; dried blood crusted his torso and legs. Old sweat coated his body.

Alec shook his head. "You need a swim."

Nolan slipped on a clean pair of breeches and carried his boots and tunic. They left and threaded through town. Nolan still got odd stares, but not as many as the day before. A few people even waved as they passed.

The air cooled his skin; the end of summer approached. The gentle breeze sent shivers over his bare chest as they continued to the lake at the edge of town.

Alec kicked off his boots and his shirt and dove in, gasping loudly as he hit the cold water. Nolan hesitated and then followed his lead.

Nolan's increased sense of touch amplified each drop on his skin. It bordered on maddening. He relaxed into the sensations and allowed his Perception to fully take hold.

Underwater, plants, fish, and other vegetation became crisp and clear in astonishing details. Nolan knew how to swim well. He'd lived near the sea most of his life, and he could hold his breath a long while. Gray stones littered the lake bottom, some as big as his head and others not quite as small as sand. Vegetation poked out in clumps, swaying as he swam past. A young catfish glided behind a plant, failing miserably at hiding from Nolan's Perception. When the burning in his lungs couldn't take it any longer, he pushed upward, breaking through the surface in time to see Alec diving in again.

Nolan took a breath and went back under, letting the sensations take over. He could hear Alec's smooth, even strokes coming toward him. When he got close, Nolan hid his Perception Shay.

They both surfaced.

Alec did an exaggerated shudder. "Crows, it's cold."

"Tell me about it."

Alec circled Nolan with even strokes, his face submerged except for his eyes. It reminded Nolan of the sharks that used to circle the boats. Nolan saw the glint of golden-yellow light flare in Alec's eyes in just enough time to hold his breath as Alec yanked him under.

The water rushed by in a current so fast Nolan's Perception couldn't see. Alec slowed his pace and they both popped above the water, gasping and laughing at the same time.

Alec's laughter stopped. He stared, an odd expression on his face. "For a second there, your eyes looked brown."

"That would be a good trick," Nolan said. And before Alec could comment any further, Nolan pushed Alec's head under.

After being thoroughly soaked and having the grime washed away, they stumbled to the shore and collapsed on the grass.

Alec pulled on his boots, his blond curls now dark and plastered to his head. Nolan had spied Alec once without his shirt in the Alton armory, but he'd almost forgotten how scarred the boy was. Even on hot days, Alec kept his tunic on. Up close, Nolan could make out all the smaller, faded scars too. Dear Brim. What had he been through? It made Nolan mad at Kardos all over again.

"How about some swords?" Alec asked.

"Ah ha! So that's your plan. Wear me out so you can beat me easier."

Alec stood, whacking Nolan with his tunic. "Nah. I can beat you without that."

"Sounds like a challenge."

An evil gleam hinted in his eyes. "More like a fact."

It was well into evening when hunger and exhaustion brought them home. Nolan ached in places he never knew he could.

"It was a good day," Alec said as they walked slowly toward the armory.

"Are you getting bored fighting me?"

Alec stopped. "Bored? Why do you say that?"

"Come now. I know you have to hold back. You'd probably rather fight someone a bit more challenging."

"I did get a chance to fight Vikas a few weeks ago before he left with Emery. He came to train me and the other Speed users." He grinned. "I surprised him."

Nolan had only met the man briefly, but he looked tough as iron.

Alec continued, "Did you know Vikas was captain of the Speed Rol'dan when Emery was general? Emery led the revolt, of course, but Vikas protected them. Still, they barely got away. Most of them didn't."

Alec became tense and silent.

"What is it?" Nolan asked.

"Well," Alec said. "When they escaped, most of the soldiers were too stunned to do anything; their general and most of his captains had turned traitor and fled. But one man fought them. Nearly killed them all. Only Vikas, Garrick, and Emery made it out alive." He pressed his lips together. "Your brother stood against them."

Nolan's chest tightened. He stopped, struggling to breathe.

"Sorry, Nolan. I shouldn't have said anything."

"It's okay," Nolan said. "I shouldn't be surprised."

"Vikas is vicious with a sword," Alec said, trying to change the subject.

"Did you win?" Nolan asked.

One side of Alec's mouth rose. "Of course."

They continued in silence. With a flare of Perception, Nolan heard the clang of Kardos's hammer and smelled the coals of his forge ahead. Nolan forced his senses back to his immediate surroundings. "How'd you learn about their escape?"

"People talk," Alec said. "You'd hear more too if you'd quit hiding."

"I have things to do!"

"Such as?"

Nolan hesitated and then quickly changed the subject. "So fighting with Vikas makes me quite pathetic in comparison, I'm sure."

"Not so pathetic," he said. "You might be surprised how well you do fight, Nolan."

"You only need to use your Speed, and you'd beat me in seconds," Nolan said. "And besides, I must cheat—as you call it—to even come close."

"It isn't like you're using your full range of Accuracy."

Nolan grinned. "At least not when you're looking."

"Oh, really?" Alec said. "Well, in a real battle, one should use whatever skills they have to defend themselves. And I suppose, considering you've only been fighting for two weeks, using your Shay power would be fair, since I've had a sword in my hand all my life. Fighting you is more challenging than fighting most of the others here."

Nolan gawked. "You can't be serious."

"You'd be a good challenge for my father," he added. "Once you've had more practice."

"Your father?"

"I'm not joking," he said. "You'll have to wait and see."

The blood left Nolan's face. "What did you say?"

They'd come to where the path separated in different directions. Alec stepped toward the armory, not answering.

"What do you mean 'wait and see?'" Nolan asked.

Alec turned with familiar mischief on his face. "Swords tomorrow?"

Before Nolan could answer, Alec flared his Speed, leaving Nolan alone with his apprehensions.

Chapter Twenty-Four

Six weeks passed without much happening. Every day they would practice, and nearly every day Alec would tease him about fighting his father.

Kardos scared Nolan just as much as any Rol'dan soldier. Maybe it was because of his fierce fighting abilities or because he glared at almost everyone. Or, more than likely, it was because Kardos had no problem injuring his own son; who knew what he'd do to someone else?

Thankfully, Kardos had kept to himself since arriving at the village, working on swords and shields. He rarely emerged from the armory, which suited Nolan just fine.

As the days passed, Nolan began seeing Alec's threats as that—only threats. Instead, Nolan focused on more important things, such as not getting sliced by Alec's blade.

The time for Emery's group to return quickly approached, and the thought made Nolan a little nervous. Would Emery detect Nolan's new power? Emery had to dig deep in Nolan's head when he'd first sensed his hidden Shay. So as long as Nolan didn't give anything away, he'd probably be fine. He wasn't going to worry about it—at least that's what he kept telling himself.

The village knew Emery was coming soon, not because of the fading summer, but because how grumpy those with Empathy and Strength had become. Rylan's grumbling and complaining could be spurred by only one thing: the closing distance between him and the Stone of Strength.

Megan entered Nolan's thoughts daily. He'd transformed in the past two months—besides the added Shay power. Nolan's pale skin had tanned, and all the training had built muscles on his normally stringy frame. The training no longer made him want to crawl in bed and die at night, and he actually looked forward to it each day. For once, he didn't feel like a mousey scribe. What would Megan think when she saw him?

Nolan stepped off early to the practice field, determined to make Alec work for his victory for a change. He pulled his sword from its sheath and slowly practiced each movement, first on the right side, then the left, and then in large sweeping arcs in front of him. Flaring Accuracy, he increased the speed, throwing offensive jabs and a slice, imagining an opponent standing in front of him.

A few people gathered to watch—which wasn't uncommon. Nolan closed his eyes, pretending the onlookers weren't there. However, the task grew harder as their whispering increased. *Do I look that ridiculous?* He summoned a small amount of Perception and listened.

"I heard he's coming to fight Nolan today," a man said.

"That blacksmith's got quite a temper. *I* wouldn't want to fight him."

Nolan's eyes popped open. He scanned the field and locked on two figures walking toward him. Nolan recognized Alec's prowling gait. He focused his Perception enough to bring their image closer to view. Kardos Deverell walked by Alec's side.

Nolan's concentration sputtered like a dying spark. Crows! What was *he* doing here?

Alec waved as he got closer, wearing an expression of excitement. He must have been trying to get his father to come for quite some time. Nolan's stomach churned, as if doing Speed-enhanced acrobatics.

"Nolan," Alec said as they approached. "Father agreed to come and watch, give us a few pointers."

"Watch?" Nolan asked. By the triumphant expression on Alec's face, it was plain he had other plans.

"Of course," Alec said.

"Mr. Deverell." Nolan bowed his head slightly.

Kardos grunted and stood to the side.

"Shall we?" Alec strapped on his scabbard and slid his sword out. His eyes locked on Nolan's as he swished the blade through the air.

"What are you doing?" Nolan whispered.

"What?" Alec answered with feigned innocence. "What do you mean?"

"You know exactly what I mean."

"I came to fight."

Nolan scowled as they squared off. "If I live through this, I'll kill you."

Alec laughed and, with a quick movement, began the duel. "Ha!"

Nolan barely blocked the blow. He deflected it and stepped back to gain some distance, his hands shaking.

"Relax," Alec said, the light of Speed flashing in his eyes.

Their swords danced. Nolan's arm remembered the moves far before his thoughts. Time and place disappeared as Nolan focused on the match.

As it progressed, Nolan's lungs burned. He grasped his sword tightly in his sweat-coated palm. Nolan's tunic clung to his chest and sweat dripped into his eyes. He blinked it away, refocusing on the duel. Flaring Perception, he focused on the design on the hilt of Alec's sword. An idea flared in his mind. He smiled and with a flick, he hooked Alec's hilt with the tip of his sword, flinging it free into the nearby grass.

Alec gawked at his open palm where his sword had just been.

People erupted in cheers.

Alec grinned. "Well done!"

Nolan laughed breathlessly. He'd finally beaten him! But before Nolan could rejoice further, a metallic flash caught his eye.

He swung, connecting with Kardos's blade.

Kardos's brows knitted, his brown eyes burning with hate. "Well done, you say?" Kardos growled. "His nightforsaken

Shay power glowed the entire time; I'd hardly call it a fair match."

"He's only been fighting two months," Alec said. "I'd hardly call it—"

"Enough!" Kardos cast an angry glance at Alec before glaring at Nolan again. "Let's see how he does with someone who won't let him win."

Nolan's arms trembled from exhaustion and fear. He knew Alec's moves. How would he do against Kardos?

Alec's eyes flared golden-yellow. "I didn't let him win. If you want to spar with him, that's fine. But at least give him a few minutes to rest."

"And in a battle, they'd give him time to rest?" Kardos said. "No. We fight now."

Nolan barely dodged in time. Kardos was on top of him, slicing with an intensity he'd never seen. His blows hammered as on an anvil. Nolan used Accuracy to avoid Kardos's angry blade. This was no sparring match. With every jarring blow, Nolan fought for his life. He dodged and parried, though his waning strength began to show.

With a flick of Kardos's sword, pain flamed through his thigh. Nolan ignored it, focusing on his moves. After some time, the battle started turning to Nolan's favor, if slightly. And by Kardos's increasing ferocity, the blacksmith saw the shift as well. Kardos stepped back as Nolan pressed forward. Nolan's anxiety slowly peeled away. He had a chance. He could do this!

"By the light! Who is that man, and what did he do with Nolan?"

Nolan's focus jarred to a sudden stop. He saw Hakan grinning widely. Both Emery and Megan stood with him, their mouths hanging open in shock.

And at that moment of distraction, Kardos lunged.

The world around Nolan jerked into one focused moment as Kardos's blade tore through his chest. Nolan's breath came out in a strangled gasp. His vision tunneled. Kardos yanked out his sword and swung back to finish the job.

Alec appeared from nowhere, blocking his father's blow. Nolan collapsed, his body shaking. He could vaguely hear chaos erupting around him. As his vision dimmed, a sudden, warm healing surged through his body. Nolan arched into the energy, gasping and coughing as his lungs breathed once again. Megan stared down at him. She shook as she pressed her hands against the sides of his face.

"Father!" Alec yelled.

"Get out of my way," Kardos said. "It's about time we rid the land of the filth."

"Filth? If you mean those with Shay powers, then you fight me as well!" Alec said, holding his sword between Nolan and Kardos.

Kardos glared, and then turned and marched away.

"Stop him," Emery said, his voice so sharp everyone stared. Even Kardos paused before continuing on.

Maska met the glowering blacksmith in three strides. Kardos threw back his blade, but before he could swing, Maska grabbed his hand.

"To the fires with you!" Kardos yelled. He struggled against Maska's Strength until a crunching pop came from his hand.

Kardos growled like a bear. "Fight like a real man, and we'll see how you fare."

"If I were to see a real man, then I might feel inspired to fight," Maska said, his face still expressionless, though his eyes glowed red like fire.

"This is our home," Emery said. "You will not come here and pick us off like vermin. We allowed you here, welcoming you into the safety of our village. Is this how you repay us? What you've done is inexcusable. You've not only hurt Nolan, but insulted the whole village with your ignorance and bigotry!"

"I'd do more than insult if given the chance," Kardos said. "You're cowards as well as Rol'dan demons. You share their power, but hide in the woods pretending you aren't them."

"So you believe us to be demons then?" Emery said.

Kardos's silence was his answer.

"Yet your son holds this same gift."

Alec held Nolan's arm, helping him to his feet. "I'm so sorry, Nolan. I had no idea—"

"I have no son," Kardos said.

Alec's grip tightened and his face paled.

Emery's Shay emerged. The purple light, which always shone brightly in Emery's eyes, glowed more intensely than before. Kardos jerked against Maska's grip as he tried to get free.

"Take your wretched hands off of me, Tala-swine!" Kardos flinched, and then the rage on his face transformed into fear.

Emery continued to stare at Kardos until a resolute expression came over his face. "Bring him to the ruins," he said. "He can face his own demons there."

***

Casual conversation had no place in times like this. Nolan walked between Alec and Megan, at a total loss for words. He blamed himself for what happened, but his logical side knew it wasn't his fault. Kardos had started it all.

Alec said nothing, either. He only stared at the ground as he trudged along. The scar on his cheek seemed deeper, as if it revealed his insides as well.

Once again, blood soaked the front of Megan's dress. Nolan had imagined their reunion differently. A nice talk. Maybe a private walk through the woods. Not her saving his life after getting a sword rammed through his chest.

They arrived at the temple ruins. Maska led the way, pushing the reluctant Kardos in front of him. When they entered, four circles of light shone on the ground. The red symbol of Strength and the purple of Empathy now joined the previous two.

"Bring him to me," Emery said.

Maska dragged Kardos forward. Like before, Emery's eyes blazed brighter than Nolan had ever seen. Kardos struggled harder, cowering as Emery's power washed over him.

Emery pointed to the light of Accuracy. "Hold him there until it's no longer necessary."

"What are you doing?" Panic spread across Kardos's face. "Let go of me, Tala-swine!" But even with the insult, Maska didn't react. He walked with determined steps and held Kardos in the light of Accuracy.

Kardos squirmed and cursed, but stopped abruptly as the pinpoints of dancing light appeared. Maska released his hold and stepped away as the light of Accuracy swelled around Kardos Deverell.

"It's not possible," Alec stammered.

Nolan shook his head, mirroring Alec's shock. *How can it be?*

Kardos rose into the air, and after the light faded, drifted down, fell to his knees, and sobbed. After several long minutes, Kardos stood, cursed, and held his broken wrist to his chest.

Megan stepped forward, reaching to touch him; he glared at her and moved away.

"Be careful of your hatred, Mr. Deverell," Emery said.

"What do you know of hatred?" Kardos said between gritted teeth. "You can never understand."

"There is a fine line between us and the Rol'dan," Emery said. "They stopped focusing on what was noble and pure when they accepted their position. We, on the other hand, must stay straight on the path of good, otherwise we lose who we are and become like them. Hate what they do, not who they are. They are lost to themselves. They deserve pity instead."

"Pity the Rol'dan?" Kardos said slowly, as if the words tasted bitter. "You want me to pity them after what they did to my dear Norah? They ravished and killed her while my boy watched. And then they blamed her for what happened, as if she were some common whore. You can't possibly understand what I've been through."

"You are right, friend. Though I don't understand completely, I do share your sorrow." An unreadable expression fell on Emery. "The biggest regret I have in my life is that I did nothing the day your wife died. Please, forgive me."

Kardos's head rose slowly, stark confusion masking his grizzled face.

Alec gasped and went sickly pale. "It was you?" he said. "You were there, weren't you? With the Strength Rol'dan who killed my mother?"

Emery's face fell. "I was. I didn't realize the captain would kill her until it was too late."

Alec's face went from pale to red. "Yet you stood there and watched him defile her?"

"I have no excuse for my past," Emery said sadly. "I ignored a lot of things then, more than I can even remember."

Kardos growled and lunged at Emery like a rabid animal. Before anyone could react, Kardos pounded Emery's face with his good hand like a sledgehammer breaking stone. Emery fell, and Kardos fell with him, continuing his relentless assault.

Maska's eyes flared red, and he yanked the flailing blacksmith off Emery.

"You gutless dog!" Kardos yelled. And a trail of every imaginable curse flew from his lips as Maska dragged him away.

Emery sat on the ground, blood pouring from his deformed nose and split cheeks.

Vikas yanked out his sword. Though he was a small man, a fierce glare shone behind the light in his golden-yellow eyes. He wasn't a man to cross.

"I'll kill him," Vikas said.

"No. Don't." Emery said. "I deserved this."

Vikas scowled. "You deserve no such treatment."

Emery put a hand on Vikas's leg. "Please, friend. In this instance, I do."

Vikas frowned and reluctantly sheathed his sword.

Megan knelt next to Emery, and the expression on Emery's broken face was horrified.

"Oh, Megan...No."

"Shh, now," she said. "Just hold still."

Nolan looked away as the green light of Healing flared in her eyes. His stomach churned with the sound of bones cracking and her whimpering echoing through the temple.

"I'm sorry, Megan," Emery said softy. "I'm so sorry."

Nolan touched the bloodied spot on his tunic and mirrored Emery's guilt.

Alec staggered and collapsed to the ground, putting his head between his knees. How much more could he take? His father had disowned him simply for who he was, and now the truth of his mother's death was revealed in the face of the man Alec respected more than anyone. Alec deserved none of this.

Nolan thought back to his conversation with Emery and all he'd gone through. If anyone understood loss, it would be Emery. And Nolan knew, without a doubt, Emery was not that same man who could watch the murder and defilement of an innocent woman.

Emery and Megan stood together. Nolan wasn't sure who comforted who—probably a little of both. They whispered to each other, his arms around her in an embrace. Jealousy flared in Nolan. There was nothing between them. That's what Emery had told him. Yet, watching them…Nolan wasn't so sure.

Alec's shoulders shook in chest-heaving sobs. Nolan slid down the wall next to him, feeling completely useless. After a while, Nolan felt an Empathy Shay pass over them. Nolan met the sorrow-filled face of Emery. His cheeks were moist, as if he'd been crying too.

"Alec?" Emery said.

Alec's head jerked up, and his eyes flared with both anger and his Shay. "There's nothing I want to say to you," he spat.

Emery flinched. "I can understand, but there is one more thing I thought you should know." He hesitated. Even when Kael had beaten him in the West Tower of Alton, he had never acted this uncomfortable; he wrung his hands together and bit his lower lip. "I want you to realize, your mother didn't die in vain. In fact, her death will probably save us all."

Alec gawked at him, the anger in his expression transforming to frustration.

"You see," Emery continued, "the night she died, I'd used my power to sense her."

"What?" Alec spat. His face reddened once again. "How could you? Did you get some sort of sick pleasure from her fear?"

"No," Emery answered. "That's what's strange. She held no fear. I felt determination and courage, not fear. Both traits I see very much in you. And when she attacked the captain, she desired to right what was wrong so it wouldn't happen again." Emery ran a hand through his hair. "I saw more bravery in that small bit of woman than I'd seen in the entire Rol'dan army the whole seventeen years I'd served. And from that moment, I realized I could no longer be a Rol'dan.

"She changed my heart," Emery continued, "and in turn, set the precedence for us to leave. Because of your mother's death, this village began. Because of her courage, we are all here. And I believe it will, in turn, save Adamah someday."

Nolan left them. Emery took his place, sitting next to Alec on the stones. They talked more, but this time the conversation was calm.

The four lights of Brim flickered as a cloud passed over them. Megan joined Nolan, silently watching Alec and Emery. Blood coated her dress and smeared across her face. Even though she was a mess, she was still pretty to Nolan.

"Hi," she said. "What a day, huh?"

Nolan snorted. "Yeah, I'll say." He motioned toward her bloodied dress. "Sorry about that."

"It's not your fault." She examined him. "You look good, Nolan. The village air suits you. And you fight well! I had no idea."

Warmth rose to his cheeks. He didn't actually think she'd notice. "Neither did I. Alec taught me while you were gone."

"You're a good student."

"He's a good teacher."

She grinned. Her teeth were straight and white, a perfect accessory to her full lips. "Or probably it's a little of both."

Nolan lowered his eyes, pulling at the neck of his tunic. Why did she always make him feel so warm?

"Emery needs me," Megan said.

Nolan followed her gaze. Alec flared his Speed and was gone, leaving Emery alone. Emery lowered his head, fingers lacing through the bloodied tangles of his black hair. Nolan had never seen him so depressed.

Megan locked eyes with Nolan. "We really haven't gotten the chance to talk much, have we?"

"It's okay. You made up for it by saving me again."

"You do get into a bit of trouble." Megan leaned in, and her breath touched Nolan's ear. "I missed you." Her lips brushed his cheek, and she darted away.

So many thoughts rushed through him: joy, nervousness, and shock. The sensation of her lips lingered—at least until he saw Megan hovering over Emery. *Crows! That girl is driving me crazy!*

He inhaled, relaxing. *Emery's not interested in her. He told me so.* But what about Megan? Every time she was with Emery, she stared at him like a smitten child. *Did she love him?* He snorted. *No, of course not. She'd just kissed me.*

Emery and Megan walked away, whispering to each other. Megan waved at Nolan as they left.

Nolan pressed his fingertips into his temples. Emery had the advantage of sensing emotions, whereas Nolan could only guess. *Sometimes life would be easier if I could read emotions, too.*

He froze.

What if he could?

Slowly, his eyes drifted to the Empathy symbol on the ground: three purple lines, crossing to form a triangle, a small circle of light in its center, resembling an all-knowing eye.

He looked around. The temple had cleared, leaving him alone.

Taking a step toward the light, he hesitated. He still hadn't completely grasped his new ability. So why would he be stupid enough to take another? Three days he'd been unconscious. Why in Brim's light would he risk his life again?

Nolan knew why. The reason came with beautiful brown curls, full lips, and penetrating green eyes. If he could find out how she felt, even for just a minute, he'd risk almost anything to know. Maybe nothing would happen. Maybe the last time had been an accident. There was only one way to find out.

Nolan took a deep breath and stepped into the light of Empathy.

Chapter Twenty-Five

Nolan stood in the white mists again. This time, a green meadow stretched as far as he could see. The mists swirled around him in thin patches, lightly caressing his skin. Ahead, a figure stood, silhouetted in a magnificent sunset.

Greer crossed his arms over his massive chest. The long grass brushed against his armored shins as hues of orange and pink outlined his formidable frame. He turned as if sensing Nolan's presence; the white light of his eyes glowed even more intensely than at their last meeting. He was more intimidating than Nolan remembered.

"It is good to speak with you again, Master," Greer said with a subtle bow of his broad head.

"Master" was an odd touch. *At least my dreams are creative.* "Where are we?"

"We are in a placeholder of your mind."

"So this is a dream?" Nolan had figured this out already.

"Of sorts," Greer answered, a smile hinting across his mouth. "Would you do me the honor of walking with me, Master?"

The sunlight faded, yet a ring of light illuminated Greer as they continued across the field. In deaf-like silence they walked, their steps soundless as they brushed through the grass. The darkness deepened with the departure of the sun, and yet they strolled as if by day.

"How do you do that?" Nolan asked.

Greer chuckled. "When one is made of light, one has little choice." He stopped and turned, towering over Nolan, making him feel like a young boy. "Our time is short," he said. "I must come to the point of this meeting. You now have four of the stones?"

Nolan's mouth opened. How did he know? But of course, it was Nolan's dream.

"Alcandor will soon sense the stones' reunification," Greer continued. "It won't be much longer until your village is in danger."

"King Alcandor knows of the stones?"

Greer frowned. "Yes."

"What should we do?"

"Your only chance will be to obtain the remaining two stones before Alcandor can find them. Then you must combine them. Combining all six will give you the answers you seek. Only then will you know how to free Adamah from Alcandor... and from itself."

Free Adamah from itself? Nolan waited for more explanation. Instead, the warrior stared into the darkness, frowning.

The last time Nolan had fallen into this strange dream, his visit with Greer had been short. That brief moment had lasted nearly three days in the real world. This time it felt like hours had passed. Nolan sucked a breath. Crows! How long had he been unconscious this time?

"Greer, why am I here?" Nolan's heart accelerated. "Why combine these stones? What do you mean by combine, and what will happen if we don't find the other two? How do you know so much? And why are you telling me all this?"

Greer chuckled. "So many questions, Master Nolan." He puffed his chest. "I believe you are here to save us all."

It was Nolan's turn to laugh.

Greer raised a brow. "Is it so difficult to consider?"

"Yes, it is. I had no idea I could dream such a self-absorbed image of grandeur."

"Ah! So you do not believe I am real."

"How can I?" Nolan said. "I've never seen anything like you."

"At one time, we walked among you."

"What are you?" Nolan asked, adding another question to the long list.

"You have asked me that question twice." Greer inhaled a deep breath, his muscular chest expanding. "I am a servant to mankind, light created to protect Brim's most favorite creation. I am a Guardian."

"Wait," Nolan said. "You said you weren't a Guardian."

"Circumstances changed my mind."

Nolan stared. "But Guardians are extinct."

Greer smiled, and one eyebrow rose over his white-orbed eye. "Perhaps we are, and this is truly only a dream." Greer's countenance changed. He glanced around and then stepped away. "Please forgive me, Master Nolan. We have run out of time again." His image began to die away. "Until our next meeting."

Greer's light faded into a darkness so thick and humid, Nolan felt as if he'd choke. Through the nothingness, a voice called out, faintly at first, then louder as his consciousness became reality.

"Nolan! Wake up."

Nolan jerked awake, gasping. His eyes popped open to Alec glaring down.

"I've been looking for you all morning!" Alec said.

Nolan blinked, trying to clear the throbbing through his skull. Daylight filtered through the domed ceiling, and a chorus of birds tweeted above, as well as the occasional bird picking morsels off the floor. Nolan still lay in the temple, though it was too early for the sun to bring the Shay lights.

"You told me you'd meet me at the practice field," Alec said, "and now I find you here? What's gotten into you?"

Morning. He must've lain unconscious all night.

Only one night.

"You slept here?" Alec said. "By the light, Nolan, what were you thinking? It's a good thing you weren't killed by the Dor'Jan."

Alec was angry. The situation with Emery and Kardos had surely dragged him down. Dark rings circled his eyes, as if he'd slept even worse than Nolan. Sadness permeated Alec, too. Nolan could feel it in his friend. But Alec tried to hide it behind his anger.

Alec flinched, his head whipping toward the temple entrance. "Someone else is here."

A strange ache pounded Nolan's head. He groaned.

Alec hesitated, still staring at the entrance. He turned to Nolan, helping him to his feet. "Are you okay?"

"I'm fine." Nolan staggered a few steps.

"You don't look fine," Alec said. At least he wasn't angry anymore; concern poured from him instead.

Alec gasped, his eyes widening.

Nolan slammed his eyes closed, but it was too late. In that brief moment their eyes connected, Nolan sensed...realization.

"Crows, Nolan." Alec grabbed his arm. "What was that?"

"Nothing!" Nolan lied, squeezing his eyes tighter.

"Your eyes were purple."

"It must've been the light reflecting—"

"Crows, Nolan. You're lying!"

Nolan turned before opening his eyes. "I'm going home. I have a headache."

Before he could take a step, Alec appeared in front of him with Speed. The Shay of Empathy in Nolan responded immediately before he could take control.

"By Brim!" Alec said with a triumphant tone to his voice. "I knew it!" His emotions were quickly replaced by anger and betrayal.

Nolan pushed by Alec, walking in determined, yet staggering, steps toward the exit.

Alec appeared in his path again, anger still pouring from him. Then it slowly switched to confusion. "How in Darkness did you get Empathy? I mean...only the king..."

Nolan wasn't sure if it was from his new power, or from Alec's revelation, but his head spun. His stomach lurched so hard Nolan thought he might vomit.

Alec was there, supporting his arm and helping him to the side of the temple wall.

What else have I gained besides these powers?

The king had obtained an ageless life. Some even said he was immortal. The horror of that thought flitted in his mind, along with so many others, he could scarcely focus. Nolan lowered his head into his hands, feeling the weight of this new power even more.

"The light," Nolan said. "I stood in the light of Empathy."

"The light gave you a second Shay?"

Nolan swallowed. *By Brim, my head aches.* "No. It gave me a third."

"Three?" Alec inhaled a quick breath. "You have Perception, don't you?"

He nodded.

"Three Shay powers?" Alec's confusion switched to a swell of excitement. "Well, it explains what happened to your eyes. I've been wondering why you haven't been wearing your spectacles." He motioned toward the light of Strength. "Would this one would work as well?"

"This isn't a game, Alec. I didn't want these powers."

Alec held his hands in defense. "Okay, okay. Just wondering, that's all."

He sat next to Nolan in silence. Nolan didn't dare look at him; every time he did his friend poured out so many different emotions it hurt Nolan's head. Finally, he met his gaze and sensed a question on the tip of Alec's tongue.

"What?" Nolan said with an exasperated sigh.

"It's just...Well, I can understand you not expecting the Perception power. But if you already knew what could happen, why would you step into the Empathy light too?"

"I didn't *know* if it would work."

"So you thought you'd give it a go, just in case?"

The sarcasm was thick in Alec's emotions. It gave Nolan an overwhelming desire to smack him. But as much as he hated to admit it, Alec was right.

"No," Nolan said. "It was because of Megan."

At first Alec was confused, and then realization—with a touch of amusement—took its place. Alec's head was like someone flipping through a book while you were trying to read the pages.

"Ah," Alec said. "It makes perfect sense to me. Why, if I could figure out what Taryn was thinking half the time, I'd be tempted to step into the Empathy light as well."

Then his emotions shifted—hardened. "Or if it could help me figure out my father. Emery seems to have this wild idea that he cares about me."

"You're still speaking to Emery?"

Alec threw his hands up. "Crows, Nolan. I don't know what to think anymore. I want to hate him, but I can't do it. Especially after everything he told me last night."

Turbulence emanated from Alec: sadness to anger back to sadness…then annoyance…

Alec cleared his throat. "Seriously, Nolan. It's a bit rude to use Empathy on someone all the time."

"What?" He hadn't noticed. "Sorry. Just not used to it, that's all."

Alec glared in warning. Nolan pulled back on his Empathy, and Alec relaxed a little.

"And then there's my father," Alec continued. "He's the most confusing of all. He disowns me one hour, and gives me gifts the next." He pulled a sword from his sheath. The pattern welded together resembled a flickering flame dancing to the point of the blade, the two different metals intertwining.

"It's great," Nolan said.

"I know. When we got back last night, I assumed he'd grab a sword and go kill Emery. Instead, he let Taryn heal him, and he started pounding on the forge."

He motioned toward the sword. "He's been working on this one for quite a while. Usually, he curses up a storm and tosses it down. Last night, though, he didn't say a word. He worked most of the night." He touched a spot where one of the lighter metals swirled. "This metal is what was left of the sword Father found at the ruins."

Nolan blinked. "He...destroyed it?"

A surge of disgust passed through Alec. "Yes. Afraid so. I guess the metal resisted him before he got his power. He worked all night on the nightforsaken thing, his Accuracy glowing the entire time. If I didn't know any better, I'd think he actually *likes* his Shay." He shook his head. "And then he gave the sword to me."

Alec fingered the blade, tracing the patterns. Nolan had never seen such a beautiful weapon—although, Nolan didn't know much about weapons. So he supposed his opinion didn't matter too much. But he assumed this sword would put the king's to shame.

"I guess I'm pretty well numb to everything," Alec said. "My father is a Shay user. If I can wrap my head around that, I guess I can believe most anything."

"Is that why you didn't act so surprised about me?"

He tilted his head, smiling faintly. It was nice to feel gladness in his emotions.

"You realize you're doing it again," Alec said as he pointed to his head. "Digging in my mind."

Nolan cringed. "Sorry. It will probably take a few days to control."

Realization washed over Alec. "Ah! So that's why you hid inside for a week. To practice your Perception?"

Nolan snickered, but stopped abruptly when another pain stabbed his skull. This Shay would take some getting used to.

"So what's Emery going to say?" Alec asked.

"About what?" Nolan asked as he squeezed his eyes closed.

"About you having more than one Shay."

"He won't say anything, because he won't know."

"You're not going to tell him?"

"No. And neither will you."

"Won't he like, um, know?" Alec asked. "Just by sensing you?"

Nolan rubbed his temple. "Last time he dug through my mind to find my Shay. It's not like he figured it just by looking at me." He shuddered, remembering.

"But he's more powerful now," Alec said.

Nolan hadn't considered that. But then he remembered last night, when he'd been searching Kardos. He'd stared at him and Kardos had squirmed. He had to dig around Kardos's mind, too.

"It will be fine," Nolan said, hoping.

"Nolan," he said, "Maybe this is how King Alcandor gained his powers. And if that's the case, maybe you can become as powerful as him."

Nolan started. "Crows! Why would I want that?"

Alec shrugged with casual indifference, but his emotions soared with excitement. "Maybe you can defeat the king. Then if we're lucky, you could take his place."

Nolan's stomach dropped, and he gawked at Alec. How could he say such a thing? He must've been more sleep deprived than he'd let on. The idea of himself as king was the most ridiculous suggestion he'd ever heard.

Nolan forced a laugh. "There is no way in Brim's light I'm going to be king. And besides, I'm done gaining powers."

"Why?" Alec said, his emotions smug.

Nolan ran a hand over his chin. "It's hard enough hiding one, let alone three."

"Then why hide?"

"Because King Alcandor is the only other person with multiple powers. What would people think? If Alcandor started like me, then what will these powers do to my mind?" Nolan shook his head slowly. "I don't know how many I can control. Three is bad enough. And if something happens…"

Alec laughed nervously. "Surely, Nolan—"

"We don't know what multiple powers can do. The only reference we have is King Alcandor, and you can see what happened with him. Promise me, Alec, if I start to act evil or something—"

Alec snorted. "You won't act evil."

"If something goes wrong—"

"Nolan, you'll be fine."

"Promise me," Nolan said. "Promise me you'll stop me if

I change."

"Change into what?"

"A monster like Alcandor."

Alec stood, annoyance lacing his emotions.

"Promise me!" Nolan said. All three Shay powers surged to life inside him. He inhaled sharply at the sensation.

Doubt and disagreement clouded Alec's emotions. He jerked his face away, his arms crossed tightly over his chest. "All right," he said in a tense whisper, "I'll club you in your sleep and tie you up if I see you acting strange."

Nolan frowned.

"That's all I can promise," Alec said, his anger swelling. "If you want to die, ask someone else to kill you."

Chapter Twenty-Six

"I can pretty much guess you're bored without sensing you," Nolan said.

Alec sighed and stood. "Sorry. It's just...well, I'm sick of sitting."

"I didn't ask you to do this, you know."

Nolan had hidden in his house the week following his gain of Empathy. Alec visited daily, letting Nolan practice on him.

"I figured the quicker you got over this, the quicker we could get back to swords."

"You do realize I'll have another advantage," Nolan said. "I'll be able to sense your fighting strategies."

"Oh no, you can't. You can only catch emotions."

He had a point. More than likely, Alec's emotion would be excitement during a duel. "Well, my Perception helped me defeat you last time."

Alec straightened in his seat, curiosity lacing his emotions. "Ah, that's better. Was getting bored of your boredom."

"So you just made that up? To play around with me?" Alec's emotions were amused.

"Of course not!" Nolan grinned. "I won because I'd focused my Perception on the hilt of your sword."

"Ha! You are such a cheater." Alec was impressed. "If you're planning on hiding that Empathy of yours, you won't be able to rake through everyone's heads all the time. You've done it so much to me, I'm starting to get numb to it."

"But you're such an easy target," Nolan said. "You give

me at least twenty different emotions in a matter of seconds."

"Are you calling me emotional?"

"More like volatile. You're about to burst apart like an overfilled waterskin."

Alec's emotions rolled, from anger to amusement to curiosity. He shook his head. "Like that, I suppose?"

"Exactly like that."

Nolan tuned his Perception outside and heard a crowd. It sounded like the village gathered at the hall. "Is there something going on today?"

"Crows!" Alec said, surging with frustration. "Emery's called a meeting. He wanted me to drag you there."

Nolan's heart stuttered. He wasn't ready. Empathy was the hardest one to control, because it took so little effort to use.

"You have to come out sometime, you know," Alec said.

"What if I make a mistake?"

"The whole village has come. There are so many Empathy users, no one will know who sensed them."

Alec was right. It would be the perfect place to try Empathy.

And so they went. Nolan was both excited and nervous. As they entered the large hall, curiosity laced the crowd's emotions. It was amazing to feel everything, all the energy in the room.

"They're all wondering what this meeting is about," he whispered to Alec.

Alec grinned wide. "And you didn't want to come."

They took a place at the rear of the building. At least a cool breeze blew through the open windows. He couldn't imagine crowding together with his enhanced smell in sticky and hot weather. This place held at least two hundred people; they pushed the limits of capacity.

He scanned over heads and found Emery and several others on a platform in front of the room. Megan stood between Flann and Emery, looking more beautiful than usual. He surged a little Perception and studied her more closely. The journey had deepened her complexion, revealing faint freckles across her nose.

"I have brought you here today to discuss the further retrieval of the stones," Emery said as the group trickled into silence. "From our recent experience, we can be certain the stones of Brim restore our true Shay powers. Certainly those of you with Healing and Speed are feeling anxious to get your turn."

"True Shay?" a voice said.

"What does he mean?" another asked.

Several more complained, impatient, probably those who were feeling the stones' pull.

A flare of light caught the corner of Nolan's eye. He turned and gasped. Greer, the Guardian, maneuvered through the group, his massive form mingling with the crowd. No one paid him any notice. Those who did only smiled and nodded as if he were one of them. Nolan pressed his eyes closed and shook his head. When he opened them, the Guardian was gone.

"Are there any questions?" Emery asked.

Several hands shot into the air.

Nolan searched for the Guardian, but he saw no one apart from the familiar faces of the villagers. His head throbbed with the increase of emotions in the room.

The meeting dispersed, but Nolan barely noticed; instead, he scanned the crowd, looking for any proof that he wasn't going insane. The image of the Guardian blazed in his head. *What is happing to me?*

Emery stepped from the platform, patting shoulders and shaking hands. His eyes would flare purple with each person, as it always did. He wanted to know how his people felt at all times. He searched the crowd, and his eyes stopped on Nolan. Nolan felt Emery's Empathy flare and fade, and then Emery pushed his way through the crowd in Nolan's direction.

Nolan stiffened and inhaled.

"You'll be okay," Alec said.

"What if I mess up?"

"Then it won't be a secret."

"Nolan!" Emery said. "How are you feeling? Alec said you've been unwell."

"I'm doing better, thank you." This was the truth, for the most part.

"He told me you've been having headaches. Hopefully it has nothing to do with the stones."

Nolan glared at Alec. What was he trying to pull?

"I hope it isn't a late symptom of stepping into the light," Emery continued. "Our whole village will soon be under the stones. I would hate for it to—"

"Oh, no, no," Nolan said. "It's probably just being in the sun too much. Alec works me quite hard."

Emery laughed. "It appears you're feeling well enough. At least I won't have to worry when we leave tomorrow."

"Tomorrow?"

Emery's smile left. "I just announced it, Nolan." Concern laced his emotions. "Flann will be in charge of the village when we're gone. I told him he could depend on you if he needed anything."

"Of course," Nolan said, though he wasn't sure how much help he'd be.

"Megan sensed the Healing stone near the direction of Faylinn. I've organized a group of our most effective Shay users, considering the risk involved. Among them are Garrick, Maska, Hakan, and Megan." He turned toward Alec. "And Alec. That is, if you'd like to come along."

"Me?" Alec said, his excitement building.

"There's none as good with a sword."

Alec's excitement wilted slightly. "But Vikas has already asked me to come find the Speed stone."

"More than likely, you'll return within a few days," Emery said. "You're traveling exclusively with Speed users, so it shouldn't take very long at all."

"Then why not have Vikas meet you?"

Apprehension swelled in Emery. He sighed. "Let's just say I don't trust him so close to Faylinn. He'd like nothing more than to repay a debt."

Vikas stood on the platform, his arms crossed tightly over his chest. Nolan summoned a bit of Empathy and shuddered.

He held more volatile emotions than Alec.

"So you're afraid he'd attack the Rol'dan?" Alec asked.

"Not specifically," Emery answered. "But if we were to encounter a situation where hiding would be preferable to fighting, I doubt he'd want to listen.

"Besides," he said, "you're a better fighter than he is—which is saying something of you, my boy. You can meet us in Caldalk after you return from finding the Speed stone. But of course, if you don't want to—"

"I do," Alec said, grinning. "Sure, I'll come along."

"I want to come as well," a girl's voice said.

Taryn appeared next to them, her violet eyes flicking from one person to another.

Alec choked a laugh.

"And what's so funny?" Taryn's eyes flared.

"It's going to be dangerous," Emery said.

"I know," she said. "But if Alec is old enough to go…"

"I've made an exception."

"Then you can make an exception for me, as well."

Megan approached. "She isn't a bad choice, Emery. We're still in need of another Healer to help confirm the stone's location."

"Surely you can find someone else," Alec said, casting a nervous glance in Taryn's direction.

"Of course I could," Megan said. "But in all honesty, her Shay power is stronger than most others in the village."

Taryn stuck her chin out like a defiant child.

"All right." Emery held his palms toward her in mock defeat. "She can go. As long as she's aware of the consequences."

Nolan gawked, not believing he'd agreed to this stupidity. "Then I should go too," Nolan said.

"Nolan, I already told you. I want you here."

"My power is as strong as Garrick's, if not stronger."

"Yes, it is. But he knows the area better than you do. He served with me while in the Rol'dan. I need him with me this time."

Nolan looked away. He was letting Taryn go? She was just

a girl, for Brim's sake. Nolan tried not to think about how most of the Shay users in the village were not much older.

"So, how's your father doing?" Emery asked Alec.

"Fine, though he won't admit it."

"I'm glad. He doesn't seem like the type of man to admit to things readily."

"True." Alec's smile left, replaced with a curious expression. "Emery, could you answer a question?"

"Certainly."

"How did you know my father had the power of Accuracy? I mean, he attended the Tournament of Awakening like everyone else, and he didn't receive a power then."

"It's the light," Emery said. "Once I stepped into it, it increased my skills—as I'm sure you'll experience once you get your turn. In the past, I've had the ability to sense a Shay power in someone if I dig deeply, but only for those who naturally come into a power. Now, if I focus hard enough, I can sense a Shay in everyone."

"Everyone?"

"Aye. They do have one, it's just not as strong as the others who emerged the typical way. Their powers are buried deeper, like your father's Shay of Accuracy."

Nolan tried to follow the conversation, but he couldn't concentrate. Alec could protect himself. But Taryn?

"Ale, sir?" Jared stood next to them, a tray of drinks in his frail hand.

"Thank you, Jared." Emery helped himself to one of the frothy mugs.

"Remarkable," Megan said. "So everyone has a Shay?"

"Almost everyone," Emery said. "I've come across one or two in whom I've felt nothing at all." He cast a purposeful glance in Jared's direction.

Jared snorted. "Ah, it doesn't make any difference to me. I'm glad I can help." His gaze rested on Nolan. "Drink, sir?"

Nolan shook his head, too foul-tempered to speak.

Jared cast Nolan a curious expression and retreated.

"I thought Jared would have a gift," Emery said. "Maybe

he does, and it's so weak my powers can't sense it. He has such a good heart. I'd hoped he could receive a Shay as well." He swished the amber fluid in the mug. "Well, at least my newly acquired skill is useful at other times, such as that incident with your father. And it could have been quite useful with my experience in Alton. Eh, Nolan?"

He smiled at Nolan, but Nolan wasn't in the mood to talk. Matter of fact, he was about to excuse himself when Emery's power passed over him.

"Something is bothering you, friend?" Emery asked

Nolan glared at Emery, wondering how—for an Empathy user—he could be so incredibly clueless. Wasn't it obvious?

Oh come now, Emery. You honestly don't know?

Emery's smile dropped. Nolan knew, too late, that he'd shared his thoughts with more than himself.

The corner of Emery's mouth twitched into a hard line. He stared at Nolan with an expression unlike any he'd ever seen. Even when Kardos had stabbed him, Nolan had never seen him this livid.

"Emery?" Megan said.

Emery didn't answer. His Empathy pulsed through Nolan, digging like before. Nolan flinched, pain stabbing his skull. Emery wasn't gentle this time. Nolan inhaled sharply as Emery's power jerked away.

"Emery? What's wrong?" Megan asked again.

"Might I have a word with you, Nolan?" Emery said calmly, but Nolan could feel the anger climbing. He grabbed Nolan's arm and yanked him away.

Megan called after them, but Emery pulled him through the crowd. With his Perception, Nolan could hear the blood pumping through Emery's veins. He pushed Nolan into the smaller room and slammed the door.

The dim room allowed meager light from a small window. But he didn't need to see much. Emery's eyes blazed purple with his Shay.

"I can explain—" Nolan's words were cut off by a power sifting inside him, so intense, he could hardly breathe. "What are you doing?"

"Quiet!" Emery snapped as he continued his search.

Nolan squirmed, his breath coming in short pants.

Finally, Emery stopped. He stared, his face turning red. He tightened his grasp on the front of Nolan's tunic, gripping it into a knot. His Empathy light intensified, and a voice spoke in Nolan's head. *By Brim! You have three Shay powers?*

Nolan turned away.

Don't even try to ignore me. Emery gave his tunic a jerk. *I know you can hear me.*

Nolan gritted his teeth. He didn't want this to happen, especially not like this. He summoned Empathy. *Yes.*

Emery shuddered and loosened his grip. "How long have you been hiding them?" he said. "For Brim's sake, Nolan, I told Flann he can trust you, and now I discover you're keeping this kind of secret? I put you in a position of leadership. If I had known back in Alton, I would have left you there. If I would have known—"

"You couldn't have known."

"Of course not," Emery hissed. "I couldn't read you like I can now. Crows! How could I be so foolish? No wonder your Shay is so strong—you have more than one!" His eyes widened and his anger flared more. "Where *did* Alec get that stone?"

"It wasn't me. I swear. I didn't give him the stone. I just received the other two Shay powers."

Emery's power relaxed, but only a little. "Then how..." His voice trailed off. Shock and fury spread across his emotions. He tightened his grip on Nolan's tunic. "What have you done to get these powers, Nolan?"

"It was the lights. The stones. Every time I stood under one, it gave me another power."

"I did the same and they gave me no such powers!"

"I know!" Nolan said. "I don't know why it worked for me."

Emery glared, the violet light in his eyes intensifying. "Then where is your Strength?"

"I haven't stood in that light."

"Then you should have no problem stepping into the light of Strength, to prove what you say is true."

Nolan swallowed hard. "I do have a problem with it, actually."

"Why?"

"Because I don't want any more powers, and I didn't react so well the other times. I can barely control what I have."

"So you refuse?"

"I didn't say I refused, just that I'd rather not."

"The lives of everyone in this village are in my hands," Emery said. "They trust me. I can't let someone absorb powers from innocent people."

"What?"

"Will you do it, if I ask you to?" Emery asked. It wasn't a request. It was an ultimatum.

"I'll do it, if that's what you want."

Emery released his hold. "Would you do it right now?"

A weight fell to his chest. He owed Emery this. He slouched, shoulders curling forward. What else could he do? "Yes."

Emery pulled a traveling cloak off a peg. "If we leave now, we'll have time to return before nightfall."

"If we want to be back by nightfall," Nolan added, "bring Maska along to carry me home."

Chapter Twenty-Seven

There were no mists this time. No strange dream. No light-filled warrior. Only agony and enveloping darkness as time crawled on. Empathy had affected Nolan's mind. Strength now transformed his body. Every muscle. Every bone changed.

He remembered the others at the trials as they thrashed on the ground. He'd always felt sorry for them. And although their suffering was bad, his was far, far worse. His Perception intensified every pulsing muscle, every twitch of his transformation, every spasm of his limbs, making the torment so much more intense.

To keep from going crazy, Nolan slept.

He heard talking, but not from specific people. He could hear heartbeats and breaths, and feel anxiety and worry. Emery visited often; Nolan recognized his thoughts, somehow. Occasionally, Nolan could even hear Emery speak to him, or maybe to his Empathy. Words such as "I'm sorry" would often break through the shadows.

Hours passed. Then days. At long last, night came and went again. Nolan felt weak, but finally in control. He pulled himself from the dark protection.

He blinked awake, and a familiar sight greeted him: a cozy fire, a table arranged with flowers, and an army's worth of weapons arranged on the far wall. Nolan slept in Alec's home.

"Nolan?"

Nolan turned. Alec sat next to him, smiling as relief and

elation oozed from him. "I didn't think you'd wake this time."

"How long?" Nolan croaked.

"Five days," Alec said. "Emery brought you here in quite a state. He's visited every day. And when he isn't here, he sends that old man…Jared, I think. Emery believes it's his own fault, somehow."

"He should," Nolan muttered, though he was also to blame. If he had told Emery to begin with, Emery wouldn't have mistrusted him.

Nolan blinked several times and pushed himself into a sitting position. Moving felt better than he'd expected. Alec talked about what happened, while Nolan tuned it out. Too much sound, too much information. Instead, Nolan let his senses roam.

He could hear Kardos in the armory. A warm fire glowed on the hearth. A large iron pot bubbled over the fire, smelling of one of Bonty's famous stews.

The front door opened, and Nolan glanced over at it, expecting Bonty or Taryn or maybe even Megan. But instead of a human, a gleaming glow preceded a light-filled warrior. Glowing eyes met his.

Nolan bolted upright. His arm swung out, and he hit something solid, but his only thoughts were with the golden warrior before him. Yet when Nolan looked at the door again, the Guardian was gone. He stood on trembling legs as Strength pulsed through him.

"By Brim, Nolan!" Alec said.

His mind cleared. Had he imagined it? He pressed his fingers to his temples.

Alec lay on the remains of a broken dining table, flowers strewn around him. He touched a trail of blood dripping from the corner of his mouth. His face contorted as he struggled for breath.

Dear Brim. What did I do? "I'm so sorry," Nolan stammered.

Alec grunted. "It's okay. You have to get used to it again, eh?"

Crows! How can he joke at a time like this?

Kardos burst into the room, a sword in his hand, and his eyes blazing sapphire blue. He looked at Alec, and with a mad sneer on his face, he stepped toward Nolan.

"Father, wait!" Alec said. "It was an accident."

Kardos lowered his sword arm. "Did you do this?" he said to Nolan while pointing at Alec with his sword.

"Yes. I'm sorry." Nolan staggered toward the door, gripped the latch, and then he tore the door from its hinges.

He ran, ignoring Alec yelling at him to wait. He ran past the rest of the village and past the target range where people gathered. His legs felt strange, as if filled with iron rods. He ran as far as he could. He didn't want to hurt anyone else.

Small trees snapped as he pushed them aside. The branches should've shredded his skin, but they didn't. Those with Strength had skin tougher than leather; the branches didn't leave a scratch.

Finally, he arrived at the ruins, kicking large rocks aside as he headed to the temple.

The morning light rose, allowing the symbols to take shape on the ground. Nolan lay on the floor in the center under the dome. He breathed slowly, taking large, full breaths. The symbols appeared around him, starting with Accuracy and then with Strength. He closed his eyes. How could a man live this way, without breaking or killing everything he cared about or loved?

He opened his eyes and stared through the open, iron rods of the ceiling. The clouds twisted strangely today. Not the typical puffy mass, but like kittens in the duke's stables when they crowded over a dish of milk. They squirmed and twisted over each other, trying to get their fill first. Nolan shuddered. Everything was odd.

Why did he keep thinking of Greer, and how did his mind keep making him appear? He rested through the morning until the sun reached its peak. It was then when his Perception heard someone approach the temple. Nolan felt a familiar presence. Emery.

He tried to get up, but a shudder ran through his muscles. He relaxed again, resting his aching head on the cool stones. Nolan inhaled and released it slowly. At least he wouldn't have to hide from Emery anymore.

"Nolan," Emery said. "Everyone's been searching for you."

"And you found me."

"Aye, I did. Are you well?"

Nolan hesitated, not answering. "How's Alec?"

"I left him with Megan," Emery said. "She's tending to his injuries."

How could he have done that to his best friend?

"She doesn't know of your powers," Emery said. "I thought it best not to tell. It'd be your choice, of course."

"The fewer people who know the better."

"I understand." Emery's Empathy passed over him. "I'm glad you're awake. I've put off our trip as long as I can. But tomorrow the two groups will set out for the final two stones.

"I'll tell Flann you're not feeling well. Considering your incident with Alec, it might be best to give you a few days to control this new ability. He can survive without your help for a while. However, I'm sure a few others will want to stop and say goodbye."

"I can control it for a minute or two."

One side of Emery's mouth rose in a pathetic, half smile. "I can see that. Considering I, of all people, have remained unharmed." His smile left. "I realize your concerns. We'll do our best to keep Taryn safe, though I hope you realize everyone is in danger, not just her. Taryn could very well be safer traveling with me than staying here. I suspect it won't be much longer until our peaceful existence will be destroyed."

"I'll keep a watch while you're gone."

"Aye, you most certainly can."

Nolan assumed Emery would leave. Instead, he lay next to Nolan, and they both gazed into the sky, watching the clouds.

Emery's mood shifted, and guilt oozed from him.

"It's okay," Nolan said, reassuring Emery's thoughts.

"You have no idea how I felt seeing you lying there, not knowing what would happen to you." He paused. "I told you of some of my experiences with the king, but I've not told you all." He hesitated and his brows furrowed. "You see...I've seen Alcandor take a person's Shay."

Nolan propped on his elbows. "Take a person's Shay?"

"Aye." Emery's mouth drew into a flat line. "When he kills them, he takes their powers. That's why he's so incredibly strong."

"So you thought I—"

"I didn't know what to think, Nolan. When I discovered you had more than one, I imagined the worst."

Nolan's stomach turned. "By Brim, Emery, I'd never do that."

"I know. But I had to be certain. I won't sit by and let my people share the same fate as Alcandor's victims. You see, those sorry people are neither alive nor dead. They are driven by only one primitive urge: to seek the Shay they've lost. And though they kill, their hunger is never sated. Only at night can they emerge, because daylight brings them pain."

Nolan's skin went cold. "Are you saying...?"

Emery nodded. "These sorry beings are lost to a fate far worse than death. They are Dor'Jan."

Nolan stared at the clouds. The Dor'Jan were real, and they used to be men. He wondered how the king did it. How did Alcandor claim a Shay? The more he thought about it, the more he didn't want to know. There had to be more to it than just killing a man. If that were the case, the Rol'dan would all have multiple powers. He swallowed; no wonder Nolan's extra powers upset Emery.

One of the clouds broke from the others, zigzagging around the sky. Nolan froze, gawking. Had Emery seen it too?

Emery rose and stretched. "I should return and let them know you're okay."

"Them?"

"Of course. You have quite a few friends." Emery smiled. "I'll send Jared to check on you later."

Emery left Nolan alone with his thoughts. At some point, Nolan must've fallen asleep. When he awoke, the lights on the ground had faded, but the strange clouds still darted in the sky. They resembled black mists more than clouds. He blinked hard and opened his eyes wide, but the sight didn't change. *What's happening to me?*

"Is everything all right, sir?"

Jared leaned against the wall, his thin arms crossed over his chest. *How long has he been here?*

"Emery asked me to tend to your needs," he said.

Nolan wasn't sure what he needed tending. But if it made Emery feel less guilty, he didn't mind. He stood, and his legs trembled, much like when Alec worked him hard.

Out of the corner of his eye, a black mist darted into the temple and out again. Nolan inhaled sharply and looked at Jared. And strangely enough, Jared's eyes rested on the spot where the mist had been.

"Did you see that?" Nolan asked, hopeful.

Jared eyed Nolan, a peculiar expression on his face. "Of course. I'm more surprised *you* saw the Nass."

"The what?" His heart pounded.

Jared turned toward the entrance. "Come with me."

They emerged outside, and Jared searched the ruins.

"It's strange for one to be so far away from people," Jared said. "Ah! There he is." He pointed to a man standing by himself, gazing into the forest.

Nolan summoned Perception to examine him closer. It was a Healer from the village, one Nolan didn't know well. Another dark mist shot from the man, wound in the air, and darted toward the sky.

Jared smiled. "You saw the Nass?"

"I...uh..." Nolan stammered.

"Very good." Jared turned and walked away.

"What's a Nass? And why can you see it too?"

Jared continued on, walking quite fast for a man his age.

Nolan followed. "Jared! Stop! Wait!"

The old man turned, and his eyes glowed with white light.

Nolan's heart stopped. *What in Brim's light is going on?*

"Yes, I can see the Nass," he said.

Nolan forced his next words. "Emery said you have no Shay."

"I don't."

"But your eyes."

He chuckled. "You still do not know, Master, after all of our conversations?"

"All of our conversations?" This was his first real conversation with the man. Jared's eyes glowed white. How was that possible? The only time he'd seen white light was… "Greer?"

He bowed. "At your service, Master Nolan."

"You're Greer?" *So they weren't dreams? How could that be?* Nolan searched his thoughts, weighing every possibility. "Did you…possess Jared?"

He laughed. "Jared is—what you might call—my disguise."

"So you're really a Guardian?"

"I am."

"And you pretend to be an old man?"

Greer chuckled again. "Effective, is it not?"

"Quite." Nolan shook his head.

They turned to the sound of footsteps against the loose rocks. The Healer came toward them, nodding as he passed. As he walked away, another Nass tore from the man's torso, turned three times in the air, and whisked toward them.

Greer flung out his hand, as if swatting an insect, and a blast of light flew from his fingertip. The dark mist dissipated into nothing.

"Annoying things," Greer said, scowling.

Nolan gawked at where the Nass had been. "What are these Nass?"

"Anger, greed, vengeance, lust, fear, and hatred summon the Nass into existence and increase the darkness covering Adamah." Greer looked into the sky. "It is not so bad here. Travel to Alton—or worse yet, Faylinn—and the skies are full. They block the light of Brim, decreasing people's powers.

That is why the powers of Brim are fading in Adamah. When his light doesn't reach man, man's temperament turns fouler, and then man increases the production of Nass tenfold."

"But you destroyed it."

"There are too many, and the Guardians are too few."

"So there are more of you?"

Greer's face tightened. "I only know of one other."

"Where is he? Is he here in our village?"

"*She* is," Greer said.

The dark sky, the Nass, and Guardians were real. And as much as Nolan hated to admit it, he wished he were still ignorant to it all. "But you can unveil yourself if you wish, can't you?"

Greer cast Nolan a puzzled look. "Yes, I can. But I have not done so since the wars."

"And in my dreams."

"Yes, there is that. But I didn't reveal myself in this world; I hid behind your mind."

"You showed yourself when you gave Alec the first stone," Nolan said. "He saw you when you saved him from the Dor'Jan."

Greer stared at Nolan. "I didn't save him. I have been here at the village for the last six years." He put his hands behind his back and paced. "Is this how you obtained the first stone? I had assumed the stone drew you, especially with the strength of your Shay power. Never did I suspect another..."

Greer walked toward the trail, this time quickly. Nolan jogged to stay at his side.

"Forgive me, Master Nolan. I must leave. I must investigate this encounter, to find out if another Guardian lives. Where did this happen?"

"South. In the forest near where the Tournament of Awakening takes place."

Greer nodded. "Then I will begin there." He stopped again as they reached the edge of the woods. "I hope you will forgive me. I will have to abandon Emery's request."

"It's all right," Nolan said, "I've never liked being waited on."

"You sound like Emery," Greer said, smiling. "Please tell Sanawen where I have gone."

"Tell who?"

"Forgive me. The Guardian you know as Bonty. Though I imagine she will be quite surprised to hear you call her by name."

"The other Guardian...is B-Bonty?"

"It pleased me when she arrived," Greer said "I had resigned myself to be alone. However, she has chosen to stay close to Kardos. He creates so many Nass she found it easier to be near him and catch them before they got away.

"She suspected you saw her this morning," he continued. "I told her it was unlikely, but now that I know it is true, it gives me great hope. The light of Brim can enter Adamah once again. It seems the more powers you gain, the more truth is revealed to you. I imagine soon I will not be able to hide from you anymore."

The sun dipped low in the horizon. Out of the corner of Nolan's eye, a brilliant light began to shine. Nolan watched in awe as Jared transformed into Greer: His stooped shoulders straightened, and his body mass and height grew. The light surrounded him, and when it finally faded, Greer the Guardian Warrior stood in Jared's place. He was more resplendent than Nolan's visions. His armor shone more brightly; his light glinted more purely.

"Remarkable," Nolan whispered.

Greer hung his head modestly. "You have no idea how good it feels to share my secret." His mouth rose in a sly smile. "Well, you, Master Nolan, just might."

"Greer, before you go. Can you get me home? It's starting to get dark."

Greer backed away, taking his circle of light with him. He smiled broadly, showing a row of gleaming, white teeth. "I believe you do not need my assistance with that particular task."

Nolan looked at himself and gasped. His skin radiated

with light. It was nothing compared to the Guardian's, but it still glowed quite well. When he turned his head to comment, Greer was gone.

Nolan held out his hand; the light glowed around his fingers. Closing his eyes, he pulled on all of his Shays at once. The light radiated from him, almost as bright as Greer's.

How is this possible? I'm no Guardian. The sun dipped behind the mountains, but around Nolan shone the light of Brim.

Chapter Twenty-Eight

Sanawen, in Bonty's stout figure, circled the busy practice field, sunlight reflecting off silver strands in her salt-and-pepper hair. An overflowing basket hung from her pudgy wrist as she continued picking wildflowers.

She'd hovered near their practice sessions each day this last week. Nolan began to wonder if there was anything left to pick, or what she was doing with all the blooms. Occasionally she would swat at the air as if fighting off a swarm of insects. Nolan was the only one who could see the bugs she fought were actually dark, cloud-like Nass.

A group drew back their bows like they had done countless times over the last several days. Regret oozed from them for agreeing to the extra practice. An air of mutiny hovered, which increased the Nass in alarming numbers.

Sanawen cast Nolan a very Bonty-like glare as she shot Nass out of the air with a whisk of her hand. Since Greer had left a week ago, she'd been left with more than her fair share of work.

And Nolan's practice sessions weren't helping.

"Let's do it again," Nolan called as soon as the arrows struck targets.

"Oh, come on, Nolan," Daren said. His mop of brown hair clung to his face. "I swear, I'm done with this." He tossed his bow to the ground. "Why should I do this anyway? I have Perception, for Brim's sake."

"Until you can find a way to smell a man to death…"

Laughter rippled over the group.

Daren scowled. "Well, I'm taking a break."

The rest grumbled in agreement.

Nolan sighed. If he pushed too hard, they'd never agree again. "All right. But swords in ten minutes."

Another dozen or so Nass tore from the group as they groaned complaints. Bonty wildly swatted the air, as if being swarmed by angry bees.

The group dispersed and trickled to the other practice area, all except Daren who marched toward Nolan, annoyance thick in his emotions.

"When I said take a break, I was thinking about a swim." Daren grinned mischievously.

Nolan moaned. A swim did sound good. "Emery told us to be ready."

"Be ready? Be ready for what?"

"The Rol'dan," Nolan said.

Daren snorted. "How likely is that? The Rol'dan aren't daft enough to wander the forest in the middle of nowhere."

"The stones might lead them here." Nolan could feel the increase of the stones' pull. If he had better awareness of the stones, the Rol'dan probably did as well.

Daren's smiled faded as trepidation lingered on his emotions.

"Come on," Nolan pleaded, hoping his stubbornness would win over Daren's. "Let's swim after sword practice?"

Daren pointed at Nolan in a mock threat. "I'll take that as a promise."

Bonty huffed toward Nolan as soon as Daren left. Her hair hung in wild strands, her cheeks were flushed, and her irritation stabbed his Empathy.

"Nolan, *my dear*," she said. "Are you planning on continuing at this pace?"

"As long as we can." He eyed the rowdy group. Rylan leapt at Daren and tackled him to the ground. "We need a lot more practice."

Daren looked in Nolan's direction, scowling, his eyes

flaring orange with Perception.

"Maybe they *could* use a break." She patted Nolan's arm in a motherly way and went off to pick more flowers.

Nolan sighed. Even the Guardian was turning against him. If the Rol'dan found them, their motley group would have little hope. Nolan had to push them harder. He had no other choice! Though, he'd need to figure out how to encourage them without them revolting and tossing him into the lake.

The group diminished from their archery session, many already taking up Daren's idea of a swim. Those who stayed grudgingly paired off with wooden practice swords.

Branded as the "expert" among his peers, Nolan walked between the rows to check holds and stances. He frowned. Alec should be the one giving advice, not him. But since Alec and Vikas left five days ago, these sorry oafs needed *someone* to help. Kardos could do it, but with his methods, they'd probably go running away in terror five minutes into practice. Nolan squared his shoulders and took a deep breath. Judging by their pathetic half-efforts, he was their best hope.

"Let's try not to use our powers this first round, okay?" Nolan suggested. "Use your skills instead of depending on your Shay. On our second turn, we'll match according to our powers."

Nolan paired with Daren who glared at Nolan with an evil smirk, ready to dish out some well-deserved revenge.

"Ready?" Nolan said. "Swords up." His Shays swelled; he pushed them back down, locking them into place. His Strength could be a little defiant, but he'd *mostly* gotten it under control.

Daren dropped his stance and stiffened, his eyes flashing orange.

"What is it?" Nolan asked.

"Someone's coming."

Nolan awakened Perception and heard trees rustling; a group ran toward them through the woods. Before Nolan could react, blurred images of people rushed in, whisked between the ranks, and tore wooden swords from their grasps.

Nolan yanked out his steel sword and sliced through the air.

Alec ducked and laughed, his arms full of wooden practice swords. "Easy there!"

The other Speed users smiled with Alec, as if they all enjoyed the same joke.

"I could've taken your head off," Nolan snapped.

"Ah, but you need to be quicker!" Alec leaned toward Nolan and whispered, "And we have something to help."

"Excellent entrance!" Vikas said. "Nolan, please inform Flann that we've returned." He didn't wait for an answer, but reached into a pouch and pulled out a stone. "To the temple!"

The newly returned group disappeared into the woods again, whooping and yelling. Not that Nolan wasn't glad they were safely back, but they could've arrived with a little less flare. Those who'd been disarmed gawked at each other. If it had been the Rol'dan, they would all be dead.

"Guess we're done for today," Nolan said.

Daren and Rylan had already stripped, leaving a trail of clothes to the lake. Nolan shook his head and trudged toward the village center. Flann would probably be at the lodge.

He turned down the first street and ran into Greer in his old man form. At his side strolled a muscular man with a square jaw and cropped blond hair. As the man passed by a group of maidens, more than one turned their head a second time.

"Nolan," Greer said, his eyes bright with excitement. "This is...my nephew."

"Please, call me Malik." He offered his hand. "I am more than honored to meet you."

Nolan grasped his hand. His shake was hard, even to Nolan's Strength-enforced grip. "It's a pleasure."

Malik surveyed the encampment. "I have been enjoying my visit thus far. I have met the man called Flann."

"I was just on my way to see him. The Speed users have returned with the stone."

Malik cast Greer a side-glance. "Everything is even more than I had imagined."

A pair of girls giggled and hurried by.

"Where is Sanawen?" Malik asked.

"Over there," Greer said. "But call her Bonty here."

Bonty walked toward them, her face downcast as she concentrated on her overflowing basket. Malik laughed heartily, and Bonty's head jerked up. She dropped the basket, spilling flowers around her feet.

"Malik? By the light, it can't be."

Malik's grin widened. "It is good to see you, Sana—"

"Bonty," she cut in.

"Ah, yes. Bonty, is it?"

She smiled. "At least right now."

The two Guardians closed the distance and met in an embrace.

"He could have chosen something less...conspicuous," Nolan said as he watched the shocked and disappointed faces of the group of young women.

Greer sighed. "He would have nothing to do with it. He didn't want to take human form at all. I finally talked him into this."

Malik spun Bonty around as they both laughed.

"They know each other?"

"Quite well." Greer smiled slyly. "When I told him she was alive, he was very willing to come with me. And after I told him about you, I couldn't have kept him away." Jared glanced toward the direction of the forest. "I believe someone is coming."

Even though Jared had warned Nolan, he jumped at Alec's appearance.

"Nolan," Alec said animatedly. "You won't believe it. It's amazing."

"Slow down," Nolan said. "Take a breath."

Alec took a few short breaths. "By Brim, Nolan, I was fast before...but now...And it's so much easier. It gave me some type of agility. If we leave now, we can get you in there—" Alec stopped; his eyes darted toward Greer.

"It's okay," Nolan said. "He knows."

"He d-does?" Alec stammered. For the first time since he'd reappeared, he was speechless.

Malik and Bonty approached, walking arm in arm. Alec's mouth dropped open.

"This is my nephew, Malik," Greer said. "Malik, this is Alec Deverell."

Malik released his hold on Bonty's arm and examined Alec with gleaming eyes. His lips spread open to a wide grin. "Alec, is it? I am honored." He grabbed Alec's hand and shook it.

Alec's gaze caught Nolan's with a "who is this guy?" expression.

Malik released his hold. "You are well, then?"

"Very well, thank you," Alec said, puzzled. He opened and closed his palm, trying to regain circulation. "Do I know you?"

Malik opened his mouth to speak, but Greer quickly positioned himself between them. "Malik, you can stay with me until you get your own place." He pulled the brawny Malik away. "I'll check on you later, sir," he said to Nolan over his shoulder.

Bonty followed behind them.

"Who is that?" Alec asked.

"Jared's nephew, I guess."

"Huh? When did he show up?"

"Today," Nolan said. He wondered how Greer had explained Malik's appearance to Flann.

"I've seen him somewhere." Alec tapped his finger against his chin. "And what's with him and Bonty? Now that's just not right."

"Bonty is a grown woman—"

"It's not that. It's something else." He snapped and held up a finger. "What if he's Rol'dan? Maybe I saw him at the tournament."

"Don't you think I would've recognized him, if that were the case?"

Alec nodded. "Maybe. But I've seen him somewhere."

"You've got a lot more to worry about than Bonty," Nolan said. "Don't you have to meet Emery and his group?"

"Yes, but I'm supposed to rest before I leave. Don't worry, I'll catch up with them. But while I'm here, you can have a go at the stone."

Nolan cast him a foul glare.

"Think of the fun we could have," Alec said. "Think of the possibilities."

Nolan grabbed Alec's arm.

"Ow!" Alec said, grinning. "Crows, Nolan!"

"Sorry." Nolan pushed down his Strength and directed Alec through the busy path, away from watching eyes behind a grouping of small trees. He lowered his voice to a whisper. "Even *if* I did step into the light, I wouldn't do it in front of anyone. Mind you, *if* I were to go, I'd wait until morning before sunrise and beat anyone coming early."

"You mean travel while it's still dark?" Alec gawked. "Let me remind you that the Dor'Jan are still out there. We saw them in the high country just last night."

"Don't worry. The Dor'Jan wouldn't dare come near us this time."

"And why's that?"

Nolan smiled. "Wait and see."

* * *

The dark roads were deserted as Nolan headed to the armory. He concentrated on the crunching of his feet against the packed earth, blocking the subtle sounds of sleep in the homes nearby. He'd augured with himself all evening, unable to eat, unable to think. Part of him wondered if the Shay powers were turning him into an arrogant twit like Kael. *Isn't four Shay powers enough?*

He inhaled quickly and released it in a long sigh. If they wanted to defeat Alcandor, if they wanted to free all the Rol'dan—including Kael—then Nolan wanted to help.

He'd become a pretty good swordsman. But no matter how hard he trained, or how much Perception and Accuracy and Strength he put behind his blade, he'd still be dead from a Speed Rol'dan before he even drew his sword. Nolan *needed* Speed.

Nolan cringed, remembering his last transformation. So much pain. But he'd seen others transform. Strength was always the worst. Speed would be easy—in comparison.

Unless it killed him.

Wiping sweaty palms on his breeches, he pushed his fears into the box with his Shays. It *could* kill him. Or...he'd gain Speed, save Kael, and—most importantly—beat the pants off Alec in their next sparring session. A smile crept to his face. Definitely worth the risk.

Summoning Perception, he heard both Alec and his father snoring softly in the armory.

He rapped lightly on the door, but Alec didn't answer.

Nolan knocked a little louder and finally heard stirring. The door creaked open, and Alec's head poked out, his hair sticking up in sleep-mangled clumps.

"Nolan?"

"I thought you were meeting me at the field."

Alec scratched his head. "You weren't joking?" He blinked, trying to focus.

"Hurry up!"

The door closed softly, and Nolan waited only a few seconds before Alec reappeared, fully dressed, hair combed, and wide awake.

"Let's grab some torches from the armory," Alec said, his eyes glowing with Speed.

"We don't need them."

Alec crossed his arms over his chest, scowling. "What do you mean, we don't need—"

"Just come on," Nolan said and stepped off.

They walked across the field, their steps crunching against the dry grass. Stopping next to one of the protective lanterns, they waited.

Alec kicked at the ground and fidgeted with the lantern pole. "Crows, Nolan. This is stupid. What are we waiting for? The sun to rise? We could've done that in bed."

"Shh!" Nolan hid a smile.

Several minutes passed, and impatience gushed from Alec.

"Relax!" Nolan said.

"I am relaxing," Alec lied. He leaned against the pole and tapped it irritably. His tapping stopped as the three shadowed figures approached. "Who's that?"

The three Guardians drew nearer, still in their human forms. Their eyes glowed white with internal light, a light Alec couldn't see.

"You invited *them*?" Alec said, confusion pouring from him.

Nolan supposed inviting an old man, a bar maid, and someone they'd just met might come across as strange.

"Evening, Master." Malik bowed. "Shall I provide our light?"

"No," Nolan answered. "I got it."

"I told you, I can get torches," Alec said. "If you just give me a second..." His voice trailed off as soon as Nolan's light emerged. Words strangled in his throat.

"Let's go," Nolan said, "before I change my mind."

***

By the time they reached the ruins, the sun poked over the mountains. Nolan decreased his Shay powers, and a blanket of exhaustion fell on him.

They arrived at the temple just as sunlight reached the high-domed ceiling. The symbols appeared, each in their turn. Nolan tensed as the golden symbol of Speed emerged.

Alec grabbed his arm. "No one is forcing you, you know." A mixture of fear, nervousness, and excitement spilled from him. "You don't have to do this for me."

"I know." Nolan smiled. "It'll be fine." Or at least he hoped it would be.

Stepping into the light, the sun warmed his skin. He inhaled and exhaled slowly, relaxing, rolling his shoulders while he shook the tension from his hands. Maybe it wouldn't work this time. Part of him hoped it wouldn't. Then he could forget the stones, or combining them, or defeating anyone. He'd finally be able to just be himself.

The sunlight sank through him, burrowing into his flesh. He clenched his fists as the light met his other Shays. They whirled and danced together inside him. Heat rose in his body like a fire, and his heart began to race.

Nolan breathed in short pants, his heart accelerating so quickly he couldn't tell one beat from another. Pain stabbed his chest, and at that moment, a golden-yellow light spilled around him and in him, coursing through his arms, his legs, his chest. His body froze, his muscles tensed, and his feet lifted from the ground. Fireflies of golden light twirled, matching the speed of the maelstrom inside him.

Slowly, the storm calmed and his feet gently touched down—just like on his first experience in the light. Unconsciousness didn't claim him. No dreams. No mists. Greer didn't enter his mind. He wilted, the tension leaving in a rush. He'd survived.

Alec laughed, relief flooding through him.

Nolan took a step and his legs collapsed. His muscles contracted and tightened like a bowstring. He cursed as another spasm took hold. "Crows! Was it this bad for you?"

Alec knelt. "Um, I didn't notice with a sword rammed through me at the time."

Nolan tried to laugh, but another spasm jerked through his body. After several more, his muscles finally loosened.

He pushed himself off the floor, but his arms wobbled, barely supporting him. When he raised his head, he forgot his discomfort. Greer, Sanawen, and Malik watched, shining in their magnificence.

Greer was as Nolan remembered: broad, glimmering, and regal. His short brown hair gleamed like copper.

Malik was much the same, with golden waves hanging down the sides of his face. However, he was even taller and broader than Greer.

Sanawen was the most changed. Nolan drew in a breath. Long, flowing, silver locks waved down the length of her back; she was…beautiful.

They all wore breastplates, leaving their muscular arms

bare. The armor was adorned with intricate vines, as well as greaves and bracers that matched. It gleamed with golden light, while the Guardians themselves glowed white and pure.

"Nolan, are you okay?" Alec asked, confused. He couldn't see them.

Nolan blinked back his gawking. "Greer. If you don't mind, I'd like to show Alec your true forms."

"Greer?" Alec asked. "Who's Greer?"

"Nolan, love. I'm not so sure," Sanawen said.

"It's okay," Greer said. "If Nolan trusts him…"

Alec laughed nervously. "What the Darkness are you all talking about?"

"He is right," Malik said. "And he has seen before."

"Nolan," Alec said. "What are you talking…" His voice trailed away as the transformations began.

Although Nolan couldn't see it, he could sense it through Alec. Alec's eyes widened, his mouth dropped open, and then he staggered backward, muttering under his breath. Fear and confusion gushed from him, and then Alec's eyes shone with Speed.

Alec ran. However this time, Nolan watched as if time had slowed. He flared his own Speed, intercepted Alec at the door, grabbing him before he went through.

"Argh, Nolan. Not so hard!"

Nolan realized his Shay of Strength was also in full force. He relaxed his hold, but not enough to let his thrashing friend go.

Like a wild animal, Alec struggled. "Let go of me!"

"Calm down, Alec. They're friends."

Alec stopped fighting, but the tension in him was far from gone.

"Alec, I'd like you to meet the Guardians."

Alec stared, his emotions ranging from horror to astonishment then finally to recognition as his eyes fixed on Malik.

"It's not possible. Is it possible? I'd almost talked myself out of it, thinking I'd imagined it after all."

Malik bowed. "It was my honor to assist you in your time

of need, Master Alec."

"It's you. You're the one who saved me."

Malik lowered his head. "Please forgive me. I almost didn't feel your presence in the woods that night. I am ashamed I nearly arrived too late."

"Ashamed?"

"If I were but a second more…" Malik continued.

"I would've died if you hadn't come. Thank you."

Malik released a breath heavy with a sob. A hint of a tear shimmered in the corner of his gleaming white eye. "Master Alec, you give me great honor."

Sanawen and Greer stood taller, their chests thrust out in pride.

Was this the only time anyone had thanked them? A simple word brought the Guardian to tears. It then occurred to Nolan: They'd protected man even after man nearly destroyed them. The Guardians disguised themselves for centuries. And they did it without a word of thanks.

Nolan knew how to hide—he was good at it. Even now, he buried his new powers from almost everyone. And it wasn't because he was in any danger, or to protect someone like the Guardians did; he did it because he was afraid what others would think of him.

The truth fell on Nolan hard.

He swallowed. He'd been selfish. Emery and the others struggled, searching for answers, wandering around the land risking their lives. And the whole time, Nolan locked himself in his cottage, pretending nothing had happened. He had five Shays now, for Brim's sake. He should do *something*.

Alec touched his arm. "Hey. You okay?"

Nolan cleared his throat and nodded. "I think so."

"No hiding this time," Alec said, excitement spilling from him. "I'll take you out to practice Speed. With swords."

Tremors went through Nolan's legs; his body adjusting to his new power. "All right. No hiding." He pressed his lips together and tightened his fist. As soon as he adjusted to his new Shay, he *would* do something, by Brim.

Chapter Twenty-Nine

For the next two weeks, Nolan and Alec lived in the forest, fighting from dusk until dawn. They sparred in small clearings, in thick groves, and even at the base of the mountains. It amazed Nolan how far they could travel within a few hours. After one such day, they ran back home. They tucked their Speed away, and the world around them skidded to a stop.

Nolan gulped in air, his lungs burning. Alec breathed heavily too, but seemed to be under control.

"Run me through next time you talk me into this," Nolan said between gasps. They'd traveled farther than usual.

"I wish I could. I can't get a blade on you nowadays." Alec leaned against an oak tree. "Though, you did cheat."

"Well, you shouldn't tell me to give you everything I have."

Alec laughed and motioned toward Nolan's sheath. "I owe you a new sword."

Nolan frowned, thinking of the two sword halves. "I suppose I did hit you a little hard."

"A little?"

"I didn't expect your sword to cut mine in two."

"Serves you right," Alec teased. "Using your Strength like that."

Nolan smiled. "I only used a little."

Though Nolan had enjoyed the last two weeks of daily combat, it was time for Alec to be on his way.

"When are you supposed to meet Emery?" Nolan asked.

He already knew, but didn't want to sound pushy.

"I was wondering when you were going to mention that." A tremor of shame flickered through Alec. "I was supposed to meet him at the inn in Caldalk two days ago."

"Two days?"

"I guess I've been putting it off."

"Not that I haven't enjoyed our matches—"

"I know, I know," Alec said, his hands held up in defense. "I need to get out there. I've just been having too much fun."

"I hope you aren't going to blame me."

"Of course not," Alec said with a sly grin. "I wouldn't do that."

"I can tell if you're lying."

"I wouldn't lie to you." There was no joking in his emotions.

They stood, catching their breath, while a cool breeze filtered through the woods. The trees were changing; orange and yellow sprinkled through the leaves. A pair of wrens flew and landed on a branch, pruning themselves before flapping away.

Apprehension formed in Alec's emotions, and a question lingered between them.

"What is it?" Nolan asked.

Alec pursed his lips. "When we bring back the Healing stone, are you going to take it?"

"Take it? As in, stand in the light? I suppose I will. Then maybe I won't have to hurt Megan the next time someone stabs me." Nolan forced a laugh, but Alec didn't. Worry lines creased his brow.

"I won't touch you if you change, Nolan. I can't."

"Of course you won't touch me; I'm fast now."

He leveled a stare at Nolan.

Nolan sighed. "You don't need to worry about that. I'll be fine. Alcandor is bad, not because of the powers, just because he is."

Alec's shoulders relaxed, and relief leaked from him. "So you're not concerned about the last stone? About the power changing you?"

"Of course not," Nolan lied. He wasn't sure what would happen, but it wasn't worth stressing his friend now.

"So, why you?" Alec asked. "What makes you different than the rest of us?"

"Don't know," Nolan said. "Some are born with extra fingers and toes. I guess I'm just strange."

"So you're a mutant?" A grin spread across his face.

Nolan snickered. "I suppose so."

They pushed off and started walking back to the village. Now that they were rested, the breeze felt cold. Nolan shivered and rubbed his arms.

"I've adjusted to all the powers," Nolan said. "A little overwhelming at times, but I've got them mostly under control. But there is still one thing I haven't gotten used to."

"Oh? What's that?"

"The Guardians. I can only see them in their true forms now. Kind of miss the old Jared and Bonty, especially when a giant light warrior is trying to make me tea."

Alec laughed. "I don't see them like you do, but I still can't get it out of my head. I'm glad they're real, though. For a while there, I thought I'd gone mad."

Nolan knew exactly what he meant.

"Poor Father," Alec said. "I think he still fancies Bonty. Didn't take it so well when she started hanging out with Malik."

"Speaking of your father..." Nolan pulled out what was left of his weapon. "You owe me a sword."

Alec slung an arm over Nolan's shoulder. "Come to the shop, and I'll get you a new one. I'm sure one or ten spare ones are lying around. Besides, I have something I want to give you."

"One or ten?"

"Production has picked up a bit."

They entered the village, where several groups practiced weapon skills. Daren waved from a distance and ducked as Rylan whisked a sword through the air. They continued past the field and through the main section of the village. Several people strolled by and waved.

When they entered the armory, Kardos looked up from his anvil. "Where've you been?"

"Practicing." Alec threw his bag on the ground. "Nolan's going to need a new weapon. My sword cut his clean through."

Kardos stopped his hammer mid-strike, and his eyes rose with interest. "Did it now?"

"One good swipe."

Kardos chuckled and wiped his head with his forearm, leaving a sooty streak. He then set the hammer on the anvil and shoved his current work into the coals of the forge. His intense eyes examined Nolan, making his skin crawl.

The last time they'd spoken, Kardos had stabbed him. Nolan felt no regret from Kardos's emotions, nor did the blacksmith say anything more about it at all. It didn't surprise Nolan in the least. He suspected the word "apology" wasn't in the blacksmith's vocabulary.

Kardos went to a row of swords displayed on the wall. After a thoughtful inspection, he took one down.

"Try this."

Nolan gripped the sword and gave it a few swings; it felt more comfortable than his last one. "This is excellent, sir." Nolan inspected the flawless blade.

Kardos didn't acknowledge the compliment, but his pride swelled. "Just finished that one last week."

"Thank you."

Kardos nodded and went back to his place at the forge.

Alec emerged from a side room, a bundle in his hands. "Here, I made these for you."

Kardos snorted. "So that's what those are for. For a while there, I thought he might build a house or something."

Nolan cast Alec a questioning glance; Alec shoved the wad of fabric toward him. Nolan unrolled the heavy bundle and the sound of metal clanged. In his hands lay a large stack of throwing spikes.

"You've been busy," he said as he tried to get a general count of them. *What does he expect me to do with these?* Nolan wondered how much weight his pouch could take. He might have to take out some stuff. His ink and quill would have to go; he didn't use them so much nowadays.

"There're about fifty," Alec said.

"Fifty?"

"Well, considering how fast you can throw, I wouldn't want you to get bored."

"Wow, Alec...I uh..."

"You don't like them?" Alec said, his excitement deflating.

"No, it's not that," Nolan said. "I'm just not sure how I'm supposed to carry them."

Alec's enthusiasm flared back to life. "I've got that taken care of, too."

He went across the room and returned with a handful of leather. "Here. This belt wraps around your hips twice." He pulled it around Nolan and buckled it into place. "It will hold thirty. The bracer goes on your left arm, and this band on your right leg. That way they'll all be in reach when you want to throw, but not encumber you when you want to use your sword."

"Impressive." Nolan fastened on the bracer while Alec shoved the spikes into place on his leg. "Did you come up with this on your own?"

A boyish grin spread across his face. "Remember, I've lived in an armory all my life."

"Don't blame me!" Kardos's face was like stone, but, humor lingered in his emotions. "I've got nothin' to do with those oversized nails. That was all his doing."

Alec shrugged. "I thought...Well, I know you aren't fond of bows, and this might come in handy."

Nolan inserted the spikes into the bracer. "This must have taken you a while."

Alec smirked. "Not *that* long."

After he'd finished inserting the last one, Nolan examined himself. The bracer he'd have to get used to, but the leg band and the belt were quite comfortable. Though he reminded himself of a porcupine, he could imagine how the spikes could function with Speed and Accuracy quite well.

"Thanks, Alec."

"It's the least I can do."

Nolan met his eyes. "So, when are you leaving?"

"You're still trying to get rid of me?"

Kardos stopped hammering. Both fear and concern lurked behind his stony frown.

"I'll be back in a minute, Father." Alec motioned for Nolan to follow him outside.

Twilight was nearly upon them. A Speed user began her nightly routine of lighting the village fires. In the past, the process was almost instantaneous, with lights appearing from nowhere. Now that Nolan had Speed, he could see the girl jogging from one lantern pole to another.

"I still wonder if you shouldn't be going in my place," Alec said.

The thought had crossed his mind more than once, but a sinking feeling of the village coming into danger kept Nolan's resolve firm. "Emery wanted me here, and he needed your sword."

"That was before you started winning."

"Well, that's only because I can cheat."

"In a real battle, cheating can be useful, especially against the Rol'dan."

Nolan looked to the sky. He still hadn't gotten used to the darkness and the constant movement of the Nass. Seeing the reality of them made his stomach churn.

"I had thought about getting a start today," Alec said, "but I wanted to spend some time with you and Father before I left. I'll leave at first light instead."

"Your father seems different," Nolan said.

"He *is* different. Something about getting his Shay power, and finding out how my mother died, gave him some measure of peace—not that he's a pleasant man, mind you. But things between us have been good."

"I'm glad," Nolan said. Kardos did seem more at ease.

"See you in the morning?" Alec said.

"I'll try, but Flann wants me out at the ruins first thing. It's my turn to watch the temple."

They stared at each other briefly, and then Nolan leaned in and gave him a hug. They clung to each other before separating.

"Take care of yourself, okay?" Nolan said.

"Of course. Don't I always?"

Nolan laughed. "As long as you keep that temper of yours in check."

"Let me know how those spikes work out."

"I'll give you a demonstration when you come home."

"I'll be looking forward to it." Alec stepped off and turned so he could walk backward to face Nolan. "Farewell, my friend."

Nolan watched until Alec disappeared into the armory. "Stay safe, my brother."

Chapter Thirty

Nolan propped a log against the outside of the temple wall, kicking a few rocks around the base to secure it. Greer stood next to him, his posture still and erect, as usual. Even in daylight, a faint glow shone from the Guardian. And with Alec gone, Greer rarely left Nolan's side.

"Numbers are up at practice," Greer said. "And they are improving, if slowly."

Brushing dirt from his hands, Nolan walked away; Greer followed.

"I've noticed the number of girls increasing as well," Nolan added.

Greer frowned. "I've tried to reason with Malik. He said he gets too hot in the tunic, and it constricts him while trying to teach. He insists the girls aren't coming for him."

Summoning Perception, the log came into Nolan's focus as if a few steps away.

"How are you faring with the new powers?" Greer asked.

Like the drum of a woodpecker, the spikes hit the log. Nolan studied his handiwork with satisfaction. "Very well, actually."

"And have you considered the stones?"

Nolan headed back to the log to collect the spikes. "Yes, but you haven't given me much to work with."

"I told you what the legends foretold, the information Brim passed on to us upon our creation."

"You've told me they need to be combined, not how I'm

supposed to do it."

"I have told you all I know."

"But you have ideas, don't you?" Nolan shoved the last spike into his belt.

"Please forgive me, Master Nolan," Greer said. "It is not my place to lead you in your journey. Considering Brim has gifted you with so many abilities, I believe the task has been assigned to you."

"Alcandor gained all six powers long before I did."

Greer's face hardened, but he said nothing, like every other time Nolan mentioned King Alcandor's name.

Nolan cleared his throat. "Well...talk to Malik again. Convince him to cover himself. It might help with the distraction problem he's having amongst the girls. And if all else fails, tell him I insisted."

"Should be effective." Greer bowed his head. "Will you be returning home soon?"

"Yes." He hurled another round of spikes into the log. "But not quite yet."

"Very well," Greer said. "I will speak to you more this evening."

The Guardian brought forth Speed and ran into the forest toward the village, leaving Nolan alone.

Nolan sighed. Once the others returned, he'd have no excuse not to combine the stones—whatever that meant.

He returned to the log and yanked the spikes free. This time, he'd arranged them in a swirled pattern. Tucking them into place in his holders, he glanced toward the temple. He didn't need to stand in the light or hold the stones. His powers stayed complete on their own. But any time he got near, they still drew him.

For a while, he tried to ignore the stones. He threw a few more rounds of spikes, practiced on his sling, and then went straight to tossing huge rocks. Finally, he couldn't take it any longer. He headed for the temple.

Nolan circled the outside of the temple until he found the ladder cut into stone on the side, leading to the top of the dome.

With a small swell of Strength, he pulled himself up. And with Accuracy, he carefully made the climb. Once he reached top, he admired the artwork of the structure. In many ways, the metal framework reminded Nolan of a half-built spider's web; the beams crossed in the middle, and the stones resembled flies carefully wrapped for a future meal.

Nolan stretched his legs apart, balancing on two metal beams as the ruined city stretched before him. Even now, in its dilapidated state, a hint of its former glory still shone. It was bigger than he'd expected; remains were scattered in parts of the forest where Nolan hadn't yet ventured.

The power in the stones pulsed, drawing Nolan to them. He shifted his foothold and squatted to study the nearest one. It rested in a perfect recess, as if the metal embraced it. Nolan reached for it, but the opening was too small for his hand.

Carefully lowering himself onto the beam, he pushed the stone upward with his fingers and grabbed it with his other hand. The Stone of Perception connected with his Shay. He closed his eyes as the power vibrated through him.

"So what am I supposed to do with you?" he said to the stone while caressing it in his palm. "How am I supposed to combine you with your friends?" He considered the small, painted rocks, the ones Hakan had given him months before. He supposed if he placed them all together in a bag, they would be combined. It wasn't a *good* idea. But at this point, he didn't have any others.

He scanned the metal dome and took note of the other stones' locations, and then his eyes caught another recess, directly in the center of the web-like beams.

It looked bigger. Not wider, but deeper than the others. Could all six fit? Could they be stacked, one on top of another? The amount of space looked right. *No. It can't be that easy.*

Stepping toward the center, he staggered, the floor below shifting with vertigo. Nolan swallowed and shut his eyes until the dizziness left. *Okay. It's not so easy.*

Instead of walking, he crawled. He made it to the center, his heart thundering. Licking his lips—which had gone completely dry—he dropped the stone into the recess with a clink. The symbol of Perception shone directly in the center of the temple floor.

He crawled to retrieve another stone and returned to the center. Sweat streamed down his face, stinging his eyes and dripping from his nose to splatter on the floor far below. Holding tightly to the Stone of Strength in his moist palm, Nolan carefully dropped it on top of the first. He lowered his head through the space in the bars to stare at the floor below him.

A circle of pure white light formed in the center of the room. But instead of two distinctive symbols, the colors melded together into parts of words.

Nolan froze. He didn't actually believe he'd see anything. He summoned Perception to get a better look, but the letters were too disconnected to discern.

Retrieving the Stone of Empathy, he dropped it on top of the others. The lines changed; the violet of Empathy joined the previous two.

"By Brim! That's it!" Nolan laughed. Though he still couldn't read the words, he'd found the answer. At least, he hoped he'd found something.

He pulled through the bars, searching for the next stone. As he rose, his Perception caught a thundering noise similar to when Vikas and Alec had arrived home with the Speed stone. Strange. Maybe Vikas had taken some villagers for a day trip. As he focused in on the noise, his heart fell into his stomach. Crows. It came from the wrong direction, nowhere close to the village.

Nolan jumped to his feet, balancing on metal rafters as he pulled two spikes, all the while hoping he was wrong. His hands shook so much he wondered if he'd be able to throw.

He swelled his Perception. The sound intensified, and the approaching group changed direction—straight toward the temple ruins.

Nolan surged all of his powers at once just as a platoon of Rol'dan broke through the trees. Golden tunics flew toward him, swords shining in the late afternoon sun. Like the log he'd been practicing on, Nolan flung the spikes toward them.

The first wave of soldiers didn't know what had killed them.

The second ranks barely noticed before the spikes embedded into their chests.

Nolan's hands shook, but his aim flew perfect. He yanked his Empathy from the horror and fear in their minds.

A few adjusted their run, diving out of the way. They yanked their swords as they ran toward the temple. Nolan leaped from one metal beam to another, using Speed and Accuracy at the same time to retrieve the stones. He flung them into his bag as a Rol'dan appeared on top of the dome.

Using all of his Shays, Nolan drew his sword, jumped toward the Rol'dan, and sliced the air as he fell.

The Rol'dan pitched backward off the temple, his head tumbling beside him.

Nolan had little time to ponder the gruesome act as he grasped the ivy climbing the temple. It slowed his fall until the ivy snapped. He increased Strength, hardening his body as his feet struck the ground.

Every bone jarred at the impact, the ground cracking under his feet.

Nolan swung around and blocked another's blow, the metal of their blades echoing against the walls. The Rol'dan soldier fought well, though not as well as Nolan. After three strikes, Nolan impaled him and turned to fight his next enemy.

Soldier after soldier, men and women both, died by Nolan's hand. And he felt everything—their fear, their pain, and the release of their death—yet he couldn't pity them...not yet. He only had time to turn and allow it to happen again and again.

After the battle ended, the few remaining Rol'dan retreated into the trees. Using Perception, Nolan heard them going farther away.

His muscles shook with tension and exhaustion. He scanned the bodies littering the ground. He had killed more than thirty soldiers in just a few minutes.

So much blood.

So many lives.

Nolan retched on a pile of rubble.

He wiped his mouth with the sleeve of his bloodstained tunic. With a shaking hand, he sheathed his sword. He must warn the others. The Rol'dan would certainly return.

"My lord," a voice said, not much past a whisper.

Nolan jerked his head around, searching for the source of the voice. A boy lay in a puddle of blood, both fear and desperation trickling from his emotions. Quickly, Nolan scanned the remainder of the bodies.

No heartbeats.

No breathing.

This Rol'dan still lived.

"My lord," the boy said again. "P-please. Have mercy. Heal me."

Nolan cringed, his muscles trembling. Crows! There was nothing he could do! He held all the powers...except the one that could save him.

"I...I can't." Nolan words stuck in his throat. He'd never felt so helpless.

What small bit of hope the boy held faded. His eyes closed, and his head drooped to the side. Nolan dove toward him, desperation driving him. If he could help. If he could save this life *Maybe I can stop the bleeding.* Nolan ripped open the boy's tunic and jolted back.

She wasn't a boy.

A wound between her breasts flowed with dark, crimson blood. Nolan pulled her tunic closed as best as he could. The wound was too deep. He summoned Strength and lifted her onto his shoulder. Though he couldn't heal her, others could.

Chapter Thirty-One

Emery Cadogan watched the girls rummage through the muck, searching for the Stone of Healing. Megan lifted a blob of mud, examined it, and tossed it aside, frustration tainting her emotions. Taryn sat in the sticky mire next to Megan, her arms buried elbow deep in the goo. Emery smiled, amused. He'd seen a lot of things over the years, but he'd never seen two young women rolling in the mud.

Hakan caught Emery's eyes. Emery put a hand over his mouth. He knew better. Megan had a temper. If she caught Emery grinning, she'd probably lob mud at him.

"Should we help?" Garrick whispered.

"Brim save the man who asks them," Emery said.

Alec jumped down from a rock where he'd been watching the girls. Tension oozed off him like a dark, stormy cloud. "Are you sure you don't need any help?" Alec called to them.

Taryn turned her head violently, flinging strings of once-blond hair now caked with grime. She answered with a glare that clearly said, "Don't even ask."

Hakan barked a laugh. "Aye, the boy will learn when to keep his mouth shut."

Alec pressed his lips together in a scowl. He paced, his emotions radiating uselessness.

"Why don't you sit and relax?" Emery suggested. "They'll be at it for a while."

Alec ignored him; Emery sensed his tension increase even more. Why was the boy so upset?

"Please, Alec. They'll be fine," Emery urged again. "Look at what a fine job they're doing."

Megan glared this time, though she didn't look very scary with mud smeared across her nose.

"But you could've been killed," Alec said. "I should've been there!"

How would rolling in the mud kill anyone? One could choke on it, he supposed. Then revelation washed over him. Alec had missed an encounter with a trio of Strength Rol'dan in Caldalk three days ago.

"It would've been nice if you were there," Emery said, "but we handled it without you. Well, actually, Maska handled it."

Maska grunted. "It was simple."

While staying overnight at an inn, three Strength Rol'dan made the two biggest mistakes of their lives. The first: trying to push their lusts onto Megan and Taryn. The second: insulting Maska. It had been a tough fight, one that almost cost Maska his life. But he'd survived. The Rol'dan, however...

A squeal came from below. Megan slipped and fell on her backside in the muck. Hakan choked a laugh, smiling broadly. Emery wisely made no expression at all.

"Are you sure you don't need help?" Alec asked again.

"No!" both girls screamed.

Alec stammered, "I...I was trying to help, for Brim's sake. I'll just go wait—"

Megan's gasped. "By the light!" she said. "I've found it!" With a sucking gurgle, she pulled it from the muck, revealing a dirty, brown lump in her palm.

"That's it?" Emery said. Though from the way her emotions soared, and how her tension suddenly vanished, they'd found the Stone of Healing.

Taryn scooted closer to Megan to admire it.

"What I wouldn't give for a painter right now," Hakan teased. "Would love to remember this vision. It'd make a grand piece to hang on my wall."

"And the next time you hurt yourself, you'll wish you hadn't insulted us," Megan said.

"A very good threat, lass," Hakan said, "but the temptation might be worth the risk. Once I get back I might try my hand at jotting it down. You know, for posterity's sake."

Megan scowled, though a smile hid beneath it. "It wasn't your posterity I was threatening."

"Come on, ladies." Emery chuckled and offered his hand. "Let's get you cleaned up before Hakan ingrains the vision in his mind."

"Ah, but it's too late." Hakan pointed a thick finger to the side of his bushy mane. "It's all here."

"Well," Megan said, "let's hope you're able to make it home alive."

Hakan threw back his head and laughed. "Indeed."

The girls trekked up the incline, slipping several times on the way. Megan grabbed Emery's waiting hand, and he pulled her up the hill before helping Taryn. When they were both on flat ground, he shook his hand, spattering mud onto the weeds.

"Hakan, can you hear any water nearby? A lake or stream?" Emery asked.

"Right on it," Hakan said as his Perception glowed orange.

Emery met Megan's eyes. "Well done. If anyone could find it, it would be you."

She smiled, and a smudge of mud cracked on her cheek. On an impulse, Emery reached up and wiped it off. Shock and excitement spiked in her. He inhaled sharply and yanked his hand away.

"Sounds like there might be a small stream," Hakan said, pointing. "But it's the wrong way from home. So if we wait a bit, then we can..." His voice trailed off.

Hakan frowned. He put a finger to his lips. Pulling his crossbow from his back, he motioned for them to follow and took off at a run.

In and out of the trees they darted, only hearing the crunch of their feet in the brush and the heavy beating of their hearts. Hakan stopped, his eyes blazing orange. He squatted in a small clearing, motioning for the others to do the same. "We're being followed," he whispered.

"Who are they?" Megan said.

"Sounds like Rol'dan. A large group of them, too. But we're in luck. They don't know we're here."

"That doesn't make any sense," Alec hissed. "If they're following us, they must know we're here."

"Not entirely true," Emery said, his eyes dropping to the stone in Megan's hand.

"Crows!" Hakan said. "They're following the stone."

"So what do we do?" Megan asked.

"We need to stop them," Emery said. "Use the stone as bait. With the element of surprise, we might have a chance." Emery turned to Megan. "You and Taryn hide until it's safe."

"She can hide without me," Megan said, annoyance tainting her emotions. "I'm needed here."

"Megan, please," Emery said.

"I'm staying."

Emery's heart sank. *Stubborn girl.* He turned to Taryn. "Run. Then hide. If all goes well, we'll see you soon."

Her eyes darted toward Alec.

"Listen to Emery." Alec grabbed her trembling hand. Emery could sense Alec's fear, not for himself, but for her.

"Go," Alec whispered.

"Where?"

"Away from us. We'll find you when it's over."

She nodded, tears streaming through the grime on her cheeks. With a last glance over her shoulder, she stumbled off, disappearing into the undergrowth.

They watched her go, then Megan took the stone and shoved it under a bush.

Emery slid out his dagger—not that he'd do much good. He had never really been a fighter. He focused his Empathy, preparing to control those he could.

Alec slid his sword free. "What's the plan?"

"You will all go to Faylinn," a voice answered.

General Kael Trividar stood at the edge of the clearing, his sword out and a confident sneer on his face. "Dead or alive," he said. "It makes little difference to me."

***

Emery's head thrummed as he teetered on the edge of consciousness. The bruising from the Rol'dan's fist had already swelled. Every time he flared his Empathy, the soldier violently reminded him to keep it put away.

He hoped Alec could hold his own with Kael, maybe even escape. There was little chance for the rest of them, and Taryn would need his help.

"Fire!"

A volley of arrows flung into the blur of sword fight, and the two figures flashed into normal view. Alec fell to ground, thrashing, while Kael grasped his arrow-pierced leg.

"Idiots!" Kael yelled.

The Accuracy archers turned white.

"Forgive us, General. We couldn't see properly."

Kael yanked the arrow free and hurled it to the ground. He then grabbed Alec by the hair and pulled him, legs kicking, toward where Hakan, Garrick, and Megan were bound.

Alec gritted his teeth. "You son of a—"

Kael kicked him in the face.

Two soldiers bound Alec's hands and feet and threw him next to the others. Several grunts turned Kael's attention toward Maska and two soldiers failing miserably at trying to hold him.

"Lieutenant, why can't you control this savage?"

"Sir," the soldier huffed, "he's much stronger than we expected."

"Break his legs if you're too weak to hold him. And while you're at it, break his arms as well. We'll see how he struggles when he can no longer move." Kael stepped closer to Maska. "How does that sound, Tala-swine?"

Maska remained silent, his face an expressionless mask.

"Nothing, then? How disappointing."

Kael nodded toward a burly soldier whose eyes glowed red with Strength. The soldier stepped in front of Maska and gave a small snort of laughter. In one swift movement, he pulled a mace, swung back, and contacted with Maska's right leg with a resounding *crack*.

Maska buckled over.

His captors pulled him upright, and the soldier raised the mace over his head—much like driving a tent spike—and smashed Maska's other leg.

Emery shut his eyes with the sound of crunching bone. *We've come so far to be stopped now.* He opened his eyes to see them repeat the process on Maska's arms. After they'd finished, Maska lay in the grass, his limbs at odd angles, and his emotions focused on pain alone. Emery's stomach lurched, his heart aching. *Oh, Maska.*

"Your freedom was short-lived, Cadogan," Kael said. "It's a shame you brought your friends into this. See the suffering you've caused."

"The suffering I caused?" Emery said, his hands shaking. "You're the one in charge of these men. Not me. And you're the puppet of the king."

"Puppet, eh? Wait until you get back to Faylinn. We'll see who's the puppet." Kael's smirk flattened. "But of course, you already know what the king can do."

Kael turned from Emery and froze, his emotions lightened with shock. "Who did this?"

Alec sat up, still bound, but completely healed. Emery could see Megan near him, her hands still tied, but her chin raised. Not that he wanted Alec to suffer, but Emery cringed. *Megan, what have you done?*

"I didn't order anyone to heal him." Kael swept his eyes over the other prisoners, stopping as he locked on Megan. He grabbed her arm and yanked her to standing. "Free her hands."

An Accuracy Rol'dan sliced the ropes at her wrists.

Kael's eyes roamed her body. He picked up a lock of her mud-caked hair and rubbed it between his fingers. Emery's blood surged.

She jerked her hair free.

"I remember you from Alton," Kael said. "You helped free Cadogan."

She glowered in silence, refusing to meet his eyes.

"And if I'm not mistaken, you healed your little friend over here as well." He tore open the fabric of his breeches nearly to his hip to reveal an arrow wound on his upper thigh. "While you are at it, you can heal me as well."

"Go get it elsewhere," Megan said.

"You will heal me. Or else you can watch one of your friends die."

That got her attention; she glared at him and reached for his face, flaring the light of her Shay. But before she touched him, he grabbed her wrist and shoved it through the tear in his breeches onto his bare thigh.

"Now heal me," he said. "And perhaps I'll let you touch me more."

The circle of Rol'dan soldiers laughed.

Megan didn't speak, but her jaw shook. She brought forth her Healing, and when the light faded from her eyes, she wrenched her hand away.

Kael laughed. But when her eyes darted to Maska, his smile vanished. "If you go anywhere near him, I'll kill him."

He motioned toward one of the soldiers. The man bound Megan again and pushed her to where the others sat on the ground.

"You're a coward, Trividar," Alec said.

A mask of curious indifference spread over Kael's face, but his emotions seethed.

"It's easy to act all brave and smug when your men surround you," Alec said.

Kael pulled his sword and rested it on Alec's throat. Alec didn't flinch; he stared at Kael, challenging him.

Kael studied him before finally turning to one of his men. "Bring me his sword."

"Sir?" the man said.

"Bring me his sword!"

The soldier returned with Alec's sheath. "Forgive me for speaking out of turn, General, sir, but the king said—"

"Then don't."

"Don't what, sir?"

"Don't speak."

The soldier said nothing else, his eyes downcast as he handed the sword to Kael.

Kael slid Alec's sword free, examined it, and plunged it into the ground next to the bound boy. It quivered back and forth before resting still. "Your father's work has improved, if that's possible. I will be keeping it once you're dead."

"You can take a closer look at it in your chest," Alec replied.

Kael laughed. "I've defeated you before, boy. Only this time, no one will heal you."

"And if I win?" Alec jumped over his bound hands and cut the ropes on his wrists with the impaled sword.

"Then you will impress the king. Which is rare."

"If I win, you'll free us." Alec pulled the sword from the ground and sliced the ropes at his ankles.

"If you kill me—and, of course, all of my soldiers here—then you may certainly go free."

"Alec, you don't need to do this," Hakan said.

"Of course he does," Kael said as he shrugged off his cape. "It's in his blood. He was bred to fight. It's no wonder he wants to die in battle." He bowed slightly. "And far be it from me to ignore his death calling."

Both Alec and Kael's eyes blazed golden-yellow. Alec threw the rope fragments aside. In what appeared to be the blink of an eye, the battle began in a flurry of ringing metal and a billowing cloud of dust.

All stared in silence, following the blur of the fight. Emery flinched as a splatter of blood hit his face. They held their breaths, waiting. Would Alec win? The fight ended abruptly at the tip of Kael's sword.

Kael yanked the blade free from Alec's chest; Alec's sword fell from his hand, and he slowly crumpled to the ground.

Megan screamed and lunged toward him. Two soldiers grabbed her arms, not letting her near.

By Brim. No...no...NO! Numbness enveloped Emery. He scanned Alec with his Shay and drew in a sharp breath.

Determination and courage—just like his mother. Alec's emotions pulsed the same as his mother's when she died. And he *would* die. Unless Alec could get healing, he didn't stand a chance.

"You fight well, young Deverell," Kael said softly, a strange mixture of pity and finality in his emotions. He knelt next to Alec.

Alec trembled. "Y...you are n...nothing." He gritted his teeth. "Nolan is t...ten times the man you are."

Kael studied him. "Yes. He is." And then he rammed his sword into Alec's chest once more.

Alec's body tensed, and he collapsed limply, releasing a long, slow breath.

Megan's sobs echoed through the silence. Emery scanned Alec, but felt no fear. To his horror, he felt nothing at all.

Kael stared at Alec briefly, yanked his sword free, and tossed it off to the side in the gently waving grass. The birds chirped. The branches of the trees rustled. And no one spoke a word. With effort, Kael stood, picked up Alec's sword, and shoved it into his own sheath.

An angry gash dripped blood from his thigh. He flicked his arm, splattering blood on the ground from another wound on his shoulder. An old Healer ran up to him, but Kael brushed him away and limped toward Emery.

"Where's the stone, Cadogan?"

Emery's mind reeled. "You killed him."

"Of course I did," Kael said. "I did him a favor." He leaned in close. "He won't have to suffer under the king, like you will."

"You can go to the Darkness," Emery hissed.

Kael smiled, though his emotions were quite the opposite. "Don't worry. I'll get there eventually. But for now, you'll tell me where that stone is, or I'll choose another to join your young friend."

"It's not here," Emery said.

"He's lying, General," The Healer said. "I can feel it. It's close."

Kael wheeled toward the man. "Well then, find it, Tiohan!"

The Healer, Tiohan, flinched and made a direct route to the

edge of the clearing toward a group of bushes lined in a row, exactly where they'd stashed the stone.

At least Taryn is gone. He hoped the girl had hidden far enough away.

Tiohan whooped in victory and emerged from the brush with the Stone of Healing in hand. As much as he hated to see them find the stone, he was almost relieved. They had no reason to follow Taryn.

"I have it, General." Tiohan's face twisted with glee.

"Give it to me," Kael said.

"W-what?"

"You heard me, Captain. Give it to me."

Tiohan trudged to him and reluctantly handed over the stone. Kael turned it in his palm and shoved it into a pouch at his waist. Tiohan continued to stare at the pouch like a starving man.

"Let's get moving," Kael said.

"But, General?"

"Heal me." He glared at the old man, daring him to say another word.

Tiohan nodded, his old face frail. "Yes, my general." Head lowered and shoulders slumped, he touched Kael's arm and healed his wounds.

"What about the boy?" a soldier asked.

"Leave him."

The soldiers yanked Emery past Alec's body. Emery searched it with his Shay one last time and felt nothing. His eyes locked on Hakan; he could hear Alec's heart if he were still alive. But Hakan's sorrow-filled face confirmed his fears: Alec Deverell was dead.

Maska yelled as they dragged him across the ground, too injured to help them at all.

Taryn was safe, at least for now. But a young, pretty girl had little chance of traveling safely on her own. She was their last hope, the only person who could tell the others what had happened. And it would be weeks before she could get home.

There would be no help.

They would have to live—or, more likely, die—on their own.

Chapter Thirty-Two

The throne room hadn't changed. It held little décor; Alcandor didn't care for that sort of thing. A large, oak throne sat at the head of the hall, and a plethora of old, oversized weapons hung on the wall behind it.

Emery looked up as they pushed him inside. The web-like beams hovered above him, like the temple at the ruins. Except here, no sunlight streamed through, no birds built their nests, and no Stones of Brim radiated light onto the floor. The ceiling had been sealed with stone long ago. The only light came from a few scattered torches on the walls.

Emery turned his head trying to see the others, but the door slammed shut, blocking his view. And worst of all, a familiar presence hovered, smothering him like a thick, wool cloak. He trembled as the memories surged over him. Every seduction. Every murder. Every birth of a Dor'Jan. Truth spiked in his thoughts, buried behind the overwhelming fear. He shook his head. The emotions weren't his. The fear wasn't his. They always came from elsewhere. Emery's blood ran cold.

"Impressive, Emery."

King Alcandor stepped from behind a pillar; the purple light in his eyes faded to frosty blue. Dressed in a black doublet and floor-length purple cape, Alcandor pushed the cape off one shoulder as he stepped toward Emery.

"You have blocked me. You've improved your skills, yet again," Alcandor said. "I'm not surprised you're behind the reappearance of the stones. You always were...resourceful.

However, I am curious how you discovered their true purpose."

The doors opened, and Kael appeared, followed by two soldiers dragging Maska into the room. Maska's head drooped, and his black hair clung to his face. They threw him to the ground—harder than necessary—turned, and left, one knocking into Maska's leg on the way out, causing him to writhe on the floor.

"The Talasian we told you about," Kael said.

"Bring me the 'light' shackles," Alcandor said.

Kael disappeared and returned with thick, silver shackles in hand. Alcandor took them and circled Maska in slow, even steps. He knelt and fastened the shackles to Maska's wrists.

"I didn't realize the gift could reach your land." The king placed his hand under Maska's chin and pulled his face up. "What is your name, Talasian?"

Maska glared in reply.

The king's eyes glowed with the light of Healing. Maska threw his head back, clenched his teeth, and growled as bones cracked and bent limbs straightened. Alcandor maintained his contact, not flinching or showing any sign of absorbing Maska's injuries. When he finished, Alcandor released his hold and studied Maska with amused interest. The king was more powerful than Emery remembered.

Maska shook his head, disoriented. When his eyes fell on the king, he jumped to his hands and knees like a wild cat, the chains clanging against the stone floor.

"Ah!" the king said. "That is more like a Talasian." Alcandor grabbed Maska by the throat, pulled him to standing, and pushed Maska across the throne room until he slammed against the wall. Alcandor reached for a collar attached to the wall and locked it across Maska's neck. Maska's Strength flared, though it did little; his efforts were pointless against the king.

"Just so you know, you won't break these bonds. They are made with a special metal unlike any you've ever known." Alcandor touched Maska's cheek, and his struggles abruptly stopped. A vacant expression fell over Maska's face.

"The interesting thing about Talasians," Alcandor said,

"is they pretend to have no emotions, but they hide intense passion." He turned a side-glance toward Emery. "But you already know this, don't you, Emery?"

Alcandor turned to Maska again. "What is your name, my warrior?"

"Maska."

"Maska?" Alcandor smiled. "I have heard of you. However, they told me Maska died. But now you stand before me, blazing with the Shay of Strength. How extraordinary. I can see how your sweet princess would risk everything for you...her inheritance...her life."

Maska's eyes jerked toward Alcandor; the control of the king no longer overpowered him. He glared with a smoldering anger Emery had never seen from him before.

"Oh, don't worry; she is alive and well. Her father brought her to me. A peace offering, he called it. However, I could sense he wanted to rid himself of her once and for all."

"What have you done with her?" Maska growled.

"Ah, see there, Emery? It just takes the right kind of motivation." King Alcandor's hand trailed across Maska's cheek. "I can help you rid yourself of those binding, Talasian chains. Like Princess Mikayla. She is free."

The anger smoothed in Maska's face as he yielded to the king's powers. His chin raised, his lips parted, and his eyes closed. Emery resisted the urge to panic. He summoned his Shay and searched Maska, feeling the passion begin to take hold. He wouldn't allow it. Emery reached deeper and concentrated on the lust, pushing it from Maska's mind.

Maska shook his head, snapping out of the desire so abruptly even the king recoiled. King Alcandor's brows furrowed with confusion, then anger, and then his fury locked on Emery.

The king appeared with Speed, his hand on Emery's throat. Emery clawed at his neck, though it was pointless. As the darkness closed in, King Alcandor released him. Emery fell to the ground, gasping for breath, allowing the world to come into focus.

"As proficient as your mind has become," Alcandor

breathed in Emery's ear, "keep it restrained. I could snap your neck with no effort at all."

"That...would...be...a loss...for you." Emery rubbed his neck.

"True," the king said casually, cocking his head. "Killing you quickly would be quite a waste of your Shay. Why, to absorb a full Shay...I haven't done that in a very long time." He yanked Emery to his feet, removed his jeweled dagger, and pressed the blade to Emery's throat. "And of course, there is still much to learn."

"I'll tell you nothing."

King Alcandor pulled back his blade slightly. "Of course not, Emery. I would be disappointed if you gave in so easily. But there are other ways to convince you."

Alcandor smiled in a way that made Emery's stomach drop. With a snap of the king's fingers, the door opened. Megan, Garrick, and Hakan were forced inside.

"Welcome!" the king said, as if old friends had stopped by to visit. "Please join us. We were having a pleasant chat, weren't we, Emery?"

Swollen and bleeding sores covered Hakan's and Garrick's faces. The sleeve of Megan's dress had been ripped away, and a tear hung in the bodice of her dress. If she had been hurt, she had already healed herself.

"Garrick," Alcandor said. "It's good to see you."

"To the Darkness with you," Garrick said.

King Alcandor laughed, and then his expression turned sour. "Is that a threat? I made the Darkness!" He swung his hand back and smashed it into Garrick's cheek.

Garrick would have fallen if the soldiers hadn't held him. His cheek split open, and a line of blood oozed down his face.

Alcandor turned from Garrick, now giving his attention to the other two. He examined Hakan, an amused expression on his face, and then his eyes flared with Empathy. "Perception, eh? You are harmless for the ox you are."

Hakan opened his mouth to speak, but froze with a wave of the king's hand.

"Pathetically weak." Alcandor motioned, and one of the Rol'dan led Hakan away, securing him to another wall.

Alcandor studied Megan next. He closed the distance between them, grabbed her head, and kissed her.

She struggled at first, and then her arms dropped to her side. She drew into his kiss, pulling him close. When they separated, Megan clung to him longingly. All the while, the king's eyes glowed with Empathy.

As hard as Emery tried to clear his mind, he couldn't. His anger roared.

Alcandor broke away from Megan to smirk at Emery, then he led her by the hand. She stared off vacantly, her expression pleasant but empty. The king had won. He'd found Emery's weakness. Emery would do anything, he'd say anything, for Megan.

"Where did you find the stones?" Alcandor said sweetly.

Emery shook with rage. "Alec Deverell found the first. The others found us."

"Alec Deverell? Ah, you mean the young swordsman. Where is he now?"

"Why don't you ask your general, considering he's the one who shoved a sword in his chest."

The king's eyes shifted toward Kael, and the king said, "I sent a group of soldiers to retrieve the other stones, but instead heard a curious tale. The few survivors told me one man killed them all. I, of course, punished them for their failure. But I can't help wondering what they saw. Might you give me some insight, Emery? I find the idea of a single man killing a group of thirty Speed Rol'dan pretty fantastical."

Nolan. It had to be Nolan. He was certain. Alcandor pressed his thoughts, but Emery shielded his mind. "Not as fantastical as you might think."

King Alcandor sucked a breath through his teeth. "You are blocking me again. Why must you make this so difficult? I will have to get more…persuasive." He kissed Megan's cheek and then whispered in her ear.

Her eyes locked on Emery. And before he could protest,

she crossed the floor to him and pressed her lips against his. They were so soft, and her familiar scent surrounded him. As he kissed her, his head swam.

Tell me what I need to know, a voice said. *Though she is under my control, she doesn't have to be. You have the power to control her. Make her desire you, then I can increase the experience. You can hold her and touch her and make love to her. I know you want her. Just tell me who killed my men, and she will be yours.*

Megan kissed him deeper, more passionately. She clung to him, pressing her body hard against his, silently begging for more. Emery groaned and pulled her against him. His hands touched her neck, her back, and her hips. She wrapped a leg around him, pressing into him. She felt so good.

With a jolt, Emery pried Megan away and drove his Shay into her mind.

She gasped and her eyes cleared, staring dumbstruck at Emery as a blush rose in her cheeks. Both of their hearts still thundered. Emery breathed, trying to calm the reactions of his body. She stepped away, a shy expression on her face.

"So this is the way we must play?" the king said. "So be it, Cadogan. I give you pleasure and you choose death instead." In a few quick strides he crossed the room, seized Garrick, and plunged a dagger into his chest.

"No!" Emery cried.

Garrick gasped, shock on his face.

Alcandor twisted the blade, all the while glaring at Emery. "Why must you force me to do such things?"

"Force you, Alcandor?" Emery said, his voice shaking. "You planned to kill us anyway."

The king's eyebrows rose in surprise. "Alcandor, is it now? If you tell me what I want to know, perhaps I might let your little minx heal him before he dies." He shoved the blade in deeper to add emphasis.

"All right," Emery said. "Let him go."

King Alcandor yanked the blade free, and Garrick fell to his knees.

Megan stepped toward Garrick, and then froze, staring off in a daze. Alcandor controlled her again.

"I-I don't know for sure," Emery said, "but I believe Nolan Trividar killed your Rol'dan."

Kael—still standing off to the side—burst into laughter. "Your Majesty, he's playing you for a fool. Nolan is my brother. He is nothing, Your Majesty."

The king's Empathy searched Emery. Emery shifted uncomfortably, letting him sense the truth from his words. The puddle of blood under Garrick's body grew.

"He is telling the truth," Alcandor said, amused interest on his emotions. "Now I really must meet your brother, General. He's become quite an extraordinary young man."

"But it's impossible," Kael stammered.

Alcandor smiled. "Of course you would think such things. You didn't even know he had Accuracy until he hit you with a jar of ink. Your little brother hides many secrets, it would seem."

Alcandor wiped his dagger across Kael's sleeve and shoved it into his leg holster. "How did he do it, Emery? How can one Accuracy user kill thirty Speed Rol'dan?"

"Your Majesty," Emery said, though the words tasted bitter on his tongue. "I will happily give you more details, but—"

"Garrick?"

"Yes," Emery hissed.

Alcandor circled the dying man, trying to find a spot clean of blood on the floor. Finally, he placed his feet and kneeled. He sighed melodramatically. "It's unfortunate he betrayed me."

Emery lunged toward them, but stopped at the end of Kael's sword. "Please. Let him die."

"And waste his power?"

Emery shook with frustration, his eyes connected with Kael's.

Kael looked away.

Emery reached with his Shay, trying to will Alcandor to stop, but he couldn't get even a meager hold on his mind.

King Alcandor lowered his lips to Garrick's as a final shudder went through him. Pure blue light streamed from Garrick's mouth to the king's. Alcandor leaned back, savoring his newly acquired power, while Garrick lay still and lifeless on the ground.

"General, we must dispose of the body before nightfall."

Emery met Kael's eyes briefly, and sadness emanated from Kael. Emery hadn't expected that.

"Yes, Your Majesty," Kael said. "Shall we have the robes brought in?"

"No. Leave him as he is," King Alcandor said. "I had almost forgotten the difference between a full Shay and those pathetic half-Shays. Perhaps I may have them step under the light before I take them from now on."

A Strength Rol'dan entered, picked up Garrick's limp body, and tossed him over his shoulder. He walked from the room, leaving a trail of blood as it dripped from Garrick's fingertips.

"So, Emery," Alcandor said casually, "you were telling me about this Nolan fellow. How did he kill my men?"

"How in Brim's light would I know?" Emery spat, his voice shaking.

King Alcandor came at Emery, grabbed him by the throat, and pushed him until he butted against the wall. He drew out a metal collar—like the one Maska wore—and latched it across his throat. The metal was warm, almost hot. It rested against stones. Shouldn't it be cold?

"You know more than you are telling me." Alcandor studied him. "You will tell me in time. You have other friends."

Alcandor untied his cloak and tossed it aside. He unbuttoned his doublet and shrugged it off, throwing it into a servant's arms. As he pulled the tie on his spotless white tunic, he closed the distance to Megan. She stared into nothing.

Emery laced his fingers around the strap on his neck and yanked. "What are you doing? Keep away from her."

Alcandor didn't answer. He didn't need to. Emery knew exactly what he was doing. As the king led her away, Emery flared his Shay and drove it into Megan's mind. She stopped and shook her head. Then a flash of pain blinded Emery's vision. When the haze lifted, Megan was gone.

Kael stood next to him, bringing his fist back to strike him again. "I don't know how you covered your lie, but there's no way my brother could kill anyone, let alone a whole platoon of Speed Rol'dan." Kael sneered, and Emery braced for another blow, but it never came. Instead, Kael turned and walked away.

A subtle grunt caught his attention. Maska struggled against his bonds, his face turning as red as his eyes. The king's power had left him.

"What are these made of?" Maska said, yanking against the clasp at his throat and then pulling the chains on his wrists taut.

"I don't know," Emery said. "But I've never seen a Strength user break them."

"Maska? Emery?" Hakan said. "I can hear you both, but I can't see a thing. This cursed strap is so tight I can't turn my head. What happened? How'd I get here?"

"The king put you in a trance," Emery said.

"Are Garrick and Megan by you?"

"No." Maska lowered his voice. "Where are they, Emery?"

As if answering his question, a servant walked from the king's chamber holding Megan's torn dress. He glanced over at them and then quickened his steps.

"Emery?" Maska said. "Where's Megan?"

"In that room. With *him.*"

A flurry of curses erupted from Hakan as he franticly pulled against his bonds. After several minutes, he stopped, heaving. "There must be something we can do."

"Not unless you can break free and kill the king," Emery said.

Maska grew silent, even more so than usual. Emery strained to look at him and saw Maska watching a pair of servants mopping the gore. "What is that, Emery? Where is Garrick?"

Emery's silence was enough.

"I would avenge him, if I could." Maska's eyes glowed

with both his Shay and an inner fire.

"And if you tried, you'd be dead, too."

Hakan's soft sobs echoed through the room, and Maska began to work his Strength at his bindings again. Even with their combined noise, it couldn't drown out the moans drifting from the king's chamber. Emery swallowed and closed his eyes.

"Oh, Megan," Emery said, "may Brim save us all."

Chapter Thirty-Three

E mery pressed his hands to his ears in a feeble attempt to muffle the sound. Time passed, though far too slowly. And with each passing hour, Emery surrendered to his memories.

He recalled his first night with the king. He'd only been in the Rol'dan for a few months. Alcandor had called for him after dinner. Emery had been nervous, for what could the king want with him? All of his speculations hadn't prepared him. He'd performed his part too well that night, for the king had called him the very next day.

The moments after the king released his hold were always the most difficult. The revelation of what he'd done—and how willingly he'd completed the task—trampled Emery's spirit. And worst of all, it never left. Emery shook his head, trying to dislodge the vivid memories, yet the images clung like a garish painting in his mind.

Soft sobs echoed from the king's bedchamber. Megan. Alcandor's power over her must be gone.

Emery longed to hold her and stroke her hair, to tell her everything would be all right. But it was a lie. Nothing was all right. He didn't know what would happen to them; Garrick and Alec were proof that things could go terribly wrong.

"Hakan." Emery's voice barely croaked through his dry throat.

"Aye?"

"Is Alcandor sleeping?"

There was silence from his friend. Emery twisted, gagging on the metal band. He caught a brief glimpse of Hakan on the far wall. "Please, Hakan."

Hakan sighed. "If his heart beats like that of a normal man, then he's at rest."

Maska stirred from sleep, though Emery couldn't figure out how he could do it standing and bound.

"Is it daybreak?" Maska yawned.

"I believe so," Emery said. "The servants are stirring. If it's not morning, it will be soon."

Maska's dark eyes frowned. It was strange seeing his emotions, even though Emery had felt his anger for years. "What of Megan?"

"She's alive and still in Alcandor's chamber while he sleeps."

Maska's eyes glowed as he summoned his Strength. He pulled against the metal strap, his mouth opened in a silent, straining yell. It would be useless, of course. No one had broken the shackles and chains before. Emery froze when a small groan came from the metal. *By Brim's light!* No one with the stones light had ever been locked in these chains.

Emery summoned his Shay, giving Maska encouragement. The metal creaked under the strain. *Maska can do this.* They could free themselves after all.

Then Maska's Strength gave way. Pain spiked in Emery's head as his Empathy slammed back into him.

King Alcandor stood before him, shirtless and barefoot, with his Empathy blazing. Maska stared into space under Alcandor's spell. Emery surged his own Empathy, ready to clear Maska's mind.

"I wouldn't do that," Alcandor said. "He is safe as he is. If you release him, then you'll leave me no choice but to kill him."

A guard came in. "You sent for me, Your Majesty?"

"My fair guest needs refreshments," Alcandor said, motioning toward his bedchamber. "She worked hard last night." His eyes never left Emery. "You will find her bound to my bed."

Emery clenched his fists, blood pounding in his ears.

The soldier bowed. "As you wish." He took a few steps toward the door.

"And Lieutenant."

The man halted. "Yes, Your Majesty?"

"Tell the general I wish to see him. And…"

The man waited silently.

"…If you touch her, you will find yourself wearing the robes of the Dor'Jan."

The man's mouth opened and closed. Emery could sense the lowly soldier's guilt and fear as he scurried from the room.

Alcandor stepped toward the silent Maska, and his eyes glowed purple. The corner of his mouth twitched into a half smile. "Remember, my dearest Emery, you determine his fate from this point on."

The blank expression on Maska's face disappeared, replaced by a moment of confusion, then a moment of rage. Then, just as suddenly, something else came over him. Maska grabbed the king's dark hair and the back of his neck. For a moment, Emery thought Maska would strangle him. But instead, he yanked the king into a passionate kiss.

Emery turned away. *How could I let this happen? But what can I do? If I interfere, Alcandor will make Maska a Dor'Jan.*

The king broke free, and Maska shook his head, coming out of his daze. The king grabbed his wrists and slammed them against the wall over his head. The clatter of Maska's chains echoed through the empty throne room.

Maska clenched his teeth, and a flurry of Talasian curse words flew from his lips. His face reddened as he strained against the king's Strength.

"I told you, Emery," King Alcandor said. "See his passion."

Maska jerked his hands, trying to free them. "You call yourself a king. You hide behind your powers because you are too much of a coward to fight on your own."

King Alcandor lifted his eyebrows. "I use my powers because they please me. And you are one to speak of such things as hiding, my warrior."

"I'll kill you!"

King Alcandor laughed and his Empathy glowed. Once again, Maska's face fell blank.

Kael entered the room. His eyes darted to the scene with a nervous twitch. He cleared his throat. "Your Majesty? You summoned me?"

"General, I need a group of Strength users to complete a task. There is a wall of stone covering the dome to this throne room. It has been there for some time. I want the stones removed."

Kael followed the king's gaze to the ceiling, confusion lacing his emotions. "Certainly, Your Majesty. Will that be all?"

"Yes, General, that will be all for now."

Kael bowed and left.

Alcandor touched Maska's cheek, tracing his fingertips lightly over his sharp cheekbone. "And now, my intriguing savage, I want to see your true Talasian passions flow."

***

Two Strength Rol'dan led Maska back to his place at the wall. Emery sensed both his shame and relief to be in bondage after the long day. The meager light of evening poured through the new opening in the domed ceiling, the removal of the stones now complete. Silence greeted them in what was left of the day, all except for Maska's escorts who laughed and walked to the king's chambers, pausing and nudging one another before reentering.

"What happened?" Hakan blurted as soon as they left.

Maska didn't answer, turning his head away.

"Did you see Megan?" Emery asked softly. "Is she well?"

Sorrow and regret clung thick on his emotions. "I saw her. She is as well as can be expected."

The soldiers returned with Megan between them. She was dressed in a silken blue nightgown with thin straps that threatened to fall down her sagging shoulders. Her tear-stained eyes met Emery's with such anguish it made his heart sink. Megan pulled her eyes from him to Maska, and then she flushed and turned away.

"She is supposed to go with the rest of them," said the taller of the guards.

"Are you sure?" the other guard said. He licked his lips.

"Aye. And you'll do as you're told, if you know what's best for you."

They pushed her against the wall near Hakan. Megan neither struggled nor complained, even when the shorter of the guards slid his greedy hand over her before the other smacked him away.

"I told you, leave her be."

The shorter guard grunted. "It's a waste, it is. Why isn't the king letting us have a go this time?"

"Perhaps he has other plans. It's none of our business."

Megan ignored the argument. Emery, on the other hand, had the urge to run them both through. If he could control their arms, they'd already be impaled on their own swords. Then an idea touched his mind. But it was so sinister. He wouldn't allow himself to—

"Ah, come on," the shorter guard said. "I'll let you go first."

Emery's rage swelled. He summoned his Shay and thrust his anger into their minds.

"I said, get your filthy paws off her. If anyone should have a go, it most certainly wouldn't be an ugly dog, like you."

"What did you call me?"

The taller man leaned over the other. "You heard me."

The shorter man lunged and threw the other against a pillar with his Strength. Ancient plaster sprinkled on their heads.

Emery increased his Shay, pushing them further.

"I'll rip out your tongue!"

"Not if you're dead, then you can rot in the Darkness."

They tumbled away from the pillar and slammed onto the floor. The taller man bashed the other's head against the ground, the stones cracking under him. The shorter man sent forth a burst of Strength and flung him across the room, missing the throne by a hand's width.

The taller man let loose a roar of anger. He took a step forward, and then Kael appeared—seemingly from nowhere—and pressed his sword at the stunned guard's throat.

The man swallowed. "G-general?"

"What's going on here?"

"I don't know, sir. He just came at me."

Emery pushed anger further.

"It's none of your business, Trividar," spat the shorter man. He yanked a mace from the wall behind the throne and stormed toward Kael. Before he took four steps, he stopped with Kael's sword in his chest, all the way to the hilt. The soldier gave a few gagging gasps and collapsed to the ground, dead.

Emery switched his power to Kael, pushing hate. Kael yanked his sword out and stomped toward the other man, eyes bulging and nostrils flaring.

"I'm sorry, sir," said the man as he cowered by the throne. "Please…"

In a gust of wind, both Kael and the king materialized next to Emery. Their sudden appearance broke Emery's concentration. Alcandor pushed Kael against the wall, his hand clenching Kael's throat. He studied him, glanced at Emery, and let go.

Kael gulped in air. "Forgive me, Your Majesty. I don't know what came over me."

"Oh, I know," Alcandor said. "I am surprised and—I must admit—a bit impressed. I haven't seen one with that ability in quite some time. Even when all were in the stones' light, it was a rare gift. And to use it in such a manner…" He clicked his tongue. "It is unlike you, Emery."

Emery's anger rose again, this time at himself.

"So, Emery." The king traced Emery's cheekbone with his finger and leaned in so his lips nearly touched his neck. He inhaled deeply and exhaled in a slow, open-mouthed breath. "What can I expect of our future? You and your friends are traitors. I *should* kill you all. But for you, Emery, I might reconsider."

Emery jerked away. "I'd rather die than get in your bed again."

The corner of Alcandor's mouth twitched. "Oh no, Emery. You won't die. I'll bring your band of traitors in, one by one, and torture them. Perhaps when they wander in the night, searching for their souls, you will finally realize there is no other choice...but me."

Alcandor strode to his throne, sat, and pulled a golden box from the drawer of a side table. "General, come here."

Kael straightened his tunic with shaking hands and approached the throne, taking care to walk around the dead soldier before bowing low. "Yes, Your Majesty."

"There are several recesses in the metal framework above our heads. Place this stone in one of them. It matters not which."

Kael hesitated then took the stone. "As you wish." He bowed once and was gone.

King Alcandor sighed and leaned back in his throne to study the empty box. He smiled faintly. "I thought it would be difficult to retrieve the other stones, considering this Nolan fellow killed my Speed Rol'dan. But to my surprise, the stones are coming to me."

Emery's heart stopped. *Why would Nolan bring them here?*

"Why indeed would he bring them so close to Faylinn?" Alcandor answered. "He must know I could feel the stones. Perhaps he means to trade them for your pathetic lives." He put the jeweled box on the table next to him. "Maybe he *wants* me to find him."

Alcandor stood and walked directly to Hakan. With a flick of his hand, he unlatched and opened the band around Hakan's throat. He grabbed Hakan by the beard and pulled him forward.

Hakan didn't respond; he only stared off, once again in the king's power.

"As impressed as I was with your skills, my dear Emery," Alcandor said. "I'm afraid you will have to pay."

Emery's heart thundered. "Then make *me* pay. Leave him alone."

Alcandor chuckled, leading Hakan to the center of the throne room. "As I said, Emery. One by one." Before Emery could cry out, Alcandor rammed his dagger under Hakan's ribs.

A spout of Talasian curse words flew from Maska, and Megan turned her head to sob.

Please, Brim, not like this, Emery prayed. The king was right. This was far worse than death.

King Alcandor threw Hakan to the ground and released his mental hold. Hakan clawed at his chest as blood gushed from the wound.

A crack of thunder sounded outside. The king looked up through the open dome.

Another crash erupted. This time it sounded nothing like thunder, but more like a part of the castle had given way. Alcandor's eyes glowed orange, then annoyance passed over his face.

A third booming crash sounded; Kael appeared with Speed.

"Your Majesty," Kael said. "There is a Strength user throwing boulders at our southern wall."

"He must be mad," Alcandor said.

"He appears to be alone."

"Is he in range?"

"No, Your Majesty," Kael said. "He's using some sort of device, a sling of sorts. The archers can't reach him."

"Certainly one man is no match for your swordsmen."

"Of course not, Your Majesty."

"That is, if you have any left to send."

Kael flinched. "We will dispose of him immediately." He disappeared just as a fourth crash resonated, this time closer than the others.

Alcandor's eyes shone orange with Perception, his brow furrowing into a furious scowl. "If you would excuse me," he said, as if speaking to guests. He bowed and disappeared.

The thunder of another stone sounded against the fortress

wall. Whatever was happening, it would keep the Rol'dan busy for a while.

"Sounds like someone is stirring up quite a bit of trouble," Hakan wheezed. "Like my kinsmen."

"Hakan?" Emery said. "Can you get away?"

Hakan coughed and a trail of blood dribbled down his chin, mingling in his beard. "Don't think so."

Megan, forgotten and unbound, cautiously stepped to Hakan, tore open the top of his tunic, and placed her hand on his chest.

"Lass, don't waste time on me," Hakan said.

"Oh, shut up." She smiled, and with a deep breath, she let her Healing come forth. A line of blood soaked through the delicate fabric of her dress, and both she and Hakan arched as the Healing power came over them. She collapsed on her hands.

Hakan—pale yet quite alive—beamed. "That a girl." He struggled to his feet. "Now, let's see what we can do about our frie—"

His words were cut off as he flew across the room, crashed against a pillar, and crumpled to the ground.

Alcandor grabbed Megan's arm and yanked her to her feet. He squeezed and she yelped. He then stuck his dagger into her side.

"Alcandor!" yelled Emery.

"Not to worry." He removed the dagger and the wound closed. "As you can see, Healers recover quite well."

He stabbed her in the shoulder and yanked it out; she screamed and began to cry as her wound closed.

"If I want to kill a Healer,"—he stabbed her again in the thigh—"the easiest way is to cut off their heads."

"Leave her alone, you piece of filth!"

Alcandor's eyebrows shot up. "Now is that any way to talk to your king? Of course, I couldn't do such a thing. She's too beautiful for something that horrific. Besides, dying quickly would be such a waste." He stuck the knife in her chest slowly as he seduced her with his mind. Her screams quieted, and she leaned into the blade, flinching and sighing with pleasure at the same time.

Emery's throat went dry.

"If one is to kill a Healer," Alcandor said as he pushed the dagger up to the hilt, "one must leave the blade in." He opened his palm, admiring the blade like a piece of art. She reached toward it, and he gently directed her hands away, shushed her, and then he released his mental hold.

Megan, coming into the shock of the moment, stared at the blade. "No. Please, no." She wrenched against him; the bloodstain spread.

"Struggle if you wish. You'll only die quicker."

Megan's face paled as her body became limp in the king's arms. He relaxed his hold, ran his fingers through her hair, and placed her gently upon the ground.

How many have lain there before? Emery wondered. *How many more must there be?*

A terrified soldier stopped near the door. "Your Majesty."

The king ignored him.

The man rubbed his hands. "Your Majesty."

"As you can see, I'm busy."

"Y-yes, Lord Alcandor, but we are under attack."

"And I assume you can defend us?"

"Yes, your grace. But...but..."

King Alcandor sighed. "What is it?"

"There are these things. Giant men. Glowing."

Alcandor froze, and for the first time in Emery's life, apprehension oozed from the king. "What did you say?"

"Two men and one woman with glowing swords. They're huge, much larger than any man. And they're setting the Dor'Jan on fire—"

"Shh!" Alcandor ran his hand across his brow, stood, and paced the floor, forgetting Megan completely. "No. No! It can't be. They are gone. GONE!"

Alcandor strode behind the throne and removed a very large sword from the wall. Emery had always assumed it more of a decoration than actually something to use.

"I will take care of this," Alcandor said, "once and for all." Shoving the soldier out of the way, he left.

The soldier cast them a curious glance and followed his king.

"Giant, glowing men?" Maska said. "What is this madness?"

"I don't know," Emery said. He had hoped Nolan had caused the commotion, but now he wasn't sure.

"Whoever it is," another voice said, "it sounds pretty lively out there."

Emery turned, as best as he could, and saw Hakan limping over. He staggered to Megan, carefully removed the dagger, and tossed it aside. Pale green light sealed her wound.

Emery laughed. "I thought you were done for."

"Nah. Been knocked around by my brothers more than that."

"She's alive," Emery said with a sigh of relief. "Take her away, Hakan. Get her out of here."

Hakan wiped a nasty wound on his forehead with his sleeve and cringed. "And where do you suppose I go? Especially with giant, glowing things and flaming Dor'Jan hanging around."

"Use your powers. Hide. You can hear when anyone gets close. Use your senses, like when we had escaped Alton. It's nearly dark. Use it to get away."

"Emery is right," Maska said. "Go while you can."

"I'll keep my ears open for a way to get you two free," Hakan replied.

"No," Emery snapped. "Save Megan."

"And if I can get you two out first, then you'll have to shut your traps and get saved." He scowled, giving a stern glare first to Emery and then to Maska and then back to Emery again.

"All right," Emery said, "but don't take any chances. Megan comes first."

Hakan hefted Megan over his shoulder and took a step.

"And, Hakan," Maska said. "Remember to keep your mouth closed. One word from you and the whole Rol'dan army will hear." A faint, teasing smiled hinted on Maska's lips.

Hakan's eyes opened with surprise. He snorted, holding back one of his bellows. "Now then, if I die, I've truly heard everything." He shook his head. "Maska? Telling a joke?" He wagged his finger at Emery. "You just wait. We might get out of this yet. As you can see, the impossible can come true."

Chapter Thirty-Four

The sea crashed against the rocks bordering Faylinn Castle. Daylight faded, painting the murky clouds blood red. No town surrounded the massive structure. No shops. No peddlers selling their wares. Just Faylinn, its vast walls, and the grassy field stretching from wall to the forest's edge. For the first time, Nolan saw the great city for what it truly was: a prison.

Nolan closed his eyes, listening, pretending he was back home in Galva. He loved the sound of the sea. But he wasn't home. In fact, he might never return home again. Tonight could be the last night he'd ever hear waves.

He took a slow, focused breath. Large square walls—much higher than the walls of Alton—jutted toward the sky. Along the wall's edge, pairs of orange lights pierced the growing darkness, pacing back and forth, scanning the dark field. Nolan hid behind the trees, out of sight of those Perception Rol'dan. They couldn't see him. For now.

As the sky darkened, the moon barely penetrated the black, twisting Nass. Nolan clenched and unclenched his fist, feeling the Strength in him lessen with the sun. Maybe they should wait until morning. The Dor'Jan were coming. He couldn't see them, but the dirty ooze of them crept through his veins. They were out there in the forest—and crows, there were a lot of them. He'd never sensed anything like it. He pushed down bile and ran a hand over his chin. He couldn't wait until morning; Megan and Emery could already be dead.

Nolan wiped his shaking hands on his breeches and loaded a head-sized stone on a sling. Flaring Strength, he lifted the man-a-pult (as Rylan had so affectionately named it) and spun it over his head. The chain went taut with the boulder's weight. He flicked his wrist and let it go—branches cracked as it soared into open space. He held his breath, following its progress as it slammed into the wall of Faylinn.

That should get their attention.

Maim, not kill. Nolan repeated the phrase in his head. Lieutenant Connelly, the girl he'd nearly killed at the ruins, had quickly switched sides once she knew she could leave the Rol'dan. Others could do the same.

Nolan loaded another stone—this one even bigger. He aimed for the dome and let it go. It cracked with a satisfying spray of debris. "Ignore that, Alcandor."

Rustling weeds and snapping twigs rushed toward him. He grabbed a spike, but relaxed when Lieutenant Connelly broke through the trees. A torch flamed in her hands, and the light danced off her bloodstained Rol'dan uniform.

"Forgive me for startling you, my lord," she said. "The others are ready to move."

Nolan shoved the spike into his belt. "Crows! I almost killed you."

Her hazel, cat-like eyes smiled. "Well, it wouldn't be the first time."

Nolan cringed, remembering the wound in her chest at the temple ruins. "I'm almost ready. Is there a good place to get in other than the main gate?"

Her smile faded. "Not really."

"Any suggestions?"

Her jaw tightened. "Kill as many as you can?"

"Maim, not—"

"Yes, yes. Although there are a few—"

Nolan leveled a gaze at her. "Tell the others to head to the gate once I make my move."

"About that Deverell fellow," she said. "He's unstable. He should've traveled to Galva with the others."

Nolan frowned. "I know. Believe me, I tried. But I couldn't keep him away."

Focusing his Perception at the gates, troops gathered—Speed users, he guessed. Kael's familiar voice barked orders. Nolan's stomach clenched. He'd been so focused on the king, he'd nearly forgotten about Kael.

Nolan loaded another boulder-sized stone and hoisted the sling over his shoulder. Lieutenant Connelly stepped back as he began the rotation overhead. The steady whoosh cut through the silence, building in momentum and intensity. Surging Speed, Nolan increased the pace. As the gates to the fortress opened, he released the stone.

The rock tumbled through the air and connected; the wall above the gates crashed, spraying rubble on a group of soldiers. Several torches and swords dropped to the ground as they covered their eyes. Kael glared in Nolan's direction. At least he was still too far away for Kael to recognize him.

Nolan repositioned his spikes: fifty deadly projectiles that would soon find their mark. A vision of dead soldiers flashed in his head. His chest tightened. *Maim, not kill.*

Lieutenant Connelly stared at Nolan, awe pouring from her like he was some sort of nightforsaken god.

"Go," Nolan said. "Get moving."

She inhaled, her face half-shadowed in the light of her torch. "Yes, my lord."

Nolan sighed. "And please, call me Nolan."

"As you wish, Lord Nolan."

She disappeared back to the Guardians, Vikas, and the other Speed users who hid at the other side of the woods. A row of Accuracy archers gathered on the wall. It was Nolan's turn. He needed to clear the path so his friends wouldn't become pincushions. As the last sunlight disappeared, he drew out his Speed and sprinted toward the waiting Rol'dan army.

The world slowed with Speed senses. Nolan cut across the empty field separating the forest and the wall. Grabbing his spikes, Nolan surged his Perception and focused on the archers. With Strength and Accuracy behind his throw, he flicked in rapid succession, and the spikes continued on what looked like a slow journey. He tore his eyes away as each spike jammed into the crook of their arms; they screamed and collapsed, dropping their bows and weapons.

Nolan thought of how many times they'd impaled him at the trials. *Let's see how they pull their bowstrings now.*

His brief moment of elation fled as a cloud of hopelessness hit him full in the chest. He skidded to a halt; his arms relaxed, falling to his sides as a spike slipped from his palm and *thudded* into the soil. He jerked from the sensation, his head whipping to the trees. In a sea of dark robes, the Dor'Jan slid into the grassy field.

Ashen gray skin stretched, dried and sunken, over boney arms and legs. Walking corpses. Men and women, none he recognized, thank Brim. Hundreds of them scurried toward him, dark and tattered robes fluttering behind. One's hood fell away revealing strands of gray, stringy hair. Nolan froze, his heart filling his ears.

Shaking away his shock, he pushed his powers just as they closed in. They reached with clawed nails and bony arms, surrounding him. The light of Brim ignited, and the creatures squealed and withdrew, avoiding the glow radiating around him. The hopelessness dropped from his shoulders like a wet cloak.

Shouts and orders of battle stopped; only the wheezing moan of the Dor'Jan filled the night air. Nolan stood in the center of the open field, a beacon surrounded by a swarm of writhing Dor'Jan. A platoon of Rol'dan stared, mouths gaped, as they waited at the open gates of Faylinn. Torches fell from their hands.

Nolan's pulsed raced, his eyes darting from the monsters to the stunned Rol'dan soldiers. He snorted, despite his terror. Bet they've never seen *that* before.

Kael's wide eyes met his. He tensed and straightened before turning to his soldiers. "What are you waiting for?" he said. "Fire!"

Nolan brought forth Speed as a dozen arrows zipped toward

him. Some came from the wall and others near the gate. Nolan caught a few, knocked the rest aside, and let loose the same number of spikes in return.

"Nolan!" Kael said.

Nolan flared Empathy and felt Kael's torn emotions. *Confusion. Concern for...me?* His stomach clenched. *Crows! If he cares so much...why in Darkness is he trying to kill me?*

Dodging, Nolan caught an arrow and sent it back with Strength behind the throw. Strengthening his light, he broke through the Dor'Jan. As they parted, cowering, he ran toward the open gate, not certain what he'd do when he got there.

Several dozen Rol'dan blocked his path, weapons raised as fear flooded from them. Glowing eyes of gold, red, and blue darted to the mass of animated death and back to Nolan again.

Nolan wiped a sleeve across his face and tightened his grip on his sword. So many. He could fight a few, but he couldn't take them all. He glanced toward the trees. *What is taking the others so long?*

Once again, the sensation of filth crept down his spine. The Dor'Jan closed in, trapping Nolan between them and the Rol'dan army. At least the creatures kept the Rol'dan from attacking.

Kael stepped forward and torchlight flickered around him, casting shadows on his hardened face. Anguish pulsed from his emotions as he drew his sword—Alec's sword. "Crows, Nolan. I can't let you. I just can't."

Just as Speed flared to life in Kael's eyes, the air around them changed. The sneer on Kael's face fell and his sword arm dropped to his side. He stared out, expressionless, toward the waiting dead horde. Nolan sucked in a breath. "No, Kael! NO!"

Nolan gasped as all five of his Shays wrenched against his chest, freezing his body in place. He increased his light, gasping as the sensation fell away. The soldiers weren't as lucky.

The Rol'dan froze, some falling to their knees. A few staggered back into the sheltered walls of Faylinn. Several others dropped their torches and pressed their palms to the side of their heads. Their faces went blank...and then they stepped into the waiting Dor'Jan.

Nolan poured everything into the illumination around him. He grabbed Kael's arm, yanking him into the circle of his protective Shay.

Kael wheezed, blinking, his senses returning to him.

"Stay with me," Nolan said.

A scream sounded as a swarm of Dor'Jan enveloped a Rol'dan soldier. One of the creatures straddled the man's torso, its fingers pressed into the soldier's skull. The man convulsed on the ground, and his body withered as if emptied from the inside out.

The Dor'Jan shrieked, frustration and desperation oozing from its putrid emotions. Nolan yanked back his Empathy, his stomach rolling from the creature's wretched desolation. The Dor'Jan screeched, raising the hair on Nolan's head. It jumped on another soldier, emptying him as well.

Kael's head jerked from one gruesome sight to another before locking on Nolan. "W-what happened to you?"

Nolan scanned the creatures and stopped on one face, his heart lurching. Dried blood still lingered on its lips. Its skin wasn't sunken or gray; it was white, as if it had just tried on death. Nolan choked back the shock, recognition washing over him. Garrick. He reached for him, but Kael yanked Nolan's arm away.

"Don't," Kael said. "The king took him last night."

Brightness burst through the tree line, and the howls of the Dor'Jan escalated into frantic screams. Nolan pulled Kael through the chaos toward the shelter of the walls. The Dor'Jan, now desperate, circled Nolan, hunger gleaming in their black eyes. They dropped away as soon as they got close enough to the torches flooding from inside the gates.

More screams drew their attention. The Guardians, massive swords raised and golden armor gleaming, surrounded Vikas and the others, protecting them from a wave of Dor'Jan. They came straight across the field toward the open gates of Faylinn.

Kael spotted them, and the blood drained from his face.

As they neared the castle gates, Kael pulled back. The Guardians slashed with their glowing swords, and the Dor'Jan fell away, engulfed in flames. They plowed through the Dor'Jan like farmers sowing wheat. As they finally raced through the gate into the paved courtyard, the Guardians parted, and the small, determined band of resistance charged.

Kael flinched, a turmoil of emotions churning within him. A few of Nolan's friends charged in Kael's direction. Nolan shook his head and waved them on. However, Kael had already raised his sword.

"Kael, we can stop this," Nolan said. "Call off the Rol'dan. We can defeat the king together."

Kael's eyes jerked toward him. "No one can defeat the king, Nolan." His voice quaked, finality on his tongue.

"Together," Nolan said. "We can do it together."

Kael's mind shifted to a glimmer of hope. But the fire building in Kael extinguished with a glance. Any chance of Kael joining them came to a violent end.

Alec Deverell stood before them, his fist clenched on the hilt of a sword, and his eyes gleaming yellow with Speed.

Chapter Thirty-Five

Nolan's stomach dropped. *No, Alec. Not now.* He stepped between them, hands outstretched, one palm open to each of their chests.

"Get out of my way, Nolan," Alec said.

Astonishment washed over Kael. "But you're dead."

"Oh yes," Alec said. "I *was* quite dead...until Taryn healed me to life."

"Taryn?" Kael's face paled, nearly draining to the ashen gray of a Dor'Jan. "No. That can't be."

"You killed me," Alec continued. "And she gave me her life. You killed her!"

"No." Kael's jaw twitched and his face reddened. "I didn't kill her; the stupid girl made that decision on her own."

"Get out of my way, Nolan," Alec said.

"If you had fought like a man," Kael said, "she'd still be alive."

"Nolan!" a voice cried.

Nolan swiveled, looking for the frantic voice.

Alec dodged around Nolan, swinging his sword.

"Alec! No!" Nolan yelled, but it was too late. Kael blocked him with a resounding clang, and the battle between them erupted.

"Nolan!" the voice called again.

Nolan tore his gaze from Alec and Kael in time to see Vikas fighting two Rol'dan. Another group of soldiers surrounded the Guardians, swords swinging.

Nolan hesitated then looked at Alec and Kael; the two dodged and parried and sliced their way toward an empty practice field. His heart twisted, but there was nothing he could do. Nolan prayed, hoping they would both come out of this alive.

He turned, pulled several spikes, and threw.

The two Rol'dan fighting Vikas fell.

Vikas immediately worked his way back to the Guardians.

Nolan grabbed two more spikes on his leg, then another pair, and another, and soon what was left of the attacking Rol'dan fled.

Greer inhaled, healing a deep gash on his arm that dripped with shimmering, silver blood. He held his glowing sword to his face, his eyes blazing with white light. And with a small bow, he gave Nolan a grateful salute.

The sound of fighting faded into an unnatural hush. All eyes rested on the doors to the castle. A Guardian, larger than Nolan had ever seen, emerged.

The Guardian wound through the awe-struck courtyard. Black hair hung, smooth and silky, down to his wide shoulders. His sharp features scowled with hate. He wore full plate armor the color of tarnished copper. In his fist he gripped a gigantic sword; it swung slowly at his side as the crowd gave way to him. Though he radiated light, it was dirty and stained. Even his eyes glowed gray, not the typical pure brightness of the other Guardians. His stare made all stop and hold their breath. He walked purposefully through the crowd, and every Rol'dan— as well as Nolan's friends—stopped and bowed. Nolan felt it, too: the forced awe. He shoved it aside. He was not dealing with just another Guardian.

Greer, Malik, and Sanawen didn't move. They stood taller: the posture of challenge.

"I should have known," the dark Guardian said. "Greer. I left you for dead."

"Did you, Alcandor?" Greer said.

Alcandor? The king is a Guardian? No. It can't be. Nolan searched the crowd. Stupid, giddy admiration was planted on their faces.

Everything made sense—all of Alcandor's powers, how he never aged. Now Nolan knew what he was truly up against: a Guardian who enjoyed killing humans. Kael was right. *How in Brim's light can we defeat him?*

A crooked smile hinted at the corner of Alcandor's lips. "I won't make the same mistake this time; I am more powerful than before."

"You stole those powers," Greer said.

"Brim took my powers!" Muscles tensed on Alcandor's neck. "He gave me no choice. I simple took back what was rightfully mine. Lay your head down, Greer. It will come off one way or the other."

He motioned toward a group of Rol'dan and then pointed to Malik and Sanawen. "Bind them. Do what you wish with them but don't kill them. I will do it myself."

The Rol'dan cheered in frenzied madness, and a mass of Nass shot from them into the dark sky. They swarmed forward, and within a few short seconds, the two Guardians were overcome.

"And this one"—Alcandor motioned toward Greer—"is mine."

Alcandor swept his sword in a menacing arch and lunged toward Greer. In a flash of white light, Greer's blade met Alcandor's. They paused, sizing one another up, and then the battle erupted.

Nolan froze at the sight. He'd never seen Greer so fearsome. Yet, however hard Greer fought, he couldn't match Alcandor's Speed and power. Greer would lose; it was only a matter of time. Malik and Sanawen were already overcome.

A twang of bowstrings sounded, and Nolan dodged the arrows. He reached for the spikes at his forearm, but the bracer was empty. His belt was empty as well. He found some on his thigh holster, dodged several more arrows, and let the spikes fly, *thudding* perfectly into the two men firing into the courtyard from the wall above.

Nolan blocked an incoming sword blow, cutting the man

before moving on. The Rol'dan kept coming, but Nolan disposed of them, dodging and cutting his way through Alcandor's army.

The Rol'dan may have been falling, but Alcandor was not. The battle between Greer and the king was not going well. Greer backed from the courtyard into the Dor'Jan-covered field, disappearing from Nolan's view.

With another sweep, Nolan disarmed a Rol'dan and made an attempt toward the gate. Rol'dan after Rol'dan pressed on him, blocking him, each taking the previous one's place.

Nolan's jaw tensed. His lungs ached. His muscles quivered with exhaustion. Another man rushed forward—Nolan swore he'd already fought him. The man's eyes blazed with Speed. He'd tear the soldiers down, and the Healers would bring them back. This battle would *never* end.

"Enough!" Nolan's Empathy swelled.

The man's sword arm hesitated.

Nolan stared at him, his muscles taught, his sword arm raised, yet the man did nothing. *Why did he stop?* Nolan inhaled sharply. Just like Emery in the prison tower: *He stopped because I told him to.* Nolan thrust Empathy into the soldier's mind. "Go!"

The man blinked twice, turned, and fled.

Nolan pushed through the crowd, influencing their minds. The soldiers parted, clearing his way. As another group advanced, Nolan made them freeze in place.

A group of Rol'dan had tied Sanawen and Malik on the ground, impaling the Guardians while laughing sadistically. Nolan's blood heated. He clenched his fist, threw up his hand, and stabbed Empathy into their minds. "Stop it!"

Confusion fell on their faces. With another quick mental jab, the Rol'dan obediently untied the Guardians.

Nolan passed them, sprinting out the gates and across the field. Pushing his Shays, his light increased. His head pounded, his body ached, and he still hadn't faced Alcandor. Trying his best to ignore the reaching Dor'Jan, he scanned the dark field and easily found the glowing Guardians.

They still battled, but Alcandor had the upper hand. The ringing Guardian steel filled the air, cutting through the night. Finally, Alcandor struck with such a resounding blow that Greer staggered and dropped his sword. Alcandor rammed his blade deep into Greer's side.

Greer roared, making the ground tremble. He opened his light-filled eyes and stared at the king with a fierce glare.

"Where are the stones?" Alcandor said. "You've gathered them somehow. I feel them on my doorstep."

"What purpose would they serve you?" Greer said, his teeth gritted together. "You are no man."

Alcandor jabbed the blade in farther. "I tire of these half-strength Shays. Give me the stones, and I will let the humans use them before I take them. Where are they, Greer?"

Arm trembling, Nolan held the bag of stones over his head. "Alcandor!"

Alcandor turned slowly, an amused smirk plastered on his face. "Has it come to this, my old friend? Have you assigned a child to carry the stones?" He bent to grab Greer's sword, and with the light of his Strength, rammed it through Greer's chest, pinning him to the ground.

Greer yelled as a thin trail of silver blood trickled from his lips. He smiled, speaking close to a whisper. "Don't be so convinced of the futility of man."

Alcandor yanked his own sword from Greer's side, and Greer's Healing light sealed it closed. Alcandor raised his sword, now aiming for Greer's throat.

Nolan drew his Empathy and jabbed it toward Alcandor.

The king hesitated, his sword motionless over his head.

"Throw your sword aside," Nolan ordered, his voice breaking. He strengthened Empathy, and the light around him dimmed. The Dor'Jan greedily pushed closer, and Nolan's Shays twitched toward the creatures. Nolan strengthened the light, his temples throbbing. A bead of sweat traced his trembling jaw. Somehow, he held the king.

The king's sword arm shook, frustration and rage spilling from him like a thick fog. Finally, he whipped his body toward

Nolan; his eyes blazed purple. "How dare you!"

Alcandor shoved fear into Nolan's mind. Tremors filled Nolan's body, and his heart raced even faster than before. Like a heavy weight, Nolan pushed the fear away.

Alcandor growled and then charged.

Nolan stumbled back as Alcandor stormed toward him. He pulled his sword just as Alcandor's massive blade came sweeping down. Their swords rang. Nolan pushed, matching Strength with Strength; Alcandor's annoyance and hate turned to puzzlement. Nolan gritted his teeth. "Get. Off. Me!" With a surge of Strength, Nolan flung the dark Guardian away.

Alcandor skidded across the long grass, surprised at first, and then golden-yellow flashed in his eyes.

Alcandor sped toward Nolan, faster than Alec had ever been in their duels. Nolan cursed, hardly able to block as he backed and stumbled over fallen bodies

They pressed closer to Faylinn, and the battle in the gates grew silent; the wall filled with watching people. Nolan's lungs burned like hot coals. Sweat poured from his face, blocking his vision, and his tunic clung to his heaving chest. Nolan couldn't keep going, not like this. Yet Alcandor didn't seem winded at all.

The king switched from Speed to Strength with a hammering blow. Nolan's sword connected with a clang. Vibrations shook the bones in his arm. Alcandor pushed, their blades locked. A warm trickle of blood trailed down Nolan's cheek and dripped to the trampled grass.

Alcandor's eyes drew to Nolan's cut. "I see Healing is not amongst your powers."

Nolan glared at the gray lights where Alcandor's eyes should have been. "Give me the Healing stone. I'll fix that problem."

"You are Nolan?"

Nolan's arms shook with fatigue.

"Yes," Alcandor answered for him. "Yes, you are. I can see your brother in your eyes." He smiled. "You could join me. Take your brother's place in front of my army."

His words tickled Nolan's mind, tempting him. He shook his head, blocking Alcandor's Empathy, and refocused on the battle. Every muscle in his body quaked, uncontrolled. He tried to push back on Alcandor's sword, but couldn't. The blade lowered, drawing closer to Nolan's throat.

Nolan groaned. All he could do was stare at the edge of the huge blade coated with both silver and red blood. He had nothing left. With his last fragment of effort, Nolan thrust his hand into his bag and tugged out the Stone of Strength. He gasped as energy poured into him; the stone's power restored him instantly.

Alcandor jerked away.

Nolan repositioned his sweaty palm on his sword, waiting for Alcandor to attack; however, Alcandor didn't move. His gray eyes fixed on Nolan's hand.

Confused, Nolan followed Alcandor's gaze to the stone. *The stone? Why would he be afraid of the stone?* Nolan shoved his hand toward Alcandor, and the king flinched, fear pulsing from his emotions. Using the distraction, Nolan swung with both Speed and Strength, coming down on Alcandor's sword with such force his massive body pivoted to the side.

The king quickly recovered, his anger flaring to madness. "How dare you! I offered you glory, yet you defy me?"

Nolan attacked again, hope rising. Every time Alcandor pressed forward, Nolan lunged with the stone.

"I will pick the stones from your dying body," Alcandor said. "And then I'll take your soul, like I did with Garrick."

Nolan opened a gash in Alcandor's side, but a muted green light closed the wound.

"And that whore Megan..."

Nolan hesitated. Was Megan okay?

The distraction was enough; Alcandor sliced, and fire shot through Nolan's arm; his sword fell from his grip.

"And just as I took her body, over and over," Alcandor said, his arrogance swelling, "I will take her soul as well."

Crimson blood streamed down Nolan's arm, yet the pain faded in the background. He glared. He'd had enough of this soulless king.

Alcandor drew back his blade.

Nolan lunged, grabbed Alcandor's wrist, and stopped the king's sword mid-swing. He squeezed, putting everything he had left into his Strength. His light faded, and the Dor'Jan closed in. Nolan didn't care. This monster had to die.

Nolan jabbed the Stone of Strength against Alcandor's forearm, not knowing for sure what would happen. Instantly, bright red beams of light burst from the stone, stretching the length of the forest and sky. Nolan blinked, blinded momentarily by the light.

Alcandor's eyes widened, first in disbelief, then in terror. "No! Get away from me!" He struggled, trying to free his arm, but Nolan tightened his hold. The red light brightened, and countless mists spilled from the stone, twisting and swirling into the sky, illuminating the darkness around them. Then each one dove toward a Dor'Jan.

As the mists hit the creatures, their gnarled bodies convulsed and red light flashed in their eyes. Flesh tone spread, fading the gray into the normal pallor of death. Their heads jerked back, dark eyes raised to the sky as a slow breaths escaped their lips. With a final shudder, they crumbled to the ground, stilled.

The remaining Dor'Jan lunged toward Nolan—eyes hungry and gnarled fingers reaching.

"Get back!" Nolan pushed with Empathy, and the creatures listened, but only just.

As the light finally died in the stone, Alcandor yanked against him, but Nolan barely noticed. Alcandor's Strength was gone.

"Let me go!" Alcandor ordered as he tried to stab Empathy into Nolan's mind.

Nolan dropped the Stone of Strength into his bag and grabbed the next. Once again, Alcandor yelled with both frustration and pain. The blue light of Accuracy spilled from the stone, and more Dor'Jan convulsed and fell silent and still.

Stone after stone Nolan pulled from his bag, until a rainbow of mists filled the sky. Swirling. Circling. Either finding their homes in the Dor'Jan or disappearing over the treetops and beyond. As the last purple mist drained from Alcandor, the dark Guardian collapsed to his knees, sorrow and defeat pouring from him.

A solitary blue mist darted around Nolan's head and then skittered across the field, finding a familiar face standing amongst the Dor'Jan. The mist slammed against Garrick's chest, and he inhaled. In that brief moment before he collapsed, his eyes locked with Nolan's. Recognition flashed in his emotions, then gratitude, and then nothing at all as Garrick Grayson crumbled to the ground.

Nolan flinched as a large hand appeared on his shoulder; Healing surged through him. Bruises and cuts and scrapes suddenly came to his attention before they dissipated and healed.

"Well done, Master Nolan," Greer said. His white light filled the dark space around them.

The remaining Dor'Jan scattered at the sight of Greer, disappearing into the surrounding woods. The haze of Nass hovered in the sky, twisting and churning.

Nolan scanned the battlefield. Corpses, both robed and uniformed, covered the grass. The wall was filled with Rol'dan, all staring with wide-eyed awe. He turned toward Alcandor just as Malik and Sanawen pulled him to his feet.

Alcandor glared at Nolan, hatred lacing his emotions. But he didn't say a word.

"Does this castle have a dungeon?" Nolan asked.

Malik beamed. "We can find something. Unless of course, we did away with him now."

"We can't," Nolan said, "at least not yet. We need to find the Healing stone and free the other Dor'Jan."

Greer nodded. "I agree. Some have waited hundreds of years to have their peace."

A twang of disappointment flitted through Malik. "Very well."

He and Sanawen dragged Alcandor toward the gate. Alcandor turned, looking over his shoulder. He glared at Nolan as revenge seeped from his emotions.

"The other stone is inside the castle," Greer said.

"I know," Nolan said as they headed toward the gate where most of the fighting took place.

Greer gave Nolan an odd look. "It calls to you?"

"I think the others did, too. I didn't recognize it at the time."

A low moan sounded nearby. Lieutenant Connelly lay on the ground, her uniform freshly stained in blood. Nolan knelt, and her hazel eyes met his.

"Greer. She's hurt."

Greer had already reacted, and his Healing light coursed through her. Her body relaxed, even as she eyed Greer nervously. Her expression softened as it fell upon Nolan.

Nolan smiled and placed the Stone of Speed into her hand.

She took a deep breath, and color returned to her cheeks. "I am in your debt once again, my lord."

"Please, call me Nolan."

"Never," she said.

Nolan shook his head. He'd deal with that little problem later. He scanned the inner ward of Faylinn, hearing faint heartbeats with his Perception. So many. Where to start? He found the nearest, a Rol'dan soldier. Rolling him over, an all-too-familiar spike stuck from his arm; he'd lost a lot of blood. Nolan yanked it out, and Greer healed him.

They proceeded for some time, healing as many as they could before Greer finally broke the silence. "Forgive me for being forward, Master Nolan, but if you were to have Healing of your own…"

"Yes, you're right. I'll come back after I find the stone."

"And what of Master Emery and the others?"

Nolan's heart jolted. *Crows! How could I forget?* "Let's hope someone found them."

Nolan handed his bag of stones to Greer. "You can strengthen them with these."

Greer's eyes widened. "No. I cannot. As you can see from Alcandor, a Guardian cannot safely touch a Stone of Brim."

Nolan hesitated. "Didn't Malik carry one? He gave it to—"

His heart jolted. There was no sign of Alec anywhere.

"Malik sacrificed much when he carried the stone," Greer continued. "His power of Accuracy is no more."

"Oh. I see," Nolan said, though he only half listened to Greer now. The last time he'd seen Alec and Kael, they'd been heading toward the practice field.

"He gladly sacrificed his power to serve man," Greer said. "Besides, compared to most of the Guardians, Malik fared well."

"You mean he's still alive, when the others are dead."

Greer nodded. "They were dark times." He healed another Rol'dan. "It was the year when Alcandor bent man's mind, making them believe we were a threat. The people attacked us, and we could merely defend ourselves. It is our sworn duty to do no harm to man. It was only a matter of time before man defeated us. Many Guardians died. Those of us who lived did so because we ran."

"So maybe there's still more Guardians somewhere? Hiding like you did?"

"Perhaps," Greer said.

"I'll find the other stone." Nolan scanned the bodies, searching for Alec or Kael. *Crows, they have to be somewhere.* Lieutenant Connelly watched from a distance. Nolan waved to her and she immediately came.

She stopped in front of him, standing eye to eye. She was tall for a girl. Her dark hair was cropped short, but her cat-like eyes sparked with a mischievous gleam. She could be pretty, if she stopped trying to look like a man.

"Yes, Lord Nolan?"

Nolan rolled his eyes. "What's your name, anyway?"

Her eyebrows rose. "Lieutenant Connelly, of course."

"What's your *first* name?"

"I prefer to be called by my surname."

The corner of Nolan's lip came up. "And I'd rather be called Nolan."

She hesitated. "My family called me Kat before the Rol'dan."

Her name fit her well. "Well then, Kat. Could you please help Greer with restoring the injured?"

She gave Greer a side-glance. The Guardian still made her nervous. "Certainly, *Lord Nolan.*" She stressed the words, a teasing air in her voice.

"Thank you, *Kat.*" Nolan shook his head and left them.

A multitude of eyes followed him, parting the way. And worst of all, Nolan couldn't block the resounding awe from their minds. It shouldn't surprise him, as much as Nolan hated to admit. He'd defeated their king.

As he headed toward the castle's keep, Nolan caught sight of a Rol'dan barracks and the practice field. He froze, his heart pounding at the sight of two figures: one kneeling, and the other lying on the ground.

Nolan stepped toward them, not daring to use his Perception; he wished to hold off the truth as long as possible. Without any Speed, he made the slow walk across the field. One way or another, by blood or by bond, one of his brothers was no more.

Nolan received his answer as soon as Alec turned.

Only one heartbeat.

Only one breath.

Kael was dead.

Alec limped toward Nolan. A large gash ran diagonally across his face, starting at his forehead, slicing across his nose and through both lips. Blood dripped from the wound, covering the side of his face in a gory mess. It would make the scar on his cheek seem like a small scratch.

Nolan knelt. Kael looked comfortable, at least: His legs were straightened, his arms neatly folded over his chest, and his eyes closed. If he hadn't known any better, Nolan might have thought he slept; however, the wound in his chest and the blood-soaked grass told a different story.

Nolan gently picked up Kael's hand, heavy with the weight of death. It was calloused and still warm. Nolan cupped it, remembering when these hands had been larger than his, when they had helped him haul in his first net of fish, or when they had playfully socked Nolan in the shoulder. *My big brother. That's how I'll remember him.*

He put Kael's hand down, leaving his own to linger on it for a moment.

"I'm…" Alec said. "I'm so sorry."

Nolan turned and found Alec staring at the ground.

"The colored lights in the sky stopped him—both of us, actually," Alec said, his voice hitching. "I tried to keep fighting, but he wouldn't. He smiled at me and at those nightforsaken lights like they were the most beautiful thing he'd ever seen.

"So I ran him through. He just stood there smiling, and I ran the idiot through, straight into his back."

Nolan didn't speak. He couldn't. All moisture left his throat.

Alec raised his injured face, and for the first time looked Nolan in the eye. "I should've listened. I should've gone to Galva with the others. I should've been there when they brought Taryn to her parents. The only thing I proved was that I'm no better than a murdering Rol'dan."

"You *have* been better, Alec," Nolan said, breaking out of his shock. "Kael was cruel."

"I murdered him, Nolan. Not self-defense, but *murder*. How is that not cruel? I wanted him to curse me and spit on me as he died. Instead, he said he was sorry about Taryn. He told me the better man had won. He turned out to be a better man than me…"

"Now stop, Alec—"

"No! I should be the one lying here. By Brim, it should have been me days ago if Taryn hadn't been stupid enough to save me. And what kind of friend am I? I killed your brother, for Brim's sake! Leave me be, Nolan. I'm no friend to you."

"You're right. You're no friend."

Alec's face jerked toward Nolan. He stumbled back a step.

"You're more like a brother."

His emotions surged, going first to shock, then to denial. "I'm nothing." Alec yanked his sword from the ground. "I have to go."

"Where?"

"Crows, Nolan. I don't know. Away from here." From his expression Nolan knew he meant, *away from you.*

"Don't go." Nolan's eyes stung. "We need you here."

Alec snorted. "You don't need me."

"*I* need you."

Surprise flared in Alec's emotions. He quickly hardened his expression.

"I've already lost one brother," Nolan whispered. "Please. Don't let me lose two."

Alec fidgeted, avoiding Nolan's gaze. Finally, he met his eyes. "All right. I'll stay. But only because you asked me."

Nolan nodded. It wasn't much, but it would do for now.

The sun finally broke through the horizon, and orange and pink hues glowed over the walls of Faylinn. With the morning light, a *caw* sounded overhead. Slowly, the sky filled with circling black birds. Another call drew attention to a crow perched on the edge of a barracks, staring at Kael's corpse, waiting to have its fill.

Nolan's stomach lurched. He reached to his holster, his fist closing around the cold steel. With a flick, he threw his last spike. A shower of black feathers erupted over the rooftop.

Chapter Thirty-Six

Soldiers parted, making way for Nolan as he carried the body of their general. Shock pulsed from them and around them, filling the entire crowd. Nolan blocked their thoughts as best he could; it was hard enough dealing with the warring emotions battling within his own mind.

Everything had gone better than he'd hoped; he never believed he'd actually defeat the king. But the death of his brother, after he'd hoped for his freedom, crushed any happiness he had.

Alec limped behind him, a shell of his former self. From the moment he'd broken through the trees in the village holding Taryn's limp body in his arms, he wasn't the same. Shame and sorrow oozed from him, making Nolan's sadness seem small in comparison. Nolan wanted to comfort him...somehow. But he just couldn't. Not with how much his heart ached.

The main entrance to Faylinn Castle was large and lavish, but not gaudy. Antique paintings and precious gem-inlaid heirlooms adorned the gray stone halls.

Nolan continued past the hanging treasures, needing no directions; the Stone of Healing called, showing him which way to go. He would mourn his brother, his cousin, and his friends later. Right now, a whole battlefield of lives needed him to be able to heal.

As they continued, a set of huge wooden doors, at least two Guardians high, loomed ahead. They stood open wide.

The smell of blood permeated the throne room when they

entered. Against the wall, Emery and Maska stood, their backs pressed against the wall, their necks secured with shiny, silver bands. Hakan and Vikas hovered, trying to figure out how to free them. None of them had noticed Nolan and Alec enter.

Nolan carried Kael to the center of the throne room underneath the light of the new morning sun. He stepped around the dark stains on the floor and gently set Kael's body down.

Alec lingered in the doorframe, staring at the dried blood. Trepidation and foreboding hung from him.

"It won't budge," Vikas said, his voice echoing in the chamber.

"Maybe we can use a sword or something," Hakan suggested.

Vikas slid his sword out and attempted to pry the band loose from Emery.

"Won't that cut Emery's throat?" Nolan asked.

Vikas and Hakan whipped around.

Hakan broke into a huge smile. A large gash ran across Hakan's forehead with traces of dried blood caked on the wound. Bruising covered a portion of his face, disappearing into his dirty beard. The front of his blood-soaked tunic was torn, revealing almost as much hair on his chest as his beard.

Nolan scanned the room and his chest tightened. "Where's Megan?"

"Resting," Hakan said. "She was hurt pretty bad."

Nolan relaxed. *She's alive!*

Vikas sheathed his sword. "Sorry, Emery. The collar won't budge."

"Here. Let me try." Nolan closed the distance and stepped in front of Emery. Emery cast him a feeble smile. His clothes were torn, his face was bruised and sunken, and his lips were cracked and bleeding. He'd aged, somehow. Nolan summoned Strength, and light flared in his eyes. He grabbed the band and pulled; it resisted him, only slightly. With a flick, the metal groaned and broke.

"By Brim's light," Hakan said."Did you just...? How can you...?"

Nolan forced a smile. "It's kind of a long story. I'll tell you later."

Emery released a breath and touched his raw neck. "You have no idea how good it is to see you, Nolan." He took a step, but his feet buckled as if he'd forgotten how to walk.

Nolan caught and steadied him. "I'm glad you're all right."

Maska grunted as he struggled against his own bonds. Sorrow flickered behind his gaze. Nolan hesitated. Was Maska actually sad? Nolan freed him, and he nodded in thanks.

"Where's Garrick?" Alec asked. He came inside the chamber, still staring at the bloody floor.

The others' eyes jerked toward him. Their emotions were more than shocked. The last time they'd seen him, he'd been dead. Even Maska's bronzed skin went pale.

"Alec?" Emery said. "For the light of Brim...how did you—"

"I didn't," Alec said. "Taryn came after you were captured."

Emery started to smile, but it quickly faded. "Dear Brim, tell me she didn't."

Alec didn't answer. "Where's Garrick?" he asked instead.

"He's dead," Nolan said softly. "I saw him during the battle. He was a Dor'Jan. He's resting now, at least. The stones released his soul, as well as most of the other Shay powers Alcandor stole. Except for Healing. I didn't have that stone. Speaking of...I need to find it."

Emery's brows furrowed. "You released his powers? Nolan, how?"

"Like I said, it was the stones." Nolan circled the room, and the Healing stone pulsed. *Where is it? I can feel it.* Nolan stood in the center of the room. "It should be right here."

The sun sent his answer; the light of Healing shone directly on him. Nolan flinched, more surprised than anything. He relaxed as the Shay of Healing worked inside him. Green lights danced, filling Nolan with Healing power. Nolan panicked when his feet left the ground. *What will happen when I gain all the powers?* But something inside him, perhaps the Shay of Healing, told him all would be fine.

When the light diminished, everyone stared.

"Nolan?" Emery finally asked. "How are you?"

The other Shays had left him in pain—thrashing, head hurting, unable to function for days. But now...well...he didn't feel anything. Maybe it hadn't worked. Maybe five powers were all he could hold. There was one way to find out.

He strode across the stones, his footsteps reverberating in the large throne room. Before Emery could object, Nolan touched his cheek, and the Shay of Healing responded.

Pleasant warmth filled Nolan, until small points of pain shot through his body. His arms. His legs. Scrapes and cuts that must've been covered by Emery's clothes. Aching bruises swelled on his face and his throat. Then the discomfort faded, covered with a soothing warmth.

Emery met his eyes. "Thank you, friend."

Nolan nodded. The Healing still thrummed inside him, making him unable to speak. He turned toward Hakan and, before he could object, Nolan touched his leather-worn cheek. Pain shot through Nolan's senses. Several cuts. Cracked ribs. Crows! His injuries were worse than Emery's. *Doesn't the man feel pain?* Nolan suppressed a groan when he finished, relaxing as the soothing warmth took its place again. He exhaled. Healing would take some getting used to.

Hakan grinned. "Thank you, lad."

Nolan smiled. "Glad I could help."

"Where is Alcandor?" Emery asked.

"Malik is taking him to a dungeon."

Emery's brow furrowed. "Malik?"

"Jared's nephew...er, sort of." Nolan shook his head. "You'll have to see for yourself."

Lieutenant Kat Connelly entered, Nolan's bag flung over her shoulder. "It's done, my lord." She handed the bag to him. "Greer will be here shortly."

"You're done already? They're all healed?"

She winked. "We work fast."

Nolan ran a hand over his chin, relieved. He hadn't been looking forward to healing a field full of victims. "How many dead?"

"Too many," Kat said. "Most of them Dor'Jan, but some Rol'dan as well. Most weren't fatal wounds, but they'd bled out before we could reach them." Her eyes traveled across the room, meeting the body of Kael. "For the light of Brim..."

"He's dead," Nolan answered her silent question.

Alec tensed, fresh guilt oozing from him. Nolan swallowed back the lump forming in his throat; his own grief wouldn't help Alec now. He eyed Alec's slashed face, and dread welled up inside him. A horrible, raw-looking wound. Hakan's injuries weren't half as bad, and they'd been painful. Nolan squared his shoulders, flared his Healing, and reached for Alec.

Alec yanked back. "Don't touch me."

Nolan stared, and then reached again. "It will only take a minute."

"Stop it, Nolan. I don't *want* healing."

"You don't what?" Nolan hadn't heard him right. But when he reached for him a third time, Alec smacked his hand away.

Alec glared at him in warning, even as the Guardians entered, all three shining with their brilliance. Hakan and Emery backed away, shock and fear coming from them.

"Master Nolan, forgive me," Greer said. "The soldiers outside grow restless."

"Sweet father of light," Hakan said. "What are they?"

Greer bowed. "It is good to see you well, Hakan."

Hakan's mouth dropped open; he stammered, then said nothing at all.

"The Rol'dan are confused," Greer said to Nolan. "In their eyes, since you defeated Alcandor, the throne belongs to you." He held the king's circlet in his open palm. "It is yours, if you wish it."

Nolan stared at the circlet, the same one the king had worn since Nolan could remember. "No...no...no. I can't be king."

"They are expecting you," Greer said as he offered the crown again.

Nolan took the crown and fingered the stone and the delicate intertwining gold band. *This is ridiculous. Sure, the*

Rol'dan would be afraid of me; I hold all of the powers, just like Alcandor did. I barely have myself together, let alone the skills to be a king. They need someone to respect, not fear. They need someone who knows how to lead.

Emery had sacrificed himself, giving up power and leadership to leave the Rol'dan. He risked his life daily for others, uplifting them, leading them, empowering them. It was an obvious choice.

Nolan held the crown to Emery. "This belongs to you."

Emery's eyebrows went up. "Nolan? You defeated Alcandor, not me."

"But don't you see? They only want me because I have all the powers."

"Yes, you are powerful. But you also have leadership abilities. I've told you—"

"No. They'll follow me because they're afraid of me. They'll follow *you* because you're a great leader." Nolan held out the gold circlet.

Emery paled. "I can't take it. I'm a traitor here. They'd rather have Alcandor back on the throne than me."

"Once, a good man told me, 'Many times, the most humble people make the greatest leaders of all.' Emery, Adamah needs *you*, not me."

Emery searched the room as if desperately seeking disapproval. His gaze locked on Alec's, questioning him. Everyone's emotions shifted. They all saw Emery's potential, too. Everyone except for Emery.

Alec pulled his sword and knelt, holding back a grimace. "My sword belongs to you."

Maska lowered to his knee. "And I would serve you with pride, my king. You are the obvious choice."

"You have my sword as well." Greer drew his glowing sword and bowed; the other Guardians followed. Emery gawked at the Guardians and took a small step back.

Nolan handed the crown to Emery. He took it, though hesitantly.

"I'll do this," Emery said as the purple light of Empathy

shone from his eyes. "I'll do it only because *someone* needs to." He placed the circlet on his head, his dirty hands trembling. "And if the army doesn't accept me, my reign might be the shortest in the whole history of Adamah. And please…stand up. Let me take this one step at a time."

They smiled as they rose. Maska congratulated him, while Greer waited his turn.

Alec approached Nolan, curiosity on his emotions. At least his sorrow was distracted, for now.

"You don't want the throne?" Alec said.

"Why? Should I have taken it?"

Alec snorted. "Darkness, no! How am I supposed to beat you in swords with you wearing a crown? Wouldn't that be considered traitorous or something?"

"Definitely," Nolan said. "Then I'd have to kill you."

Alec laughed, though it sounded forced. "You'd *try* to kill me,"

"I could do it," Nolan said. "I defeated a Guardian on my own. I think I could take you on."

"A Guardian?"

"Alcandor is a Guardian."

"Alcandor is a…Guardian?" He whistled, but stopped, wincing with pain. The cut across his lip pulled open, oozing fresh blood.

"Crows, Alec. Let me heal you."

Alec took a step back. "I told you: I don't want to be healed."

"Why not?" Nolan asked, frustrated.

Alec's eyes drifted to Kael, and guilt flowed from him. "I want to look at myself in the mirror and remember to never lose my temper again."

"Your Majesty," Greer said to Emery, "you should address the Rol'dan before their patience breaks any further."

"Yes, I suppose I must." Emery stepped toward the exit, Greer following at his side.

Emery paused, obviously startled by the Guardian standing next to him, but curiosity laced his emotions. "Forgive me, sir," Emery said, "but what *are* you?"

Greer laughed. "I am a Guardian."

"A Guardian? How remarkable," Emery said. "All these years I wanted to believe Jared, but found it harder and harder to do so." He paused to study Greer. "I know it may seem odd, but I feel as if we've already met."

Greer laughed again. "Master Emery, I am sure you will be surprised at how true that observation is."

They left, their laughter echoing down the corridor. Alec turned to follow, but Nolan grabbed his arm. Self-loathing and guilt was so thick on his emotions. "Alec, can you do me a favor?"

Alec shrugged him off. "What kind of favor?"

"In the center of the dome there is a place where all the stones fit together, one on top of another. Back at the village, I put a few stones in and I found a message hidden in the light." Nolan shrugged, feigning indifference. "Perhaps it's nothing, but Greer thought it was important, that the stones must be combined. Can you do it for me?"

"Why can't you do it?"

"I should stay out of sight for now."

Alec nodded, though irritation oozed from him. He yanked the bag from Nolan's hand. "Sure. I'll do it…in a bit."

"And take the Stone of Healing to Alcandor and Megan."

Alec sighed and swung the bag over his shoulder. "I'll tell you what happens."

Nolan watched the others leave. Hopefully, the Rol'dan would receive Emery well. He had a hard road ahead of him; some would still look at him as a traitor. How long would it take before one of them tried to kill him? Where would Adamah be then? Leaderless. Kingless. They didn't even have a general.

Nolan studied Kael's broken body. If Kael were still alive, would he protect Emery? Would he lead the army to follow? Nolan remembered the tower and how Kael had strangled Emery. Maybe Kael would kill Emery himself; he sure didn't like him.

He'd gone through so much before death. Nolan knew that

now. He only wished it could've ended differently. He wished he could've saved Kael, somehow. Kael had still *wanted* to be good; Nolan felt that from him in the end. He would've done the right thing, despite his feelings for Emery. Nolan was sure of it. But it was too late now. Kael was dead.

Nolan stared down at his blood-smeared hands as an epiphany stirred inside him, making his blood run cold. Though Nolan couldn't be Emery's general—the Rol'dan would treat him as king even though Emery wore the crown—Nolan *could* help. Emery *needed* Kael.

Chapter Thirty-Seven

lec Deverell took off with Speed, beating the others
outside. He stopped abruptly, staring at the largest
gathering of Rol'dan he'd ever seen. The courtyard
teemed with soldiers. They crowded around the base of the
steep steps to the castle and continued on, filling the space
until they met the huge walls. Even without Empathy, Alec felt
tension in the air. He could see it on the Rol'dan's faces and
their uptight postures, and by their loud-mouthed groans and
complaints. Alec huffed. He still hated the Rol'dan.

As the doors to the castle opened, the hum drifted into
silence. The fidgeting stopped and the crowd became still.

Greer's light emerged well before he did, as well as that of
the other two Guardians.

The crowd leaned forward expectantly.

Greer spoke, his voice amplified louder than a normal man.
"Nolan Trividar has declined to take the throne."

After a shocked silence, a curse rang out, followed by a
chorus of others. Hostility spread like flames. Greer held out
his hand, and the crowd grew reluctantly silent. Greer waited
until the last complaint dribbled away before he spoke.

"However, Lord Trividar has chosen your king. He is one
who led you once, and recently led the army who won this day.
I present to you Emery Cadogan, the new king of Adamah."

Emery stepped forward, and a swell of angry voices
greeted him.

Alec placed his hand on the hilt of his sword, his heartbeat increasing. He could take quite a few of them, if he needed to, though his injuries would slow him. Maybe Emery was right about the shortest reign ever. Alec tightened his grip and flared his Speed, and then a strange calm fell over him.

And it wasn't just Alec, the entire courtyard relaxed. Fists fell limp and the angry voices faltered. Alec scanned the crowd, confused yet calmed. Then he saw Emery; the light of Empathy blazed brightly from him. His eyes roved the crowd, soothing them. Emery was good.

"I know you were expecting someone else," Emery said. "Frankly, I expected someone else as well. But it seems our fates have taken a different path.

"I don't come to you with vast powers, except to sense your happiness or pain." He hesitated. "And perhaps refocus you, when needed. But I know what you have endured. I have been there myself."

A murmur in the crowd swelled and then calmed again.

Emery walked along the landing, hands behind his back. His stained and torn clothes looked as if they'd been worn for a week. His tangled hair hung in his dirty, thin face. Even with this haggard appearance, he looked like a king.

Emery continued, "For the past six years I have gathered many who had the same goal as myself: to use our Shay powers to better ourselves and our world, and to live free of the king's tyranny and control. We have strived to be as normal as we can, to love and to laugh, to live life, and to better the lives of our fellow man.

"Together, we can continue this goal. We can make Adamah safe and build a land where the Rol'dan lead and protect. Not because the people fear us, but because they respect us. If you will have me, I will repair this land. Starting with our own hearts, the healing of Adamah can begin."

There was silence, then a few grumbled protests. But the murmuring dimmed as a solitary soldier pushed through the crowd. Alec recognized him, had met him before. The first time was at the Trial of Awakening—he'd healed Alec more than he wished to remember. The second time was the day the coward stood and watched while General Trividar killed him.

Tiohan climbed the steps, his shoulders hunched with age. When he reached Emery, he slowly lowered himself to one knee.

"I will serve you," Tiohan said, "with whatever years I have left to serve, Your Majesty."

The crowd mumbled, all with varied states of emotional highs and lows.

Emery touched his graying head. "Tiohan, it's good to see you."

The old man smiled. "I'm *very* glad to see you."

Gradually, they approached, each bowing on one knee. Emery touched them, his eyes flaring violet. They didn't deserve him.

Alec pulled in a deep breath and scanned the crowd, still seeing scowling faces. Groups held back, clustered together as they whispered. Hopefully they would appreciate him... eventually.

Hakan's barrel chest appeared, pressing into Alec's face in a bone-crushing hug. When he finally released him, the cut on Alec's face screamed.

"Did you ever see such a beautiful thing?" Hakan sniffed and brushed away a tear. "And I'm so proud of you too, my boy. You took out that general, all on your own."

Alec stiffened, his face still blazing. He'd only won because Kael had stopped fighting.

"He was the best swordsman in the land," Hakan said. "I guess you get the title now, eh? It's not like it's unexpected..." He snuffled again, his tears welling up. "Though I'm sad Taryn is gone, I'm happy to see you again." His eyes crinkled into a sad smile. "You know, if Taryn hadn't done what she did, none of this would've happened."

Alec stared at Hakan. "W-what did you say?"

"Well, you'd be dead, and Taryn would still be trying to get back to the village or Galva. Nolan wouldn't have known about our capture and, more than likely, Emery and me and Meg would all be dead too." He sniffed. "Taryn was such a sweet lass."

Alec's vision shifted. He hadn't considered it that way. Not only had Taryn given her life because she cared for Alec, but because it was the only way to save the others. She wasn't fast enough to reach Nolan and the village in time. But Alec was.

Alec shuddered as his stomach turned. Crows, what a decision! She'd known exactly what was at stake. Taryn was the real hero. Alec sniffed back tears. He'd spilled so many in the past two days, he didn't know how they could still come.

The line in front of Emery grew.

Alec snorted. Rol'dan. A whole army full of murdering Rol'dan. And Emery was trying to salvage them, trying to save them, trying to unite an army of filth. Alec scanned the soldiers' faces, searching, trying to dredge his buried memories. Was his mother's murderer still here? He'd blocked out the details; he could hardly remember. Years of hatred bubbled to the surface, and he despised them all over again. He had promised Nolan he'd stay, but he couldn't. Not now. Not so close to all these nightforsaken Rol'dan. Not for Emery. Not even for Nolan. He needed some space, some time to get away.

Alec rubbed the bag's strap around his neck, reminding him of Nolan's request. Nolan's eyes were so kind when he'd asked, it made Alec's stomach turn. Why did he have to be so kind? *I killed his brother, for Brim's sake, and he still treats me like a best friend? It would be better if I just got away from him.*

But first, Nolan wanted Alec to combine the stones— whatever that meant. Well, he couldn't. The urgency of leaving pressed on him too much. Nolan would just have to do it himself. Stepping off his perch, he headed toward the castle.

"Where you going, lad?" Hakan asked.

"I have to give Nolan something." *Before I go.*

The castle was quiet without the Rol'dan, and probably smelled better too. It would probably take a while for Emery to talk to them all, and the castle would be flooded by their foul stench again. He stepped through the large throne room doors and froze.

Nolan squatted next to Kael's body. The fabric of the corpse's shirt was ripped away, revealing a bare patch of death-pale skin. Nolan's hand rested on Kael's chest, his fingertips spread apart as his green light of Healing glowed.

Alec gasped; his heart twisted. "Nolan! NO!"

Nolan's head snapped up and their eyes met.

Flaring his Speed, Alec raced toward him. But after only two steps, every muscle in Alec's body jerked to a sudden stop.

Nolan stood, his hand held out and violet light blazing from his eyes. Alec struggled, trying to move anything, but he couldn't. Crows, he couldn't. Nolan was so strong now. Why did he have to be so strong?

"You shouldn't be here," Nolan said, his voice breaking.

Alec tried to speak, but his lips wouldn't move. *Don't do this, Nolan. Don't do this.*

"I have to," Nolan said, as if he were trying to convince himself. "I've sensed the Rol'dan; they won't follow Emery without Kael. Adamah is in danger. Emery is in danger. If Emery can do anything to help, he'll *need* Kael."

Nolan was worth more than all the selfish, dimwitted people of Adamah. They could all rot in the Darkness as far as Alec was concerned.

Nolan walked toward Alec and looked in his eyes, his jaw trembling. "I know Kael isn't easy to love. Trust me, I know. But the king tortured him, turned him. He deserves a chance, like I got. Love him, if you can." Nolan put a hand on Alec's chest, over his heart, and a tear drew a line down his cheek. "Thank you, my brother…for everything."

Alec's mind screamed. Even his tears seem stuck, unable to escape. *Nolan! Don't!*

With hesitation, Nolan removed his hand, stepped away, and went back to Kael. He took a deep, stuttering breath and looked at Alec one last time. "Goodbye."

Nolan's eyes glowed green, at first dim and then brighter. His hands trembled as he laid them on his brother's chest. His head jerked backward, and he gritted his teeth, holding back a scream before he let loose a series of choked cries that stabbed

Alec's soul. A spot of blood grew on Nolan's chest, increasing and soaking through.

Alec panted, his heart thundering. He didn't want to watch, but he couldn't turn his head. The battle with Kael replayed in his mind, except this time, Alec pushed his sword into Nolan instead of Kael.

Kael's hand twitched at the same time as a muscle twitched in Alec's arm. If he could just get free, he could break the connection and stop this madness. Nolan's hold lessened little by little, and Alec's voice finally broke free.

"Nolan!" Alec screamed. "By Brim…no, no, NO!" He strained, moving his head ever so slightly. Alec pulled harder against the bonds.

Kael twitched.

The binding weakened again, and Alec could almost move his arm.

And all at once the binding fell.

Alec collapsed.

Nolan crumpled.

And Kael's back arched. He grabbed his chest and gasped like one who had been underwater for much too long. He rolled to one side, clutched his stomach, and retched.

The world around Alec slowed. He staggered to Nolan and fell to his knees. Nolan wasn't moving; brown hair sprawled around his head. Alec turned him over and blue eyes stared into nothing. Sticking his head to Nolan's chest, warm blood smeared across Alec's cheek. He listened for the heartbeat that was no longer there. Gripping the front of Nolan's tunic, Alec shook him as hard as he could.

"Nolan!" He couldn't be dead.

"Let him go, lad," a voice said.

Alec looked up. Hakan, Emery, and Greer had arrived— probably from hearing all the commotion. They stared, their faces pale and painted with shock. Hakan's red eyes were moist.

Alec let go and Nolan crumpled. Then a hand touched Nolan's head. It was Kael. Alec didn't know how to react.

At first he considered blocking Kael, refusing to let him see Nolan. But the expression in Kael's eyes—the surprise and utter disbelief—Alec knew far too well.

"Please tell me," Kael said, his hoarse voice above a whisper, "that Nolan didn't have the power to heal." His face pleaded. "Please tell me."

Alec could only nod.

Kael released a stuttering sob, scooted in closer, and pulled Nolan's head into his lap.

Alec withdrew to the wall, turning away. But morbid curiosity brought him to watch again.

Kael stroked Nolan's hair gently. He wiped the torn sleeve of his tunic across his eyes and sniffed. "What in Darkness were you doing, Nolan? Everything was as it should've been."

"He made his own choice," Greer said.

Kael's head jerked up. He tried to jump to his feet, but his legs were too weak and he fell. Greer offered his hand to help him, but Kael dragged himself away.

"I'm sorry for startling you. Allow me to introduce myself."

"W-what are you?"

Greer bowed slightly. "Greer is what I am called. But in the years past, when we walked freely among man, we were called Guardians."

Kael's eyes found Emery, and then drifted to the circlet on his head. "Where's Alcandor?"

"Imprisoned and powerless," Greer answered.

"He's fallen?" Kael ran a hand over his chin, a mannerism quite similar to Nolan's. "How?"

Greer smiled. "Nolan defeated him."

Kael choked out a laugh. "Little brother, you have surprised me more in the last few months than our whole lifetime."

For the first time, Alec couldn't help but notice how familiar Kael's eyes were. However, the sparkle Nolan's held wasn't there. Instead they held sadness and fear.

Alec reached into the bag—Nolan's bag—and grabbed the Stone of Speed. He recognized it by the way it pulsed in his palm. He withdrew it and handed it to Kael. "Hold this. It will bring back your strength."

Kael hesitated and then took the stone. As soon as his hand wrapped around it, the color returned to his face. He gawked at it and rolled it around in his palm. "What magic is this?"

"One which Nolan brought back to us," Alec said, trying to keep his voice from breaking. "If it weren't for him, these stones would still be lost." Alec glanced at Malik, "Well, perhaps all but one."

They all mourned. Even Kael. For a moment, there were no Guardians. There were no traitors. And there weren't even any Rol'dan. They were all Nolan's friends and family. And they missed him. Whether they agreed with his decision, or even liked each other, it didn't matter. For those few minutes, they were unified.

A purple cloak, looking as if it had belonged to the king, sat crumpled in a heap. Alec lifted the heavy cloth; it was soft to the touch. With a quick upward jerk, he let the exquisite fabric flutter downward and cover Nolan's body.

After a long while, Emery left with the Guardians. He had to finish what he'd started outside. The others soon followed.

Alec sat next to Nolan after all others were gone, still trying to fathom Nolan's decision. Alec's world had been uprooted. *My best friend and Taryn, both dead.*

Alec rocked back and forth. He had no direction. No purpose. No real reason to live. The only thing keeping him from falling on his sword was dishonoring Taryn's sacrifice.

Nolan's bag slipped from Alec's shoulder. He stopped rocking and studied the worn leather. Memories of Nolan flooded into his mind. He cried again, and then stopped abruptly. He flared his Speed, clutching the bag to his side. He wouldn't forget Nolan and what he'd requested before he died.

Try to love Kael.

Join the stones.

One request would be much easier than the other. Right now, General Trividar was the last thing Alec wanted to look at, let alone love. Yet, for Nolan, Alec would try to do both.

For now, Alec would start with the stones.

Chapter Thirty-Eight

It took hours for the crowd to clear. Rol'dan after stupid Rol'dan came forward, and Emery was as kind to the last one as he was to the first.

Kael put on a good show, too—arrogant and pompous as ever. And every person who touched him acted as if he were some sort of god. They had probably never seen anyone resurrected by a Healing Shay before, especially in the selfish Rol'dan army. Alec snorted. He wondered what those same people would think if they knew another resurrected person stood a few steps away.

Finally, all the Rol'dan cleared. Some returned to their barracks, some took posts on the wall (probably out of habit), and others went outside the great walls to clean the battlefield.

While Emery and the others retreated to the castle, Alec made for the dome. He climbed the stone steps as a cold breeze whisked through the air—winter would be coming soon. The waves lapped, spraying sea foam onto the rocks bordering Faylinn. For the first time, Alec saw the sea.

He inhaled sharply. By Brim, it was beautiful! Nolan had told him about the sea, had shared his love of it with Alec. He'd even told Alec he would take him there, someday. But Alec would never see it with Nolan. He lingered, staring at the waves, all the while thinking of his friend. Alec swallowed a lump in his throat and then pulled his eyes from the waters to his task at the top of the dome.

When he reached the top, he peered into the throne room

and stared at the strange vision below: three massive, glowing warriors, a king in rags, and a body forgotten on the floor. It was surreal, as if all of this had never happened, and Alec watched a long and very tiresome dream from someone's overactive imagination.

He grabbed the metal bars, crawling toward the middle of the dome. He took care not to make any movements that would send him down next to Nolan on the floor. When he reached the center, Alec pulled out the first stone. He studied it, wondering if he needed to put it in a special order. Maybe he'd put them all in only to have to rearrange them a second, third, or fourth time. No matter how long it took, Alec would get the job done.

He slid the stone into the crevice and carefully inserted the others, clicking one on top of another, until the last, smooth stone joined the others with no space to spare.

When Alec reentered the throne room, Emery, Kael, and the Guardians circled the spot where the colored images flickered. Lines of orange, blue, red, purple, gold, and green interchanged and disappeared again.

"It's the clouds," Alec said. However, no one listened to him. They all focused on the indistinct letters on the floor.

"Remarkable," Greer said. "After escorting the stones for so many years, I had no idea this would happen when they were joined."

"What does it say?" Kael asked. "It doesn't make much sense."

"There isn't enough light," Emery answered.

Time passed more slowly than usual. Finally, the dark clouds parted and a beam of light shone, revealing a message. They all stared in confusion at the foreign symbols. They meant nothing.

"Greer, do you recognize this?" Emery asked.

"It's the ancient text. I am unable to read it."

"What about the other Guardians?"

"No," Greer answered. "None of us can read."

They all stared at Greer.

"You can't read?" Alec asked.

"Why should we?"

"You know, to send messages or…well, for everything."

Greer glared with his light-filled eyes. Alec cringed. *Crows, he's frightening.*

"This text was not created for Guardians, but for man," Greer said sternly.

"Nolan translated the text in the lost temple," Emery said. "He could read it."

Kael gawked. "He could?"

"Yes, surprisingly well."

"He had some books," Alec said. "I picked up a few of his favorites when I passed Alton last time." Alec's soul wilted. It was supposed to be a surprise. He just never had a chance to give them to him.

"You went inside Alton Manor?" Emery asked, scowling.

Alec shrugged. "They didn't even know I was there."

"Where are the books now?" Emery asked.

"On their way to Galva. I stashed them into one of Nolan's crates."

"Galva?" Kael asked.

"Nolan had everyone leave after the Rol'dan attacked."

"Why send them to Galva?"

"He has an uncle who might get passage for them—" Alec stopped. "Your aunt and uncle."

"I can get the books." Kael fidgeted, like he didn't know what to do with his hands. "I know where my uncle lives."

"And everyone in our group would try and kill you when you show your face," Emery added.

Kael nodded, though the scowl didn't leave. "I suppose you're right."

"I'll go," Alec said. He needed something to do anyway, otherwise he'd scream.

"That settles it," Emery said. "Alec, you get the books. The rest of us will salvage what's left of the army."

"You know, even if we translate it," Alec said, "It doesn't mean we'll actually figure out what it means."

Emery sighed and ran a hand through his hair. "Yes, I know. But it's all we have." He looked at Greer. "And you're certain this message is important?"

Greer nodded. "Yes."

"It would've been easier with Nolan here." Emery's words lingered with pained silence.

"I'm pretty certain," said a low voice, "the text says, 'Wake up, sleeping one. Rise from death. Take up Brim's light and let it shine.'"

Everyone turned slowly. A Guardian glanced over Alec's shoulder, concentrating on the text. Alec didn't recognize him. The new Guardian was a lot shorter than the others. And he didn't wear the typical golden armor of the other warriors. He was naked, apart from a purple cloth tied around his waist. His broad chest and wide shoulders emanated power and strength, and his brown hair waved with highlights of gold that shimmered even in the faint light. He joined their circle, making no sound as his bare feet hit the stone floor.

The strange, new Guardian stared at the text. He rubbed his chin in concentration, furrowing his brow. "Yes, that's what is says. I have the 'rise from death' portion figured out, but I'm still not sure about the second half."

He met Alec's wide-eyed gaze. Where a Guardian's white lights should be, eyes as blue as a summer sky pierced into him. "What do you think, Alec?"

Alec couldn't speak. Who was he? Was he a man? He looked like a Guardian more than a man. The Guardian waited for an answer, with a bit of mirth behind his stare. Alec sucked in a breath. It was an expression he knew very well.

Alec pulled his gaze toward where Nolan's body had lain. He wasn't there. Only a few blood-soaked shreds of cloth remained. Slowly, he turned back to the new Guardian and sucked in a shallow breath. "Nolan?"

Nolan held out his arms, examining the defined muscles. He opened and closed his fists, like an infant first discovering their hands. "I didn't expect this at all."

"Though it would appear the stones knew of this event

before you were even born," Greer said casually.

"I guess so." Nolan ran a hand slowly over his face.

Emery and Kael still hadn't spoken. Their mouths hung open.

How could Nolan be alive? Is he alive? Crows! What is he? He isn't really Nolan, is he? He's more Guardian than human now. Questions piled in Alec's mind so quickly he couldn't keep up. He pressed his eyes closed as his head throbbed. When he opened them again, this new version of Nolan was still there.

Nolan adjusted the purple cloth, which Alec now knew to be the king's cloak. "Thanks to whoever left this. My clothes tore off me. I'm sure my appearance shocked you enough without showing…the entire transformation."

Greer was the only one to laugh.

"What in the nightforsaken Darkness are you?" Kael spat finally.

Nolan smiled, but it didn't reach his eyes. "It's good to see you alive, brother."

"Am I your brother?" Kael said. "I'm not so certain, considering I don't even know *what* you are."

Nolan touched his face. "I suppose I am a bit changed."

"Changed? You look like one of them!" Kael pointed at Greer.

The size difference between them was obvious. Greer still towered over Nolan, yet compared to the rest of them, Nolan had most definitely grown in mass and size.

"You look like a Guardian," Emery said, finally regaining his composure. "Though not exactly."

"He is not a Guardian," Greer said. "I can still sense his human presence and his human strength. The Shay is alive in him, though I cannot deny the light of my Guardian warriors in him as well. If I would have to answer, I would say he is both Guardian and man."

Nolan nodded slowly and raised his face skyward. A deep furrow formed in his wide brow. "Greer? Has it gotten worse? The darkness is so thick now."

"What darkness?" Emery asked. "The king is imprisoned and the Dor'Jan are nearly extinct."

"The king and the Dor'Jan are the least of our problems," Greer said. "I know you all can't see them, but there is a darkness—the Nass—which hovers over us. The dark clouds are more than what they seem." He turned to Nolan. "A little worse, Master Nolan. However, you just see things more clearly now."

Nolan jerked his face from the clouds and scanned the others. "My eyes. What color are my eyes?"

"They're blue," Alec said. "They look the same as before."

Nolan's wide shoulders relaxed slightly, and he released a quiet breath. "Blue. At least I still have that."

"Is this Nass another of Alcandor's abominations?" Emery asked.

"The Nass are born from the people," Greer said. "Each of you, I'm afraid, has added to it. The Nass cover the light of Brim, lessening your powers."

Emery blinked. "So *we* are responsible?"

Greer nodded.

"Can we reverse it?" Emery asked. "What can we do?"

Nolan reached to the beam of light and stiffened when the colors reflected onto his palm. His square jaw clenched as the message rippled and faded with the clouds. He filled his lungs slowly and released it in a rush. "It's me. The light must shine from me."

***

Nolan stood frozen in the light as the ancient text reflected on his face. Maska and Hakan, both hearing Nolan now lived, came to see for themselves. Each one, in their turn, had no words to express their shock—except for Hakan, who muttered a faint, "What in the light of Brim?"

Greer and Alec remained in the throne room with Nolan, though there wasn't much to see. Alec sat on the ground, watching Nolan, while his injuries throbbed even more intensely. His face burned the most, as if a forge-heated sword raked across his skin. In a moment of weakness, Alec thought about asking Greer to heal him. He gritted his teeth and resisted; he needed that scar to remember.

Alec glanced through the open ceiling. The sky was dark, yes. But clouds always covered the sky. Though, he had to admit, it appeared darker here in Faylinn, as if a storm approached. Alec squinted, trying to see these strange Nass creatures. Nothing but a crow flew by.

Then Greer joined him. The Guardian stared upward. "They have grown stronger."

"So you can see these…uh, things?"

Greer nodded but said nothing.

Alec shifted his position, but regretted it as pain shot through his thigh. "What exactly are they, anyway?"

"They are creatures born of the darkest parts of man. As they increase, man's connection to Brim weakens, his Shay falters, and his discontent grows."

"So we need to get rid of them to feel better?" Alec asked. "Everyone's a bit off from time to time."

Greer frowned. "It is more than that, Master Alec. If left unrestrained, the Nass could take complete control."

Alec shook his head. How could a few ill feelings destroy them? *If that were the case, the Nass would've controlled me long ago. Father is the master of foul moods and bad temper.*

Alec found the whole concept confusing. Everything had changed. Even his best friend had become something strange and foreign. Alec stood with a wince and limped closer to Nolan.

Nolan's face held the same expressions and mannerisms. *Why didn't I recognize him?* Alec leaned in to see if Nolan still breathed.

"How much longer can he stay like this?" Alec asked.

"I am not certain," Greer said. "Brim's strength grows in him. Perhaps we will see his light this day."

"His light? You mean Brim's light?"

"Yes."

"And how's it supposed to shine from him?"

Greer crossed his hands over his chest. "I'm not certain, Master Alec. But I believe it will be something so magnificent, its story will be passed through the ages."

Alec leaned closer. *What's taking him so long?* Nolan's eyes popped open and Alec flinched in surprise. Nolan's familiar eyes had changed. His blue irises sparked with hints of white light.

"Nolan? Are you okay?"

Nolan gave a slight nod, but his body trembled.

Alec touched his arm, but yanked back. Nolan's skin burned.

"Greer! We need to get him out of here!"

"No," Nolan said. "Have to f-finish."

Finish? Alec looked into Nolan's eyes again; they glowed brighter than just a few minutes before. Nolan stared back, his teeth chattering.

"Master Alec," Greer said. "We should wait for Master Nolan outside."

"I'm staying," Alec snapped.

"It's okay," Nolan said. "G-go outside." He attempted a smile. "I'll b-be there s-soon."

Alec hesitated then pulled away. Nolan closed his eyes in deeper focus.

"Come," Greer said. "We should go."

Greer led Alec outside and toward the fortification's main entrance. Instead of going to the battlefield, Greer turned and climbed the stairs.

"Shouldn't we wait for Nolan?" Alec asked.

Greer ignored him and kept walking up the stairs.

Alec struggled to keep up; his leg throbbed, and he wasn't in the mood to use Speed. By the time they'd reached the top, he was ready to stop. Alec leaned against the thick, stone wall and peered over the edge. On one side of the wall, the entrance to the castle loomed. On the other, Alec could see the trampled grass and corpse-strewn battlefield.

Soldiers stacked mounds of bodies, more than Alec could

imagine in his nightmares. Though most were the freed Dor'Jan, it still made his stomach turn.

Time passed as the morbid cleanup continued. Alec was about to suggest they see what had happened to Nolan, when the sky dimmed. The sun's position marked midday. It looked as if they'd get some rain. The sunlight darkened yet again. This time, all the Rol'dan's faces turned upward. They'd noticed too.

"Greer?"

"Yes, Master Alec."

"What's happening?"

"It appears that Master Nolan has started."

The clouds began to separate. Instead of the typical dark mass, shapes started to form. They moved gradually at first, and then they increased in speed, darting all around.

The sunlight dimmed again, like a sudden storm. A woman pointed skyward at the horror. One of the clouds whipped around several others as if propelled by some invisible force. It darted in a circle, and Alec ducked as it whisked past.

"What in Darkness is this, Greer?"

The Guardian smiled. "Exactly."

The dark clouds soared over the crowd. People screamed, and dark forms pulled from them and joined the previous manifestations. The strange creatures whipped in and out of the people and disappeared into the black mass above.

Alec's heart thundered. He gasped and threw himself to the wall's edge. A faceless, black mist whirled near Alec's head and flew into the morphing, twisting sky.

The Rol'dan pushed against each other, and the creatures poured from the crowd, adding to the truth: the darkness, created by man.

A light appeared from the castle, cutting through the dark mists. Nolan walked stiffly through the oversized wooden doors, dressed only in the purple cloth around his waist. His muscled skin glowed, and white light rose above him like steam. Alec blinked; Nolan shone so brightly, it was hard to look at him. The Rol'dan, now silent, watched Nolan's slow progress across the courtyard and out the gates to the field below.

Alec dove to the other side of the wall, gripping it hard, while he watched Nolan appear on the field.

A few soldiers who had been working there left their task and sprinted toward the gates of Faylinn to join their fellow soldiers.

Nolan stood alone: behind him, a backdrop full of corpses, above him, a whole host of black mists. The creatures circled overhead, increasing their urgency, flinging down on Nolan, and, just as quickly, flinging away. They seemed worried, as much as a faceless vapor could be.

Greer's massive presence appeared behind Alec's back. "Master Alec. Whatever happens, hold on as tightly as you can." He then encompassed Alec with his body, placing one hand on either side of him, gripping the edge of the wall with his massive hands and bracing his feet as if he were about to push a very solid stone.

Nolan raised his arms as if reaching for the heavens. Then his arms fell outstretched to the side, palms up, his face to the sky.

"Hang on!" Greer commanded.

Alec grabbed the wall just as Nolan's light exploded, like a star dropping to earth. The force hit them like a hammer blow.

Screams filtered through the force of the wind, though Alec could no longer see. The light blinded him even with his eyes closed. He gripped the wall, and another wave, even more violent than the last, hammered, yanking Alec's hands free.

He slammed into Greer, the blustering wind pushing him against the Guardian's chest. Greer protected them both from being thrown from the wall.

The third blast hit, and Alec held on to Greer, hoping the Guardian was strong enough to hold them both. Then just as suddenly, the wind stopped. Alec dropped to his knees, as did Greer. He opened his eyes and could see nothing at all.

"It is done," Greer said.

Slowly, images began to surface in Alec's vision—blotched

shapes still white with light. Alec groped and found Greer's large arm. "Greer, I can't see."

The Guardian touched Alec's face and healing energy pulsed into his eyes. His vision opened to a sun brighter than he'd ever seen and a sky as blue as the sea. Alec gawked. It was stunning.

Alec staggered to his feet. The word "chaos" wouldn't be enough to describe the scene: Healers ran frantically, healing eyesight and broken bones, stones were missing from places in the castle, and worse yet, the neatly stacked corpses were now blown in grotesque piles against the foot of the wall. Even the forest appeared to have taken damage; trees were bent or half pulled from their roots. Never had Alec seen something this devastating. Yet even with such a disaster, Alec felt free.

He laughed. "Greer, I can't believe it."

The Guardian didn't answer. Instead, his eyes fixed on the field.

Smiling, Alec followed his gaze, and the happiness left him instantly. The figure of a man lay crumpled, a charred ring of earth surrounding him.

Alec's throat clenched. *Please Brim*, he prayed, *please, don't make me lose him twice in one day.* He summoned his Shay and ran as fast as Speed could carry him.

Chapter Thirty-Nine

Familiar white mists filled Nolan's vision, stretching out farther than he remembered. He turned, searching. No grass this time. No sunset. No sky. And no light-filled Greer. Just a sea of white splayed out before him.

He held up his hands; they were small, with normal fingers. His eyes traveled down his naked body, and he was thin. Unchanged. The "old" Nolan. He released a long breath, relief flooding through him. It had all been a dream.

In the distance, a light broke the mists, and pain shot through Nolan's skull. He blinked until his eyes adjusted, and then he staggered toward it, his feet swishing through the swirling clouds. As he got closer, the light took shape, forming into a man.

He froze. This man had no face, and the power emanating from him took Nolan's breath away.

Nolan dropped to his hands and knees, choking in gasps.

"Don't be afraid, my child," Brim said. "You have done well."

A memory of exploding light surfaced in his mind, the vision of lying in blackened grass. *I must be...dead.*

Brim chuckled. "No. You are still alive and well."

Slowly, Nolan looked up. A feeling of peace passed over him. The faceless figure solidified, transforming into a man in the middle of his years—dark hair, dark eyes. He reminded Nolan of Emery.

"Does this make you feel more comfortable?" Brim asked.

Nolan nodded feebly, though his heart still thundered. It did help, a little.

Brim sat, and the mist parted from him, grass taking its place. "I will keep our time brief; your loved ones are waiting for you to awaken. Let me start by saying: I am proud of you. Alcandor has been causing trouble for quite some time. I appreciate you putting him back in his place."

Nolan leaned back on his feet, his knees tucked under him. He was thankful the mists swirled, covering him to his waist. The overwhelming fear had passed, and Brim's soothing voice caressed him. Nolan sighed. "What should we do with him?"

"With Alcandor?" Brim asked. "I haven't yet decided. Leave him where he is. He should cause no trouble...for now."

For now? Nolan didn't like the sound of that.

Brim brushed non-existent lint from his spotless, white tunic. "I did not come to discuss Alcandor, my son. I have another job for you."

Nolan blinked. "Another job? For me?"

"Take the stones out into Adamah. Tell the people of their abilities. The people most likely won't listen, but do your best. The Nass appear only from those who have not taken the light. So until they see truth and take it, the Nass will never truly go away. You've damaged the Nass for now, but they will return."

If they won't listen, why bother? It sounds like a hopeless cause.

"Difficult. But not hopeless," Brim said, answering Nolan's thoughts. "But you will do well."

"Why me?" Nolan asked. "Surely someone else—"

"Only you hold all the powers."

Nolan's jaw clenched. "What am I? A Guardian? A man?"

Brim smiled. "Yes. And yes. You are both."

"But how? Why no one else?"

Brim steadied his gaze. "You will find out eventually. But for now, do not worry about such things. Focus on your task. Be my Emissary."

Brim stood and stretched. His disguise began to fade, light taking over his human facade. "Oh. There is one more thing, child. Stay with the stones. For as powerful as you are, you are equally as weak. You can no longer gain strength from the sun; your Guardian abilities block it from your Shays. The only way to restore your strength is from the stones' light. Without them, you will die."

Cold fingers jolted his chest. *I will...die?*

The white mists darkened, and Brim vanished into them. Then the landscaped darkened to black.

"Go get Emery," a voice said. "He's waking."

The darkness lifted as light filtered through Nolan's eyelids. He imagined himself tucked in a feather bed in Alec's house while Bonty fixed a stew and baked fresh bread. The Guardians weren't real. His powers weren't real. His conversation with Brim, of course, wasn't real. Nolan brought his hand to his face—an unfamiliar face—and reality returned.

He was changed. Changed like no other person. His new life began when he'd awakened naked on the throne room floor, his clothes torn away by the transformation of his body. Nolan Trividar was no more.

The light inside Nolan lingered, though it was faint, not like the outpouring in the darkness when he'd destroyed the Nass. He opened his eyes and focused on a figure sitting on the edge of his bed. She looked at him, wonderment in her emotions.

"Your eyes are still the same," Megan said. "I couldn't believe it at first, but now you're awake..." Her small hands slid across the blanket and held his.

Nolan appeared to be in a sick room, not Alec's house. Drying racks strung with herbs covered the far wall. Bottles of different sizes and shapes, holding a variety of colored liquids, lined a shelf. A silk banner hung next to it, adorned with the Healing symbol of the Rol'dan.

The door creaked open, and Emery entered, wearing a deep blue doublet, blue breeches, and a blue cloak, made with some sort of thick, expensive fabric. Several emotions flickered through him: affection...concern...compassion. Emery's gaze dipped to their joined hands, and his emotions revealed shock at first, then resignation.

Nolan quickly withdrew his Empathy…and his hand.

Emery smiled. "It's good to see you awake, friend."

"How long?"

"Five days," Emery said. "At first we weren't sure if you'd live, but you've steadily improved. We would've used the stones, but Greer didn't want us to risk it, seeing as you're half Guardian and all."

Nolan propped himself on the bed, and the cover fell away. Chiseled muscles covered his chest, his arms, his stomach. He traced the lines of hard muscles with his large fingertips and then held up his hands. No wonder Megan's had felt so small.

Megan followed his inspection. Her eyes flicked up to his and her face went scarlet. Heat rose to Nolan's face as well.

Nolan turned away, avoiding her gaze. He ran a hand down his smooth jaw. No half-grown stubble. His arms and chest had no hair, either. He flipped the cover back, wondering about his legs.

Megan gasped, and Nolan quickly repositioned the blanket, heat rising to his face, yet again.

Nolan cleared his throat. "I don't suppose I can find some clothes?"

Emery pushed down a smile and pointed to garments carefully folded on a chair. "I had the palace seamstress make these for you. I told her not to create anything elaborate." He held out his own arms with disgust. "However, I can't make any promises. I told her the same for me."

"You look very regal."

Emery laughed. "Regal? Yes, I suppose."

Nolan moved to get up and then hesitated. Megan and Emery turned around.

Rising to his feet, the world swirled. He grabbed the wall until the dizziness passed. He slid on the breeches. They were a perfect fit, the fabric soft and warm. Nolan wondered how the seamstress sized them so well, but decided he didn't want to know.

A full-length mirror stood near Nolan's bed. He stared

at the stranger, the one with the strong brow and chin. He touched his hair; it was softer than it used to be, and shinier too. The color was almost metallic, more Guardian-like. And his familiar eyes appeared threatening and strange.

He lowered his head and stared at the floor. Even his feet looked different. A wave of mourning hit him for the old Nolan, the weak Nolan, the uncoordinated Nolan. As much as he'd always hated his awkward self, at least he'd known who he was.

Nolan cleared his throat. "So where are the stones now?"

"We separated them," Emery said. "The Rol'dan go in shifts to take the light."

"And Alcandor?"

"Still in the dungeon," Emery said. "Although, it's difficult to find soldiers willing to guard him. They aren't convinced his mind control is gone."

Emery glanced over his shoulder and noticed Nolan was dressed. Both he and Megan turned around.

"And his Healing?" Nolan asked.

Megan smiled, though bitterness tainted her emotions. "I took it from him myself."

Nolan studied her, which made her blush.

Emery cleared his throat. "Should you be out of bed so soon?"

"Isn't five days enough?" Nolan walked toward the door and turned to speak again. But before a word left his mouth, a sharp and sudden pain erupted in his head, followed by vibrations so hard he could feel the outline of his skull. He staggered, grabbing his scalp. When his vision cleared, he searched for his assailant: the now-broken doorframe.

Nolan caught Emery in what was left of an amused grin. Nolan closed his eyes and flared Healing. When the throbbing ceased, he looked down at his friends. He couldn't believe how short they seemed. And, of course, the doorframe as well.

"Are you okay?" Megan asked.

"I'm fine. Just have to watch doorways."

Emery chuckled. "Yes, otherwise you'll end up back in bed."

Nolan ducked through the door and emerged on the field where Kael had died. A large group of Rol'dan practiced with swords. Kael stood in front of them, quite alive. He yelled orders with his typical general flare. But even though he was working them into exhaustion, the emotional atmosphere of the group leaned toward joy.

"Soldiers, attention!" Kael yelled in the distance. The whole group stopped in recognition of their king.

Emery casually waved.

"Where's Alec?" Nolan asked.

"He went to Galva, to tell the others what happened." Emery inhaled and released it slowly. "He's angry with you, Nolan. He thinks you threw your life away."

Nolan frowned. "I didn't throw my life away."

"Give him some distance. I'm sure he'll come around."

"I suppose he still hasn't let anyone heal him?" Nolan asked Megan.

She held up her hands in defense. "Don't look at me. He wouldn't let me. He's stubborn and determined to suffer on his own."

"Speaking of stubborn," Nolan said, eyes on Emery, "are you and Kael getting along?"

"He's still one of the most arrogant men I've ever known in my life," Emery said.

"So he's fine then?"

Emery laughed. "He's loyal to me. There's no doubt in his emotions. And though he's not always loved by the Rol'dan, he's respected."

The Rol'dan troops trained, but Kael watched Nolan, arms crossed over his chest. Nolan pushed Perception and saw a smile on his brother's face. Then, in a flurry of Speed, Kael appeared next to them.

Nolan saw him coming, but Emery did not.

Emery gasped and held back a curse. "General, you will lessen your Speed before you approach, giving me ample warning."

"Sorry, Your Majesty," Kael replied, though his emotions

revealed nothing apologetic. "May I speak freely?"

"Of course, General," Emery said.

He grinned, examining Nolan from head to toe. "You look well, I suppose."

"Now what's that supposed to mean?"

Kael shrugged. "You tell me. You're the one with Empathy."

"Are you being disrespectful to my friend?" Emery asked.

"Oh no, Your Majesty," Kael teased. "I'll treat him as I would my own brother."

Nolan rolled his eyes. "Now *that* isn't very reassuring."

They entered the castle and headed to the throne room. A group of Rol'dan waited for their time in the light under the dome. Nolan ignored their gawking stares as best he could and strode to the three Guardians watching over the proceedings.

"It is good to see you awake, Master Nolan," Greer said, his straight posture more erect than usual. "I hope you are feeling well?"

"A little weak, actually."

"It is expected, considering what you have accomplished."

"So the Nass are gone?" Nolan asked.

Greer smiled, though his emotions were tainted with apprehension. "For now."

Weakness washed over Nolan. He steadied himself on Greer's arm.

"Master Nolan?" Greer said.

"I...I think I need to stand in the light again."

Emery motioned toward a group of Rol'dan.

Kat approached. Her eyes traveled up and down Nolan, and her emotions were...well, Nolan tried to ignore her emotions. "Yes, Your Majesty?"

"Go to the top of the dome and combine the stones again," Emery said.

She bowed, but her gaze stayed on Nolan. She smiled and left to complete her task.

Nolan turned, and Kael stared at him, puzzlement radiating from him.

"What's wrong?" Nolan asked.

"Well, if I didn't know any better, I would say Lieutenant Connelly fancies you."

Nolan coughed, nearly choking on his own breath.

Kael grinned. "I'm right, aren't I?"

"I don't see how this is any of your business, General," Emery added.

Kael straightened, but amusement spilled from him. "I'm sorry, Your Majesty. It's just, well, Lieutenant Connelly has always been more man than woman. It took me by surprise."

"More man than woman?" Nolan asked. "Why? Did she reject you?"

Kael barked a laugh, though annoyance spiked from him. Nolan had struck a chord. "She dresses like a man and is as tall as one. One could easily mistake her for a man." Kael grinned. "Or maybe she really *is* a man, and is fooling us all."

Nolan huffed. Kael was so ridiculous sometimes. "Oh, for Brim's sake, Kael. She's a girl."

Kael's eyebrows rose, satisfaction sparking his emotions. "And you can prove this? You know from personal experience?"

"No! Not like that," Nolan added, redirecting Kael's less-than-pure thoughts. "I'd almost killed her. I'd stabbed her in the chest and I...uh...checked her wound."

Kael threw back his head and laughed. "Oh? Did you, now?"

Megan frowned and quickly averted her eyes.

Crows, what does she think of me? He considered reading her, but quickly changed his mind. He didn't want to know.

"Well," Emery said a bit louder than necessary. "She's done already."

The light of Brim shone in a single circle, the spectrum of colors dancing on the floor. Nolan pushed aside Kael's teasing and his thoughts about Megan and Kat. He staggered forward, tuning out the watchful faces.

He stayed in the light for quite some time, and slowly his exhaustion ebbed away. Brim was right: He needed the light. He froze, the memory of his vision flooding back. Without the stones, Nolan would *die*. His breath hitched. The vision had been real? Brim was real? He swallowed back his dread. Brim had a job for him.

Emery's brow furrowed. "Nolan, is something wrong?"

Nolan met the faces of his friends, concern on their emotions. Crows, he didn't want to leave them. "I..." Nolan said, his voice breaking. "I have to go."

Emery relaxed, and a smile hinted on his face. "You don't need to leave, friend. Most of them have accepted me as their king. Your presence here won't interfere—"

"No," Nolan said. "It's not that. I need to leave with the stones."

Everyone stared, confusion coursing through their emotions.

"What do you mean, Nolan?" Emery asked.

"I need to share the stones. I must take them to the cities and villages. The people need to know of their hidden powers."

Emery nodded, his emotions contemplative. "So why leave? The people of Adamah are welcome here."

Nolan took a deep breath. "Brim told me to go."

Silence followed, shock in their emotions. Megan stared at him with an intensity that made Nolan squirm.

"When do you have to leave?" Greer asked, unshaken.

Nolan hesitated. "Soon, I think."

"I can go with you," Megan suggested, hopeful.

Nolan shook his head. "No. You can't."

Her recent grief flooded into him, along with a multitude of other, more intimate feelings. Nolan really liked her, but things had changed. She needed to find someone normal and move on.

"I don't care what you look like," she said, her voice trembling.

"It's more than that, Megan."

"No, it isn't," she said, desperation tainting her tone. "You're still Nolan. I see it in your eyes."

"I'm not the same. Nolan Trividar died—"

"You aren't dead," she snapped, anger flaring. She reached to his face, and Nolan caught her hand, longing to let her touch him.

"I am only half human," Nolan said. "I may never grow old, or be able to raise a family. And now I have to carry the stones."

"Why you?" she stammered, yanking her hand away. "What about the Guardians? They can take the stupid stones, and you can stay here with me."

"Megan, they can't even touch them."

"Then let me go with you!"

Nolan met her eyes, wishing he could say yes. She'd been through so much. But he couldn't take her; she'd only distract him. "You can't come, because I don't want you to."

She startled and stepped back, rejection striking her.

Nolan turned his head, unable to look at her, his lie stabbing him. Nolan risked a glance and saw Emery holding Megan as she sobbed in his arms. Emery and Nolan's eyes met. Emery's emotions snuffed like someone throwing water on a flame. He'd hidden it too late. Emery *loved* Megan.

Emery's voice appeared in his mind. *Don't tell, Nolan. Please.*

Nolan nodded once to reassure him. This secret wasn't his to tell.

"So, Lord Emissary, when do you plan to leave?" a voice asked.

Nolan jerked toward Kat. "What did you call me?"

"Emissary, of course," she said. "You said you must spread the knowledge of Brim to Adamah. The term 'Messenger' doesn't seem a grand enough word to use."

He couldn't speak at first. *Why'd she use the same title Brim had?* Finally, he cleared his throat. "You could just call me Nolan."

She feigned a shocked expression. "Call you Nolan? Never."

Emery led Megan from throne room, still sobbing in his arms.

"So, will you need assistance on your journey, Emissary?" Kat said, pulling him to her conversation.

"Maybe. I haven't thought much about it yet."

"Then may I request to assist you?"

"Wouldn't you rather stay and serve under General Trividar again?"

She laughed, and then stopped abruptly, scowling. "That cad? I'd rather you tried to kill me again."

Nolan raised his eyebrows. "Would you, now?"

"Especially now that you heal."

Her eyes roamed over Nolan, causing his face to warm; he'd been doing a lot of that the last hour or so. Across the room, Alec entered: A perfect excuse to leave.

"I'm sorry, Kat. If you'd excuse me?"

He ignored her flare of disappointment and closed the distance to Alec. The gash across his face had scabbed over, puckering the skin.

"I just got back," Alec said. "Heard you were awake."

"Obviously."

Alec examined Nolan and shook his head. His emotions felt so heavy. "I still don't know how I'm going to get used to you." He hesitated then held out his hand. A new leather belt and straps lay in his open palm. "Here. I made you some new ones."

Nolan didn't need his Empathy to see the turmoil of emotions behind Alec's brown eyes.

"Thanks." Nolan took the straps. "How's my uncle?"

"Not well. He seemed better after we talked, though I can't imagine why."

"If Taryn loved you, he would too."

Alec looked at his feet. "The Trividar family is an odd group."

"That's why you fit in so well."

He smiled faintly and then licked his scabbed lip. "There's something else I wanted to give you." He unbuckled the sword and held it out.

Nolan stared at it. "Alec, I can't. Your father made it for you."

"And it's given me trouble since the day I touched it. Besides, my father created it from both the steel of a Guardian sword and of man." He shrugged. "It seems more fitting for you."

The sword meant a lot to Alec. Nolan couldn't take it.

"Please," Alec said. "Every time I look at it, I think about it causing the death of Taryn, Kael, and you. And don't tell me it isn't true." He held the pommel toward Nolan. "Please, Nolan. Take it. For me."

Nolan didn't want to, but he took it. For Alec.

As soon as he touched it, the light of Brim swelled and spread into the sword. The Guardian steel came to life, glowing as if a living flame took shape in the blade. Nolan swung it in a slow arch. A line of light traced the path as if the sword *had* been made for him.

"Nolan?" Alec said.

Nolan stopped mid-swing, catching the tortured expression on Alec's face.

"That day in the throne room, when you brought back Kael..."

Nolan's gut wrenched. "I...I didn't have a choice."

"Everyone has a choice!" Alec snapped. "Taryn had a choice. *You* had a choice."

"Kael's my brother. What did you expect me to do?"

"I know he's your brother. But crows, Nolan. You made me *watch*." Alec's face trembled, his eyes pooled, and a tear fell down his cheek, running through his scar. "You died in front of me, and I felt like I pushed the blade in myself."

Nolan jolted back. He'd only stopped his friend, he didn't think about what he would see. The same wound that killed Kael was the one he'd absorbed to die. And he'd frozen Alec so he had to watch the whole thing. What had he done? "Alec. I'm so sorry."

Alec scowled and walked away.

"Alec! Forgive me!" Nolan said.

Alec paused, his back to Nolan. "I will. Someday. But not now."

Nolan ran a hand over the smooth contours of his new face. He'd hurt the two people he cared about the most. But as much as he regretted it, they would both forgive him...eventually. Families did that for each other.

He looked to the light of Brim as it shimmered and changed on the floor. It was ironic how the very stones that gave him his powers were the ones that would keep him alive. And now, Nolan had to carry them around the land and hope people would listen. Though he knew he must travel throughout Adamah and spread the knowledge of Brim—alone for the most part—he also knew he'd always remain in the hearts of friends. And their friendship was more precious to him than all the stones or powers in the world. He'd just have to make Adamah believe in the stones, whether they wanted to or not.

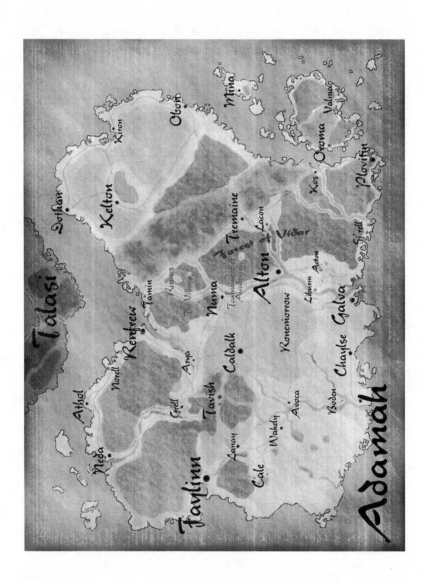

The Six Shay Powers

Empathy

Accuracy

Speed

Perception

Strength

Healing

ACKNOWLEDGEMENTS

Firstly, I would like to thank the staff at Month9Books for allowing THE EMISSARY to finally become a reality. To Georgia McBride for creating the opportunity, and to Courtney Koschel for being such a rock star editor and support person— this project has become so much better with your hand. To Zach Schoenbaum for his wonderful artistic talents on the cover. And to the rest of the staff of Month9 behinds the scenes, thanks to all of you as well.

I also want to thank the many people who helped me on my way to publication:
Firstly, to my friends: Michelle Gregory, who has read this story almost as much as I have. Without her, I would've struggled getting past the first draft. Michelle McLean, who has been a great partner in publishing crime. Thanks for letting me whine to you for so long. Thanks to my other writing friends from Operation Awesome Blog and the Query Tracker forum. I appreciate your support, especially early on. And to my local critique partners, Wayne Saap and Joan Mauch, who've been great friends and emotional support for me over the years.

To the folks and beta readers of Slinging.org forum: Your expert advice about slings was ever so helpful and fun. Also, thank you for becoming my mini fan club in a time when I needed it the most. You have no idea how much that meant to me, and how it helped me to go forward when the path to publication was the darkest.

To my best friend, Barb Pope. Thanks for being a cheerleader and support system for so long.

Lastly, to my family: My mom, Karen Davenport, who has been a great reader and supporter for me. And my kids who've had to put up with me and leave me alone while I worked. And to my husband, Peter, who helped me not to look as stupid, by giving me great advice on blacksmithing and other skills, and for having to generally put up with me through the emotional rollercoaster of publishing. I love you. Thank you for being so tolerant with me and encouraging for so long.

To everyone else who has read my book and given me advice, suggestions, or just kudos, thank you.

And lastly, thanks to God, who forced me to have patience. Though I might have not liked the long road, it has taught me much. Thank you for being my rock, and for giving me stubbornness, so I would keep going, and to giving me the creative gifts which allowed me to write this book in the first place.

KRISTAL SHAFF

Kristal Shaff grew up with books (and used to drive her mom crazy when she wouldn't leave the library); her first job was even shelving books at the library. She loves anything creative, and you can often find her exploring strange and fantastical worlds in her choices of movies and fantasy fiction. Kristal resides in Iowa with her farmer husband, numerous pets, and 3 awesome kids (plus one more on the way through the journey of adoption). When she isn't writing, she is a professional face painter who enjoys making children smile.

OTHER MONTH9BOOKS TITLES YOU MIGHT LIKE

BRANDED

INTO THE FIRE

PREDATOR

CROWN OF ICE

ENDLESS

PRAEFATIO

THE LOOKING GLASS

OF BREAKABLE THINGS

A MURDER OF MAGPIES

LIFER

A SHIMMER OF ANGELS and A SLITHER OF HOPE

SCION OF THE SUN

CALL ME GRIM

FLEDGLING

NICOLE CONWAY

THE
DRAGONRIDER
CHRONICLES

AVIAN

NICOLE CONWAY

PAB SUNGENIS
SIDEKICK
THE MISADVENTURES OF THE NEW
SCARLET KNIGHT

One slave girl will lead a rebellion.
One nameless boy will discover the truth.
When their paths collide, everything changes.

LIFER

BECK NICHOLAS

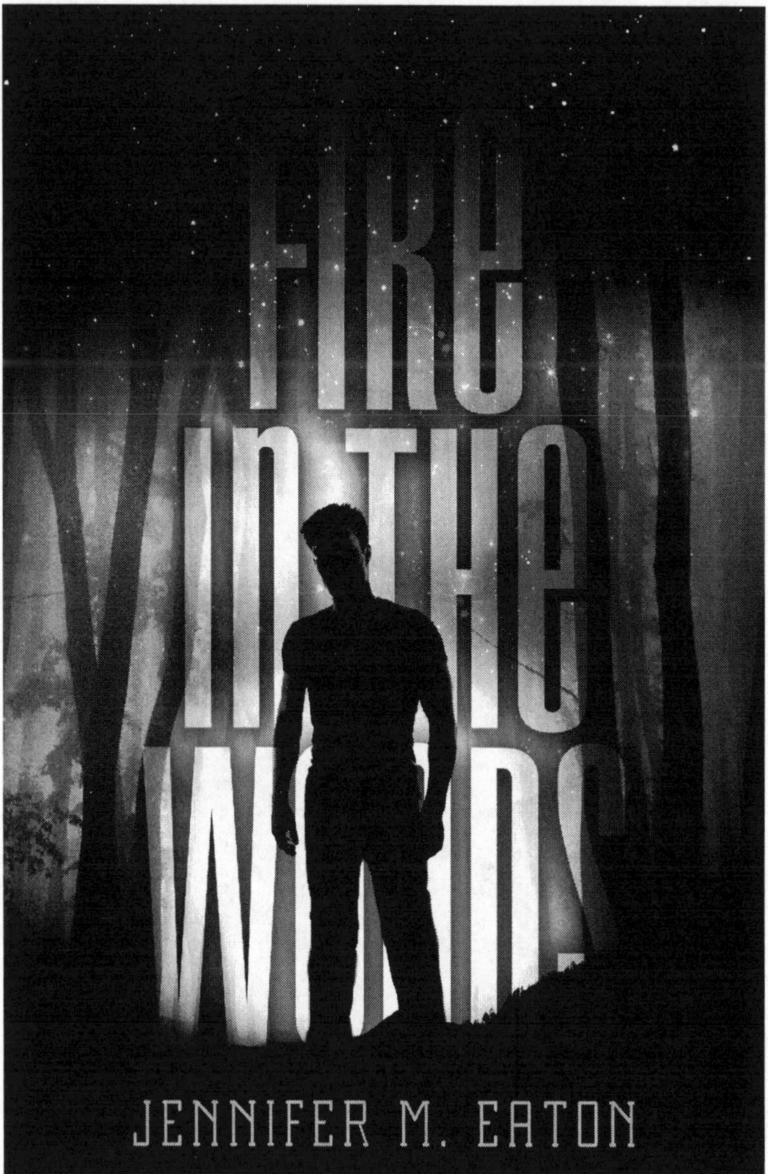
FIRE
IN THE
JENNIFER M. EATON

Find more awesome Teen books at
Month9Books.com

Connect with Month9Books online:
Facebook: www.Facebook.com/Month9Books
Twitter: @Month9Books
You Tube: www.youtube.com/user/Month9Books
Blog: www.month9booksblog.com
Request review copies via publicity@month9books.com